McCabe, Ed.

Against gravity

$22.45

DATE			
DEC 5 '90			
NOV 12 '98			
1-26-98			
OCT 1 0 2000			
OCT 1 8 2001			
OCT 0 1 2007			

9th RALLYE 1987—NEW YEAR'S DAY
PARIS—DAKAR

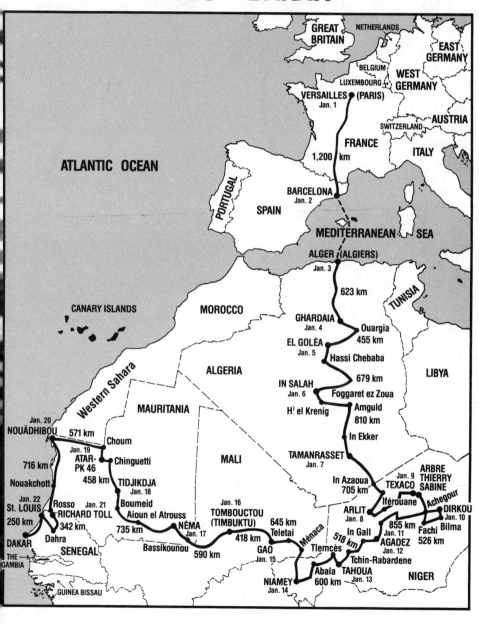

AGAINST GRAVITY

AGAINST GRAVITY

From Paris to Dakar in the world's most dangerous race

ED McCABE

WARNER BOOKS

A Warner Communications Company

A Warner Communications Company

Printed in the United States of America
First Printing: June 1990
10 9 8 7 6 5 4 3 2 1

LIBRARY OF CONGRESS CATALOGING-IN-PUBLICATION DATA
McCabe, Ed.
    Against gravity / Ed McCabe.
      p.   cm.
    "From Paris to Dakar in the world's most dangerous race."
    ISBN 0-446-51454-3
    I. Title.
    PS3563.C3337A7   1990
    813'.54—dc20   89-40460
                                                                                    CIP

Map illustration and book design by Giorgetta Bell McRee

Dedicated to those who do.
To inspire those who don't.

ACKNOWLEDGMENTS

The author wishes to acknowledge the following people whose contributions, large or small, made this book possible:

David Abbott, Scott Andrews, Andy Arghyrou, Jean Pierre Audour, Alain Bardy, Helmut Barthel, Nancy Belli, Pam Bernstein, Pietmor Bienhaur, Jacqueline Borderes-Levet, Simon Bowden, Phyllis Brown-Norman, John Buffum, Patricia Cartier-Millon, Robert Combas, Bob Cranny, Frances Edwards, Jim Fitzgerald, Suzanne Fournier, Milt Gravatt, Bernard Gruber, Roger and Eve Hachuel, Jacky Ickx, Susan Isaacs, Sylvie Jolimoy, Richard Kaan, Yvon Lambert, Richard Lopinto, Alan Mahony, David McCall, Jackie Merri Meyer, Laura Morton, Bob Needleman, Phillipe Nicolas, Nikon, Inc., Jean Clement Oodomanfaib, Christine Oppenheim, Mel Parker, Bill Pekala, Chuck Pfieffer, Frank Perdue, Christian Potocmik, Martin Ford Puris, Michel Richardot, Norbert Ruthofer, Corky Severson, Dr. Chandra Sharma, Dr. Rajendra Sharma, Bob Sharp, François Siegel, Corinna Snyder, Vic Spector, Steyr-Daimler-Puch, Buzz Stoner, Kathryn Suerth, Yves Tourre, George Tradewell, Carol Volk, Dena Walker, Peter Wegel, Frank Wells, Ralph Wild, Bill Wildprett, Jack and Helen Zalinger.

It would be unfair not to single out Lulu Anderson, whose patience and support made the writing almost a pleasure. And Carolyn Jones, whose adventures spirit made a dream come alive.

THANKS

To any whose names are missing, sorry.

AGAINST GRAVITY

Compared to Fontainebleau or Vaux-le-Vicomte, the Palace of Versailles is no graceful beauty. It is a great, gray, stone pile with a mansard roof, arranged in a massive horseshoe. Subtlety is not one of its virtues. Apart from its ranging enormity, it is also perhaps one of the tallest three-story buildings in the world. It overpowers you and makes you feel ridiculously small with every aspect of its scale. Excepting the beautiful outbuildings and breathtaking gardens, the main attraction is a stout and overbearing affair that screams for attention, like a fat old king with gout.

Louis XIV built Versailles, it is said, for political self-defense. Even if that wasn't his motive, it had the desired result. By moving his court from the Louvre in Paris, which teemed with aristocratic plotting and intrigue, he, in effect, declawed the cats. Out here, on his own meticulously groomed turf, he kept all the noble schemers under his beady eye, thwarting every slinky move they tried on him. He reigned for seventy-two years.

But this is not about Louis XIV. It is about the tenth Rallye Paris/Dakar, the official start due to occur here at Versailles any minute now.

Here where Louis once ruled, pandemonium now reigns. A half-million people—more than the entire population of Louis's Paris—mill among the cars, trucks, and motorcycles, gawking, touching, dreaming. And today Louis is either rolling over in his grave or wishing he was still around to order up his fastest coach.

The contestants and their hyper-powered chariots are jammed side to side into the Place d'Armes—the cobbled court in front of the Grand Palais. There are row upon row of them, lined up like so many tin soldiers arrayed for mock battle. Looking toward the palace, from right to left, there are three long rows of motorcycles, about fifty in each line. Tilted

1

over on their stands and up on tall, spindly, studded tires, they look like infantrymen standing at cockeyed attention. Down the center the ranks are made up of seven rows of cars, mostly four-wheel drive jeeplike vehicles. These look like armored cars and form practically solid lines of steel, as they are more closely spaced than the motorcycles, which look weak and vulnerable, almost human, by comparison. All the way over on the left in two long semicircles is ranged the big stuff. The artillery, so to speak. These are the trucks. Some are turbocharged behemoths that belch flames and billow smoke from towering chrome stacks. There are long and high eighteen-wheelers as well as more modest rigs with as few as six wheels but no shortage of power.

This army does not wear camouflage. It bristles with advertising. Each member is gaudily painted and covered with numbers and colorful stickers hawking cigarettes, airlines, soda pop, candy, auto parts.

In the cold, morning half-light, between the bikes, cars, and trucks, a mass of spectators stumbles drunkenly over the ancient domed paving stones like sardines inching around on their tails. I am one of these odd fish.

How familiar it all seems. The noise, the breathless babble of the overattenuated emcee, the powerful engines revving, the people reveling, some still clutching their blown-out noisemakers and bottles of leftover flat champagne.

At least it's not pouring with rain like last year. Last year! It doesn't feel like a year already. It feels like weeks. In some respects, it feels like centuries. It also feels strange being here, being a spectator instead of a concurrent, which is what the French call these crazy, macho adventurers about to speed off toward the Sahara Desert in what has come to be known as the world's most dangerous race.

Last year they crowded around me, pressing for autographs while I huddled inside my rain-streaked, mud-caked car. The cold, the wet, the discomfort, the anxiety, they were all part of it. This year it's just plain cold. And in this crush, it is hard to get to my friends to wish them well. "Bonne chance! Bonne année!" the words clatter and ring in my ears, sweep me back to this same place, same time, last year.

Car number 248. That was our number. We were squeezed into our slot under the never-ending downpour between cars 247 and 249. What little space existed between the cars was consumed by people. Occasionally there would be a tapping on our plastic side windows and one of us would slide open the small "door" we'd had cut into each panel. A small hand clutching a pen and a piece of paper, belonging to a child held up by his father, urged itself inside for an autograph. Annoying, these interruptions. We were in the final countdown, both of us a tangle of jangled nerves, studying maps, checking equipment, each doing the best we could to calm the other, both probably wondering how the hell we ever got here in the first place. And why. At least I was.

This was the culmination of nearly a year of planning, preparation, and training. For us, this race began eleven months before when we first made the decision to do the ninth Paris/Dakar Rallye.

We were about to begin the longest, toughest, most hazardous race in the world. Over eight thousand miles, most of it through the Sahara, an area so vast you could superimpose the United States over it and still have room left over for duplicates of some of our biggest states. The course would wind its way through five North African countries, not all of them hospitable, over some of the most inhuman terrain God, nature, and the Rallye organization could devise. Twenty-two days, that's how long the ordeal would last. If we would last. Most don't make it to the end. Typically more than a third of the field has its dreams, cars, or bodies smashed by the third or fourth day. Oh, well, we were as ready as we'd ever be. We were also both emotional and physical basket cases. Well, not quite. Physically we were both strong, probably as fit as either of us had ever been. Still, I was fighting the flu, had been for two or three days. I had the sniffles and was aching, running a slight fever. She was having migraine headaches. Not surprising considering what we'd already been through, the frantic pace we'd been keeping for months. And it was about to accelerate.

Yes, I said "she." Carolyn was my codriver, navigator, riding mechanic, fiancée. We were probably the most unlikely pair in the race.

She, tall, thin, twenty-nine, beautiful, a New York fashion photographer who had absolutely no prior experience at this sort of thing. Me, short, skinny, just turned forty-eight, an advertising executive who after thirty-three years had just dropped out to, as they say, "pursue other interests."

This wasn't really one of them. This was just something I was going through on my way to somewhere else. Just another way of fighting gravity.

People pushed and shoved all around us, clamoring every so often for autographs or for a word with us. We were the only Americans demented enough to show up for this contest. Our car was a bright white (to reflect the desert sun) Mercedes-Benz Gelandewagen specially built for the event. It glowed a dim pinkish-blue in the pre-dawn light like a fluorescent tube in its last seconds of existence. Every so often it seemed to flicker back to life, whenever a beam from one of the big, theatrical arc searchlights orbited past.

Next to us Guy Dupard, the driver of car number 247, was holding a makeshift press conference. Floodlights suddenly lit up by the camera crew made obvious the slanting rain. We'd lived under it for two months in France. We were taunted by a bright, clear picture of the drear we'd been so long hoping to escape. Dupard stood beaming through the downpour, chug-a-lugging from a magnum bottle of champagne and posing for the cameras while his copilot passed out miniature bottles of chianti, salamis, matchbooks, and autographed posters. The sponsor of his car was the Casa Nostra Pizza chain and his team was earning that sponsorship. One of our sponsors was Perdue Chicken. PERDUE FRESH YOUNG CHICKEN was painted in bright red letters all over the front of our car. I could have put Dupard in the shade if I'd had a few cases of raw chickens to pass out.

Perdue as a sponsor was a possible source of amusement to French- and English-speaking people alike. First the irony. The young, inexperienced female copilot who had been attracting so much attention just because she was a girl, a pretty one at that. This, juxtaposed with "Fresh Young Chicken," attracted even more notice. Then there was the fact that in French perdu means "lost." And becoming lost in the desert is one of the greatest hazards of the race. I thought it was all kind of funny and got a kick out of it when people asked, seriously, if I was aware of the secondary messages being sent out. Carolyn was not amused. Lately nothing seemed to amuse Carolyn much.

To the other side of us, in car number 249, was a young Englishman named Gooding. He was driving a factory-assisted Mitsubishi. As if to flaunt his Englishness, it was right-hand drive. Earlier his copilot had helped Carolyn cut up and organize some of the maps we'd need in Africa. Now Gooding was out in the rain, checking the locks on his hood.

"What's with the locks?" I called out through my sliding peephole.

He shoved his way over and told me that in Africa thieves often sneak into camp while competitors sleep, open the hoods of cars, dismantle the engines, and cart the pieces off into the desert. I noticed Dupard had engine locks too. Here I was, a man without a chicken, and not a lock to my name. What was I getting myself into? I didn't know it then, but the mother of invention was to provide me with a rather obvious solution to the no-lock problem. No sleep.

But I'm getting ahead of myself.

Forget for the moment the subject of sleep, of locks, of chickens, of lights, cameras, autographs, rain, crowds. Defer for a while the distorted blare of the announcer who was calling the cars to the starting ramp, the trucks and motorcycles already having been flagged on their way. Let us leave the marshalls in their bright white coveralls who arm in arm formed a cordon against the crowd and were gesturing to us to start our engine and move out. Toward the ramp. Toward Africa. Toward what?

What were we doing here, a couple of amateurs about to begin a race even professionals regard as the toughest there is? More to the point, why? Is this the kind of thing anyone in his right mind would want to do with his time, his money, his loved one; to say nothing of his own life? I wasn't sure. I sat there with a lot of questions and no answers. The biggest question was what would I do with my life when this race was over. Maybe by the end of it I'd have an answer. Maybe by the end of it I wouldn't have a life to wonder about. But I was a little too busy to worry about that just then.

1

About five years before, a young woman, American, visiting Paris on a photography assignment, chanced upon the spectacle I've recently described. She was swept up by the excitement and imagined herself dashing off into the unknown at great speed with all the other mad adventurers. Years later, it would be my fate to fall in love with this dreamer and to become the Svengali who would help her realize that dream.

We met through friends. A model I knew in New York and her boyfriend brought Carolyn to my apartment for dinner. Friends were always introducing me to attractive, available women as if I were a Venus's-flytrap that would bloom when fed the perfect fly.

There was no evidence that Carolyn could ever be that one. On the contrary, this had all the makings of a mismatch. She was much younger, much taller, and very different. She, much more than me, seemed uncomfortable with those differences. She was twenty-eight, trying to launch her career as a fashion photographer. Carolyn led a bohemian, spartan existence in a loft downtown. I was forty-seven, at the peak of a successful advertising career and lived in a style consistent with that success. I could see that she regarded my midtown apartment with disdain and my life-style with suspicion. She cringed when my butler came in and offered her a drink. But she was very good looking. And you never knew what might happen.

Her hair ran from light brown to blond, in streaks, and she had it pulled back severely into a pony tail. She had a high and open forehead with pronounced cheekbones. Her cheeks then narrowed abruptly and disappeared into the largest set of dimples I'd ever seen. When she smiled, which was often, everything widened, the greenish eyes, her mouth. And when her mouth went wide, the dimples deepened, mak-

6

ing her into a bold caricature of a beautiful woman. In every other way she was an understatement. Hers was a natural beauty. She wore no lipstick or makeup of any kind. No nail polish, no perfume, no jewelry. And she was dressed all in black, which lent a bright whiteness to her naturally pale skin.

Her entire wardrobe, I would learn, was either black or white, consistent with her views on a variety of subjects.

Carolyn was a good three inches taller than me, in flats, and had the look of a girl who worked in front of a camera, not behind one. As I'd spent my life in advertising, I was familiar with the New York photography scene. We had many mutual acquaintances so were able to communicate with each other, at least on a superficial level.

She was a bit of a joker, a clownesse. In the sixties we would have called her "kooky." She would wink or rearrange her animated face into a variety of funny expressions, sometimes erasing one dimple and increasing the size of the other. She did this often, for she had a quirky sense of humor that seemed to require frequent excercising.

Before the evening was over, I found myself staring at her and smiling a lot.

I pursued her relentlessly, concocting all kinds of specious reasons for calling her or visiting her at the studio where she worked and lived. It soon developed into an all-out, albeit protracted, campaign. For many months it remained an on-again, off-again type of affair. One day I seemed to be be doing fine with her, the next she wouldn't answer my calls. I likened it to playing hockey. Every so often I'd be cited for some infraction and find myself in the penalty box. I'd sit there waiting for the time to run out so I could streak back onto the ice and bash my brains out yet again. I have always been a sucker for the difficult, a riser to challenges, and this was a big one.

Every time things seemed to be going well, something would happen to change it. If the romance became too intense, she'd retreat. A small disagreement or an argument would abruptly lead to a period of es-trangement. Or the sudden appearance of someone from out of her past would lead to a crisis. I believed she was testing my conviction, plumbing the depths of my ardor. At least that's what I wanted to believe. I tried that much harder, sending even funnier notes with bigger bunches of flowers, though I must admit I was growing a little weary of riding this particular seesaw. But I remained convinced that the prize was worth the contest.

I decided to get out of town. This was part tactic, but even more, a necessity. When I met Carolyn, I had been planning on taking a sabbatical but put it off, hoping our relationship would seek some comprehensible level.

Finally I was happy to be getting away. I needed some time on my own, to think, to ponder my career. I had been in advertising for thirty-two years. Recently, something inside had been telling me it was time to take a peek at the world outside. Was this the career I would choose for myself if I had the choice to make over again? I didn't know. I was president and creative director of an ad agency I'd cofounded nineteen years earlier. It had become big and successful by dint of hard work, good luck, and some talent. I was sitting at the top of my profession, with more to look back on than forward to. I had a comfortable job and a comfortable life, but I was uncomfortable in my comfort. I felt uneasy, stifled, frustrated. I spent most of my time trying to teach others what I already knew, but I was learning little. To me this seemed like dying. It's learning that's living.

What if I were to apply my talent to something new? Maybe I could write, maybe produce or direct films; exactly what I didn't know. All I knew was that it was time I knew. At forty-seven, having made a name and some money for myself, I would never be in a better position to decide.

The sabbatical was to be more than a period of self-indulgent introspection. It was also an act of self-preservation. My doctor ordered it. Years of stress, smoking, drinking, bad eating, and hard living had taken their toll. For the past two years, he had nursed me back toward good health with a strict diet and total abstinence from all that had gone before. I was making headway, but the job was far from finished.

My doctor advised me to take four months off. But two months was all I could swing. In the advertising business, four months is a lifetime. Four might have been twice as good as two, but I figured two was twice as good as none. Besides, in my current state of mind, it was just possible I would decide to leave my company. It wouldn't have been fair to go away for four months, then come back and just go away.

Aspen is where I was headed. The Volvo (my company's oldest and one of our most visible clients) wagon was loaded with more than its fair share of my worldly possessions. A computer for writing, all my ski gear, my youngest son's guitar. I had this silly notion I might learn to play it while away. These and other assorted personal items crammed the car. Much of it was the kind of stuff that normally stays stashed in a basement at home but which inevitably accompanies you to a house you've rented for two months' vacation. Where it also goes unused.

Carolyn had come to my place to help me load up the wagon. I was to drop her off at her studio downtown near the Holland Tunnel, which I would then take out of Manhattan on my long trip west. We set off down Second Avenue. It was the middle of January, cold, with snow on the ground that was almost white, a rarity in New York. It was one of those brilliant bright days with a deep blue sky, it having been brushed clean by the recent snowfall, which lay there, barely soiled from its labors.

There was traffic. Morning rush hour in New York. These people were all going to work. For a change, I wasn't. And I was happy at the prospect. Yet I was a little sad to be leaving behind this beautiful girl who was now radiating "on." The fact that I was going away seemed to have thrown the magic switch.

We were talking. The talk was of skiing, of writing, of, how can I bring myself to say, "midlife crisis." As we inched our way downtown, the talk somehow turned to dreams. Not the kind that visit you at night. The kind that haunt you for life as long as they remain un-realized. I always had a few of these. To sail around the world, to fight a bull, to drive a bobsled down an Olympic run, to find *the* woman. Daredevil dreams mostly. I told her about some of them. She didn't give me the typical "Boy, are you crazy" reaction girls give you on those rare occasions when you spill your innermost thoughts. She had an adventurous spirit too. For about a year before I met her, she'd spent her weekends parachuting out of planes.

Carolyn was a bit of a rebel and a tomboy. That's what the black sweaters and jeans she usually wore were all about. Sort of a young, fashionable, guerrilla uniform. She'd been brought up well, in a small town in the East. Her father was successful and well off. She had even been a debutante, though she now seemed more dedicated to refuting that upbringing by spurning financial aid from her family and doing wild and dangerous things. A very independent lady. She cultivated the friendship of starving artists, writers, musicians, and a potpourri of downtown whackos. There was little "normal" about her, and that's what appealed to me. She threatened many of the conventions I had adopted over the years, and I found being with her both refreshing and stimulating, although people who knew her "when" thought she had gone a little off. Her young nieces had taken to calling her "Crazy Aunt Carolyn."

"I've always dreamed of driving in the Paris/Dakar Rallye," she said, as casually as some girls talk about having their nails done.

"Oh? We could do that," I said in reply.

As soon as I said it, I realized I'd made a fateful pronouncement. It never ceases to amaze me how easily I seize the impossible and start running with it. Had she dreamed of climbing Mount Everest or of walking across Antarctica, or swimming the Pacific, it wouldn't have made any difference. Maybe it would have taken me two or three seconds before saying "Oh? We could do that." But this response was not that carefully considered. In fact, it was so spontaneous that she was now giving me one of those "Boy, are you crazy" looks.

Maybe I was. Maybe I always had been. Certainly I've always gone against the grain of what "normal" people call normal.

When I was born, I wasn't even supposed to be. I popped out of the oven two months premature, fingers and toes still unglazed. I was put in a real oven to cook some more. Once out I made a mission of doing what I wasn't supposed to. It was a habit I carried with me from birth, one that had been formed genetically then hardened in an incubator.

In my youth I went to a Catholic grammar school and began to make good on the promise I showed at birth. I went to war with the nuns. I rebelled against the way they tried to make me just like everybody else. They rapped me on the knuckles with rulers whenever I wrote with my left hand. But it was a habit they couldn't break me of, no matter how hard they tried. I smeared my bloody knuckles around on my paperwork and defied them with my eyes to give me bad marks for neatness. If it hadn't been for their trying so hard to make me into something I didn't want to be, I might have ended up right-handed anyway. I only write and throw left-handed. In everything else I'm a natural righty.

My father died when I was eight. I didn't cry at his funeral. I even turned my head away when my sobbing mother tried to kiss me. That kind of stuff was for babies, forever behind me. I had become the man of the house, I thought. My mother interpreted these as signs of disrespect rather than the symbolic display of maturity that was intended to fortify rather than upset her. It was a stoic acceptance of responsibility and a radically different future from the one I had grown to expect. From then on, my mother and I rarely approved of anything the other did. I was nine years old when I took over.

I got a job selling papers at a newsstand on weekends. After school I delivered papers, soon working myself up to three routes. I even took on the tough one, the collection run. This entailed delivering papers to everyone who hadn't paid. It was tough because I couldn't just fold and fling. I had to walk up and knock, then put the arm on them. All the shirkers seemed to live on the third floors of the buildings I delivered to. Also most of them worked, so I couldn't get them after school. I had to wait and go after dinner. My mother didn't like me going out so late, but it paid the best of all my jobs. I got a percentage of the take.

The way I'd collect the money from the scofflaws, when they'd answer the door, was with an appeal of disarming directness, a tech- nique I would use in later years in advertising with great success.

At first they wouldn't even see me. They'd look right over my head, peering out their screened back doors in the dark. I was small even for my height, beneath most people's notice.

"Good evening, I'm your newsboy and here's your paper."

"You didn't have to ring." Most of them said something like that as I handed over the paper.

"I'm sorry to bother you, but I need you to settle up your bill for the papers. My father just died, my mother isn't working, I go to a Catholic school, and if I don't collect it's going to come out of my pay and, believe me, I need the money more than you do right now."

So I'd go, door to door, collecting much more effectively than the big bruisers who'd ring the bell and say, "Duh, you gotta pay up."

I never told my mom what I was saying on these rounds. She didn't like me working nights in the first place. I'm sure she would have been horrified, thinking it was beneath our dignity for me to use our un- fortunate circumstances for commercial ends. Already I had a great load of pride, but this didn't ruffle it in the least. There is always pride in the truth. I seemed to instinctively know this. I didn't beg or whine or ask anyone to feel sorry for me. I just stated the case and stuck out my hand.

My mother remarried. A nice guy but I hated his becoming my stepfather. A truck driver. I thought *he* was beneath our dignity, and I let him know it. My mother thought I was becoming unmanageable.

I got thrown out of my genteel Catholic high school. Thrown out for fighting. No, worse than fighting. I sent a big bully to the hospital for a long convalescence. The police got involved. I was sent to a vocational high school. So unenthralling few of us going there went. We learned more on the street. My mother and stepfather thought I was going to school. I was. But rarely. Most of my classes were held in pool halls. I'd hustle. I never stopped working, just changed the nature of my business activities. When pool didn't pay, I'd join the winos in the bowling alley setting pins. But that was hard, rough work. And it stank back there. The alkies were forever busting their bottles of sauterne and cutting themselves up. And each other. I'd pick up a couple of dollars this way then move on to sell popcorn, peanuts, or soft drinks at Wrigley Field just so I could get into the high-stakes card games with the vendors afterward. I was almost fifteen. I had tattoos. And then I got into real trouble.

It wasn't anything heinous. It was just another rebellious kid thing. But the cops made it clear to me and my mother and stepfather that I wasn't to be allowed one more thing. I either had to go back to school and keep my nose clean or drop out, get a job, and stick to it. If not, they'd see to it that I was put away. All that hypocritical talk about what I needed for my own good. That's what got me. It came after they'd beat the shit out of you with the rubber pipes. They'd always hit you on the neck with them, where it would really hurt without showing bruises. And, of course, they always punched you a few times in the stomach so you couldn't inhale the proferred cigarette even if you wanted to. As if it was a precious gift or something! But that's the way it was in those days. Bogart smoked, so it was cool. Daley's cops held up grocery stores and hauled away cartons of stolen cigarettes in their squad cars in broad daylight. The surgeon general was off screwing around with polio or something, so nobody knew any better. And, of course, everybody liked Ike.

I quit high school. The employment agent I went to said, "I'll send you to an ad agency. They'll hire anybody!"

Through study and struggle, I grew out of the mailroom. I started by reading the dictionary. It was the only place I could think of where I would find everything ever written. For education I read the Harvard Classics. Then I read just for the sake of reading. Kafka, he was hot then. Shakespeare, naturally. And Kerouac, who helped explain me to myself. I even began to write. Poetry, short stories, mostly for myself. No delusions. For a time I thought I might someday write the great American novel. I put that dream back in my pants and got on with a career in advertising.

Business associates told me to take college night courses. I couldn't tell them I hadn't even done high school. I'd lied about that, and about my age. It seemed logical to me that if I worked twice as hard as a normal person, in four year's time, I'd know more and be ahead of anyone just graduating college.

Eddie Fisher sang "Oh, Mein Papa." "Earth Angel" played, and Elvis Presley was coming on strong. I heard it in the background. What little time I wasn't working, I played with girls and cars. I'd met some people who were into sports cars and the bug bit me, too. Soon, I started rallying, then racing.

I'd just missed Korea. One day I went pheasant hunting with a guy who hadn't. He shot a cow for kicks. Glad I missed Korea.

Moved in with my mechanic. He couldn't cook. Neither could I. I bought the *Escoffier Cookbook* and learned, the hard way. Our apartment was just to one side of the Chinese laundry we used. The guy who ran it didn't like us. I think he was jealous, watching all the girls coming in and out. He used to starch our sheets and nothing we yelled at him would make him stop. Whenever one of us had a hot date, we'd break open a freshly starched set, place the pieces on the bed, and burn the skin off our knees.

Had a bad racing crash. Selective Service called me the week after. Me, on crutches. Great timing.

The ads I was writing were winning awards.

One weekend I made a pit stop in a race. A gorgeous number in short-shorts was sitting on the hood of a Corvette. We stared at each other.

"Later," I said to her before peeling back out onto the course.

Later she was there, having dumped her date. It turned out she wanted to learn how to write advertising copy. I just happened to be able to help. Six months of nights I taught her. She then decided she wanted to go to New York to look for work. I'd just quit a job, so I went with her. She immediately got work as a copywriter. At first, I couldn't get a cold, so I contracted a cashier's job in Schrafft's.

Once I connected, my New York career began to soar. People stopped liking Ike. JFK came to pass. Chubby Checkers had everybody twisting their nights away. J. D. Salinger reacquainted me with myself. I wore Brooks Brothers suits and for sporty social occasions put Band-Aids on my bare arms to hide my tattoos. I started racing again, driving better, faster cars. Changed girlfriends, got married, had a son. Stopped racing. Gave my all to advertising. The marriage ended in divorce.

By now I had my own ad agency. Worked hard, traveled widely, lived well. Penned a succession of successful ad campaigns. People said I had a way with words. My mother said I'd always had the gift of blarney. Got it from my dad. My peers said I was one of the greats, installed me in the Copywriters Hall of Fame. That happened when I was thirty-five. The others were mostly older, mostly dead. I was flying high.

Met another girl, got remarried. Moved to Connecticut, had a second son, continued to build my business. All along I fit the mold I was born in. One time when my wife and I visited France, we went to the Domaine de la Romanée-Conti. What Lourdes is to Catholics, Romanée-Conti is to oenophiles. I was becoming interested in wine and had a small collection. A snooty Frenchman was there with us buying some wine. He looked at me with a superior air and asked if I collected wine, if I had a "wine cell-air."

"Yes, I have a few hundred bottles," I told him proudly.

"A few hundred boo-tells? Monsieur, you do not have zee wine cell-air, you have zee wine closette!"

I'll show this creep, I thought. The next day I went back to New York and ordered two thousand bottles of wine, sneaking them into the house a couple of cases at a time so my wife wouldn't freak at the scale of my revenge.

Carter was out to get the "two-martini lunch." It seemed like a good time to sell the company. Money came. Moved back into the city, built a palatial weekend house, bought a forty-six Ford convertible, just to remind me of who I was. Got divorced again. Didn't know if it was me or my all-consuming drive. She didn't know you're not supposed to kick a man when he's up.

Entered my wine, women, and Wong period. Consumed more than my fair share of the first two. Wong was my Chinese houseman who saved his only English for just after dessert.

"One pirrow or two?"

If there was a great party in L.A. or Sydney or Hong Kong, I'd be there. Five in the morning at the bar of a splendid hotel in the south of France, my drinking partner, a famous film producer, announced, "We'd better make this the last one, Ed. I hate to keep the plane waiting." Time to find some new tracks to put my life back on.

Unhappy, unfocused, I had everything a lot of people think they want. Having got it, I knew that wasn't it. I got sick. Got rid of Wong, hired a man who knew how to cook health food, sold my country house. At night, I sat in my apartment and moped. I lost interest in women. I lost interest in my company, in what it had become, and in where it was headed. And in so doing, I lost interest in life. I had nothing new, nothing exciting, nothing impossible to look forward to. When Carolyn and her dream of doing Paris/Dakar turned up, I had a vacancy. Both moved into the shell of my life.

Sitting in the Volvo, in traffic, Carolyn stared at me, wide-eyed, like I was nuts. And suddenly I found myself selling her on the feasibility of her own dream.

"We could do that. Really, we could. I used to race cars. I'm too old and too rusty, but I think we could pull it off. I could teach you what you need to know. I've got connections in racing circles. I could use my advertising contacts to get sponsors."

"And I'm very handy with mechanical things," Carolyn chimed in with equally naive enthusiasm. "I rewired my whole studio myself."

And so it began, the doing of a dream. An idi-oddyssey that would span a year, involve thirty-five thousand miles of travel, taking both of us from New York to Aspen to Las Vegas to New York to Austria and back again. Then to Georgia, Massachusetts, Ohio, Massachusetts again, Georgia again, and then from New York to London to Austria, Italy, Germany, France, Spain, North and North-Central Africa before coming home again.

Between the dreaming and the doing, there lies a great abyss filled with ignorance, blocks, hurdles, expenses, threats, realities. It is the fear of entering this void that keeps so many dreams undone, so many flights of fancy tethered to the ground. How many dreams never live to see the light of day? How many remain behind in how many unmade beds simply for want of trying? What a crime. All reality starts out as a dream. To deny one's dreams is to thwart reality, the same as killing a living thing. At least that's the way I see it.

By the time we got to her studio, a plan was evolving in my mind. I went inside and began making calls. I wanted to get the ball rolling. My car was not equipped with a phone and while I drove cross-country to Aspen, I didn't want this project at a standstill. So I started things in motion from there. Carolyn's mouth was now as wide as her eyes as she watched me swing into action. At first, she couldn't believe that I had actually taken her harebrained dream seriously.

We needed all kinds of information on the Rallye, its history, its dangers, its rules, its weather conditions. So I was calling around looking for information. I never do anything impulsive without first learning everything about the subject. It's a thoroughness that lives just outside the obsessive-compulsive border.

The Paris/Dakar Rallye was thundering into Dakar at that very moment. If we were serious about running the next one, we only had eleven and a half months to get ready. My instincts and experience told me that would barely be enough time. It would be a race just to get to the race.

We'd need a car, a very specialized kind of car. I'd have to do a lot of research on this. We'd need a sponsor, or many sponsors, to help defray some, hopefully all, of the costs. No way I was going to pick up the tab for the whole enterprise. I had to start doing homework and begin preparing a budget.

Carolyn needed to be trained in competition driving, navigation, mechanics. I needed retraining. It had been years since I'd raced a car. We'd both need competition licenses, a lengthy process that had to be started soon.

Both of us would have to start working out. The skiing would be a good beginning for me. But after, I'd really have to knuckle down. I was a wreck that needed to be overhauled, rebuilt, and restored from the ground up.

Meanwhile, the team, if it could rightly be called that, was still unengaged in a tenuous relationship. Would it ever come together and settle down? Would we ever get this Paris/Dakar pipedream off the ground? If so, *could* we do it? Realistically, I still held a demanding and time-consuming job. How could I keep all these balls in the air, me, who was supposed to be taking time off to relax, rest, recover?

These were some of the questions crowding my mind as I roared into Pennsylvania at over a hundred miles an hour. I was already practicing. And it wasn't long before I hurtled past my first hurdle: a Pennsylvania state trooper. His radar clocked me going eighty-six. It could have been worse. He could have been lurking on a downhill stretch instead of an uphill one. Now I had to creep toward Aspen. Well, relatively, anyway. I just couldn't afford to risk losing my driver's license. Without that, I couldn't get a competition license. No competition license, no Paris/Dakar. I'd have to save the racing for the race.

Where would we practice? With what? My mental gears meshed on into the night. If I couldn't practice speed, at least I could work on my endurance. I drove as fast as I dared for as long as I could and grabbed five hours' sleep somewhere in Indiana.

As I drove across America, I was possessed with a feeling of dawning potential. My life, which had been sidetracked, now bubbled with promise. I was in love and had little doubt I would win the girl. An exciting, dangerous, and nearly impossible challenge now gripped me. It was there for the doing. I vowed my enthusiasm and seriousness to Carolyn via a succession of pay phones as I hightailed my way toward Aspen.

Throwing myself into the spirit of the adventure, I converted a boring cross-country drive into a training routine. I had an instinct that becoming mesmerized by the dull, flat sameness of the desert was something I needed to prepare for. What could be closer to that than the turnpike through Indiana, Illinois, Iowa? I drove along, fighting off the mental wanderings. Who had more eighteen-wheelers on the road, Preston 151 or the Yellow Line? I'd snap myself back to attention and concentrate on the endless gray rolling ribbon. Where I was going mental distractions could prove deadly.

Instincts are what I've always lived by. Some people think things through, then act. Often after the optimum moment for action has passed. I've always acted instinctively, you could even say impulsively, then later reviewed what I was doing, checking up on my gut with my mind. That's what I was doing then, crossing Illinois and Iowa, reviewing my actions, intellectually assessing the situation my instincts had gotten me into.

Why had I seized upon this particular piece of craziness so readily? It must have had some logical fit in my agenda. What was it that attracted me? As always the pieces began to fall into place.

I honestly believed I could do it. In my younger days, I had raced cars, wasn't bad at it either. For a time I'd even thought of forgetting advertising and becoming a professional racing driver. My first marriage annulled that fantasy. A good thing, because by now I'd probably be too dead to once again consider risking my life. But the idea of reviving this long-lost dream, perhaps for the last time in my life, had a strong appeal.

Paris/Dakar could make the romance. It was an exciting, involving pursuit in which we had a mutual interest. It could pull us closer together as we worked toward a common goal. It could also break us apart what with the time pressures, the work, and the danger. A decision either way was a positive thing, I felt.

If I were to leave my job, my profession, Paris/Dakar would fill the vacuum during a critical time. Many make such a decision only to go rushing back to what they've left out of boredom, not allowing them-selves adequate time to discover the opportunities that wait. Certainly I wouldn't be bored.

If I stayed in my job, the Rallye would be an exciting interlude, an injection of life that could bring me back to advertising revitalized. It would also be good practice for any new career I was likely to choose. Pulling this project together, organizing it, preparing for it, selling sponsorships, was almost like producing a film, one of many possibilities I was considering.

If nothing else I could write about it. As a writer of advertising, certainly I could transition myself into writing articles, a screenplay, maybe even a book, using the race as a vehicle. Between this and whatever sponsorship I could round up, I might someday recoup my investment, might even make a little on it. If I didn't, what the hell? More and more I was beginning to think this was the kind of experience that could be amortized over a lifetime.

Carolyn could photograph it. Together we'd have the words and the pictures. She was a fine fashion photographer but was interested in other kinds of photography as well. Here was a chance for her to break out and demonstrate competence in another area.

Then there was the sheer challenge of it. No American had ever finished this race in a car. An American biker finished second in the motorcycle category two years before. But we could set a record in our category. An over-the-hill guy and a totally inexperienced girl finishing Paris/Dakar! No small accomplishment.

Also there was the sheer physical and emotional thrill of it, the kick. Both of us found going fast a turn-on. To go fast, to fly against for-midable odds was an idea that appealed to both of us. And I had this tremendous additional rush that rose out of a collision of conflicting emotions. I was overwhelmed by the basic, powerful urge to protect the life of the one I was becoming convinced I loved, while in the process of doing something that threatened it.

Most of all, it was an opportunity and I felt I had to seize it. If you miss an opportunity, it moves on to someone else. Opportunities always take the path of least resistance.

2

There I was, newly arrived in Aspen, which boasts some of the most magnificent ski slopes anywhere, and what did I do? I hit the phones. The first person I called was an old racing crony from Chicago. I planned to call everyone I knew, anyone who knew anything at all that could help me.

"I'm thinking of running the Paris/Dakar Rallye," I told him.

"You're crazy. People get killed doing that."

"With my girlfriend as codriver," I went on.

"Why not? As I said, you're crazy. You're too old, you're not good enough, and you're not man enough, but you're rich enough and crazy enough, so why not?"

Jack was always a joker. This was exactly what I wanted to hear. Recognition of the difficulty, with conditional approval. Jack knew me. We'd raced together for years. If he thought I couldn't do it, he would have come right out and said so.

"I need a car. What do you think?"

"Why don't you call Volvo? After all you've done for them, they should give you a car, spares, *and* a support team."

"I called them just before I left New York. They're thinking about it. But they said two-wheel drive could be a problem."

"Maybe so. Where are you?"

"In Aspen, skiing, getting in shape. I'll be here for two months."

"Good. Then you can break a leg and drive Paris/Dakar with another handicap. Good luck."

This was not unlike many other conversations I was to have about Paris/Dakar, although most of the warnings weren't couched with such lighthearted jocularity. I called all over the world in my quest for information. Nothing I heard was as positive and encouraging as the chat I had with Jack. They were all gloomy variations on the same gravity-laden theme.

Through my friends and contacts at the automotive magazines, I got the name of an American who had entered Paris/Dakar the year before. I tracked him down in California. I said "entered" because he didn't finish. This guy hadn't even run for long. He was knocked out on the first day with mechanical problems. Another member of his team hadn't even fared that well. He didn't make it to the starting line. He was knocked out in the Prologue, the time trial that takes place two days before the start to establish starting positions. A former winner of the Indy 500, he had crashed, breaking his nose and his kneecap. I was finding that just talking about Paris/Dakar hurt.

The California man also informed me that "the Dakar" presented another kind of hazard altogether. The first night in Africa their camp was raided by desert marauders who stole most of their gear.

I asked him what he thought I should do to train for the event.

"Running a marathon a week isn't enough" is what he said.

In Detroit, I contacted a guy who had gone along with the Rallye the year before, scouting it for an American car company that was thinking of entering a factory team. He began by asking me all kinds of questions I couldn't answer.

What kind of support team will you have? What kind of car are you driving? Will you have factory backing? And so on. I informed him that I was in the early planning stages, that I had no idea what kind of car I'd be driving, that I would do it with my girlfriend who was totally inexperienced, that I had little hope of factory backing and that we would in all likelihood be providing our own mechanical assistance, that we were doing it not so much for victory or glory but for fun.

"It would be fun to enter the Olympics too," he said.

I considered this guy a real jerk. Here we had a spectator, a knowl-edgeable spectator maybe, being sarcastic and patronizing to someone who might actually do it. I have no use for these negative types, deflaters who come up with all kinds of reasons why something can't or shouldn't be done. They give you negative inspiration. Rather than tell you the problems and encouraging you to find ways around them, they backwash you with their own fears and limitations, hold you down to their level. They make you want to do something just to show them. Thirty-inch yardsticks. That's what I call them.

Water was the biggest thing on this boy's brain. He kept going on about the problem of water and how he'd found a way to lick the water contamination problem and the plastic-tank taste by putting a half-bottle of Scotch in each tank for two days before the Rallye, then dumping it and refilling with fresh water. Something like telling a downhill ski racer that wearing a sweater will help with the cold.

I thanked him for his help, made a mental note of the water business, and never called him again.

I'd left a message for Pietmor Bienhaur, the head of the BMW motorcycle racing team, which had done very well over the years, winning in the motorcycle category four times. He called me from Hamburg where he'd gone for a meeting. Most of the people I talked to were generous, accommodating, and helpful like this busy man proved to be. I told him what I was up to. He was succinct.

"Prepare. Prepare. Prepare. It's the hardest race in the world."

"Harder than the Baja 1000?"

"It's like twenty Baja 1000s, back to back."

I thanked him for the advice and resolved to thank him in person, somewhere in Africa, I hoped.

Sometimes it took six or eight calls before I was able to connect with someone I wanted to reach. By the time I left Aspen, my phone bill had nearly won a race with my rent.

Of course I made quite a few calls to Carolyn, too, finally coaxing her to come out to Aspen for a visit. The reunion was great. We got her outfitted in ski clothes, black and white, naturally. In her tight black ski pants, she was a standout even in Aspen, which is where the standouts go to stand out. I did my best to teach her how to ski. The first day I pushed her hard and she fell down a lot but progressed rapidly. I don't think either of us ever laughed so hard in our lives, rolling in the snow, shedding tears of happiness. Either our long separation or my method of ski instruction seemed to bring us closer together than we had ever been.

My rented chalet was on Red Mountain, facing the World Cup downhill run, which snaked down Aspen Mountain, directly across the way. The owner was a very successful and well-known composer of popular music. So the place was not only equipped with an enormous Jacuzzi but with a wallful of gold records hanging over a perfectly tuned and incredibly shiny black piano. Carolyn played Bach on it. I cooked mountain trout on a grill in the fireplace. Love was great. Unfortunately, it was fleeting. She could only stay a few days before returning to work in New York, leaving me unhappy and alone.

Meantime, I kept compiling info on Paris/Dakar with a belief so strong that it was as good as knowing that we were going to end up together, that we were going to do Paris/Dakar. It was going to be a great adventure.

On the International Calendar of Motoring Events, Paris/Dakar is not classified as a race or a rally, but is the one event categorized as a "Raid." It is a motorsports mutation, combining the worst elements of both racing and rallying.

Unlike endurance races such as the Daytona twenty-four-hour race or the twenty-four hours of Le Mans, Paris/Dakar is not held on a fixed circuit. It follows a different route every year. Which countries it travels through and the exact course to be followed is kept a closely guarded secret until three weeks before the start, which for the last few years had been in Versailles, just outside of Paris.

It usually begins on New Year's morning and always ends up in Dakar, Senegal, on the west coast of Africa. In between lie eight to nine thousand miles of hellish terrain to be traversed in daily stages. As a result, the cars that run it are more like off-road vehicles than conventional racing machines. It takes twenty to twenty-two days to get to Dakar, depending on the length of the course and the whim of the organizers. It is so brutal that the vast majority of the five hundred or so contestants never make it to the end. Usually, fully a third of them are knocked out in the first couple of days.

Like most rallies, Paris/Dakar is made up of two kinds of stages— liaisons and speciales. Liaisons are relatively tame tours designed to move the contestants along at a good clip to a predetermined point. After the initial liaison stage through France to the boat that takes the drivers and vehicles to Africa, most of the stages would be speciales—full-blown races. Each of these is like a separate race, so you can perform poorly in one and still come back and improve your standing on subsequent days. The objective is to complete each day's speciale in the minimum possible time. Often these individual legs are so long and the going so arduous that the days slop over into the nights. Physical and mental exhaustion play major roles in Paris/Dakar. The winner is the one who uses the fewest hours, minutes, and seconds in getting to Dakar.

In setting up the course, the organizers plan it for the fastest competitors and make no allowances for slowpokes, breakdowns, accidents, or navigational errors along the way. They establish a maximum time you are allowed to complete each stage. If you go over that, you are penalized additional hours. This pushes you still farther behind the leader, forcing you to take greater risks to catch up, increasing the likelihood of disaster.

Disaster has dogged Paris/Dakar since its inception in 1978. To the best of my knowledge, there had never been a year when someone, either a driver, a navigator, or a spectator, wasn't killed. Twenty-six people have died in its short history. And hundreds have been injured. Some of those so severely it could be argued that they'd be better off dead.

The Paris/Dakar Rallye originally began as a race for motorcycles. Contrived by a swashbuckling Frenchman named Thierry Sabine, it has become more than a race for death-defying cyclists, more than simply a race. It is a uniquely French expression of "the great adventure." It pits humans and machines, now cars and trucks as well as motorcycles, against a variety of hardships and dangers in the hope of showing the world how people under extremes of stress display uncommon bravery, sometimes heroism, occasionally desperate and fanatical determination.

This aspect of "the Dakar," as the French call it, was perhaps best exemplified in 1985 by the motorcyclist who ran out of gas and pushed his bike for many miles, for many hours, through heavy sand under the blazing sun. Miraculously, he made it to the finish line that day, only to fall from exhaustion as he crossed it, dead. The ultimate finish. It is high drama. And the French relish it, promising in each year's entry form a fleeting glimpse of some of the world's most awe-inspiring scenery and ever new opportunities for adventure and heroism.

In 1986 Thierry Sabine himself was killed in a helicopter in which he and three others were out looking for stragglers. It was blown into a sand dune during a sandstorm and crashed, killing everyone aboard.

When the subject of Paris/Dakar comes up, horrible tales of fatalities, injuries, and misadventures like kidnapping, robberies, strandings, and the like are about all you hear. Seldom do you hear of the money that is donated by the Rallye organization to the poor African countries the Rallye traverses. Or the pumps they donate to bring water to remote villages. This is the fault of the organizers themselves who are proficient at generating adverse publicity but are public relations neophytes.

When compiling background information for this book, I tried to get statistics on Paris/Dakar injuries and fatalities directly from the organization. I was told that they had no data on this and, besides, it was something they didn't like to have publicized. As an advertising man who has made a career out of understanding human nature and communicating with the public, I could have told them that nothing makes steam escape like trying to keep the lid on the pot. The imagined and speculated dangers of the Paris/Dakar Rallye are probably far, far worse than the actuality due to this stupid and shortsighted attitude.

The Paris/Dakar Rallye has generated a legend far greater than its short life span would seem to deserve, largely due to the controversy, the "incidents," and the carnage that the media gobbles up and spits out in magnified form.

I was a long-time automobile afficionado and former sports car racer, yet "Paris/Dakar" had seemed even to me as one of those racing legends that had always been around. That it was a part of motoring history like the Indy 500 or the Vanderbilt Cup. Not some crazy idea that got cooked up in 1978. Of course to the average American, the Paris/Dakar Rallye means little, if that much. But to car enthusiasts and to the general population of the rest of the world, it's big. Right up there with the World Cup in soccer, the World Series in baseball, the Super Bowl, or the Kentucky Derby, though to much of the world those last three are just glorified local events. They're also highly specialized, professional.

To a Frenchman, Englishman, Spaniard, Scandinavian, Italian or German, doing the Dakar is a dream real people can still have, even amateurs like me and Carolyn, and like themselves. So it has a cachet most Americans would find hard to comprehend. In France, the Dakar gets three weeks of continuous television coverage. Open, say, a Dutch newspaper on any day the Rallye is under way, and you'll find a good half-page devoted to it. On New Year's day, millions line the roads of France to get a glimpse of the blurs going by, to scream their "*Bonnes chances.*" In Barcelona, where the Rallye embarked for Africa the year Carolyn and I were running, more than a million people packed the streets. At three o'clock in the morning. But, again, I'm getting way ahead of myself.

Winning the thing was a notion that never entered either of our heads. So why did we even think of entering a competition we knew we couldn't win? Isn't that downright un-American?

Maybe, but winning Paris/Dakar was simply unthinkable. The past few years Porsche had dominated it. Their methodically organized and well-equipped team of professional drivers and state-of-the-art four-wheel drive racing cars had torn through the desert at 150 miles an hour and left most everyone else back somewhere choking on their dust.

Automobile companies such as Porsche use Paris/Dakar as a proving ground for new technology, as a showcase for their products' performance and reliability. They don't pinch pennies on this ego trip. Neither do the Japanese, with teams from Toyota and Mitsubishi. Nor the English with their desertproven, soupedup Land and Range Rovers. Nor the French with their Peugeot and Renault teams. That took care of, at least, the first ten places.

After the factory teams, one had to pay heed to at least a score of teams underwritten by wealthy private individuals or consortiums whose cars would also be driven by professionals, some of them world class Formula One drivers out to prove themselves in another class of competition. Optimistically, that would put us down to about twentieth place. Then there were dozens of private entries, piloted by serious drivers who received financial and mechanical assistance from factory teams running the same make of car. Thirtieth? Fortieth?

And that's without considering the other hundreds of hopefuls. The Belgian garage mechanic who saved up for a lifetime to run the Paris/ Dakar. The royalty. Prince Albert of Monaco had run the year before. Princess Stephanie had tried to. The truck she was in crashed fifteen minutes into Africa. The movie stars, the rock stars, bored South American businessmen, the dozens and dozens of eager young Frenchmen who see Paris/Dakar as a way to prove or enhance their virility, the adventurers, the thrillseekers. Those who have nothing much else to live for, so why not? One couldn't just dismiss them all. Fiftieth? Maybe fiftieth. If we were lucky. In an event where more than 75 percent of the starters don't finish, finishing alone is considered something of a victory. But winning? Come *on*.

In Aspen, my files and scribbles continued to grow until they stood in a teetering pile on the coffee table in front of the fireplace in the chalet. I'd managed to get a copy of part of last year's route book. It arrived, all in French, and was gobbledygook to me. I started calling around for a French teacher, preferably one who understood something about navigational terminology.

I'd formulated a budget. There were still a lot of variables, so I figured, roughly, somewhere between $125,000 and $160,000, depending on the type of car we chose. That was the biggest variable. The Volvo people had been very helpful, but in the end we decided I would need a fourwheeldrive car, something they didn't make. This meant if I couldn't coax some car company into lending me a car, I would have to buy one or have one made. Add to this the cost of research and training, our travel and living expenses, our supplies— tires, oil, gasoline, spare parts, tools, camping gear—and transport for it all. To make Paris/Dakar affordable (it wasn't affordable, let's say possible), I had to try to accomplish one of two things: (1) Get a car for nothing or next to nothing, or (2) sign a sponsor or sponsors to the tune of $160,000.

That was if we did everything ourselves, on a shoestring. If we had mechanics or other assistance like serious competitors had, flying along in the Rallye's chartered planes, it would cost more, maybe as much as $250,000. Even that was a pittance compared to the factory teams that also entered teams of trucks to transport parts and support their entries. They invested millions to bring cars across the line. For reasons both financial and romantic, Carolyn and I would be doing the Dakar with no outside help. We would be the pilot, the copilot, and the backup team, all in two. Rather than seeing this as a ridiculous handicap, I viewed it as an additional incentive to press on. It just made the challenge that much more worth meeting. I liked it like that.

I now had all the information I needed to make a decision whether or not to go ahead. All I needed to know was whether or not I had a girlfriend who was going to go with me.

I invited Carolyn out to Aspen again. Again, the separation seemed to have had a salubrious effect on our relationship. This time her visit was better, more fun and longer lived, but also too short. She had to get back to her photography business. Before she left, though, we resolved that we were a team, romantically and for Paris/Dakar. Now my work could really begin. I could actually start calling car companies for a car and potential sponsors for money, without worrying that I would be spouting off about some half-baked proposition that might never come off.

My youngest son, Colin, who was eleven at the time, came out to ski with me toward the end of my stay. He was disappointed to find that I wouldn't be skiing with him as planned. During my sixth week there, the day before he was due to arrive, I took a nasty spill, skiing way too fast for the conditions, and fractured my leg in two places. I now had the handicap Jack wished on me.

Carolyn came out a final time. We decided to make the most of my unfortunate situation. We shipped most of my stuff back to New York, packed up the Volvo, and headed for Las Vegas, a treat for Colin who hadn't been enjoying skiing too much without me anyway. As for me and Carolyn, the drive from Aspen to Las Vegas and then back to New York would give us valuable seat time together. I would begin coaching her and filling her in on all I'd learned we were up against.

My leg was in an inflatable cast and hurt like hell, particularly when I drove and had to depress the clutch. I regarded this as just another part of the training. I had an instinct that driving in pain was a skill that might be required.

3

En route to Las Vegas, I made another significant decision. And once there I acted on it. I sat in an overdecorated suite in Caesar's Palace composing letters of resignation to my soon-to-be former partners on the casino's stationery.

This makes it sound whimsical, I know. But it was not a decision I had taken lightly. For years I had been thinking about it, worrying it into a large, tight knot I kept in my stomach. More recently, I'd agonized over it. What I came to was the realization that anything that caused me such aggravation was probably something I could live without. It was that simple. Even the most worrisome things usually are.

Colin was making himself mindless on electronic games in Caesar's arcade. Carolyn was sunning herself by the pool. And I was writing my associates to the effect that we'd had a great run, but now it was time for me to pick up my winnings and walk away from the table. I wished them many sevens and elevens. It seemed fitting. Years before, when we'd first started out in business together, a couple of us had stood at a crap table in Las Vegas into the wee hours flushed with our small winnings and the excitement of the adventure we were just then beginning. For me, it was now ending, almost the way it began. And I could already feel the knot loosening.

Money was a concern but not a big one. We'd sold the company a few years before for a ducal sum (compared to what ad agencies are being sold for these days, I could hardly call the sum princely) and had gone on managing and building it. We'd taken it into the list of twenty largest ad agencies in the world and had an enviable reputation for our creativity, winning all the awards it was possible to win many times over. We had more than a thousand employees in offices all over the world. We had an impressive list of blue-chip clients. We had everything anyone in advertising could hope for.

I had one of the best jobs in one of the best companies in its field. But I didn't want that job. I wanted to build something new for myself. Luckily, I could afford the luxury of taking some time to figure out what that might be. So I wouldn't be riding in limos and flying Concorde all over the world anymore. I worked long and hard to earn the right to do that. Hadn't I also earned the right to stop?

The advertising business had changed a lot since I got into it in 1954. At that time, advertising was a magnet for the creative, which is to say the odd and interesting. Creative departments teemed with budding musicians, artists, novelists, and playrights who needed to feed their families. These people naturally gravitated to advertising, a business where they could get their kicks and get paid well for it too.

But over the years, the kicks became harder to get. Advertising got more businesslike, more scientific. A business-school mentality gradually seeped in through the cracks. Advertisers wanted to know the results of an ad or commercial before the fact. This led to a lot of research and testing. Which in turn led to a formulization of advertising approaches, anathema to the truly creative. Many moved on.

In the early seventies, they bailed out in droves. The passing on of these creative types whose primary interest was not in advertising was not all bad. Many believed, myself among them, that as talented as some of them were, they were only half there. But their leaving was the symptom of a disease that was infecting advertising. Like fish, they couldn't survive in the polluted water.

Pay scales in other areas had begun to catch up with advertising too. A business long famed for its inflated salaries entered the real world. Ad agencies simply couldn't pay as well as they once did. They had become less profitable. All the new scientific services had to be covered by the same 15 percent commission. And even that was beginning to be whittled away by tightfisted advertisers.

If the work produced by the advertising industry is a help-wanted ad for the industry as well as a selling tool for its clients' products, and that's what I believe it is, what came out during the 1970s was enough to send all of America's brilliant young minds racing for more fertile fields.

Our company successfully bucked this mediocre trend all through the 1970s, creating work that stood out from the prewashed, preshrunk, pretested invisibility that dominated our newspapers, magazines, and television screens. As a result, we attracted more and bigger clients and got large, as large as many of the giant, less creative agencies at whose expense we had grown. But keeping it up was a struggle.

Hordes of kids just out of business school were given responsibility for running clients' brands. But most didn't have a clue how to communicate with the public, much less move it. Yet they were given decision-making power over advertising. These were people conversant with numbers, trained to focus on short-term results, with little ability to see the longer view or the need to break rules rather than blindly follow them. I found myself working with too many of these middle managers—an apt term, "middle managers"—because it not only signified their level on the corporate ladder, but delineated the parameters that contained their minds.

I was spoiled, having worked over the years with great entrepreneurs like Charles Revson of Revlon and Frank Perdue of chicken fame. I'd worked with many characters like these, dynamos whose approach to business was anatomical. They built empires on brainpower, gut instincts, and balls. Unlike so many of the B-school boys, they knew how to make tough and daring decisions without first having to consult *In Search of Excellence* or some other book that encouraged following the genius of others as a guide to success. Success maybe, but it ain't excellence.

Don't get me wrong. There are still some very bright advertisers, quite a few talented creative people, and even some visionary middle managers involved in advertising. But they're becoming rare as hell. For a creative man, the business isn't as exciting as it was. And not as free of bullshit. I'm sure there is no more bullshit in advertising than there is in any other business. It is just the bullshit with which I am most familiar, and therefore despise with greater expertise.

American business, in general, isn't what in once was. It has lost its spirit of energy and adventure. It is peopled by paper shufflers trying to protect a mediocre status quo. Contrary to popular opinion, I don't believe American business is technologically inferior. Neither is American business the victim of an inability to control costs. American business is in trouble because it is no longer able to cope with change, much less cause it. It is being strangled by a middle management mentality—by people who are dedicated to keeping anything new, or original, or brilliant from happening.

My reservations about advertising, in particular, and today's business climate, in general, aside, I had always been eager and willing to struggle and fight for an ideal. But I was unwilling to settle for the kind of success I now saw coming out of it. I've always viewed growth and profit as a natural by-product of doing something very well, not as a goal in itself.

"Do great work," I used to tell people who worked for me, "the money will come."

Now part of a large publicly traded communications conglomerate, I had been feeling more and more lonely holding this view. I had no intention of changing my act. So I decided to change audiences.

Of course, had I wanted to take some time off, do Paris/Dakar and come back to the agency, I could have arranged to do so. But then my nagging doubts, my unhappiness would have continued to hang over me. I would have returned with nothing resolved. Also, I felt it would be bad for the company. How do you tell your clients or prospects that they can't see or talk to the president for a few months because he's racing through Africa trying to sort out his midlife crisis? I wanted to leave the company, not wound it. No advertiser wants to place its account in the hands of people who give off any scent of disorganization or confusion. No, I had to leave, for both our sakes.

Then too, I had this idea deeply imbedded in me, a foundation probably laid somewhere in my youth, that a person can only do one thing well at a time. In order to build a new life for myself, I had to first move out of the old one.

To have acted in any other way would have been inconsistent for me. I have a history of taking leaps without a safety net. Once, very early in my advertising career, just before moving to New York, I quit a job without having another one lined up. I had been working in the advertising department of this big industrial company writing ads addressed to their customers. They appeared in trade publications. I spent nearly two years there learning my craft. When there was nothing left for me to learn in that company, I left. Just walked in one day and quit.

This was a huge stuffy outfit and they had forms for everything. You had to fill out forms to get in and out in the morning and evening. I even had to complete a form giving my reason for leaving. I didn't want to put "stultifying bureaucracy!" on the form, so I wrote "The food in the company cafeteria." Would you believe that my boss called me in and asked me to change it? He was a real Caspar Milquetoast kind of guy, a nice man but quite meek. One day he got in a serious accident driving to work when he swerved to avoid running over a caterpillar. That sort.

"Why do they ask if they don't want to know?" I asked him.

All he knew, he said, was that if I didn't change it, *he'd* get in trouble. It would make him look bad. I don't know why I'm telling this story. I'm not sure it makes a clear and obvious point. Yet I'm convinced that there is some nugget of information buried within it that helps to explain me.

Another time I was working for a big ad agency. By then I had a semi-important, high-paying job. It was the holiday season and a lady came around passing out Christmas bonuses. She stopped at my office and brought in an envelope. I was surprised since I had only been working there a few months and had contributed little. I opened the envelope and just sat there staring at what was inside in astonishment. I took the envelope and ran, literally ran, to my boss's office, barged in on him in the middle of a meeting, and said, "I have to talk to you about this."

"What's the matter? It's not big enough?'

"No. It's too big. I don't deserve this. I want to give it back."

"You can't give it back." He laughed at me. "Enjoy it. This company is famous for its generous bonuses."

Here, I didn't have to fill out a form explaining my reason for leaving. I told them right out, saying to my boss, "I can't work in a place that doesn't understand the value of money."

I found a job in another ad agency for half the salary I'd been making. I just couldn't see myself in an outfit where people were rewarded by policy rather than merit, even if I was a beneficiary of their cockamamie policy. Taking a 50 percent cut in pay turned out to be one of the smartest career moves of my life. Within a year I was making much more than I had been making in the previous job. And I was happier. Because I earned it.

Most people's egos would never allow them to do what I did. How could they ever explain to anyone that they were moving backward in salary? This is what so few people understand. They don't *have* to explain it to anyone. Only weak, insecure people regard the money they make as a measure of their worth anyway. They only do so because they have no meaningful values to go by in their lives. It was second nature to me, just good common sense to know that the ultimate ego-gratification lies not in money but in knowing that you are right.

During the very short time I spent in high school, I would sometimes come across a test paper with a confusingly worded, irrelevant, or incorrectly phrased question on it. Instead of guessing and groping for what might be the right answer to the capricious question, I would scrawl "Stupid question!" or some similar sentiment on the paper next to it and leave it unanswered. I was failed often for this. Then I became bored with high school, quit, got into advertising by accident, created work that helped set new standards for the industry, built an empire within it, and made millions of dollars as a result. Who is to be the arbiter of failure?

You might wonder what place all this has in a book about a car race. This is not a book about a car race. This is a book about a guy who walked away from everything most people hold dear and went off to do something else, the first of which just happened to be a car race. It is a metaphor for a much more significant and universal topic: life. Or one man's view of it. A soupçon of this, a dash of that, these are critical ingredients to your appreciation of the fruitcake as a whole.

I laughingly refer to what I was going through as midlife crisis. I don't really see it as that at all, never have. My problem, if I have a problem, is that I started working too young. After toiling in one field for more than thirty years, most people are nearly ready for retirement or some form of crop rotation. Because I started in advertising early, at fifteen, I peaked earlier than most, way too soon for retirement. It's not unlike mountain climbing. Those people who conquer, say, Mount Everest, they plan, they work, they dare, and when they make it to the top, what do you think they do? Do they just sit up there gloating? No, they come down and do something else.

People need convenient, understandable terms for things they don't understand. "Midlife crisis" is such a one. Probably coined by some embittered workaholic, hopelessly committed to a function for which he no longer had explanation or justification, but by God he'd find one to explain away the actions of those who would not be immobilized by such ignorance. "Dropping out" is another one. That's the way the "droppees" see it. The "droppers" of course see it another way altogether. It's really dropping *in*. Leaving behind the predictable, the expectable, the safe, certain, and secure (which, by the way, is only safe, certain, and secure in desperately hopeful imaginations) to become part of the stream of life in which one experiences the very essence of what life is, and that is *surprise*.

The three of us spent a couple of days in Las Vegas checking out the sights. Colin wasn't allowed into the casinos, but one time I dropped a quarter into a slot machine, and Carolyn, who'd been hiding Colin in a doorway nearby, rushed him in so he could pull the handle. He hit the jackpot.

We put a happy and richer eleven-year-old on a plane for New York (his mother was waiting at the other end) and drove off on the first leg of our adventure together.

From the outset, I made clear to Carolyn that since we were involved in a dangerous venture, that since it would be a costly undertaking for me even if we were to sign generous sponsors, that since I had some prior experience with racing, though ancient, the one-eyed would be leading the blind here. We were a team, but I was to be the captain of it. We were in love, and in matters of love we were equals. But when it came to Paris/Dakar, I was the teacher and she was the student. That was the only way I'd have it.

Had I been in her shoes, I might have found this situation, this dichotomy of roles, difficult to live with. But it couldn't be helped. We were to face many urgent and threatening choices. Collaboration wouldn't always be possible. Often, she'd have to just let go and give herself up to my instincts. Handled with intelligence and sensitivity, I felt we could, somehow, keep our adventure and our relationship in separate compartments, keeping one from confusing and contaminating the other. How well we'd fare was just another one of I didn't know how many unknowns.

Of course, the biggest unknown of all was me. Acknowledging that my health was iffy would be lying on the optimistic side. I was weak, burned out, underweight, my constitution was downright feeble, rejecting most everything I would try to feed it. For two years I had survived on gruel and vegetables. I was now eating brown rice, some raw vegetables and salads, and a little fish or chicken. That's about all I could stomach. On my current diet, I couldn't hope to get through thousands of miles of nutritionally barbaric North Africa. I was having trouble foraging my way across North America as it was. It's hard to believe how little healthy, wholesome food finds its way to the roadside stops of America.

At five feet six and 120 pounds, I was a shadow of my once robust self. About 35 pounds lighter, in fact, than in my pre-salad days. Could I pull myself together in the less than nine months that remained? Could I sustain such an arduous pace—not only during the race itself but during the months of preparation as well? Back in Aspen, one of the first calls I'd made was to my doctor.

"Am I physically capable of running the Paris/Dakar Rallye?" I asked him point blank.

He's a Brit, of Indian heritage, has some familiarity with the event. He responded equally to the point, "No."

Sensing his indecision, I pressed, "Come on. We've got plenty of time to get it together."

"You really *want* to do this?"

"If there's any way."

"Let me do some homework. I'll think it over and send you a letter on the subject."

"Thanks, Doc."

"Why don't you do something easy? Take up professional hockey or something."

Some people would view this conversation as negative and let it corrode their resolve. I'm an optimist, hearing "yes" where others only hear "no." I saw this interchange with my doctor as tantamount to receiving his wholehearted approval, so I continued to move ahead as though everything was okay. But down deep I couldn't lie to myself. I had to face the very real fact that between us and Paris/Dakar, I was the biggest stumbling block. And it was going to be a hell of a job getting over it.

Was there an automobile manufacturer out there who would just hand over a properly prepared car to a guy and his girlfriend, neither of whom had a track record in this sort of event? Was there a sponsor out there who was equally naive? To me, the sheer unlikelihood of it, rather than being an obstacle, was an asset. The outlandishness of the request was attention-getting. I saw in it opportunities for generating publicity that no conventional, professional racing team could ever dream of.

But would I have time to structure the proposition, make the contacts, package and sell the deal? It's not as though I had a lot of time on my hands. It was April. Already I was beginning to feel that we were running out of time. Even though I would be leaving my company, I was obliged to finish out the year in my job. I would be a lame duck with more time available to me than usual, but even so, would it be enough?

Did I still have it as a driver? If not, could I get it back?

I never viewed myself as a great racing driver. At best I was a good one. I was never the fastest, but I was always dogged and determined to hang in and finish. My best events had always been the long ones, the endurance tests. In these, the fastest cars would often crash or break down. I always laid back and strategized, often beating faster cars with better drivers in the end. This is what gave me hope for Paris/Dakar. It was the endurance test to end all endurance tests, my kind of event.

I thought about this, mentally licking my chops, thinking back to racing days when my lie-back-and-wait tactics paid off. When I raced a Lotus, I remembered, there was a guy with a car no faster than mine, maybe even a little bit slower because it had chronic overheating problems, but he was a faster driver. To remedy the heating condition, just before the start of the race, he'd pack ice cubes all around his radiator.

Early in the race, I could never get past this guy. He was just too fast through the corners, and I didn't have quite enough to pass him on the straights. I'd stick on his tail so close you couldn't slip this page between us, but my car and my head would pay an awful price. Going through the turns, his ice cubes would fly out and come rocketing back at me, knocking dings into my thin aluminum bodywork, clanging "bong" off my helmet, occasionally even slicing past and drawing blood from my face. I'd push him like this until the ice cubes were all dispensed or melted. Then he'd start to overheat and slow down. With me back there, close as his own back pocket, he'd have to push his car harder, take risks to keep his lead. This overheated his car still further. After a while, he'd have to pit. I'd slow down, relax, and be in front at the finish.

Naturally this kind of tactic wouldn't work in a short sprint race. Then I'd just plan to lose, but in comfort. And in style. In one such race, I jumped the starting flag twice, causing false starts. By the third attempt at a start, the whole field was so rattled and confused that I was the only one off the line with a perfect start and shot through the first few turns in first place. After a while, the ice man caught up with me and went on to win but not until the rest of the field had already borne the brunt of his deliveries.

I had faith that my doggedness would compensate for my lack of out-and-out speed in Paris/Dakar. Or was I conning myself? As a teenager I had been a good roller skater too, skated in the Junior Roller Derby in Chicago. Two years ago someone had shown up at my weekend place in Connecticut with a pair of roller skates. I put them on and went bumbling, spinning, and falling all over the place in a hail of laughter. Were cars any different? Or would I just be making a bigger fool of myself on larger wheels?

Then there was Carolyn. Looking beyond her enthusiasm, I didn't know if she was capable of handling a car at high speeds over hostile terrain. I didn't know if she could repair a car or learn complex navigation. I didn't know if she could take the abuse, physical or mental, that she was letting herself in for. Most of all, I didn't know if she could take me.

I can be an impossibly demanding person. A perfectionist, I will go to ridiculous extremes to do a thing, any thing, well. People compared working with me in advertising to being in Marine Corps boot camp. Now I had better reason than ever for being a perfectionist. It wasn't an ad or a commercial or an account or a job that was at stake. This was really important. I was shouldering the responsibility for our very lives. And I would take every measure I could think of to make sure we kept them.

Heading East in the car, the pain in my leg was excruciating. This didn't bode well for my future physical training. If I favored it while working out, I'd end up lopsided. If I waited until it was completely healed to begin, I might not become strong enough, soon enough.

Carolyn was doing most of the driving, and I was coaching her.

"*Please* try to avoid the bumps." I was saying, pointing to the leg. It had become "THE leg." At times it pained so, I'd have to sit in the back seat with the front passenger seat folded down, "THE leg" stretched out on top of it. Wherever possible I was teaching her to downshift—changing from a high gear to a lower one by double-clutching and revving up the engine so it would be running in harmony with the lower gear when they met to mesh. I advised her in basic driving skills, although she was already far better than many people I've met.

We are a nation of mediocre drivers. This is heresy, I know, for we are also a nation of macho fatheads who think we're the best drivers in the world. Believe me, we're not. The typical American drives with his head up his ego. He turns and talks to people riding in the back seat, thinks rear and side-view mirrors are things for his wife or girlfriend to apply makeup in, decides to turn before turning on signals, "parks" in the passing lane, and when you honk or flash your lights, acts as if you've threatened his masculinity. He also tends to sit all hunched up over the wheel so in an emergency he can't turn it quickly enough to take effective evasive action. Carolyn had few of these basic faults.

On our way across the country, I pointed these people out to her so she could see how ridiculous most drivers look and how downright dangerous so many of them are. I coached her in a fundamental driving concept that has always held me in good stead. When you drive a car, always act as though you are driving five cars: your own, one immediately in front, one immediately behind, and one on each side.

Even when driving alone on an open road, drive five cars. You become intimately aware of the ramifications your actions will have on other cars, and the effect their reactions will have on yours. It becomes ingrained in you that a car suddenly braking directly in front of you is a threat to your *rear*. You learn to squeeze the brakes on gently rather than jab at them, allowing the maximum distance for the less able driver *behind* to slow down. And so forth. Of course this sort of driving requires intense concentration. Good drivers make lousy conversationalists. But then you generally arrive alive and are able to talk with them afterward. This is not always possible when riding with blabbermouths who don't pay attention to what they're doing.

Somewhere in Arizona, Carolyn got a ticket for going ninety. Boy, was I mad at her. Not for going ninety or for getting a ticket, but for getting caught the way she did. When I got nabbed in Pennsylvania, it was the unavoidable result of running through a radar speed trap. The trooper who got Carolyn clocked us at ninety by following behind. That meant she hadn't been watching her mirrors. An expensive lesson for her. And now we both had to be extra careful to protect our precious drivers' licenses.

It was the second week in April when we got back to New York, and Carolyn had a much better idea of what she would be up against. She had also progressed from being a good, basic driver and was well on her way to becoming a proficient, aware driver, which is exactly what she had to be. In six weeks I would be taking her to an advanced racing drivers' school where you're expected to know how to run before they teach you to fly.

4

Soon after returning, I called our creative staff together and, paraphrasing Richard Nixon's infamous line to the press, announced that as of the end of the year, "You won't have me to kick you around anymore."

Why Nixon, I don't know. It just popped into my head. Then I sent a memo to the rest of the staff, telling them that I had come to a point in my life where I needed a limb to climb out on and that I would miss them all. I would be leaving on December 31st. And the day after that, I would be out on a very shaky limb indeed. But in the interim, there was much to do.

For the next few months, I set about wrapping up my past and organizing my immediate future. Each was a full-time job. As if two full-time jobs weren't enough, I also bought a building in downtown Manhattan. This would be both my home and headquarters for whatever enterprise I might dream up after Paris/Dakar. If there was an after. This was a thought that sometimes intruded on my mind as the pages of my desk calendar brought us closer to Paris/Dakar.

As if two full-time jobs and moving weren't enough, Carolyn and I became engaged. Our relationship, as I had anticipated, blossomed and flourished under the light of our shared adventure. We were now spending all of our time together, planning, preparing. She would have her photography studio in the new building. Life was both blissful and exciting.

This was a transition period for us. Knowing what we were working toward and where we were headed, realizing that there was an outside possibility that we might never come back, we lived.

We went to the Caribbean for a long weekend, which is where I popped the question. Back in New York, I designed and had an engagement ring made for Carolyn. It was beautiful, but she thought it was too big and said she felt a little uncomfortable wearing it. She'd just have to learn to wage her guerrilla insurgence against a background of wealth and privilege while slightly out of uniform.

Life wasn't all bliss, though. My stepfather, to whom I'd become very close since my mother's death the year before, was critically ill in a hospital in Chicago. During this period, I made three trips to Chicago, none of them for pleasure.

Any doctor or psychologist can tell you that the five things in life that cause the greatest stress and are the most serious threats to one's health and well-being are: (1) changing jobs or careers, (2) changes in close personal relationships, i.e., marriage, divorce, (3) changing places of residence, (4) death or serious illness in the immediate family, (5) financial pressures.

I had BINGO!

On top of all that, a letter had arrived from my doctor telling me that in his view I was taking a serious risk, that in my present physical condition there was considerable doubt in his mind as to whether or not I could survive the ordeal. But if I was determined to go against his judgment, he would help prepare me for it as best he could. He had really done his homework. In his letter, he addressed every medical and nutritional concern even down to vaccinations, food, and drinking water. And he outlined a training regimen that would have brought Charles Atlas to his knees. He also advised me to begin yoga instruction immediately so that when the time came, I would be able to suffer pain with greater equanimity.

He ended by counseling me, as he had for the last two years, that the most important thing for me was to avoid stress and aggravation.

I called him immediately and told him that I appreciated his thoughtful response and that I had already begun acting on his advice by quitting my stressful, aggravating, high-pressure job.

We can always find reasons for not doing something. Doing anything entails risk. Making any decision at all exposes one to possible unpleasantness or failure. Such exposure generates enormous fear. This is why the most easily and often rationalized thing in life is ennui.

There is a recurring theme in my life, a rallying cry that always gets me going, a motivator much more powerful than the promise of money. It's the simple phrase "You can't do that." Oh, no? Watch. Looking back I think I can honestly say that nothing I've ever done was considered possible. There was always someone around, shaking his head, saying, "You can't do that" or its pathetic equivalent.

"You can't have a successful career in business without a college degree." I did it without a high school diploma.

"Today you need an MBA." B.S.

"You can't reorganize this, say that, do such and such, go there, dream of that." "It would be fun to enter the Olympics, too." Great towers are built despite such babble.

Discretion may be the better part of valor, but when my doctor posted his reservations, he didn't say I couldn't. He said I shouldn't. There were at least a hundred other reasons why I shouldn't. I was taking a calculated risk with all of them. This one wasn't even that much of a risk. I could always abort the mission later if I didn't feel able. I would lose nothing. I could only end up ahead, by pushing myself more quickly toward better health and fitness. The world is full of people who throw in the towel for fear of getting punched. I'm not one of them.

Against a background of stressful uncertainty, we worked to make the dream a reality.

The first thing I did was create a list of priorities that would give us a guideline to work by, something to help us keep our perspective. A marketing plan for a dream: "1. Survive 2. Finish 3. Finish well 4. Break even."

It was too soon to tell how we'd do with items one, two, and three. So I worked on number four.

Learning of my intent to compete in Paris/Dakar, my good friend and client Frank Perdue, the man who produces Perdue chickens, generously came forward and offered to sponsor us. I turned him down. I felt that since this was an international event and his products and people's knowledge of them is confined to the eastern United States, the offer was flattering to me but the expense wasn't justifiable for his company.

Ideally, I wanted a big, international company who could benefit from the overseas publicity as well as what we got back home. I was making progress on the U.S. publicity angle, signed agreements for us to cover Paris/Dakar from inside for both *Esquire* magazine and a new automotive publication, *The Automobile*. This would not only allow me to write about the event and Carolyn to photograph it, but it would also help defray a few expenses and "legitimize" our being in the Rallye in the first place. In addition, it gave us a captive publicity outlet to use as leverage in selling sponsorships.

My client, Nikon, declined my request for sponsorship owing to the fact that they already sponsored the car of one of the leading professional drivers, the driver who, in fact, had just won the most recent Paris/Dakar. But they generously volunteered to supply the camera equipment Carolyn would need to photograph the experience along with all the complex rigging, including the services of a technician, a man who had done camera rigging for the space shuttle flights and other sophisticated camera installations.

I began work on a press kit, themed "Doing the Dream." This would include information on Paris/Dakar and an outline of our ambitions, along with a comprehensive resume of our lack of credentials. I never completed it. We were becoming desperately short of time. At this point, other concerns had to take precedence.

It was already May and I was beginning to realize that finding sponsors with both vision and the ability to make a decision according to the needs of our timetable was the highest form of wishful thinking. I'd made a few contacts and so far had struck out on all of them. Or I was left dangling in the air for want of a response, positive or negative. In retrospect, I should have approached one of the sports marketing companies that specializes in lining up sponsors for people like us. That I didn't is excusable when you take into account two facts. It *was* number four on the list. And I am not perfect. My personal opinion notwithstanding. Recognizing this, I put getting sponsors aside for the moment.

Friends put me in touch with Kathryn Suerth. She was a yoga instructor who had studied under THE acknowledged master in India and now had many big-name clients of her own—the New York City Police Department among them. We began to stretch and breathe our way into shape. Also, Carolyn enrolled in a gym downtown near her studio. I found one near the office. We also found a French tutor to come to my apartment two evenings a week and torture us verbally. I was still doing research on Paris/Dakar, trying to get our competition licenses and racing practice lined up. I was also trying to disentangle myself from my job.

But the most urgent need at this time was for a car. We still had no idea what kind of car we wanted or whether we'd be able to get one in time. I had contacted Land Rover and was being delayed to death. I had also written to Mitsubishi, this year's winner, the Porsches having all crashed or broken down. They were interested but wanted to know more about my racing record and requested specific information about my off-road racing history. A history that didn't exist. I smelled a run-around leading to a dead end. I began to realize I'd probably have to shell out for a car.

About this time I was walking down Fifth Avenue and saw a Mercedes 280GE go by. You don't see many of these, as they are not officially imported into the United States. I had an instinct. This car just *looked* right to me. I ran back to my office and scoured my Paris/Dakar files, which by this time had grown obese. Sure enough, one of these cars had finished tenth in the latest Paris/Dakar. Three years ago, before Porsche, one of them actually won. Once again, I hit the phones. One call led to another and another and another until I found myself on the phone to Graz, Austria, speaking to a man named Richard Kaan. Kaan had been an engineer at Steyr-Daimler-Puch, the company that builds the 280GE, or Gelandewagen as they call it. He was instrumental in the creation of this particular vehicle and had gone off to start his own business preparing custom cars and competition cars. It sounded like I was calling the right place because our conversation was a particularly positive one.

"Hello, Mr. Kaan?"

"Yes."

"My name is Ed McCabe, and I'm calling from New York. Vic Spector of Orion Motors referred me to you."

"Yes."

"I understand you know something about the Mercedes Gelandewagen."

"Yes."

"Well, I'm interested in one. I'm planning to run the Paris/Dakar Rallye, and Vic said you might be able to help."

"Yes, we could do that."

"Well, I don't know if such a car presently exists that we could buy or whether we'd have to have one built, but Vic told me either way you were the man to talk to. Is this the sort of thing you feel you could handle?

"Yes."

"Well, fine. I suppose you'll need a couple of days to think about this, to figure out costs, schedule, and so forth. So why don't I call you back, say, day after tomorrow and see what can be worked out."

"Yes. That would be fine."

Why I don't know, but I hung up feeling like I had actually accom-plished something.

Later when I told Carolyn I had spoken to the man about the car, she said, "Great. What did he say?"

I thought for a minute.

"He said yes," I told her.

Two days later I called the yes man back. Only this conversation wasn't so positive. It was memorable, though. He told me that no such car existed, that it would have to be specially built but that he had checked with the factory and they could build it in September after returning from their summer break. That would give him October to fully prepare the car for competition. This was precariously close to the start of the race. It would leave only November and part of De-cember for us to familiarize ourselves with the car and get it finally outfitted and provisioned. This made for an impossible timetable even if everything went off without a hitch. And when it comes to cars, particularly racing cars, *nothing* ever goes off without a hitch.

I told Kaan this was cutting things awfully tight, that I was nervous about this schedule. He suggested I fly over to Graz, Austria, for a meeting with the factory engineers and that maybe something could be done to speed things up. Finally he said, and I'll never forget his words, "Before ve undertake to build this car for you, Mr. McCabe, there's something I vant you to understand. Paris/Dakar is a *very* dangerous race. It vill cost you a lot of money to have a little fun . . . and hopefully not for dying."

Kaan's phraseology was to prove a never-ending source of amuse-ment over the months ahead. His English was good enough to make clear what he had on his mind but just bad enough to always come out a little funny. I had a client who spoke in a similar fashion, always to be counted on for the definitive malaprop. He was a Swede. Once when his company was having problems with its computer systems, he called in the sales and technical people from the computer supplier and lashed them mercilessly in an hour-long tirade. He ranted and raved about all the problems they had been having. Finally, frothing and foaming, banging his fist on the table as he neared verbal climax, he said, "In short, gentlemen, I want that computer out of here! That machine is an *orange!*"

Kaan's English took similar twists and turns, but beneath it was always the stern, serious Austrian whom I was giving the job of building our car. We had flown to Vienna and driven to Graz to meet him, not really knowing what to expect.

"A girl? You're going to drive Paris/Dakar with a girl!" he spluttered in disbelief.

Those were Richard Kaan's first words when we arrived at the greasy little outdoor café where we had arranged to meet him for dinner. I hadn't told him on the phone that my codriver was also my fiancée and therefore a member of the opposite sex.

He looked too young to be so narrow, so conservatively opinionated. Early to midthirties from the look of him, and built. I wouldn't want to tangle with this guy. I figured him for one of those men whose greatest passion in life was for a set of barbells.

I introduced him to Carolyn. He presented his other passion, his wife, Herta.

We sat down. He turned to Carolyn with an indulgent smirk and asked, "So tell me, Carolyn, have you ever held a wrench?"

Carolyn calmly informed him that she was quite handy and what she didn't know she was prepared to learn. He looked at me, with one of those male-to-male grins, as if to say, "I guess we'll both have to humor her."

Next he came after me. "Order a lot of food, Edvard. You look pretty skinny. Do you think you're strong enough to drive Paris/Dakar?"

"I will be."

That's all I said. But the way I have of saying little often says a whole lot more. Implicit in my flat, determined answer and steady glare was the pugnacious question, "Look, buddy, you want to fuck around or build racing cars?"

I didn't want to overtly antagonize this fellow. We had to get him to like us. If he didn't, it could creep into his work and that might kill us. I wanted more than a pair of expert hands. I wanted his passion or as much of that as he was capable of mustering. I wanted him to jilt his barbells in favor of us, at least for a couple of months.

I could tell in the quick glance we had exchanged earlier that Carolyn already hated his guts, but she also understood the need to go easy. We needed Richard Kaan. At this late date, where else could we turn?

Practically everything Kaan said could be interpreted as either an insult or an order.

"You vill finish tenth!" he pronounced, brightening.

Tenth? Why not ninth or eleventh, I wondered. He proceeded to tell us how they had analyzed the cars that were likely to be entered, knew the capability of the car we would be driving, factored in the weight we would be carrying in fuel, spare parts, and equipment. What he meant was that the *best* we could hope to do was finish tenth.

The car they were building was not a lightweight powerhouse but a proven tank capable of going to hell and back under frightful conditions. The factory knew what they were doing, he told us. They had built the car that finished tenth this year and had also built the car that won three years ago. They knew what was called for. In this case, a strong, safe, reliable car. Not a contender but one that could, and would, turn in a respectable performance.

"The question is not the car," Kaan said. "It vill finish. The question is you. Can *you* finish? Make him eat more, Carolyn."

Back at our hotel after dinner, I joked to Carolyn, "You vill finish tenth!" mimicking Kaan.

"What a chauvinist!" she said.

"He thinks we're dilettantes," I explained. "A couple of amateurs out for a lark."

"Aren't we?"

"He may think so and you may think so, but I don't think so," I said. "We're going to do this thing right, and we're going to do it well or there's no point in doing it at all."

I suppose I must have sounded a lot like Richard Kaan at that moment. "Vee vill!" But I didn't hear that in myself. If I had, I probably wouldn't have thought it the least bit unusual, being half-German myself. I was becoming obsessed with putting in a good showing.

I didn't care if Kaan was a chauvinist or an orangutan, I was only relieved. Relieved and pleased that we had found this rigid, humorless, grating Austrian whose apparent dedication to thoroughness and efficiency hid any trace of softness or sensitivity. We would just have to play along for a while and do our best to win him over.

The next day, we visited Kaan's workshop and there he proudly showed us the work he was doing. Restoring old cars, repairing and tuning competition cars, building recreational vehicles and what looked to me like German "pimpmobiles." Top of the line Mercedeses that rich Germans or Austrians wanted dolled up. Here these cars were lowered, fitted with wider wheels and tires, had fiberglass "spoilers" added on, and so forth. After the tour, we met over money matters. Carolyn brilliantly wandered off somewhere, sensing, probably correctly, that Richard felt such topics were not suitable for women's tender ears.

The car was going to cost me about forty-five thousand dollars, payable in Austrian *schillings*. That was at the current rate of exchange, which was going the wrong way for me daily.

The business discussions over with, we drove up into the hills outside of Graz. There Richard had arranged for one of the factory test drivers to meet us with a car similar to the one that would be constructed for us. The site was an old logging camp. The "roads" running through it were rocky trails lined with trees on one side, sheer drops into oblivion on the other. This was a test, not so much for the Gelandewagen, which was built specifically for this kind of terrain, but for us. I think they wanted to see if we would sweat or puke and go running back to America with our tails between our legs.

I paid no attention to the terrors of the trail. I watched the driver and every move he made as we took our familiarization laps. I needed to know what gears he used, when he switched in and out of four-wheel drive, how to work the differential locks, whether the car over- or understeered, how badly it leaned in the corners, and so on.

The driver was an Austrian mountain man and an experienced professional rally driver. He knew his stuff, I'll say that. We flew around corners and over huge boulders to the tune of horrendous crunching and banging as the car caromed over rocks and fallen trees. Inside, the car was almost quiet, like being in a church while a bombing raid was going on outside. I was not frightened and only a little impressed. Good as he was, this man could show me nothing.

A few times, I had ridden with Gunnar Anderson, one of the world's greatest rally drivers, on trails such as these in Sweden. Gunnar was Volvo's number-one test driver and delighted in making folks sweat and puke. He'd race down trails like these going so fast we'd never be pointing in the direction we needed to go. We'd be perpetually sideways on the narrow, little dirt roads. The way Gunnar changed direction was by sideswiping trees or piles of logs stacked alongside the road. At the end of a session with Gunnar, all you wanted to do after cleaning yourself up was go home, buy a Volvo, and drive it very slowly.

I took my turn at the wheel. Never having driven a four-wheel-drive car before, I learned my first lesson immediately.

As I took off, the test driver warned me, "No thumbs! Keep your thumbs on the outside of the wheel."

On this car the front wheels were drive wheels as well as for steering. When you hit a rock or a hole at speed, the steering wheel jerked violently and the spokes of the wheel could easily break your thumbs with the force.

"Very painful, broken thumbs. You'll be out of the race."

I had to learn a whole new driving technique, made a mental note to start driving everywhere with my thumbs out, creating a habit before the race.

Carolyn took her turn going around with the driver and then driving the car herself. She came back beaming, with a slightly glazed expression on her face. Up until then Paris/Dakar had been all talk and I had been doing practically all of it. Now Carolyn had gotten her first taste of the action that was in store for us, firsthand. Though it was a small taste, just a sip, for a while she carried the slightly crazy, serene expression of someone taking drugs.

We both loved the car. But I wondered if it would be fast enough. I asked Richard about this later.

"Fast enough to finish," he answered.

"Couldn't we soup it up a little?" I pressed him.

"No!" he bellowed. "Vee vill take zis engine apart, polish and balance everything, vee vill test it on a dynamometer to make sure vee haf za maximum horsepower it vas designed to produce. Vee vill do nothing that could make it less reliable."

"How about putting in a five-litre V-8 then?"

"No!" he blustered at me again. "It has been tried before and always failed to finish. Zee front suspension cannot carry the extra weight. Please, Edvard, vee know vot vee are doing."

Good, I thought. *Just testing.*

At lunch, I asked the test driver if he could think of anything else we should watch out for besides our thumbs while doing Paris/Dakar. He had run the Tunisian Rallye the year before, so he had some desert racing experience.

"Yes," he said. "Sand vipers and scorpions."

I made another note. To contact the Poison Control Center in Atlanta about carrying antidotes.

"Anything else?" I asked.

"Yes. Be very careful when jumping off the tops of dunes. Get out and take a look first. One of the greatest hazards of the race is coming down on top of a downed motorcycle."

For whom, I wondered, filing my most morbid mental note yet.

The meeting with the factory engineers held few surprises for us. They were every bit as rigid and dictatorial as Richard Kaan. As a customer ordering an expensive custom-made car, I had this ridiculous idea that I should be telling them what I wanted and that they should comply with my wishes. I also felt they should be anxious to cooperate with me, as I was in a position to bring fame and glory to their car. It was becoming clear to me that these people were not in the market for fame and glory. They too were ordering me around.

"Zee car vill of course be za long-vealbase model," one of them began.

"Why long wheelbase?" I interjected.

The three engineers stared at me, then turned to Kaan, patiently waiting for the nursery school teacher to enlighten the unruly foreign tot, such fundamental stuff obviously beneath them.

"Edvard, za long vealbase vill be more stable for this race. The short vealbase vill pitch and gyrate. It vould be too uncomfortable," he explained with strained patience.

"Yes, but isn't it also heavier?" I asked.

"Yes, Edvard, also safer. Didn't you tell me safety and reliability were your foremost criteria?"

These people were beginning to impress me. And though my constant questioning was bugging them, I could see that it was also bringing them around. They were starting to take us seriously.

We went over the whole car, item by item, piece by piece, point by point. When we came to the transmission, I balked.

"Vee vant to fit zis car vis an owtomatic gearbox," one of the engineers let casually fall.

"No way!" It was my turn to bellow. "What is this, some kind of a sissy racing car? I never heard of such a thing!"

They worked on me gently, matter-of-factly.

"You know, zis is a very long race, you vill become very tired, it is inevitable zat you vill make mistakes. Zis is von less mistake you can make," one of the engineers lectured.

Kaan gave me one of his Edvards.

"Edvard, how much off-road racing experience have you had? Have you ever raced in sand, deep sand? For sure you vill burn up the clutch."

"If you lose za clutch, you vill be OUT!" A young engineer chimed in. "It is too complicated a procedure for you to replace it yourself in za desert."

They went on and on at me like this, telling me that they felt all the clutch or transmission problems cars they had built had had in the past would have been eliminated by going "owtomatic."

"Ve gave za same advice to za man who finished tenth zis year. He didn't listen to us. He could haf finished fifth or sixth but had gearbox problems," the head engineer said.

"Isn't the automatic heavier?" I asked him.

"Yes. Twenty-eight pounds heavier. Zis is nossing. Za car is already too heavy to be considered truly competitive. And you haf no assistance. You vill carry a heavy load of equipment and spare parts. Vot difference is twenty-eight pounds?" His argument was persuasive, but I didn't completely buy it.

"I'm not interested in being a guinea pig," I told him. "As I understand it, no Gelandewagen with an automatic gearbox has ever finished either. Also I'm becoming very concerned about weight. When do you need my answer on this? I want to think it over."

We agreed that I should let them know within a couple of weeks, but they reiterated their strong feelings. We also established a timetable. They would complete the chassis before their summer break in July. It would be a specially strengthened version of their stock long-wheelbase model. It would travel down the line labeled "Paris/Dakar Car." All the workmen would know that people's lives would be riding on it, taking extra care and effort at reinforcing and tightening critical points. The engine would be delivered to Kaan the beginning of September for dismantling and "tuning."

In late September the engine would be installed, the body by then would be built and bolted on top of the whole thing. At that time the car would be thoroughly tested and assuming everything was okay, shipped to me in America on October 5th. That would give us approximately five weeks for testing, fiddling, provisioning, and whatever else needed doing before shipping the car to Paris in time for the start. It had been a profitable trip. We had gained two to three precious weeks on the originally proposed timetable.

Before we left Austria to return to New York, Kaan called me aside and said in an uncharacteristically kindly manner, "Edvard, you must start working out, zer is not so much time."

"I know," I said. "You'll see, I'll be ready."

"Oh, and Edvard, zer is somsing else I vant you to know," he continued.

"What's that?"

"No amount of money could get me to do vot you are about to do."

A friendship had been struck. Or at least the beginning of a mutual respect.

My reluctance to go "owtomatic" wasn't as reasonable as I'd made it sound. I was on a stupid ego trip. I was afraid I'd be viewed as a wimp, driving a car in a race with an automatic transmission. Also, I was loathe to admit that I had wasted many hours teaching Carolyn to downshift, which with automatic would be unnecessary. For the few weekends we had had, between returning to New York from Colorado and before leaving for Austria, we had gone out to the country in my Ferrari and I had taught her how to downshift and "heel and toe." This is working the brake pedal and the accelerator at the same time to effect the gear change without losing stopping power, an essential technique in racing. Greater love hath no man than letting his girlfriend practice on his Ferrari. An old Ferrari, at that. Over the years I'd assembled a small collection of interesting old cars. Carolyn thought some of them were show-offy and refused to ride in them. But the Ferrari, for that she made an exception.

As soon as I realized my true motives on the automatic issue, I telexed back my go-ahead. Now the telexes were really flying. Between me and Kaan and Paris/Dakar headquarters in Paris. We were back in New York. I still had some advertising business to attend to. Extensive remodeling was soon to begin on my building. I gave my butler three months' notice and put my apartment up for sale. I started preparing equipment lists, hit the phones yet again, looking for information, advice, insights, maps, weather information, navigation instruction, sponsors, competition licenses, and much, much more. I also had to fly to Chicago again. But I did have one less thing to worry about: wheels. Now my biggest worry was whether or not we'd be good enough to drive them up to their potential.

5

You don't get an International Competition License mail order or by walking into a drugstore and asking your pharmacist for one. You have to work at it. It can take months, sometimes years. I'd started working on getting ours back in February.

We first had to join the Sports Car Club of America, the licensing body with which I was most familiar. Assuming we were accepted for membership, we then had to apply for Regional Competition Licenses. To get one of these, you have to attend an accredited racing driver's school. After obtaining a certificate there, the conventional route is to compete in at least five regional races, finishing in the top four places in at least one of them. Then you can apply for the national license, which you must hold before applying for the international one. This procedure fit neither my timetable nor reality. We had nowhere near the kind of time this process required. And we didn't have a racing car set aside, waiting, with which to pursue our licenses. This situation had all the makings of a "You can't do that."

Some rules and regulations had to be bent or broken. In this case it was made easier by virtue of the fact that I had held National and International Competition Driving Licenses for many years, though many years before. Through a variety of lengthy discussions with cooperative and understanding people, I arranged for us to get both national and international licenses pending satisfactory completion of a driver's school. But these would be special restricted licenses, for Paris/Dakar only. In other words, we would be licensed to kill, but only on foreign soil, out in the Sahara where no one would notice.

There were many driver's schools we could have attended in order to meet the licensing requirements. But I wanted the best. I wanted to maximize our chances of doing well in Paris/Dakar, slim though they were.

I called Bob Sharp, head of the Nissan Racing Team. Bob and I had met through mutual friends. We had also been racing contemporaries, although then, our paths hadn't actually crossed. Bob was, and still is, a car dealer. In the old days, he had raced production cars, hoping to gain favorable publicity for the types of cars he sold. Then I drove modified cars, prototypes built by people like Ferrari and Lotus, so we competed in different categories, raced in different events. Also, he was a more successful driver, a two-time national champion. My best ranking had been eighth nationally.

Paul Newman, the actor, drives for Bob's Nissan Racing Team. I had the thought that if we could get Newman to put us through our paces it wouldn't hurt with publicity or sponsors. It turned out he wasn't available. Bob arranged for us to get our training time with Jim Fitzgerald, another member of the team. Jim had won more U.S. road races than any other driver. He'd trained dozens of America's top-flight racers and was a national champion a couple of times himself.

We went to Road Atlanta, a winding two and a half mile road racing circuit in the Georgia hills. It was a sunny, warm, early June day outside. I remember because my mind was outside, not inside the stuffy classroom with my body. It was me, Carolyn, and a couple of good old boys from North Carolina, Bobby Williams and Haskell Willingham. Haskell was boning up for a big Grand National stock car race to be held there July Fourth weekend. Bobby was his friend and sidekick. Jim Fitzgerald was at the blackboard, giving us tips on points of entry and exit for various turns, pointers on hitting the apex just right, positive and negative steering characteristics, and so on.

I was having trouble concentrating. We had begun our gym and weight training, our yoga and French lessons, and I was tired into the deepest recesses of bones I'd forgotten I had. I was in a state of zombiehood. I just couldn't focus on what Fitzgerald was saying. Besides, I already knew this stuff. I was wondering if all these stock car racers had the same mother. Their names all sounded alike. Darrell Waltrip, Cale Yarborough, Billy Joe Harcastle. They all seemed to have handles like that. And here we had Haskell Willingham. Why is that, I was asking myself when I became aware that Fitzgerald was saying something to Willingham, saying my name, saying that McCabe was driving the world's hardest race and would probably end up dying in the desert because of his lack of concentration. I snapped out of it and they all had a good laugh, but from then on, "Fitz" rode me hard, really all over my case.

I don't know if he was upset with me for not paying attention, if he just plain didn't like me, or if he was aware of the hazards I would be up against and was just doing what he felt he had to do. But by the time he was finished with me, I felt about him the way shavetail recruits feel about drill sergeants.

Fitz was a big, overweight, florid-faced Irishman who stood about six-one. Curly white hair and an ample paunch gave him the look of a pregnant priest. Sixtyish, he showed signs of being what he was. A veteran racing driver. His complexion looked like it had been grafted back on after a bad burn and he wore only three fingers on his right hand. Some questions are better left unasked.

I was zooming down the back straightaway, going about a hundred. The car was a Nissan 300ZX. Fitzgerald was strapped into the seat next to me. We were rushing up on a little snap jog at the end of the straight. I flicked the wheel just a hair to the left and, at this speed, the car shifted its weight and itself from the far right of the road all the way over to the left edge, practically off on the shoulder. Then we headed uphill toward a sweeping right bend under a bridge, the hardest turn on the course. We couldn't see it because the turn itself was blocked by the hill. The road fell away to the right, just past the crest. You entered this turn fast and blind, on faith that the road would still be there, where you remembered.

I braked, gently at first, then downshifted from fifth to fourth, the bridge still flying toward us. We were doing between eighty and ninety. I applied more brakes. Suddenly, over the roar of the engine, I heard this screaming in my ear.

"STOP! STOP!" Fitzgerald was yelling at me. I had my hands sort of full just then, but I applied more brakes.

"STOP! STOP! STOP!" he screamed at me.

Stop? I couldn't believe what I was hearing. I'm all set up for this killer corner and this guy was howling at me, gone all purple in the face. I downshifted to third, mashed on the brakes, and squealed to a stop at the outside of this treacherous turn, pointing off the road. A more dangerous place to STOP! I couldn't imagine. Carolyn and Willingham were out on the course too, and I was worried about one or both of them plowing into our rear end.

"You're dangerous," Fitzgerald said. "When I say stop, I mean stop."

"I thought you meant *brake*," I told him.

"I'm not interested in what you *think*," he said. "Just do what I tell you. Are you trying to kill me? Now let's go."

He never even told me why he was shrieking "STOP!" in the first place.

We went around again, through S-bends, through an easy constant-radius, through turns with personalities, increasing radius, decreasing radius, up and down and around and through the Georgia hills. On the shoulders, on the insides of the turns, were pieces cut from old tires, painted white.

"HIT THEM!" Fitz barked at me. "I want you to *hear* and *feel* them going under you. I want you to use *all* the road!"

Back on the straight, over a hundred, I made the twitch, shot up the hill, downshifted, hit the brakes. So far, so good. Then, an echo. I had an echo.

"STOP! STOP!" This time he was really bananas. This time I didn't hesitate, I STOPPED! coming to rest under the bridge, off on the shoulder on the inside of the turn, a much safer place to STOP!

"You're dangerous!" he shouted at me again. "You're going to die in the desert! You're going to kill yourself and Carolyn. Now let me out of this car before you kill me too."

On our way into the pits, he finally softened and started to elaborate. "You're babying the brakes. You're braking too soon, too gently. You're going up to the turns too slow and through them too fast. You're coming out too soon, too wide. Do that in Africa and you'll go off a cliff. I want you to go into the turns faster, deeper, STOP! Then get back on the gas and get out of there."

"I've been trying to save the brakes," I told him meekly. "I've got to get through eight thousand miles with them in the race."

"WRONG!" he jumped on me again. "First you've got to get through *this*."

Fitz was getting to me, but what he said was getting through. I went out and around and around and around again. For hours I did this. All the time getting faster, smoother, safer. Occasionally I'd have to pit for water, for a breather. Sweat was pouring off of me, and most of the time I was all cotton-mouthed from dehydration and fear. With all the exercising I'd been doing, I became easily dehydrated. In my old racing days, I'd sucked lemons to stave off the thirst. The old days were old. Gone. I'd better forget them. This was a whole new game, a new test. Besides, there were no lemons where I was going. Only scorpions, sand vipers.

In the pits, Fitz would amble over, shaking his head from side to side, as if to say, "What am I going to do with you, you turkey?"

"Coming around the downhill right before the pits, you're hitting over a hundred," he said.

"Too fast?"

"No, good. Very good. But you have to hold it inside longer coming through there. You're letting it too far out, the car is driving you. You're going to come crashing over the pit wall and kill us all!" He never let up.

Out I'd go again, occasionally lapping Carolyn. I'd woosh past coming out of a turn and give her the "thumbs up" as I went by. She looked serious, her face a pale extension of the white helmet she wore. Emotions collided in me again. Here she was, on a racetrack, doing very well. I was happy about that. But she was belted into a car, wearing a crash helmet, driving faster than she'd ever gone before. A risky business.

Once I was overtaking her, coming up fast into an S-bend she was in the process of negotiating. She lost control and went spinning wildly off the course in a great cloud of dust. I came around and into the pits and waited for her. After a while she came in, slowly, shaken.

"Lost it, huh?" I said, trying to keep it light.

"I didn't know if I was upside down or right side up. I lost all sense of where I was," she said.

Good, I thought, *she's going fast enough to learn*. But I was torn. Very torn.

I never expected Carolyn to be Mario Andretti. I was going to drive Paris/Dakar. I figured she might have to drive some of it, but only when I became too exhausted to drive or if I got hurt. But whatever little she did, she had to be 100 percent ready.

We were getting ready. One of the most arduous and humiliating routines at Road Atlanta was practicing on the wet skid pad. We went there early every morning. A big asphalt slab had been installed alongside the course. A circle maybe fifty feet in diameter had been painted in the middle. High-pressure nozzles fired continuous thick streams of water onto it.

The idea was to drive around the circle, stand on the accelerator until the car broke into a skid, "throw" the wheel full lock in the opposite direction and with the accelerator, push the car around and around the circle in a continuous controlled skid.

The objective was to familiarize the driver with how to control a car that left to its own discretion and momentum would be totally out of control. Also to speed up your hand movements. Fitz had accused me of having "lazy hands." Getting around the wet skid pad with lazy hands is simply impossible.

Once I had the car in the skid, had thrown the wheel opposite lock, I kept it there with quick little flicks of the wheel back and forth and more or less throttle as the feel in the seat of my pants dictated. This part of the drill was exasperating and exhausting for me. If I didn't get it just right, and in the beginning I rarely did, the car would snap into a spin, throwing me all over the inside of the cockpit. Too much or too little of a flick, too much or too little gas, and wham, I'd be going round and round, my head whipping like a berserk pendulum from the G forces being exerted on it. Once I got the car into the controlled skid, the G forces would push me so strongly into the door that at the end of a session I'd limp out, my left side bruised and aching all over.

At times, I'd practically crawl from the car all dried up inside, my outside as wet with sweat as the skid pad itself. The dehydration was also giving me splitting headaches. And it would be worse in the desert what with the sun and the heat. There would be no air conditioning in the car. It would rob power from the engine. And add too much weight. We would be sealed inside a stripped-down machine with little or no creature comforts, no ventilation, a safeguard against the intrusion of suffocating dust.

Safeguard? These were the kinds of thoughts that ran through my groggy and aching head as I sat beside the skid pad, recovering, watching Carolyn take her turn. I was also thinking about trying to book some time on one of NASA's G-force machines to help acclimatize us to the extreme gravitational forces that would be working against us for ten or more hours every day. I wondered too if anyone had a shaking machine, something like the vibrators paint stores use to shake up cans of paint, but for humans. That might be good conditioning for the bumps. It was a good thing Carolyn couldn't read my mind.

How, I would ask myself, how could we fit it all in? And how, if the warm-ups were killing me, how could I ever hope to get through the real thing?

We got our certificates. Now the licensing procedure could begin.

Before leaving, we made appointments for a refresher course in mid-
October, as close to the start of the race as we could dare push it.
Any later and the weather might be too bad for us to practice. I wasn't
particularly looking forward to another three days with the sergeant
or to taking any more licks on the wet skid pad. But an instinct told
me that was the most valuable of all the training we'd gotten there.
More than the road course, more than the timed races we'd run on a
short little course through pylons. Driving eight thousand miles on
dirt, sand, and rock, I had a hunch I'd most have to know how to
control a car that wanted to be out of control. Short of racing on sand
itself, the wet skid pad was it.

But I wasn't about to enter Paris/Dakar without some experience
running on sand. To get that, we set off for Martha's Vineyard next.
This was to be a combination of business and pleasure. We needed
the pleasure part. The constant demands of the preparations were
beginning to get to both of us. Romance had been playing second fiddle
to the Rallye, adding to the strain. Our personal lives had been almost
nonexistent. Kissing is uncomfortable in a yoga position, and hugging
is hard while your hands are full of weights. We needed time alone
together.

We were each having trouble with different phases of our training.
I was almost enjoying the yoga. The deep-breathing exercises put me
in a state of meditative, almost blissful relaxation. They were having
an adverse effect on Carolyn, giving her deep and disturbing insights
that upset her and had her almost constantly on edge. I was physically
spent from the calisthenics and weight training, whereas for Carolyn
that part was almost a breeze. She was running over three miles a day
now, in addition to all the other exercises she was doing.

I'd arrive at the Sports Training Institute at Fortieth and Park in a
sweat, jogging there from my office at Fiftieth and Third. I'd do it
around noon, when the sun was at its highest and hottest, wearing
heavy sweats as per my doctor's instructions. Remember, it was exertion in desert heat I was training for. I'd go from machine to machine,
pushing my pulse rate up to one of the ceilings the doctor had set for
me. I'd do the rowing machine, the bike, the whole gauntlet of Nau-
tilus, the calves, the thighs, the back, the shoulders, hamstrings, quad-
riceps, biceps, wrists, a lot of work on the wrists.

When I became desperate for a rest, my trainer, Nancy Belli, would
sit me on a bench with my arms extended straight out in front of me,
in driving position. She would give me weights to hold there, rigid,

immobile, timing me. A minute was an hour. Whenever it didn't feel that long, we'd do it again, this time with heavier weights. When I became too tired to move and on the verge of giddiness, we'd turn to the easy stuff.

Fifty push-ups, fifty sit-ups, a couple of sets of chin-ups, twenty-five apiece. Always water in between. No time to breathe, just drink. Four litres a day now. Moving toward the seven-litre goal the doctor had set for me for the race. I worked out like this four days a week. The other three I'd do an hour of yoga positions, calisthenics, and stretches. I did the breathing for an hour and a half every day. In two forty-five-minute stints.

At the start of a gym session, I'd bounce in, hearing in my ears, "Da, da, daaaaah, da, da, dah," the theme from *Rocky*. At the end of a session, I'd be too wobbly to climb back into my underwear. Unable to lift my foot high enough, I'd often snag my toes on the elastic band, trip, and keel headlong into the wall of metal lockers. I'd stumble out tired, so tired, I'd be hearing Mozart's *Requiem*, as though it were being played at too slow a speed. Nights all I wanted to do was sleep. Carolyn thought something was wrong with her.

Back to the office in the afternoons, on the phone. A French meteorologist whose specialty was North Africa. The Defense Mapping Agency in Washington. The Poison Control Center in Atlanta. A U.S. Army Intelligence expert who had spent World War II in North Africa. Camping equipment people. "Yes, Richard, I'll send another payment." Health food suppliers. Where were the sponsors? No time to call let alone write. Expedition outfitters.

Early evening, French. The tutor would come. Two hours. I'd be fighting to stay awake, to learn, to think, to remember. My name. What was my name? Yes, Eduard. That's it.

Then forty-five minutes of yoga breathing. Blackout. Almost blackout. Purple visions in the cerebellum. Peace.

Then dinner. Jesus, it was ten o'clock already. Eat, review the day's progress. Did she contact the guy about the compasses? I couldn't get the anti-venom. It must be obtained locally. Did the Algerian maps arrive yet? Not the large scale. Just the small-scale aerial reconnaissance. Keep trying.

After dinner, French practice. *Je t'aime* you too, honey. But sleep, I must have sleep. Carolyn thought something was wrong with her.

Every day got a little harder. And our relationship became a little more strained. Carolyn was chafing at the rigorous preparations I was putting us through and was feeling unloved. We seemed to be bickering a lot. It was her misfortune to be involved with someone who had such a long climb back to fitness. Even though my health and strength were improving by leaps and bounds, the preparations sapped every ounce of energy I had and there was little left for her.

In the morning, Carolyn and I would meet Kathryn, our yoga instructor, at my apartment. The idea behind the yoga was for us to be able to control both our minds and our bodies. We were making rapid progress at this.

The sessions lasted about an hour and a half. Yes, we stood on our heads. We also would twist, stretch, and contort our bodies into shapes normally only seen in a plate of spaghetti.

We'd do deep-breathing exercises, lying still on our backs, breathing in slowly to the relentless tock of the metronome, twenty-five seconds in, twenty-five seconds out, try not to think, clear the mind, the lungs won't break, control, control. Tomorrow, thirty seconds. Next week thirty-five. Where would it end? An hour in, an hour out?

Already we could control our pulse rates. I could stand on one leg with the other foot folded up into my crotch. I could just stand there, and stand there and stand there. How long could I do that, I wondered. How many minutes, hours? Days? Through special breathing techniques, we learned how to massage and relax our internal organs. Through meditation we learned how to revitalize ourselves when tired, how to summon up energy we were sure we no longer had. We were a long, long way from ready. But we were getting somewhere. Every glimmer of progress was an incentive to keep going, get better. Every setback was an inducement to work harder, to try with greater determination.

We were so busy we didn't have time to ask ourselves if it was worth it. Of course it wasn't worth it. Nothing could have been easier than justifying and rationalizing quitting. All the more reason to keep going. It was just another nail in the challenge.

Carolyn often asked if I hadn't missed the point. Couldn't we just go and have fun? We weren't professionals. Why did we have to go through all this? I had all the answers. To do it wrong wasn't worth the work and expense *that* would entail. It was too dangerous to play at. I could see us dangling upside down in our safety harnesses, our blood irrigating some dried up old Sahara wadi. Because we weren't ready. Because we were too tired. Because we weren't fit. Because we didn't know what we were doing. Because we weren't good enough. Because we just went to have fun.

No, we weren't working this hard because we were professionals or had professional pretenses. We worked this hard because we were amateurs playing at a game that was out of our league. I was building us a safety net. Fun wasn't just going and having fun. Fun was going and coming back. I was incapable of approaching it any other way.

Naturally we drove to Massachusetts. More seat time. I felt we needed all we could get. We left the Volvo in a lot and boarded a 10:00 P.M. ferry for the Vineyard. By the time we found a place to collapse, it was well past midnight. The next morning, we skipped our yoga breathing. This was a vacation. But I felt guilty about it, like we had lost a day.

We wandered around, sight-seeing. The day was beautiful, bright, and clear, with a hot summer sun pulsing its unimpeded rays down upon our skin. It was one of those ten-on-the-Sunburn-Index days.

We found a car rental place, one that had a Jeep. The woman there didn't want to rent it to us. She didn't want to rent it to anybody. She told us they had been burnt too many times by kids who tooled around in the sand, not knowing what they were doing and as a result burned out the clutch or transmission. We sweet-talked and cajoled her.

"What experience do you have driving in sand?" she asked me. I couldn't tell her "None." Nor could I tell her I was about to race through thousands of miles of it and was soon to become one of America's foremost experts on the subject.

"I own a Jeep, left it in the city, and flew up," I lied.

Carolyn chimed in with her most innocent and dopey, and therefore utterly believable, smile. "He's good. Very good, drives it on the beach in the Hamptons all the time."

"Well, okay," the woman said, "but only if you sign a paper saying you'll be the only driver and leave a five-hundred-dollar deposit."

I agreed. Carolyn was crestfallen. But practice for one was better than practice for none.

For three days I drove the Jeep all around the beaches of Martha's Vineyard and Chappaquiddick Islands, getting the feel of the sand. One of the first things I learned was how to dig a car out of it. We got stuck, sunk in soft sand up to our axles. We dug trenches on each side between the front and rear wheels, sweating under the powerful sun and the tutelage of a lone surf fisherman who taught us this technique for getting out.

We explored, stopping occasionally for rests, for swims, for yoga exercises on a deserted beach. I practiced going fast on sand, watching out for beach patrols. The faster I went, the less likely I was to sink down and become stuck. At slow speeds, the pressure of the sand on the front wheels had the effect of steering the car. The faster we went, the freer the wheels became from the influence of the sand. But there was also less bite. I had to exaggerate the movements of the steering wheel in making turns. It felt like driving on the wet skid pad but required bigger flicks.

Carolyn began to figure out camera angles. She'd lie on the hood as we went along, looking through a little viewfinder. Or she'd clamber down and ride with her feet resting on the front bumper while hanging on to the grill, examining a lower angle. It was bumpy and I was nervous with Carolyn dangling out there in front of the car as we bounced along the beach. Sometimes I was just overcome with admiration for this girl. She had guts. Guys with guts are rare enough, but girls with guts you don't often see. Oh, I'm sure they're out there. I'd just never seen one this close before.

I was not at all concerned about having a female codriver being a handicap in Paris/Dakar. I was concerned specifically about Carolyn's lack of experience. I was concerned about her driving and navigational skills. And I had reservations about whether or not she had the mental toughness and emotional stability that would be required. These concerns were born out of a recognition of my own weaknesses. I was pushing myself to the limit. In no way did I feel capable of "carrying" someone else during times of danger or stress. I would need support, not dependency.

The pressure had been getting to both of us. But Carolyn had started having bad migraine headaches. We talked about this. I told her right out what my concerns were and that if she didn't feel up to going forward, I would understand. We could pack it in and get on with our lives, together I hoped. A few times before, I had expressed the same reservations. We were coming to the point of no return. Soon so much money, time, and effort would have been spent that turning back would be next to impossible.

It wasn't just her. I was getting scared about all the money going out and no sponsors coming in to offset the huge expenses. I was having second thoughts of my own, about whether I would be physically ready, about her stability under pressure. This concern led me to apply even more pressure to see if she'd crack. Better now than later, I felt. This unnerved her further. She felt I was vacillating, watching and weighing her, playing God. I was. Lacking omniscient counsel from the real thing, I would just have to do.

We returned the Jeep, returned to New York, feeling a little more rested and a little more resolved. We had agreed that we were going ahead, sponsor or no sponsor. I would bite the financial bullet and hope we could find a sponsor between then, late in June, and December. If not, so what? It was going to be the experience of a lifetime. Still, some of my reservations lingered.

We took a few days off and flew to the south of France. It was to be a final fling, a last good-bye to an old life-style that I would be leaving behind with my job. And, hopefully, a last period of calm before the onset of the storm of activity that would soon engulf us.

It was the time of the Cannes commercial film festival, my last opportunity to say farewell to all my international advertising friends and acquaintances. We stayed in nearby Cap d'Antibes, having a good time for a while. But Carolyn began to feel uncomfortable among all the glamorous and successful people we met and hung around with.

Back in New York, she felt more in her element. Though one night we went to a big party at the Explorer's Club in honor of someone who had just returned from an African safari. The invitation said, "Dress for the occasion." Most people showed up in pith helmets and khaki. We arrived in full native regalia, which is to say totally nude. Carolyn got a makeup artist to cake us completely in mud and stick some clumps of dried grass onto us. We wore only strands of shells and feathered headgear. I carried a spear and we strolled in behind a herd of goats. I rented them from a company that supplied animals for motion pictures. No designer dress, no diamond ring. Carolyn was the happiest I'd ever seen her. I was just cold. We had to leave after the first course. I couldn't take it any more.

By now, the entry forms for Paris/Dakar had arrived in the mail. We sat down one night and filled them out together.

After filling in all the answers to the questions about the car, the crew, our racing license numbers—they too had recently arrived in the mail—we came to the part requesting our racing records. I listed all my impressive twenty-some-year-old finishes. Then came the three big questions. "Why do you want to do the Rallye Paris/Dakar?"

We answered, "For the adventure, the challenge, the sport and the fun of it."

"What are you doing to prepare for the Rallye?"

We wrote, "We are practicing by doing repeated cross-country driving, attending road-racing driver's schools, attending U.S. Pro Rallyes, talking to previous Paris/Dakar participants, working out regularly with weights, taking yoga instruction, navigation and medical training, orienteering, studying French, conditioning ourselves for desert survival by working out in saunas and steam baths, running in the noonday sun. We started in January of 1986 to prepare for the 1987 Paris/Dakar."

"Are you aware that this event entails certain risks?"

"Yes," we wrote. "And we are doing everything possible to minimize them."

The form also asked us to provide our blood types. Neither of us knew them. The next day we went to a lab to be tested. Carolyn grew faint when she saw the needle.

T he question naturally arises, were all these elaborate preparations necessary? Would my preparatory zeal kill us before we met the real threat?

I sincerely doubt there was ever much danger of that. As to the first question, I can't honestly say. Maybe I was going overboard. Maybe we could have prepared ourselves for Paris/Dakar with less loony and compulsive determination. I didn't know. Despite all my homework, Paris/Dakar, the reality of Paris/Dakar, remained one of those black voids full of pitfalls I could only imagine.

Words rang in my ears and I could only heed them. "Prepare, prepare, prepare, it's the hardest race in the world." "People get killed doing that." "Running a marathon a week isn't enough."

Maybe we weren't doing enough. That's what I was thinking. At the time, the thought never occurred to me that we might be doing too much. I had done everything I could that time and propriety would allow. I'd even been pushing that. So many telexes full of questions had arrived at TSO (Thierry Sabine Organisation) headquarters in Paris, I was later to find that the staff there referred to me as "Mr. Telex."

Never do too little. Always do too much. Prepare for the worst. Nothing good is easy. These are the kinds of cornball sentiments I've always lived and worked by. Burned into my being at an early age by my parents, by my somewhat provincial Midwestern upbringing, they always have been and therefore probably always will be part of me.

"Shoot for the moon. At least you'll hit the fence."

That's one of the things my mother always used to say to me. To her the sky was not a limit. It was something you went through on your way to somewhere else. Her advice to be daring blended with

65

my father's flair for making grand and outrageous gestures and state-
ments. My memories of him are few, but those that remain are deeply
stamped. Once when I was five or six, I overheard a "discussion"
between my mom and dad. I don't know why this particular incident
should have stuck in my mind. Maybe it's because, at the time, I didn't
know what circumcision meant. My mother wanted to have me circumcised.

"Circumcised, hell! Let him wear it off the way I did!" was my
father's response to this suggestion.

Another time he took me to Riverview Amusement Park. I remember the ice-cream cone I was licking. Vanilla it was. No ice cream has
tasted as good since. My dad was short, bald, overweight; it was
summer, a hot, sunny day. He wore one of his white linen suits,
chamois-lined, for he perspired heavily. His Panama hat was the color
of my ice cream. Yellower than now, vanilla was then. I remember
noticing because the ice cream was dripping onto the brim of his hat.

I was riding on his shoulders. So high up in the air it seemed. To a
three- or four-year-old, life is an exaggeration. Short is tall, good is
great, bad is awful. He took me to a stand, a concession where people
threw baseballs at stacked-up milk bottles. Not real milk bottles. These
were fabric, upholstered bottles with stupid, tasteless designs on them
and fringe all around. Not real milk bottles.

My dad swung me down to the ground, a long fearful trip. It was
shady and cool under the awning. We stood there, me finishing my
ice cream, my dad mopping at his brow and his brim with a handker-
chief. He hoisted me up to the counter, holding me by the waist.

I wanted a teddy bear. The concessionaire handed me a baseball.
So big and heavy. Even small and light was big and heavy then. I
threw, missing by a mile. I threw again, missed by a block. Again,
I threw. Closer but close didn't count. Only three balls to a customer.
My dad put me down.

I started to cry. I wanted a teddy bear. He picked me up again.
Again I threw. Again I missed. And again. With the last ball, I hit
the pile right in the middle with all my mini-might. The bottles didn't
move, didn't even rock or sway. I began to bawl. Bad was awful. It
wasn't fair. My dad put me down. I pressed my head into his thigh,
making dark, wet patches on his crisp, white trousers. We didn't leave
right away. He was talking to the man behind the counter.

Then my dad began handing me teddy bears. Stacks and stacks of
teddy bears. So many I couldn't carry them all. There were so many

teddy bears even my father couldn't carry them all. Together we went home, covered in smiles and teddy bears. Those we couldn't carry he would send for later. He had bought them all. Cleaned them out, every last teddy bear was mine. Good was great. Great was fantastic. My dad was great; no, better than that. And the ice cream we had later on was too. That's one of the things I remember most about the time when my father was alive. Ice cream tasted better then.

That was my dad. That was partly me now too. That, combined with my mother's urging to dare. To try to go farther than I needed to go. No one needs to go to the moon, but if I tried, maybe we would get to Dakar.

During July and August, I spent like a lunatic, buying the whole stand. Anything I thought we might need, I bought. Any skill I thought we might require, I obtained. I didn't want to find us wanting for some small yet urgent thing at the last minute. At the last minute, there is always too much to do. Do everything and more, now. Later might be too late. I was preparing us for awful. If it proved to be only bad, well, lucky us. Then it would be a piece of cake. Down deep I didn't believe this. I felt we had to do still more. There would be better cars and better drivers in Paris on New Year's Day. Our only hope was to be better prepared.

I'm the same way in business. Stories went around the advertising business about my determined bent. Or bent determination, depending on how one viewed it. It was said that my creative staff had to come in early every morning and run through tires. Once I was in the toilet at an industry dinner and overheard someone asking an art director who worked for my company how it was going.

"Do you get to see much of your family?" the person inquired.

"Once a month!" I shouted out from my stall. "We keep their families in camps."

My employees once presented me with a whip as a Christmas pres-ent. A joke that I accepted with a joke.

"Take off your shirts," I told them.

Writers working for me found it difficult to get their work approved, sometimes having to rework a piece of body copy (the words that go into an advertisement after the headline) dozens and in a few instances more than a hundred times. Why would they subject themselves to this? Because they shared my sense of perfection. Because they knew that their best work would actually run.

Clients often tear apart or kill the best work done by advertising creative people. Usually, if they got it past me, it would appear with little or no change. It had already been picked and perfected to death. Because they knew that I cared. Because they knew that my goal was great advertising, not appeasing clients. Because they knew that once I'd approved their work, I'd fight like a fiend to preserve its integrity. Because they knew that if they'd had to redo their work a hundred times, it was still okay because I had reworked mine two hundred. Because as much as I demanded of them, I always demanded still more of myself. In any event, many of the best people in advertising always wanted to work for me. The best people in any field are always a little weird.

My relationship with Carolyn had started as a romance that developed into an adventure that was now beginning to show signs of frailty as a result of building pressures and an already frantic pace.

Carolyn was still involved in her photography operation, and I was carrying most of the Rallye workload. I asked her to take over chasing down maps and compasses.

"I've got a business to run," she said.

"The business or the Rallye, it's your choice."

I was pushing her to do more Rallye work, but her response made me feel like I was forcing her to do her own damned dream. It was as though we were in a power struggle. And the struggle was beating us both. There was little time for the nicer, more romantic aspects of our relationship.

Friends who knew me well warned me that no relationship could stand such a bashing. Easy for them to say. Easy for me to see, now, that in their objective ignorance they were able to divine a truth that I could not or would not see. At the time, for me, and perhaps for her, such perception was impossible, unthinkable. We were possessed of a blind, childlike, and unshakable faith in our ability to beat the odds against our emotional as well as physical survival. True love could stand the test. If it didn't, it wasn't meant to be. At least that's what I thought.

Carolyn had a dream about the Rallye. Not the kind that haunts you for life. The simple sort that troubles you at night.

"How'd we do?" I asked her.

"Good, we finished."

"Well?"

"In the top twenty-five."

"Great. Anything else?"

"Yes, there was trouble," she went on. "There was a war, some kind of skirmish. We were being shot at."

That day I went to a firearms store in New York, one of those places that gives the appearance of catering to hunters out for duck, but you just know that they're also supplying munitions to mercenaries who use them to kill people. There I ordered a 26.5mm Heckler & Koch flare pistol. A huge, black thing that looked like a forty-five but bigger. I had told the salesman that where I was going conventional firearms would not be allowed but that a flare pistol would be, that I wanted one that could be used for self-defense as well as for emergency use. So he specified this particular piece of rocketry, assuring me that it could eliminate two with one shot.

As a rule I'm not superstitious. But some signs seem so clear, it's stupid to ignore them.

I was behaving like a creative person. Over the years I've observed that this kind of constant pushing and driving is the hallmark of the creative personality. It's the major difference between creative people and those who are not. People who are not creative don't know how to start. Those who are don't know how to stop.

So, I had my gun. All I had to do was figure out how to smuggle it into France. The same with the ammunition. Initially, I thought I'd just stick it in the car when we shipped it back to France. Pretty obvious that a racing car bound for Africa, being shipped from New York to France, should have a flare gun. Nothing untoward there. The only problem was that the car wasn't coming to America and then being shipped back to France after all.

There had been delays, problems. There always are. Anything having to do with racing cars, other than racing, is slower than it's supposed to be. I didn't like what I was reading between the lines in my incoming telexes from Kaan. So in late August, I made the decision to pull up stakes and move to Europe earlier. We would go in October, immediately after our last racing practice at Road Atlanta. I'd worry about the gun later.

Now we really had to push. As if we hadn't been pushing already. It was nearly September. We both had business affairs to wrap up. We still had equipment to get, more sand and racing practice to do. We had to organize accommodations in Austria and in Paris. There were hundreds of details and less than eight weeks left to tend to them. We now had to accelerate our yoga, gym, and French training as well. I never did have time to mount a serious effort at raising sponsorship money.

Carolyn concurred that moving to Europe was the right thing to do. We would go to Graz where our mere presence would be a spur (thorn?) in Kaan's side. We would be able to have a say in final design details. We would have more time to familiarize ourselves with the car, participate in the testing phase, and better learn how to maintain and repair it. We would be closer to the Paris/Dakar action. Geographically, we'd be in a better position to meet other competitors, compare notes, and learn. After Graz we would go to Paris and live our French lessons. Some specialized equipment would be more accessible there. It was a good decision. In Europe we would be able to concentrate on the job at hand without all the disruptions and distractions we had at home.

I remember only the vaguest snatches of my life during these weeks. The whole time I was blinded by the sweat of training, the blur of details, and the bright hope of getting away to Europe. For the adventure, for the dream.

In the gym, the strains of *Rocky* grew in volume and duration as did my strength and endurance. Mozart's *Requiem* died away. We were having yoga sessions every day now. Forty-five seconds in, forty-five seconds out, for thirty-five minutes. I could not only touch my toes, I could bend over and put my palms to the ground I was so limber. I could sit completely still, cross-legged for ages, and just think away the pain. We knew how to relax any part of our bodies, independently from any other. We were so energized, four hours' sleep was all we required. When we became tired, we would meditate for twenty minutes and come out of it as refreshed as if we'd had another four hours' sleep. I was up to five litres of water a day.

I flew to Chicago again. My stepfather was having major surgery to relieve an arterial blockage. It didn't look good.

Later, we flew to Martha's Vineyard. Our schedule was too tight to drive there this time. We rented a different Jeep, with less hassle. This time we were both able to drive and get some practice. I remember driving it fast, along the narrow, undulating beach on the marshy side of Chappaquiddick Island. We were bathed in the last rays of the late summer sun, which in late afternoon shone a powerful yellow-orange. The blue water had an orange coating, the green marsh grass appeared golden yellow, the pair of hawks that rose up in front of the flying

Jeep seemed an iridescent steely blue. We chased them for miles as they soared along the chromatic coast, flapping effortlessly.

We had the windshield folded down. In that crisp, rushing air, everything swathed in unbelievable colors, I felt, in the moment, as free and detached as those hawks. I hoped they would fly on forever and that we could go on following them for that long, indefinitely postponing reality. Eventually we ran out of beach on which to run. We sat quietly, watching the hawks fly on, until long after they had passed from our sight.

We flew to Ohio, to a big U.S. Pro-Rally being held there. I wanted Carolyn to talk to some navigators, to pick their brains on both techniques and equipment. I remember watching the high-powered cars blast through the forest, down tiny gravel trails, showering us with stones from their churning wheels as they went past. I imagined myself doing the showering. I especially wanted to talk to U.S. Rally champion John Buffum. He had been very helpful to me on the phone, but I'll never forget his face-to-face advice in Ohio. He told me not to get all hung up on fancy navigation equipment. "Just get in the car and drive it as fast as you can."

In Ohio, I made the decision to go with simple, straightforward, mechanical mileage counters, passing on more sophisticated electronic gear. I met a man who said he could get what I wanted and send it to me in New York. I also met the head of the Audi Competition Department in the U.S. I told him we were going to do Paris/Dakar. He told us to be sure and say hello to his old friend Jacky Ickx. The mental note I made here would later prove to be a valuable one.

In October, we went back to Atlanta and spent more hours on the wet skid pad. Only now I could get out of the car like a human. Not so sore. Not dehydrated. I was up to five and a half litres of water a day, engaged to Carolyn, but married to the men's room.

This time in Atlanta, the actor Tom Cruise was our only classmate. We spent three intense days together. Paul Newman had turned him on to the idea of racing when they were making the film *The Color of Money*. He seemed a nice, unpretentious fellow who was fascinated with our yoga skills. Between stints in a car, I would stand on one leg and touch my toes or do some crazy stretch. He couldn't help but notice.

This time Fitz was easier on me. He said my attitude had improved. Maybe it had. Now I was stronger, more alert, my mind on the business at hand, my body now fully capable of following through on it.

One evening we met Scott Andrews for dinner. Scott was the camera technician Nikon was lending us. He lived in Atlanta and would be coming over to Paris to do the camera rigging on our car. Nikon would provide his services, but now that our travel plans had changed, I had to cover his airfare to Paris and his expenses while there as well. In for a dime, in for a dollar.

Scott was one of those technical-genius types who gets gaga over gear. The way Scott talked about remote electronic shutter releases and omnidirectional ball sockets was the way most guys talk about tits and ass. At dinner, he showed us machine-shop models of the camera mounts he'd developed for our car. They had been made out of cast aluminum in deference to our need to save weight. Even so, I thought they were too heavy.

"Drill them out," I told him. "Make them look like Swiss cheese. Keep only as much metal as you need for strength and rigidity." This was a racing car first, a camera car second. Even though it sometimes seemed as if Carolyn saw it the other way around.

Scott was a good guy, but he went on and on so about technical stuff that we were almost asleep by the end of dinner. Industrial-strength boring. We agreed to send him tickets and would meet him in Paris on November 20th. We would also be putting him up. After our dinner, we decided that should be in a location convenient to, but separate from, us.

Back at the track, our driver's ed continued. I had the skid pad down now and actually enjoyed the sliding around. This time I didn't get nearly so much time on the road course. After a couple of hours of STOPPING!, I burned out the brakes. Fitz was happy. We celebrated our regraduation in a smiling group photo. Cruise asked for the name and number of our yoga teacher. He also gave me his private number. I was reluctant to take it, knowing that stars rarely return calls.

"No, really," he said, "take it. I'd like to hear all about how it goes."

Twice I called him to keep him apprised. He never returned the calls.

I don't know if he ever called Kathryn. I was far too busy to remember to ask.

7

Arnold Schwarzenegger was born in Graz. How Arnold Schwarzenegger ever got to be Arnold Schwarzenegger on the food they eat there is beyond me. Greasy fried stuff, pork, sugar, dough for dumplings and dessert, these are the staples of the local diet. All these delicacies are *verboten* to me. And to Carolyn, who is a virtual vegetarian.

"In German, *graz* means 'grease,'" I joked with her.

Too big to be a village, too small to qualify for major cityhood, Graz is a town of about a quarter million people. It's located at the point of an upside-down triangle, the upper two corners being Vienna and Salzburg. It straddles the River Mur, as though unable to decide which side it is supposed to be on.

It's not a particularly pretty town, though at times it's quaint, in places picturesque. Mostly, Graz is gray. Dark and dour, its countenance has been stained by centuries of uneventfulness. Not unpleasant but unmemorable. Its major contribution to the world being, apparently, Arnold Schwarzenegger. Which is a hefty one at that.

We arrived in Graz on October 30th, the day before Halloween, about to be tricked rather than treated. On the way we had spent a few days in London. There we went to a racing driver's store and bought new helmets (the ones we'd bought in New York were too tight to accommodate the intercom system we learned about in Ohio and picked up in London). We also bought some lightweight flame retardant shoes with nonskid soles and other racing paraphernalia. As a nation of shopkeepers, England justifies that claim to fame by providing a shop for *everything*.

I made a few visits to my doctor, receiving a final barrage of vaccinations, along with plenty of vitamins and supplements to take away.

He handed these over, along with a few of his concerned and worrying glances. I felt as good as could be expected under the less-than-perfect medical circumstances. Not good as new but an artfully restored old. I was still carrying the scars of an "interesting" life, skinny as a rail but now just as hard. I resolved to do everything possible to put on weight between then and New Year's Day. In the race itself, I'd start losing weight for sure. And I hadn't an ounce to spare.

Once in a long, hot race, I'd lost 14 pounds. I'd be running the equivalent of twenty-two such races. All longer. All hotter. If my past experience was a valid indicator and if the formula was projectable, I could arrive in Dakar weighing *minus* 185 pounds.

I was really very concerned about this. But in Graz I didn't worry about it nearly as much as the subject warranted. The available food didn't allow it. The Schwarzenegger diet just wasn't what the doctor ordered. And here, too, there was not enough time to worry about it.

The weeks we spent here were a whirl of reluctantly ingested, badly digested grease; dirt and grease applied lavishly, externally, and enormous loads of laundry from which both dirt and grease refused to be completely freed.

To me, *Graz* will always mean "grease."

We slid into town in a Mercedes we rented from Hertz in Vienna, driving there at a breakneck pace. More practice. Once there, Richard Kaan supplied us with a beat-up old VW wagon with no brakes. I felt completely at home driving it, having so recently been without any in Atlanta. He also supplied us with an "apartment." I'd asked him to find us something cheap. He bettered that, finding a place that wouldn't cost us a pfennig. It wasn't worth a pfennig.

Number 6 Bindergasse was a narrow, humorless five-story building in the old part of town. I never could tell if that made it fifteenth, sixteenth, seventeenth, eighteenth, or nineteenth century. Fifteenth century it must have been. There was at least six centuries of dirt built up on and in it. More than enough to keep its exact vintage cloaked in dismal mystery.

We entered the building through a gray, wooden door, thick and stolid enough to keep anyone who didn't belong inside out. As if anyone outside would want to go in. Next to the entrance on the ground floor, there was a beauty parlor, permanently closed. *An ugly parlor*, I thought.

The building fronted on an also narrow but somewhat humorous street, old Bindergasse itself. *Gasse* is the diminutive of *strasse*. In

English, we'd call it an alley. Facing the front of our building—we quickly adopted it as "our building"—was a jewelry store. The identity of the jewelry store was heralded by a large sign out front to that effect. SCHMUCK it read. I guess in German, schmuck means jeweler, or something like that. Where I come from, that word is used differently. In New York, it's used to describe people who allow themselves to become involved in situations such as the one in which we then found ourselves. Every time we went in and out of that building, the sign yelled at us: "Schmuck, Schmuck!"

If coming in and out was a joke, going up and down was an adventure. We ascended to our flat via a unique winding staircase with unevenly warped and worn treads. So irregularly "settled" with age they were that I could actually step up a tread and end up slightly lower than I had been on the tread from which I had just departed. When the lights were out, which was often, the simple act of going up and down presented us with a serious test of our finely honed balance and equilibrium. On our inaugural attempt at entry, we were like Sisyphus, getting nowhere with our loads of luggage. Fortunately, our destination was the third-floor landing, not the fourth or fifth.

The flat itself was spartan, as you might imagine. This was not one of Ludwig of Bavaria's playhouses. It was a room maybe ten feet square. Two large windows faced the "schmuck" sign and the gray buildings across the Bindergasse, which was so narrow we could almost reach out and grab the milk bottles off our facing neighbor's windowsills. The sun was shining outside, but it bounced off the grimy windows and only a dim duskiness streamed in.

There was one table, two chairs, a bare light bulb dangled above. Two small wooden beds wore thin, very thin, foam-rubber mattresses with no bedding. On the left was a small sink, then a free-standing stall shower, then a kitchen sink, a hot plate, and a tiny refrigerator under that. This is mostly useless information. There was no heat or hot water. So washing or showering was impossible. The temperature was in the mid-twenties to low-thirties the whole time we were there. So there was no need for a refrigerator, either. Completing the dreary picture was a wooden wardrobe with doors that would not close, the floor under it was so warped. All the "furniture" was done in dirty blond wood, standing in sharp contrast to the deeper, darker, richer dirtiness around it.

"Very nice, Richard," I said.

"We can clean it up," Carolyn said.

"Not fancy, I know, but the price is good," quipped Richard.

We were all standing there speaking in monosyllables. Anything longer and our teeth would start to chatter over them.

"Where's the toilet?" I asked.

"Down the hall," said Richard.

I went.

Finding it, I opened the door. We shared it with the birds. No kidding, birds lived there. Probably pigeons. From the looks of the encrusted guano and feathers stuck everywhere, I guessed the bird population to be about a hundred. Upon reflection, I lowered my original estimate. A hundred pigeons couldn't possibly have fit in there. Probably it was just a well-fed family of four or five. From the looks of things, about five generations of them had taken refuge and relieved themselves there since the housekeeper died.

It took us a few days to clean everything up and make the place somewhat livable. Carolyn is the "Clean Queen," so I was in the wrong place with the right person. When it comes to things like cleaning and laundry, she was as fastidious as I was about most every-thing else. The birds moved to the windowsill outside, which was the same as staying inside because the window lacked a major pane. But our mere presence seemed to intimidate them somewhat. At least they left evidence of their cohabitation with us with less reckless abandon.

To be sure, the feathers still flew. Especially when one of us made one of our nocturnal visits there, which for me were quite frequent. I was now up to six litres of water daily. Whenever I'd get up in the middle of the night, wearing two layers of long underwear and groping my way toward the door, Carolyn would stir and groggily ask where I was going. "To beat the bird," I'd reply. We kept the broom we bought in there. A club that could also clean.

Sleep was next to impossible. The beds were too short, even for me. Worse for Carolyn who was quite a bit taller. At night I'd lie there feel-ing the thin foam rubber compress itself under my weight into a sort of hard Styrofoam case for my body, rendering me as immobile in the morn-ing as a toy store robot, batteries not included. That being the only other thing that I can think of that's packed in a similar fashion.

We were sore, we were dirty, we were cold, but we were coping. We found the town's one health-food store. Also we found the morning market to be a good source of vegetables and a few other things that we could eat. We even came across a good seafood shop. So we rarely went out to restaurants where we found eating both expensive and nauseating. We would come home from Kaan's shop beat, eat and try to sleep, every so often getting up to stretch or go beat the bird. We'd get up early and do some yoga. Kathryn had cautioned us to go easy on the deep breathing here. The Chernoybl reactor had recently blown, allegedly scattering much of its fallout into the area. So it was mostly stretching. Calisthenics we got plenty of over the river in the shop.

After the morning exercises, Carolyn put together breakfast. We didn't need the refrigerator. We just left perishables out in the room. The cold kept everything crisp and fresh, except for us. It made us tense, short-tempered, and snuffly. I'd trundle out with our almost daily load of laundry, making a game out of descending the tricky stairs. Once outside I'd run to keep warm, always trying to avoid direct eye contact with the SCHMUCK sign.

Frau Boder was a nice little old Austrian woman who ran the *waschen-putzen* down the street and spoke not a word of English. The ritual with her went like this. We'd exchange "*Morgens*," smile at each other, and carry on a lively conversation, not having the foggiest notion what the other was saying. I found that the easiest way to get by in the German language was just to add an "en" to the ends of all the words and keep nodding and smiling. Otherwise it was hopeless. "Moren, dirten, greasen" I'd say in a dopey sing-song cadence. She'd smile as though she understood, taking pieces of greasy laundry out of the sack one at a time, holding them up in the air for the whole crowd there to see, as she counted out the pieces with maddening enthusiasm. "*Ein, zwei, drei, vier, funf, sechs, sieben . . .*" and so forth, writing all the numbers down.

The count complete, I'd say something I thought would pass as civil like, "Veeren, colden, morgen." Or "Haven ein guten dayen."

She'd radiate a big pink smile, replying as though she had completely understood even the inscrutable nuances of whatever gibberish I'd uttered. "*Ja, ja, guten dag, ha, ha, vedershein*," and I'd be on my way. Then I'd go into the health food shop next door and ask for an "orangen juicen fer taken homen" for Carolyn.

Oscillating my way back up the downity stairs, we'd sit and shiver through breakfast. I'd always have a laundry tale or joke to tell.

"I'm convinced she thinks I'm Austrian or German," I said to Carolyn one day, stony-faced serious. Carolyn looked at me like I was insane and laughed at me. That's right, I would think, better to laugh than cry. My visits to the laundry and my German were about the only things we could laugh about in Graz.

The first few days we got lost a lot. Graz is not a big town, as I said. But it's a maze. To get to the shop, we had to start out by driving in the wrong direction. I had problems with this process conceptually. I'd insist on starting off in the right direction, which invariably proved wrong. We'd find ourselves on some streets where vehicular traffic was *verboten*, inching along, arguing with each other about where I'd gone wrong, while one of the tandem streetcars, which was the town's major form of public transport, clanged angrily at us from behind to get out of its way, to get off the tracks, to get the hell out of town. I wanted to comply with this last clanging wish, but couldn't.

"You're the navigator," I'd say to Carolyn. She'd reply to this with something noisy and unprintable.

"The river!" I said, having a sudden brainstorm. "If we find the river, we can find the shop."

Then we'd dodge around until we saw an amiable-looking pedestrian. I'd pull up. The visual appearance of this car was shocking enough—bright green, freshly hand-painted as though with a broom, on top of dents of every imaginable shape and size—but when Carolyn rolled down the window and I let go with a sing-song "Morgen, vanten to finden ze rivern!" we'd get a dumbfounded, astonished look as though we were visitors from another planet.

"I just don't know what's wrong with these people," I'd say to Carolyn. "I sprecken zee perfecten German."

Eventually we'd laugh and argue our way out of the maze and by some miracle find our way to the shop.

It was located in a Bauhaus-era industrial park on the outskirts of town. Once out of town, finding it was a cinch. It was a well-designed, tannish, graystone building of about four stories. It stared out at us from its rather indistinct background because the architect made the windows larger than the building seemed to deserve. It sat there bug-eyed, welcoming. Like one of us, it, too, looked tired and appeared to have bags under its eyes.

I'd wish the brakeless wagon to a stop alongside the building. It looked somehow correct there. It was the same green as a park bench and had been painted over just as many times.

Kaan's office was just a suite. Most of the building was occupied by an industrial-design firm and an international group of construction engineers. We'd go through the wide glass doors, up to his office. Inevitably, we'd beat him there.

"Mr. Kaan comes," was the way his secretary, Claudia, usually greeted us. She was very young, nineteen or twenty, and was soon to be married. Perhaps, as a result of this fact, she applied the totality of her brainpower to dreams of dumplings and other domestic things, for she offered no evidence of aptitude whatever. Claudia, pronounced Cloudia, would make Carolyn her morning coffee and me my morning tea, and we'd wait for Kaan to come. This was in the beginning, before we were allowed to go directly to the shop and work with "the boys." For now we were at the mercy of Kaan's orders, which were apparently "You vill vait!"

Kaan would come and we'd exchange morning pleasantries over coffee.

"Have you been working out, Edvard?"

"Living in that apartment is a workout, Richard."

He would lift an unsmiling eyebrow.

"Soon, Carolyn, ve vill see what you can do, ha?"

We had concluded that most of the things Richard said that sounded so authoritarian were really not intended as such. Something about the way German translates into English makes the words come out in a seemingly dictatorial pattern. Gradually we were finding Richard Kaan to be a kind and warm fellow who was oblivious to his own off-putting manner. When we intellectualized it, we could overlook it. The problem was, we didn't always have time to intellectualize it. Sometimes he'd say something Kaanlike, and we just wanted to strangle him.

The car was completed. That is, it existed and ran. The basic competition modifications had been made. Now came the work of making it ready to race, the final equipping and preparation. Our timetable allowed two weeks for this phase, then we were moving on to Paris where we would wire up the cameras and do all the final organization and provisioning. Days were dwindling down to the precious few.

In the shop, "the boys" teamed up on the car. Kaan employed between five and eight men, depending on the work load. We had the full complement going now. Kaan called them "the boys," and some were little more than that, young apprentices learning their metal. Everyone called Kaan "Mister Kaan," those being the only words of English most of them spoke.

The foreman was Helmut Barthel. Helmut was a master mechanic. If there was a higher title, he'd have it. "Doctor of Cars" is what he really was. And specifically, of this car, the Gelandewagen. Helmut was a miracle man. We'd ask for a miracle, he'd frown, groan, then produce it. Without Helmut, our chances of having a car ready for Paris/Dakar would have been less than "nossing." Kaan treated Helmut with kid gloves, always calling him "Herr Barthel." Helmut wore a spotless tan lab coat, which made him look more like a doctor than a mechanic, certainly no grease monkey. He was tall, thin, and narrow-faced with twinkling blue eyes. He had sandy hair and a reddish blond moustache, a silly, scraggly little thing that made him look like a boy trying to appear grown up. Helmut would dive into the engine compartment for some complicated procedure and emerge cleaner than he was before he began.

"Ver goot!" He'd beam. Then he'd show us how to clean tools.

An early lesson I learned was that the worst offense we could make in Helmut's eyes was to fail to return a tool to the exact place where we'd found it, cleaned. He'd stand there holding the item aloft with a pained expression on his face, shaking his head with his eyes closed, saying, "Dis is no goot, Edvard."

That was no good for two reasons. First, because I might have replaced the tool in other than its precise home or had failed to return it in spotless condition. Second, because I had used one of the shop's tools at all. They had prepared a tool kit for us, the size of a doctor's bag. In it was everything we would need to perform any maintenance or repair, reduced to the smallest, lightest minimum. We had been instructed to use only this kit. In that way they could determine if there were any items lacking and fill it in. Also, it would help us build familiarity with our own kit. In the desert, there would be no handy, wheeled stands full of tools to pick from. From the day we arrived, Helmut regarded our use of any tools other than our own as cheating.

The shop consisted of one big room in a bunkerlike cinderblock structure behind the main office building. There was room inside for about eight cars. There were only four cars here now. Ours was the centerpiece. The remainder of the available space was taken up by boxes and boxes of spare parts and equipment the contents of which would somehow find their way into our car in some organized way. Though it was hard to fathom how that would be achieved.

They were fitting us to the car. Special racing seats had been installed, chairlike buckets that hugged our hips, made by a company named ASS, the kind of twist I appreciate. Ours would be strapped into them from five points, with safety belts running down over both shoulders, across our hips from both sides and up between our legs, where they would all join in a central locking device situated approximately where the stomach meets the rib cage. The belts were fastened to the frame and to the aluminum roll-cage whose members criss-crossed their ways down each side of the car, across, under the dash-board, and up over our heads.

Getting in and out of the car wasn't easy. We had to unlatch our belts, open the door, hoist ourselves up with our hands on the edges of the seats, and swing our bodies up and over the roll cage and down to the ground. I made a mental note to practice evacuation, to eject ourselves out of the car and onto the ground, rolling away from the car, in a simulated fire emergency. But first I'd have to find a place with soft dirt or sand. This was a very high car, and I winced at the thought of falling out onto concrete from that height.

Fire is a great hazard in the Paris/Dakar Rallye. Both from the extreme heat and the fact that the cars are little more than stripped-out shells filled with fuel. We carried the main fuel tank of fifteen gallons in the tail. In addition, there were two small bladders of about five gallons apiece, riding higher and off to each side of the main tank. About a foot behind us was a huge two-hundred-litre auxiliary tank that had been specially made for the race. Fuel lines connecting the various tanks ran all through the car, as did fuel system venting hoses. The interior of the car smelled like a gas station, definitely a no-smoking area.

The main control valve for the fuel system, which had to be thrown when switching over from tank to tank, was located on the floor between our seats, just aft of a large fire extinguisher. Mounted just below the dashboard, which was looking less and less like the dash of a car and more like the cockpit of a Concorde, what with all the clocks, timers, mileage counters, and assorted other navigation gear, was the main electrical shut-off switch. In case of trouble, that switch had to be thrown first or an electrical spark could ignite the whole contrap-tion, blowing us to kingdom come.

Most racing cars have this sort of arrangement, and fear of a fiery death makes using it second nature. One time when I was racing the Lotus, I got a wheel off the road and into some loose gravel at over 115 miles an hour on a long sweeping turn on a race course in Con-necticut. The car snapped ninety degrees, shot straight up in the air, and soared over the road. I remember sitting there looking down, as though in a plane, while other cars raced past beneath me. As the car flew over the road and its nose pointed down toward a deep ravine, I went over my checklist: fuel pumps, off; main electrics, off; wheels, straight; legs and arms, braced; and so forth. People often ask how I had the presence of mind to think of such things at a time like that. It's easy. You either keep your wits or you cry for your mommy. Those who select the second option don't usually live to tell about it.

There was a problem with the main electric switch on the Gelande-wagen. When strapped into my seat, I couldn't reach it. I pointed this out to Kaan, who responded by saying, "You're too short, Edvard." This was a fairly significant problem. The location of the electric shut-off, not my height. That's an insignificant problem. But I concurred with Kaan that there was simply nowhere else to put it, so crammed was the cockpit. I practiced throwing it with my foot, a practical compromise.

We also had a main electrical shut-off outside the car. A box with a blue lightning bolt painted on it identified its purpose. If the car started to leak fuel or developed electrical problems, we could shut it down from out there.

Because of my height, the driver's seat was set almost all the way forward on its travel, which meant the seat belts weren't long enough to reach up and around me from their mounting points behind. Racing belts are not adjustable like those in a family car. After again saying "You're too short, Edvard," Kaan suggested extending them with steel links where they attached to the frame.

"No, Richard, I'm not too short. You should have waited until we got here to install them. They have to be moved," I told him.

This was an expensive and time-consuming proposition I could see he wanted to avoid. But I would make no compromise where our safety was concerned. The links Kaan suggested, strong as they might be, were an interruption in our lifeline. They could become kinked and in the force of a crash, might shear off. Also, this was against the technical and safety rules established for the proper fixing of seat belts for the race. I was inflexible about the belts. Richard spent days trying to track down longer belts, but in the end he had to move the fixing points.

These are the kinds of details that occupied us in our early days in Graz. These and trying to find edible food and arranging to get heat and hot water in the flat.

After the first few days, Kaan suggested we take the car for the weekend, drive somewhere, and familiarize ourselves with it, making notes for any changes and adjustments that would be required. He also wanted to give "the boys" a good rest. After we returned, we would all be working days, nights, and weekends.

We picked Venice. This would be our last opportunity to have a couple of days off in a civilized place with decent food for months. Paris wasn't going to be a picnic or even much of an enjoyable experience the way our schedule was beginning to shape up. Also, Venice was an easy drive from Graz. We could drive down leisurely on Saturday morning and back on Monday afternoon. Monday was a national holiday, and Kaan wanted "the boys" to have it off.

The three things we wanted most out of Venice were food, heat, and showers. We hadn't had much food, any heat, or a shower in days. After that, we would be happy with a little rest and sight-seeing. And, of course, there was the excitement of the car. Neither of us had driven it yet. Kaan had run it on the dynamometer a few days before and pronounced the engine "strong."

It was important to get miles on the engine. It had to be "run in." The objective was to have ten thousand kilometers on it by the time we started racing in Africa. It would then be at its absolute peak of performance, the engineers had predicted. The drive to Venice and back would pile on the first critical thousand kilometers.

I don't remember if we were more excited about the car or the prospect of showers as we set off on Saturday morning. The cold had moderated into the almost balmy lower forties. It was sunny and we were as children with new toys on Christmas morning. As we drove, I talked and Carolyn made notes. Mostly about seat, pedal, and mirror adjustments, obvious things like that. After a while, the observations would become more critical and subtle. After two or three hours of driving, being careful to avoid running at a constant speed, which can cause "flat spots" in a new engine, I began to open the car up.

There are two schools of thought on this. One dictates running an engine in slowly, being careful not to put a strain on it too soon. The other advocates pushing it sensibly to its limits, in short bursts, varying speeds as much as possible.

I belong to the latter school. If there was a flaw in this powerplant, I wanted to find it fast. Later would be too late. So I pushed, got it up to 106, going slightly downhill on the autostrada. No problem with the engine.

The problem with this car was aerodynamics. It was very high, as I said. In sailing terms, it had a lot of windage. So it was all over the road. Where most cars knife through the air, this one barged through and became the victim of its own turbulence. I wasn't surprised. The Gelandewagen wasn't designed for fast, flat-out running. It was designed to make molehills out of mountains. In Paris/Dakar the route would be a virtual obstacle course most of the way, so extremely high speeds and aerodynamics would seldom come into play. Even so, there was a downside.

Because of its aerodynamic inefficiency, we were burning fuel at a frightening rate. The engine had to work hard to push the thing through the air at any speed. I could see where losing the brakes wouldn't be a major problem. All I had to do was take my foot off the gas and the car would stop. We calculated that we were getting slightly more than three kilometers to a litre. We carried a total of three hundred litres, more or less. That put us precariously close to the required range for Paris/Dakar, which is eight hundred kilometers. Maybe the mileage would improve after the engine loosened up. But it was sure to get worse under racing conditions when the engine would be constantly revving at maximum revolutions per minute. We made a note to discuss fuel efficiency and capacity with Kaan.

Driving along close to top speed, learning the car's fuel consumption and high-speed handling characteristics, feeling a sense of exhilaration at having come this far from our original almost casual discussion about doing Paris/Dakar in the first place, I forgot that I was supposed to be varying the speed. I'd been going a hundred miles an hour or more for about twenty minutes. Way too long. In a cold sweat, I slowed to fifty, which felt like a crawl. Cars we'd gone flashing past now overtook us, the passengers giving us strange looks as they went by, perplexed by our inconsistency. I was praying that I hadn't caused a flat spot in the engine. Oh well, at least it would be where it would cause the least problem, up near the top end.

Venice was crowded, even though it was off-season. We parked in a garage outside of town, after waiting in a line for two hours to get in. Then we dragged our three enormous duffel bags onto a landing and boarded a waterbus. We were living out of the bags we would take along on the Rallye, one for Carolyn, one for me, and one for joint gear. This one was now filled with cameras. Carolyn had brought along a bunch of cameras and lenses, which added much to our burden. We carried all the photography equipment with us from New York. Nikon had been more than generous with what they loaned us, so we carried it with us everywhere, concerned for its safety. There were at least nine cameras, two of them with bulky 250-frame magazines, which would be built into the car. Each camera had a complete battery of lenses and special filters. There were also strobe lights and a variety of other accessories. We could have stayed in Venice and opened a photo store.

During whatever free moments she had, Carolyn was testing the cameras and lenses. Later she would make a final equipment selection and ship the remainder back to Nikon in New York. As always, we carried a lot of laundry, hoping to have it nicely done by the hotel. Entering Venice we looked more like an Italian family emigrating to New York than a couple of New Yorkers visiting Italy.

We checked into the Danieli, a nice, somewhat commercial hotel on the Grand Canal. In my old business, which is to say expense-account days, I would have headed straight for the Cipriani. Now, the Danieli was more than extravagant enough. Most of the hotels were full. We were lucky to get a room anywhere. So we couldn't complain that we were put in a dark room off to the side over a particularly smelly little canal. This would put a damper on our deep breathing. But at least the shower worked and the room was warm. We each took two showers, as if that would help make up for the days we had spent without one.

Suddenly, we were alone together with no pressing duties other than our regular exercises and yoga. It was almost like meeting for the first time. We began to act like lovers again instead of teammates under extraordinary pressure. We held hands and strolled through the Piazza San Marco, saying little, the peace being meaningful enough. It was drizzling as it so often does in Venice, but rather than being a discomfort or annoyance, it was sublime. We held our faces up to the falling drops, as though to a shower, basking in the ablution of our many tensions. We walked and walked, not minding that our feet were becoming soaked.

Other than wearing sneakers, we were dressed properly for the weather. We had on our bright blue and black windbreakers, which were our racing uniforms. They were waterproof, had rain hoods with cuffs that sealed tight with Velcro tabs. Just right for the weather but exactly wrong for Venice and the somewhat fancy restaurant we were headed for. It didn't matter. I was having that sensation so many people feel when they visit Venice. Like having walked out of the audience and into some lively opera with an ornate stage set. Our costumes served to heighten the out-of-place feeling, seemed to increase our feeling of foreignness in the surroundings, and made greater the joy of finding ourselves here for the moment without a care. Like a couple of kids in blue jeans crashing a black-tie party without an invitation but being asked to stay because our audacity was admired.

We ate in Venice as though each meal would be our last. That night I remember having soup and pasta and risotto and roast chicken with rosemary, the restaurant's specialty.

The reality of Venice is its lack of it. From the restaurant, gazing through the falling rain, we were transfixed by the sight of a small square lined with buildings overlapping each other, jutting out from one another at absurd angles. Leaving one, you would have to walk over the stairs of another to enter or leave the square. The entire square was bathed in a warm, pinkish glow as though projected over the unreal scene by some lighting engineer. We sat and ate, waiting for the cast to come on stage.

We spent the whole next day walking in the intermittent drizzle. Days in Venice are as fictional as the nights. It seems as though the thousands of people scurrying across the ever-changing scene will sud- denly be gone, back to wherever it is they came from. And it happens that way. You walk down a crowded, narrow, cobbled street, turn a corner, and stand facing a totally deserted square. In a matter of feet and seconds, thousands have disappeared! The phenomenon also occurs in reverse. Traversing the lonely square, you unexpectedly come out facing a grand canal, perhaps *the* Grand Canal, crowded, boisterous, humanity clotting on the banks, all watching a regatta of floating busses, wedding barges, funeral biers, water taxis, and gondolas ply their way in, out, around, and miraculously not through each other.

I was awed by the unreal nature of Venice on this trip, more so than usual because in such an unlikely setting, I was often struck with thoughts and images of dazzling and sometimes frightening reality. Walking across a bridge to visit a museum, we came upon a young man and woman who looked like hippies out of San Francisco in the sixties, unchanged in the interim. They were sitting on the bridge, as were many others, selling trinkets. This couple had a small carpet set out and on it they displayed their handiwork, beaded wristbands that tie on, the type so popular with teenagers. We stopped to talk to them. It turned out they were Canadians vagabonding their way through Europe, earning their way as they went.

I bought two wristbands to send to my boys in New York. As I admired my purchase, I thought of my boys and their possible reaction to receiving these gifts from me. It was then, standing there on that bridge in that fairyland, that the too-real fact of my mortality finally dawned on me. This could be the last gift they would ever receive from me. It might be the last word they would ever hear from me.

Would I ever see them again? Was I soon to become only the memory of their father like my father was to me?

For a moment I was shaken, scared, on the verge of tears. I had been so absorbed with Paris/Dakar I had never considered the possible out-come of my absorption until then. There on that bridge mentally cling-ing to my previous life and wondering about its significance to others.

All these months, I had been hearing of the dangers of Paris/Dakar, was even planning and preparing for them. Yet they had been abstrac-tions as unreal to me as Venice was now. I think Carolyn was having similar insights, for soon after this incident she told me of her desire to fly back to the States for Christmas to see her parents. I told her that I doubted our timetable would allow for that. I couldn't tell her that on Christmas Day we'd be changing tires in the rain in Versailles.

Our last hours in Venice were spent wandering around, keeping our maudlin and troubled thoughts to ourselves.

That night we had dinner at Harry's Bar. When the food is "on," it can be among the very best in Venice. Also, it's crowded, lively. That's the kind of atmosphere we craved. There was nothing anything like it back in Graz. And beyond Graz, who knew? While we were eating, a group of five people sat down at the table next to us. I saw they were all advertising people I knew from New York. One of them was the head of the ad agency that did the advertising for Mercedes in the U.S. I had called him a few months before to enlist his help in getting Mercedes to throw some PR support our way. Here I was again in another of those real/unreal juxtapositions, the house specialty in Venice.

"What are *you* doing here?" my friend asked. "I thought you were off racing somewhere in Africa."

"I am, I mean I will be. We're putting the car together in Austria and just drove here for the weekend to shake it down. And to have a last good meal."

After I'd said it, I realized the ironic significance and didn't think it was very funny.

They were all fascinated, wanting to hear the stories of our prep-aration and training and to know more about the race. It was the last thing in the world I felt like talking about in my current state of mind. Seeing real people from a real place just added to my mounting anxiety. It made me even more aware that I was living a dream, a potentially deadly dream, one from which I might never awaken. At that moment, I couldn't wait to return to the familiar nightmare of Graz.

8

Upon our return to Graz, we found heat and hot water. We took showers immediately, not believing the good fortune could last. It couldn't. There was only enough hot water for one hot shower. Rationing would follow, showers by appointment only. But we were finally able to move our perishables to the windowsill outside, like all the other schmucks who lived along the Bindergasse.

That evening we met Kurt Knilli. He was an old acquaintance of Richard's who would also be running Paris/Dakar. Kaan was maddening because he was dictatorial and curt. Kurt was annoying because he came on like he knew it all. He had never run Paris/Dakar before either, but he talked to us like a man to children. He asked if we had moved our calisthenics and weight-lifting inside the sauna yet. He was putting in three hours a day there, he said.

We didn't believe him. He would have looked like a prune. He didn't. Kurt had a face like an overripe cantaloupe wearing glasses. On top of the melon was a mop of gray hair. He also had a soft, quiet, monotonous tone of voice that lent undue seriousness to all the bullshit that droned out. He talked of sharing his support truck with us, of letting us share the services of his mechanic, of taking us to the Mitsubishi test track outside town where we could practice, of our flying to Africa with him to avoid the uncomfortable ship's crossing. It all proved to be hot air. Over time we even grew to like him too. Shared adversity makes strange bedfellows.

Hidden in among Kurt's B.S. were some valuable odds and ends that I gleaned and filed for future reference. One such tidbit was the importance of making an appointment with a carwash outside of Cergy-Pontoise, a suburb of Paris. That's where we would drive the Prologue, the time-trial in which the lunatics are paraded before hundreds of thousands of crazed spectators. Our finishing time in the Prologue would also establish our starting position when the real racing began in Africa. Kurt told us that in running the course, our car would become caked with well over a hundred pounds of mud. If we didn't get it washed off fast, it would solidify and there would be no other opportunity to have it removed. This guy seemed to have done his homework. I began to wonder if we were going to be so well prepared after all.

The next morning I told Kaan of our meeting with Knilli.

"He's a nice guy, but take everything he says with a grain of salt," Richard said.

I told him the weight-lifting in the sauna story.

"Three hours a day!" I laughed.

"The heaviest thing Kurt ever lifted vas a hamburger!" Kaan said. "Is he still fat? I haven't seen him for a while."

"A little pudgy."

"I can't imagine Kurt in Paris/Dakar," he went on. "I don't even know if he knows how to drive. He'll never finish!"

This sauna business I should explain. Part of the training routine is desert conditioning. The nearest thing to that is a sauna or maybe a steam bath. The idea is to condition your body to exertion in extreme heat. If Knilli had already moved into this phase, he had moved too fast. You wanted to work up to a peak. We'd calculated six to eight weeks in the sauna, three to four days a week, starting out at half an hour and working up to about an hour toward the end would be about right. Even then it wouldn't be perfect because the worst of the heat wouldn't occur until the second week of the race. During the week in between, our systems would begin to adjust out of the heat conditioning anyway. We would begin this phase in mid-November in Paris, hitting our peak on New Year's Eve. Kurt was wasting hours of his precious sweat on the cold weather in Graz.

Acclimatizing ourselves to the desert was the reason we'd been drinking a lot of water too. Particularly me, for I was prone to dehydration. That's why my doctor had set as a goal seven litres of water a day. The desert sun beating on my arm through the car's windows could dehydrate me in twenty minutes, he'd said.

We carried twenty gallons of water. I had four five-gallon tanks installed behind our seats. This would not only give us ready access to the water, but it would serve as a liquid safety barrier between our backs and the two-hundred-litre fuel tank just behind. We'd suck the water into our mouths as we drove via a system of tubes I'd designed, which Kaan, Helmut, and the boys were installing now. Knilli told us he'd devised a plastic bladder that would be mounted on the roof of his car. That was when we really knew Kurt was full of it. What if he rolled? And if he didn't, the water he'd be carrying up there in the sun would be of a temperature more suitable for our shower in Graz than for his big mouth in the desert.

Carolyn was not feeling well, yet in the shop she showed a toughness and mechanical aptitude that made me proud. While I worked on designing the water supply system, on determining the strategic place-ment of navigation equipment, on rigging our helmets for sound, on wiring the automatic tape recorder that would record our dialogue. While I sorted, marked, and shuffled tools and spare parts, Carolyn methodically, under Helmut's expert guidance, dismantled and reas-sembled the car. What she was doing while feeling unwell would be hard work for a healthy experienced mechanic.

She removed and remounted the shock absorbers. This entailed jack-ing up each wheel of the car and removing all four wheels and tires. Each of the giants weighed between ninety and a hundred pounds. Then the hard work began. She had to break loose all the nuts and bolts that had been tightened with a passion by the factory workers who knew what kind of torture the car was being built for. As she went she marked each nut with two numbers. On the shock absorbers for example, she'd mark 24/120. That meant a twenty-four millimeter wrench was needed to loosen these nuts and that they should be retightened with 120 pounds of torque. There would be no time in the race to fumble around looking for the right-size wrench or to look up in a manual the proper amount of torque.

By the time we left Graz, every critical nut and bolt on the car would be loosened, tightened, and so marked. During the race the engineers had determined we would have to replace the shock ab-sorbers at least twice. We were being drilled on all these scheduled maintenance items, as well as on repairs that were not scheduled but highly likely. In one day Carolyn removed and replaced the wheels and shock absorbers, the fan, the alternator, the fuel pump, and the fuel filter. Then would come my turn for some heavy work while Carolyn painted millimeter numbers on the tools for ease of identifi-cation, sorted gear, etc.

Kaan and the boys threw us a curve. The following day they asked me to redo everything Carolyn had done the day before.

"Why?" I protested, "Carolyn knows how, isn't that enough?"

"No, Edvard, zis is best. If von of you forgets, za uzzer vill have to remember. Better get to vork," said Kaan, brooking no shortcuts on our part.

He was right. And so it went for days. Each of us would repeat the work the other had already done. And that's what we'd talk about night after night.

"Isn't that third nut on the manifold heat shield a bitch?" I'd complain.

Carolyn would recollect, "That's a ten millimeter, isn't it? I remember. I think it's easier to use a box wrench on that instead of the ratchet with the short extension."

That's how we would feed each other. Before we left, we'd know the car, its maintenance, and repair in our sleep. We weren't getting much of that, though.

Carolyn came down with a strep throat and ran a high fever. Probably from lying on the cold concrete under the car for hours on end. She wouldn't take a day off. There was so much to be done.

Every day there would be a little surprise waiting for us. I swear Kaan and the boys would meet at night after we left and concoct little trials for us. We'd drag ourselves out of bed, to the laundry and out to the shop, every morning arriving a little duller-eyed with our limp tails dragging.

"Carolyn, Edvard, this morning we are timing you. We bet you can't change the starter in less than an hour."

Kaan would challenge us with his diabolical smirk. We'd done this once each before. After the first time, we'd asked them to cut a hole in the transmission tunnel and install a removable plate over the hole. That way one of us could release the starter motor from inside the car. It would drop down into the hands of the other who was beneath the car. The new starter, which Carolyn had pulled from one of the spare parts cases now built into the back of the car, was pushed up into position by me from underneath. While down there I also reattached the wiring while Carolyn, from inside, tightened the starter back into place with a flexible ratchet we'd had specially made for this job. The plate screwed back over the hole, we both jumped back from the car, threw our hands in the air, and yelled, "Time."

"Not yet," Helmut said. "First start za car!"

"Damn!" I reached in and turned the key, smiling with relief as the engine roared to life.

"Ver goot!" said Helmut. "Forty-eight minutes."

"Next time we'll do it in thirty-nine," I said.

Then Helmut would check the quality of our work. He'd inspect the tightness of the nuts, the neatness of the wiring. Smiling out at us from beneath the car, he'd say, "Goot. You're getting goot."

There were still many things that weren't so good. I was sweating out the arrival of the navigation equipment that had failed to show up in New York as promised by the guy in Ohio. We needed it within the next few days or we'd be in trouble. I was nervous about the ability of the Ohio guy to come through. So we'd been calling all over Europe to locate two Halda Twinmasters. These particular models were nowhere to be found. We called the factory in Sweden. They had none in stock. The last two had just been shipped to someone in California. I called the guy in Ohio. He reassured me that I'd have them for sure within a week. They would be arriving in California any minute now.

"Oh, God!" I groaned. This was typical. Racing! Only in racing could you find yourself waiting for equipment to be sent from Sweden to Austria via California, Ohio, and New York. I was beside myself. Guess who was paying for all the shipping? And every pair of hands cut themselves in for a little piece of the action. But I had no choice except to wait. And pay.

I had been doing this with every part or piece of equipment that wasn't being supplied directly by Kaan, backstopping, double-checking, making sure we were covered and not stuck waiting for something important at the last minute. I spent a lot of time on Richard's phone, calling all over the world. Guess who was paying for that? My sponsors, I still hoped. But busy as we were with everything else, my hopes on this were dimming.

Safety matters were still unresolved. I was unhappy with the way the sand tracks had been mounted in the rear of the car. The sand tracks were four latticed aluminum strips about a foot wide and five feet long. Should we become stuck in the sand, we would put one in front of each wheel and ride out of the predicament on these rails. They were mounted on their side edges in a channel that traveled the length of the car, just strapped in place with nylon belts. I was con-vinced the sharp treads of these tracks would chafe through the nylon tie-downs in no time. Worse, I thought that in a panic stop or crash, momentum would shoot them forward, turning them into deadly projectiles that would go right through Carolyn.

I insisted that their mounting be reengineered. An aluminum endpiece was constructed and riveted into place, the nylon straps were lined with leather to protect from wear. The battery mounting needed to be reengineered as well. It was held down by a single nylon strap. If I turned the car over, a frequent occurrence in Paris/Dakar, the battery would break away from its tray and it would be impossible to remount it. Using long bolts and nuts and aluminum angle brackets, we improvised a more permanent fixing.

There were dozens and dozens of details like this still to be attended to. Everyone's patience was wearing thin. People were blowing up at the drop of a wrench. Nearly every day the dashboard had to be torn apart, either to make room for some other piece of equipment or because someone had installed a piece of gear without consideration to the accessibility of something else. A light had been mounted over the stopwatch and clock, blocking our access to the speedometer cable, which at some point would probably need to be replaced. Even the Teutonic thoroughness was breaking down under the pressure.

We had spares for everything. This wasn't a car. It was Ed's Ark. There were backup fuel pumps, fans, belts, a water pump, a windshield, fuses, a starter, an alternator, backup navigation equipment, lights, fuel filters, a master brake cylinder, distributer cap, hoses and lines, a battery, three sets of spare shock absorbers, brake pads, spark plugs. Think of anything. We had it. What do you think I'd been putting into all those telexes?

The heaviest stuff would ride in a pair of chests packed in foam aboard trucks that were also competing. I had contracted for this space months before. I had even taken the precaution of specifying that each chest be carried on a separate truck so that if one of them went out we wouldn't be left high and dry. Each truck would also carry a spare wheel and tire. We had two of our own inside.

The lighter stuff, along with our sleeping and cooking gear, was carried in a nest of aluminum cases strapped into the back. Wherever possible, backup systems were built in. If the main fuel pump went out, I could switch over to a spare by flipping a switch on the dashboard. We were labeling all the switches and knobs with a Dymo, otherwise we'd never remember what they were all for.

The camera mounts were giving "the boys" nightmares. There were to be five cameras mounted on the car. We'd brought the mounts with us, and they were being installed here. The cameras would be affixed and wired by Scott Andrews in Paris. In the front, a Nikon F3 with a 250-frame magazine would ride just behind and below the bumper. Part of the body was being cut away to allow for it. Also a special screened aluminum cowcatcher was being built over the front end to protect this camera, as well as the radiator, the oil cooler, and the powerful rally lights, all of which, incidentally, I carried spares for just in case. There was a cut-out in the screen, and they were mounting a piece of clear Plexiglas there to protect the lens. The whole camera unit would be encased in a plastic bag to protect it from dust. The same with the other exterior mounted camera, which would be riding in a specially-designed cage on top of the right front fender.

"The boys" were bending and welding and cursing the tubes for this cage. Inside, two cameras would be mounted to the roll cage behind our heads, pointing out the windshield providing a pilot and copilot's eye view. Finally, another 250-frame F3 was being mounted inside, up against the rear window looking out behind. This and the outside lower camera had the giant magazines. Since they required the biggest, strongest mounts, these cameras would be the hardest to get into, the film hardest to change. That's why they had the big magazines. We carried three hundred rolls of film in addition to all the other apparatus I described earlier. Kaan and the boys weren't happy about all this camera business. Of course, Kaan told me I'd have to pay extra for this work. In for a dollar, in for two.

Costs were rising, tensions were mounting, and time was running out. Every day became harder and longer. We had wanted to be out of there and on our way to Paris before the tenth of November. No way we'd make that date anymore. We were running a week behind schedule. The camera work had slowed everything down. And we were still waiting for the Halda Twinmasters to orbit the globe and catch up with us. Meanwhile we were learning the car. As our patience ebbed, our knowledge and proficiency soared. We learned how to weld. Our support truck carried tanks for welding. I thought we ought to know what to do with them just in case. Some signs it seems stupid to ignore. So we spent a couple of days ruining scraps of metal. This was not our best event. But Carolyn had a better touch than I did, so we made her team welder.

One cold bleak morning we arrived at the bunker early, having taken a day off from the laundry. The boys were all standing around the car in a semicircle with serious expressions on their faces. No work was going on. I wondered what was up.

"Start za car, Edvard," Helmut said glumly.

I got in and turned the key. The starter cranked and cranked, but the engine would not fire up. I gave Helmut a quizzical look.

"Find the fault and fix it, Edvard and Carolyn." He smiled, starting the stopwatch he held in his hand.

I pulled the metal pins that fastened the hood and opened it up while Carolyn ran for the tools. She handed me two 17-millimeter open-end wrenches, the only size we had two of, specifically for this operation. We were working like a surgeon-and-nurse team. While I loosened the brass nuts on the intake to the fuel injection system, she had taken another tool and had begun to loosen the main power lead to the distributor cap. There was an emergency starter switch under the hood. We both carried keys for it on leather thongs around our necks. I cranked the engine. Fuel came spurting out. That eliminated the fuel filter, fuel lines, and the fuel pump as possible problems. I then repeated the operation on the fuel return line, cranked the starter again, and found fuel. That eliminated the injection system.

"I've got spark to the distributor," Carolyn announced. That eliminated the alternator, the electrical box, and the coil. While she put that back together, I began unplugging the leads from the distributor to the spark plugs, one at a time. Now Carolyn cranked the engine while I checked to see if a spark traced between the sockets and the screwdriver I held in my other hand. I had a spark from every one. That eliminated the distributor.

"Plugs!" I said. "The problem has to be the plugs. We've eliminated everything else." But it didn't seem logical. When the problem is plugs, it's one or two of them. Then the engine will run rough, but it will still run.

I grabbed a plug wrench anyway and climbed up on top of the engine. The car was so high you couldn't lean into the engine compartment. You had to climb in and straddle the engine while working on it. I pulled a plug. It looked clean. I pulled another. Clean too. Then I looked at the plugs in profile. The devils had removed all the plugs and closed the gaps so they couldn't emit a spark.

"Ver goot, ver goot," Helmut congratulated us. So did all the boys who smiled around their approval.

"Six minutes, forty-five seconds," beamed Helmut, holding up the stopwatch as proof. "Ver, ver goot."

Then everybody stopped laughing and got back to work. That day we ate lunch with the boys in the shop, the first time a girl had ever been accorded such an honor or probably any outsider for that matter. The conversation was limited, owing to the language problem. But not much more limited than the conversations held in our normal daily lunches with Kaan and Claudia who would just sit there smiling emptily.

It was clear we were nearing graduation. And we could tell that they would all be very pleased to see our commencement. They had been going full-tilt for over two weeks and were starting to balk at any new request.

Other than little last-minute niggles, the car was finished. Mostly, what remained was tightening down and testing. For example, we'd installed an oil temperature gauge by rolling the car out of the shop and up a handy concrete ramp out front and off to one side. Helmut climbed beneath and fastened the sensor for the gauge by drilling it into the brass oil drain plug at the bottom of the engine. I always checked every bit of work that went into the car. Not because I didn't trust anyone. But because I needed to know exactly where everything was, exactly how it worked, and what its function was. And, of course, because I really didn't trust anyone.

I looked at the sensor installation and didn't like what I saw. Originally, the car was meant to have an aluminum shield running underneath to protect from damage from flying rocks or crunching along over boulders. The engineers had changed their minds on this. They felt that it would be too heavy and that it would also act as a trap for heat, which they wanted to dissipate. Particularly heat from the "owtomatic gearbox."

Anyway, the sensor that Helmut had installed was up behind one of the beefier front suspension members. Other than that, it was just hanging out there. Easy prey, I thought, to getting knocked off.

"It's too vulnerable there. We'll lose it the first day in Africa," I told him.

He always had a ready response to my misgivings. He'd shrug his shoulders and say, "Test it."

Out behind the bunker, Kaan had his own private test track. It was a little one but okay for shaking things down and people up. Kaan's track was roughly the size of a football field but not as flat. Far from it. It looked like the kind of place the army might test tanks.

Two straight rows of trees running the length of the field split it approximately into thirds. The left and center thirds were just grass straightaways between the trees. Which one you raced down depended on how acute a turn you wanted to make at the end of the straight. Go down the leftmost strip and you got two ninety-degree turns into the rightmost third of the course. Go down the center strip and you had a 180-degree turn into the far right strip, which was a miniature mountain range. There were three hills of varying height and steepness. You could drive onto or off of each of the hills from about three different directions so small as it was, Kaan's track could simulate a variety of conditions.

I jumped into the car, strapped myself in, and shot down the left third as fast as I could go. This was my favorite way because I could take the two ninety-degree turns as one, in a full sweeping 180 in a beautiful controlled skid entering the first uphill at maximum speed. This hill was just short of straight up. Any steeper and you'd fall off backward. The top of the hill came to a point, so shortly after you ran out of land, the front end pitched down the other side, dropping you on your front-end into soft dirt with a terrific jolt. Then up the middle hill, which was less steep but very rocky and bumpy, also taller than the first. Coming off the mounded top, you hit a plateau placed just under the peak, so the car bounded up radically, reversing its own momentum. Then you dropped down into a little valley before ascending the third and nastiest hill.

This third one was a driving test as well as a car test. There were three ways you could take it, three different mistakes you could make. You could go straight over the top too fast and pitchpole end over end down the other side. You could make a right turn off the top, going too slowly and roll down the hill side over side. Or you could split the options and go between. But if you went too quickly, you'd slide off the side of the hill at a crab-angle and crash into one of the trees lined up alongside. Also, visibility on this little track was always horrible. Generally, the testing would be taking place at dusk in a cold, gray mist. It was a diversion from the bunker, though. I took it around a few times, the car sliding, leaping, pitching, yawing, plunging, shaking, twisting, as the track was designed to make it do. It also rearranged all my personal plumbing.

Back at the shop, Helmut looked underneath, picking clumps of earth and grass out of various places so he could get a clearer picture.

"Sensor is okay, it hasn't moved. Dirt not near."

"Okay, Helmut, whatever you say, but I don't think so. Two days. I give it two days."

This was a Saturday evening. The next day we were taking the car out for a few hours drive to give it a longer but less violent shaking down. Home, we shook ourselves out of our filthy coveralls and took showers. We'd each get wet, turn off the water, wash, then rinse. It was the only way we could get two showers out of the miserly hot water tank. Drying my hair with the dryer, a fuse blew. A key fuse blew. No heat, no light, no hot water. The temperature was in the low twenties. It was too late, too cold, too dark, and we were too tired to worry about it. We fell into bed exhausted.

In the morning, we saw a neighbor outside our building. The whole time we lived in Graz, we never saw a living thing *inside* our building other than the birds. I said, "Morgen, blowen a fusen," and got him to help. He spoke a little English and told Carolyn where to find an electrician. She ran off to track him down. In the meantime, the man, the tenant of a nearby building, came with me to the fuse box and began juggling fuses. The fuses were as old as the building. Some of them were as big as your fist, others the size of your little finger. He played a shell game with the fuses, moving them around in every conceivable combination.

Eventually he sorted them so that we had light and hot water but no heat. I can only imagine what some of the other tenants, if any, lost for us to realize this gain. God, we were so sick of being cold and dirty and uncomfortable that we were both near cracking. There was always some problem like this, every day we were in Graz. I thanked our neighbor for his help. Carolyn hadn't been able to locate the electrician. We'd try again later or tomorrow. I think we were both hoping the car would break down on our test drive so we'd become stranded and never have to come back to this place and face the lack of heat.

We were near the Yugoslavian border when it looked like we might be granted that wish. Driving down a little dirt lane and sliding around a right-hand turn, we both became nauseous and our eyes began to tear. The car had filled with asphyxiating fumes. We opened the filtered vents that I'd had cut in the roof. The side windows were useless for ventilation. They were solid Plexiglas panels with tiny little sliding openings, useful only for reaching out to adjust the mirrors. I'd drive along and the fumes would clear, but after every right-hand turn, we heard a hissing sound and would begin to choke all over again. I couldn't figure this out. The hissing confused me, made me think it was some kind of hydraulic problem. My instincts told me it was a bad fuel leak, probably from the big auxiliary fuel tank. But why so bad only on right-hand turns? And why the hissing? The symptoms were unclear.

We choked our way back to the shop, whenever possible going out of our way to avoid right-hand turns. It was Sunday afternoon, and the shop was closed when we got there. We left a note on the dashboard, describing the strange symptoms so they could get a head start on fixing it in the morning. We were supposed to be leaving for Paris in two days, assuming the Haldas arrived the next day as the man in Ohio had assured us on the phone on Friday. He had them in his possession and was shipping them overnight air. They would be in Vienna Saturday, Graz on Monday, he promised.

We weren't anxious to return to the flat to freeze. So we found a single shaft of sunshine hitting a bench next to the shop. We sat there breathing in the cold, fume-free air in greedy gulps, pointing our gray faces up to the warming sun. We unpacked the lunch we'd thrown together for our aborted jaunt in the country. In silence, we ate our potato sandwiches. I remember wondering what the rich people were doing.

That night the electrician came with fuses and everything was back to normal. Normal? If that's what this was, what was abnormal? Two more days! That thought was the only thing that kept us going.

When we got to the shop the next morning, Richard told us they had already found and fixed the fumes problem. Rolf, one of "the boys" who had a nose for fuel problems, had discovered a pin-point leak in one of the many hoses that made up the fuel breather system. They had replaced it, tested the car on the track, and there were no fumes. To me, it had smelled a lot worse than anything that could be caused by a pin-point air leak. But if there were no fumes . . . maybe.

The Haldas arrived. Helmut and I worked on installing one, me, underneath, doing the dirty work of course. The other Carolyn wrapped, catalogued, and stored with all the other spare parts destined for the trucks. Then we began to address one of the final and most perplexing logistical problems of all. What to do with our fourteen wheels and tires. We had six road tires, four for the car and two spares. We would need these for getting to Paris and back.

Yes, we would have to come back, Richard had just informed us.

The factory wanted to give the car a final going over, a tune-up, some adjustments. Also, it would receive a final paint job. By then I'd know who our sponsors were, if there were any, and their names could be painted on. We'd also change from road shocks to racing shocks. We didn't want to put any wear on them so far in advance of the race. Also, they were very stiff and just driving around on them would be jarring and uncomfortable. I dreaded the thought of coming back and having to meet and beat the bird. But there was no alternative. Besides, there wasn't enough room in the car to haul all the wheels and tires and spares in one trip.

Aside from the six wheels with road tires, we had an additional eight wheels mounted with desert racing tires. Four of these wheels were lightweight aluminum alloy and had been custom-made for an Austrian armored car. We found them stored in the rafters of Kaan's shop, and he sold them to us for a pretty good price. They were each twenty pounds lighter than the steel wheels that came with the car. That was not only eighty pounds less weight in the sand, but changing them was easier.

Anyway, we would leave carrying six steel wheels mounted with road tires, four on, with two matching spares. We would also carry all the spares and equipment that had to go into the cannisters on the trucks. We would then squeeze in two desert racing tires mounted on steel wheels. These would go on the trucks as well. We'd leave our spare road tires in Paris when we came back and pick up the other six racing tires and the remainder of our spare parts and equipment, the items that would ride the race with us. How we were going to juggle all these wheels and tires for the race itself remained a mystery that would haunt us night and day until I finally figured it out four days before the start.

Tuesday morning, November 11th, I had a budget meeting with Richard. We were seventeen thousand dollars over budget. This was due to the extra work on the camera mounts, the additional wheels and tires, and assorted other extras. But the bulk of the overrun was due simply to the drop in the value of the dollar since I'd placed the original order in May. The car was now up to sixty-two thousand dollars and counting. And some of the work that remained to be done was still unaccounted for. By the time I was all finished, adding in the extra spares and equipment I was still to gather in Paris, the grand total for the car alone would approach ninety thousand dollars.

We took the expensive Gelande out to the Mitsubishi/Denzel test track to put it through its final paces. It had been raining for the last day and a half, so the track turned out to be too wet and slick for the car and its weight. It would just slide sideways off the slippery hills, and we could hardly drive it there at all. Richard was concerned that we'd roll it and then he'd never get rid of us. At this point they were just as anxious to be free of us as we were to get away from them. So we went back to the shop and each took turns pushing the car through the short torture test on Richard's track. A couple of loose things turned up here and there, otherwise the car seemed perfect. "The boys" gave it a last going over and tightening on into the evening.

That night the head engineer from Steyr-Daimler-Puch came by to give the car a final visual inspection, to check on Kaan's handiwork, and to give me and Carolyn some last-minute tips. He went all over the car, grunting his approval and firing a barrage of questions at Kaan and Helmut. He asked about the thick, two-inch-wide nylon straps that chained the engine to the frame. Kaan explained that they were there to keep the engine inside the engine compartment should it break away from its mounts if we took a bad jump off a dune.

The engineer also wondered why we had installed little rubber pads on the bases of the hinges joining the hood to the cowl. This was one of the few tips we had gotten from Knilli that made sense. One night he had dropped by and told us everything that we were doing was wrong. He told us these hinges crack from the intense vibration and that we would be wise to cushion them. We passed this intelligence on to the engineer. He understood and approved. Then he told us which oils to use for what and when to check the various reservoirs.

"And never," he said, "never vipe za dipstick for za owtomatic gearbox viss a cloth. Use only your fingers."

He went on to explain that even microscopic shreds of fabric entering the gearbox could put the kibosh on the whole shebang. Not in those exact words, of course. Carolyn scribbled furiously into her notebook, which was now thick with maintenance information.

Free at last! We woke up buoyant for the first time since our arrival, in honor of our impending departure. We picked up our final load of laundry from Frau Boder. By this time we had grown so attached to her and she to us that we posed for a photo with her and her son, Zoltan, in front of the little shop. We gabbed and smiled between ourselves like crazy people, which we must have been because she didn't understand an iota of what we said any more than we could understand her. Maybe it was something in the soap she used. Got into our pores and made us all cuckoo.

I met Richard at the bank, losing still more money converting cabled dollars into Austrian schillings. Not my favorite part of the trip, though I'd be hard pressed to pick *any* favorite part of this trip. If you pushed me, I guess I'd have to say the best part was leaving.

Then we all went out to the shop and got the title and registration and insurance organized. While Richard and I attended to the paper-work, Carolyn supervised the loading and packing of the car. At two in the afternoon, we were finally ready to hit the road. Helmut bestowed upon us his personal tire gauge, one that had been in his possession for ages. We presented all of "the boys" with a powerful little "boom box" of a radio we'd bought in a department store in downtown Graz. This was both a thoughtful and cruel gift. Like giving the precocious child of people you hate a gift of a set of drums or carpentry tools. Richard disliked noise in the shop. He'd be ordering them to turn it down for months. We figured they'd all get a big kick out of that.

As we pulled out of the shop, Richard and "the boys" all stood shoulder to shoulder and beamed like we hadn't seen them beam since the day we arrived, their relief to see us go clearly written on all their faces. We tried to hide our ecstasy at leaving Graz behind. We'd been there less than three weeks, but it felt like forever.

You have never seen a more shocked, then depressed, then sullen group of people than Richard Kaan and "the boys" as we pulled back into the shop an hour later. I think we arrived in the middle of their celebration of our departure. We saw their joyous expressions collapse into ones of sad defeat. A half an hour out, the car had filled with fumes again. It had been a tough choice, choking to death or turning back to Graz. We chose the slightly lesser of the two evils.

We could see ourselves having to stay in Graz for days, maybe weeks, until this problem got diagnosed and fixed. We were bananas. But at that moment, we tried not to show it. There was more than enough unhappiness to go around.

It took more than an hour to unload the car before we could even begin to look for the problem.

Helmut took it out on the test track and after a few minutes came back and pronounced it "Bad, ver bad."

We already knew that. "The boys" covered the car like ants, sniffing, squeezing, poking. At one point Rolf, "the nose," announced that he smelled fuel coming from the big auxiliary tank where the thick rubber neck entered through a hole cut into the aluminum shell. There was nothing for it but to take the tank completely out of the car, open it up, and inspect it. This was easier said than done. First we had to find containers for two hundred litres of fuel and siphon it all into them. We had topped up just before leaving. A couple of hours later, the gas drained, the tank now sitting on the floor of the shop along with all our gear, they began to open it up.

Here was the problem or at least one of them. Inside the aluminum shell was a huge rubberlike bladder. The neck of the bladder came out through the top where it hooked into the filler elbow. At the bottom, the bladder had a smaller tube that fed the gas into the fuel line. The hole it passed through in the aluminum shell was unfinished, jagged metal. The shifting of the bladder in the shell had pushed the tube up against the sharp edges, which had cut a gash into it, causing a trickle of fuel to work its way out into the pan under the tank. I went berserk. This was worse than incompetence. This was an act of aggression on our lives. The danger of explosion or fire was apparent here.

"Why there isn't even a grommet around the hole! Blind people must have put this tank together!" I bellowed at Kaan.

I'd had it with his superior dictatorial attitude. And now this, this was too much. I called him aside and told him I was very worried. What other death traps might be lurking in this car? How could such a thing happen? Richard was quick to blame the problem on the people who built the tank.

I bellowed at him again, "*You* picked them!"

He didn't understand, the tank was certified. The people who made it did tanks for Formula One cars.

"Well, they really fucked up this time! And so did you," I told him.

Carolyn came over to drag me away. While Richard started making angry phone calls to the tank people, she tried to calm me down.

"Take it easy," she whispered to me. "Having a fit won't do any good now."

"This isn't one of his goddamned pimpmobiles!" I said. "I should have known. First the seat belts, then the sand tracks, now this. This guy's learning at our expense. What next?"

We had a mess on our hands. And we had to get it resolved fast. It wouldn't be easy. We were caught up in another racing Catch-22. The people who fabricated the bladder, which was now ruined, were

located in Milan, Italy. The people who built the shell were in Stuttgart, Germany. The result of his phone calls was that Richard would
send the bladder to Milan for replacement or, if possible, repair. We
would repack the car and head for Paris, dropping off the shell in
Stuttgart on the way. He would have the Italians ship the bladder to
Stuttgart, and we would pick up the complete unit on our way back
to Graz. He had a little less than a month to get it all together.

You don't need to listen in on our Stuttgart rantings and ravings,
so I'll spare you the specifics. We'd stopped in Salzburg for a few
hours' sleep and got back on the road early. We were due at the shop
in Stuttgart at noon. We drove a hundred miles past it and lost nearly
four hours. We finally arrived hating the world, and that now included
each other. Needless to say, the Stuttgart people blamed Kaan, said
he should have finished off the hole and installed a grommet. At this
point I was less concerned with affixing blame than I was with ex-
tracting some professional workmanship from both sets of boobs.

You also wouldn't have wanted to be in the car riding with us from
Stuttgart to Paris. Carolyn had gotten quite hysterical with the people
in Stuttgart for taking apart all her packing unnecessarily while trying
to unload the tank. A planned twenty-minute stop had turned into a
two and a half hour ordeal. An hour of this was devoted to getting
the sand tracks back into their slots. They didn't have to come out in
the first place, which made Carolyn crazy. But once out, we found it
practically impossible to get them back in. This made us both crazy.
Still another Kaan foul-up. Obviously they hadn't bothered to test
getting the sand tracks in and out of the car quickly. The way they
were mounted now, if we became stuck in the sand, we'd croak for
sure, so much energy was required to load and unload them. I was
going to have a long, serious telephone conversation with Mr. Kaan.

Up until then, Carolyn had hardly ever complained. Through all
the adversity in Graz, she was stoic. Whereas I bitched like crazy,
about everything. If I didn't give voice to my discomforts and frustrations, I became difficult and short-tempered. So rather than hang on
to it and let it congeal into a highly flammable lump, I pissed it out
in little spurts. Carolyn was the opposite. She'd hold it all in, then
dump the whole, vast accumulation. This invariably led to explosive
fights between us. This was one of those times.

Carolyn had gotten into a hysterical rage at the Germans, tears and
all. Heading toward Paris afterward, she smoldered, a pestle being
worked against the world. Just outside the town of Saarbrücken, she

blew. We became involved in what now seems a classic, comic fight, although it didn't seem so funny at the time.

We were lost again. Neither of us had the faintest idea of where we were or which way to go. I told her she was a lousy navigator and that we were certain to get lost and die in the desert if she didn't get her act together.

She called me an insensitive and cruel SOB and blamed everything bad that had ever happened to anyone, anywhere, on me. She was crying again, and I was getting riled as hell. I could visualize myself in the Sahara, lost, with my sobbing navigator. I suggested that if I was so awful, why didn't she just get the hell out and go away? This was more a statement of exasperation than a serious suggestion on my part, but she chose to take it seriously.

The problem was, the car was still moving. We had slowed to turn off at a cloverleaf exit whose signs now indicated that we were definitely headed the wrong way. She opened the door and began to swing herself out of the moving car. I slowed down so she wouldn't kill herself, but she jumped out onto the grass before I could find a place to stop. I went on about a hundred yards before I could safely pull over, the passenger door still flapping. I walked back to where she was sitting, on a little grass triangle in the midst of three exit roads that curved around the triangle off the autobahn. It was night, dark, around 8:00 P.M., but the whole triangle was lit up like day from powerful gas vapor road lights.

She was sitting there under the lights, crying. I tried to reason with her, told her this was ridiculous, to please come with me back to the car. She wouldn't. In fact, she unleashed another torrent of invective at me. I now thought this was funny and began to laugh. Rather than calming her down, this made her even madder. She jumped up and began to attack me physically as well as verbally, pounding at me wildly with her fists.

It seems one of the more peculiar lots of a man's life is to be called insensitive and unfeeling, always by women, and generally by those pummeling you with their fists or lunging at you with a kitchen knife. After, they tell you that you're neurotic. True to that diagnosis, you later rationalize their eccentric behavior by convincing yourself that it was you who somehow asked for or deserved such treatment. Men are strange. As a *very* experienced friend of mine once put it, "No man is a match for any woman."

Carolyn wouldn't let up. I began laughing even harder, trying to let her know that the joke had gone far enough. This made her madder still, and she pounded on me harder yet. I grabbed her hands to protect myself and tried to pull her back toward the car. She refused to listen or to come.

So I told her okay, to have it her way. I let go of her and started walking back to the car. That's when I noticed all the cars that were slowing down and people staring at her standing there, sobbing. I got back to the car, threw it in reverse, and backed along the shoulder, back toward where she was standing. She saw the car coming and began to walk away! She headed for the far end of the triangle. As I came closer, she moved even farther away until she was backed all the way into the narrowest corner of the brightly lit triangle. I leaned across and opened the passenger door.

"Get in," I said, no longer seeing the humor in the situation.

I don't remember if she said nothing or something I didn't like, but I hoisted myself down to the ground, went over and tried to reason with her to get back into the car. Cars were slowing down all around us now, the passengers staring at us.

"Please get back in the car, we're making a big scene here," I said, trying my last bit to reason with her. She wouldn't budge.

I opened the back of the car, grabbed her duffel bag, and threw it on the ground.

"I'm leaving here now," I said. "Do you want to come or not?"

She said nothing. I said nothing. I just got back into the car and drove away.

I guess it took me ten or fifteen minutes to work my way back around the system of cloverleafs to where she was standing next to her duffel bag. The tears had been replaced with a look that could kill. Again I got out. I grabbed her bag and asked her to *please* get back in the car. Again, she walked away. That's when the police arrived. With me holding the bag and her walking away. Christ, they even had a siren or some bells going. I can't remember the sound track. The picture was memorable enough.

Two big German cops got out of the car, hands on sidearms, thankfully not yet drawn, and came up to me. What kind of words could I put "en" at the end of to talk my way out of this one? That's what I was thinking. They yammered at me in German, and I spoke calmly to them in English.

"Just a little family dispute, officer." Something like that.

They spoke very little English, but they seemed to get the drift of what I said. One went to fetch Carolyn. He came back with her in tow. I looked around. It was as if we were the main attraction at a suburban mall opening. It looked like people were coming from miles around to get a look, win a prize.

"Do you vant to go vis zis man?" one of the cops asked Carolyn.

"For Christ's sake, tell him you want to go with me! You can leave me later!" I said, verging on hysteria myself.

The bigger of the two cops glared at me and put his hand back on his gun.

"Do you vant to go vis zis man?" he asked her again. "If not, you can stay here vis us."

I think that finally did the trick. As bad as I was, I gained some appeal by virtue of the comparison.

"Yes, I'll go with him."

"You don't haf to," the cop went on. "Are you sure you vant to?"

"Yes, I want to go with him," she told him. Then everybody relaxed. The cops began chasing the audience away. I asked for directions to the road that went most directly to Paris, being very careful not to lapse into "vanten ta finden za vay to Paris."

There were a few more tears, some controlled arguments, and at one point we pulled over to the side of the road to kiss and make up.

Around 11:00 P.M., we ran into a wall of rain, got lost again in the poor visibility, and ended up spending the night in a hotel near Charles de Gaulle Airport, which was nowhere near where we wanted to go. Not an auspicious beginning for the next-to-last leg of our journey to Dakar.

It was after three in the morning before we got to sleep. In spite of all that had transpired, I was happy. I think Carolyn was too. We were out of Graz, had let off a lot of the steam that had been building up in us there, and we were safely, almost, in Paris.

To this day I swear there must have been something funny in that soap.

9

In our imaginations Paris had been a bright, shining jewel. A diamond glowing, glinting, beckoning. It turned out to be a zircon in the rough. Paris didn't shine. It only rained. The normally beautiful and spritely city had turned in on itself, as though a person hunching up to escape the cold. And cold it was, as well as flat, gray, blustering. From the time we hit the wall of rain, to the time we left Paris the day the race began, we saw the sun two, maybe three times.

This was one of those precious days, our first day in town. Our initial excitement and relief at being there urged us up and out early. We drove to Neuilly, a district at the north end of Paris where we have an office. I say "we" because the company has an office there. And I was still president of the company. My resignation became effective December 31st, in six more weeks. But I had already begun to feel like a man without a country, when I let myself feel or think about it, which wasn't often. Sometimes it was unavoidable, like now, driving toward the office.

I'd put my career, my past, and my future away in a mental box, which I wasn't going to open until after the Rallye. Aside from the occasional twinge of doubt or regret, the occasional wistful recollec- tion, that's where they remained. But I felt a little sad and displaced heading for the office, like you do when you come to the end of a summer rental.

They gave me a hero's welcome. Not only was I the president, a renowned advertising creative man, but now I was also a *concurrent* in the Rallye Paris/Dakar. To the young people in the office, I was the daring American with the blond beauty who was living out one of their most cherished and wistful dreams. They, like everybody else,

108

seemed to think I knew what I was doing. I felt like a fraud, yet was as unable to relieve anyone of their grandiose beliefs in me and what I was doing as I was incapable of explaining myself to myself.

Mail and supplies had already begun to trickle in to the office for me. Jean-Pierre, the head of the Paris office, had arranged for an apartment, a garage, for interviews with the advertising and the sports press. And, as I feared, for a luncheon with the creative staff. This was work, part of a job I no longer wanted. Yet I felt obligated to do it both out of a sense of professionalism and in return for all Jean-Pierre had done for me. I hated to relinquish even part of a day. Our schedule was that tight. I put off making a specific date, told Jean-Pierre I'd have to let him know when I could fit it in, the same with the advertising trade press. But the sporting press, the sooner the better. I was still trying to get sponsors and thought publicity could only help.

Jean-Pierre's secretary, Lise, Claudia incarnate, went with us to the apartment. It was ridiculous trying to squeeze another person into the car. We had to put her on Carolyn's lap. Both she and Carolyn were tall, so every time we hit a bump, Lise would hit her head on one of the tubes of the roll cage, which thankfully was padded with rubber.

The apartment was in the Sixteenth Arrondissement, just off of Avenue Foch. I had told Jean-Pierre nothing fancy. He put us in this splendid section for practical reasons, he said. It was located midway between the office and the garage. Everything within walking distance. For people in training. The apartment was dark, dingy, hot, stuffy, expensive, and had bugs. The halls reeked of Arabic cooking. But after Graz we couldn't kick. We hauled all our personal gear upstairs, then went on to the garage where we would be living most of the time anyway.

We drove down Avenue Foch to the Arc de Triomphe, around the Etoile, and out into the Champs-Elysées. It was sunny, balmy, and alive, Paris at its best. Three blocks down the Champs, we came to the garage. I had to hand it to Jean-Pierre. Our garage was smack on the Champs-Elysées, a more central and pleasing location we couldn't hope to find. Well, it wasn't exactly on. It was in a sub, sub-basement, smack under. As we pulled up to the entrance, which was around the corner on Rue de Berri, Lise explained that this was the only garage they could find in Paris that would accommodate a car of this height. After I had sent Jean-Pierre the car's dimensions, Lise had gone around measuring garage entrances, she told us, giggling.

We drove in. The roof scraped the top of the doorway, and the car became stuck in the entrance. Lise put her hand over her open mouth, and assumed a startled expression, as though she had just seen a unicorn and a pterodactyl, golfing. Carolyn and I just looked at each other and giggled in sympathy with Lise's stupefaction. I got out of the car and let some air out of the tires. Our height thus reduced, we skimmed through the opening and descended the ramp with excruciating slowness in case we encountered something else that didn't measure up.

Our space was a box with locking doors. About nine feet wide by fifteen deep, it had light, power, even water, everything I had specified in my many telexes to Jean-Pierre. Lise went back to the office via taxi. We began unloading. One corner of the box was already filled with cartons that had been shipped over from America. These contained dried food, batteries, camping gear, rolls of foam rubber, tape, adhesives, the nuclear flare gun, and other supplies. There were about ten cartons in all. We emptied them and organized the contents by destination.

At the far end of the box, we put cartons containing items that would be shipped back to America before the race or simply thrown away. In one corner, we stacked the wheels and tires. Against the right wall, we put tools and accessories like jack stands and working lights. Against the left wall, we piled all the cartons whose contents would go with us in the race or into cannisters to be hauled by the trucks. The cannisters would be delivered to us here, empty, in a couple of days and picked up on Christmas Eve, packed. Along this wall we also stacked the aluminum cases from inside the car. Now the car was stripped clean and the next morning we'd get to work in earnest.

We spent many hours in this subterranean prison every day for seven weeks. I'll never forget how it sounded down there: hollow, cavernous, the emptiness rushed in our ears. How it smelled: like urine, the air was stale and dank. After breathing it for just a couple of hours, we were stricken with headaches and shortness of breath. This was a parking garage, not a working garage. As we had all along, we would be making the best of a bad thing.

In the garage we had no sense of time nor of place. We might as well have been in Milwaukee.

Back outside, it was already midafternoon. We enjoyed the fresh air, the bustle on the Champs-Elysées. We strolled back toward the apartment, walking around the Arc and up the Avenue Victor Hugo, stopping occasionally in little food stores for fresh vegetables and other things we could eat. But our first night in Paris, we were eating out. After unpacking, after yoga, after exercises and after finding a laundry, we were going to Chez André, a crowded, noisy little Parisian bistro where I always try to eat on my first night in Paris. It's a place that, to me, feels like Paris.

If the two plus weeks we spent in Graz were a blink, the seven weeks we spent in Paris were a blur. Back in the summer, which seemed like an eternity ago, when we decided to move our headquarters to Paris for the final preparations, we'd made a pact. Carolyn, as though able to see into the future and hating what she saw, made me promise that we would regularly take some time off for ourselves to see Paris. She thought it would be a real shame to spend so much time there and not enjoy it. I agreed. But it was not to be. I've done more and seen more of Paris in a weekend than I did in the weeks we lived there. We had a handful of dinners out, went to one museum, briefly. The rest was all work. It wasn't that I was still driving us like maniacs. The clock now drove us, even more relentlessly.

We got life down to a science quickly. Mornings yoga breathing. Then errands; shopping, laundry, and such. Then to the garage on the metro. Walking took too long. Also it rained, a cold, knifing rain, every day. We'd work on the car. There was still so much to do that I was seriously worried that we wouldn't be ready by December 28th, the day we had to be in Rouen to present the car for inspection.

A thousand little things needed doing, things you'd never think of unless you were going racing in the desert. There was a thin coating of Cosmoline on many parts of the car. That's sticky stuff that protects vulnerable parts from corrosion. There was no fear of corrosion in the desert. I was concerned that it would act as flypaper, attracting a heavy buildup of many pounds of sand. Also parts would become encrusted, making them difficult to service. We were stripping the car of Cosmoline with toothbrushes dipped in benzine, foul-smelling stuff whose fumes made us dizzy but at least masked the smell of urine.

Driving to Paris from Graz during the day with the sun behind us, I'd been getting glare in the rear-view mirrors off the rubber strips that ran down each side of the car outside. We were sanding them down, roughing up the surface to reduce the glare. Carolyn's head blocked my view of her outside mirror, so we needed to install another one on her side of the car. We'd have one for her and one for me. At night, the dashboard lights had been too bright. To reduce eye fatigue, we were removing the bulbs and painting them red. The lights from some instruments still cast glare onto others. We were making individual shades out of black cardboard to go around the offenders.

In the morning, Philippe would come to the garage. Philippe was a chauffeur for a Paris limousine company I'd used in my executive days. Now he was working as a "gofer," running errands for us in his spare time. I'd give him a list. He'd always look at the list, then look at me as if to say "You've got to be kidding."

On the list would be a mind-boggling assortment of strange requests. "Four toothbrushes" (for cleaning), "44 cloth diapers" (one each for twenty-two days to use as face wipes, towels, then rags), "bottle of red nail polish" (for marking), "10 feet of garden hose" (to hook up to our water spigot in the garage), "one roller skate key" (to turn on the spigot), "10 quarts Castrol 20W50 motor oil" (obvious), "10 Scotchbrite Pads" (to use as dust filters for vents), "one electric drill" (Scott Andrews would need), "20 feet of bubble wrap" (for packing spare parts), "two quarts of Scotch whiskey" (for conditioning the water tanks, remember? I had). Philippe didn't have the benefit of the parenthetical explanations, so his confusion was understandable. He'd come back at three in the afternoon with his daily load. Then we'd lock up and head for the gym. Five hours in the garage was the absolute most we could take without a lengthy breather.

We found a nice gym a few blocks from the garage in the Hotel Royal Monceau. Walking there in the rain, we'd always stop into Neuhaus, the Belgian chocolatier, for our one daily treat, a single small piece of white chocolate.

In the gym, we'd do forty-five minutes to an hour of stretching and calisthenics. Then Carolyn would take a gymnastics class while I worked out with weights. After that, I'd take some small weights into the sauna. There I'd spend half an hour doing sit-ups, push-ups, leg lifts, and arm work with the weights. My two one-litre bottles of Evian were always just outside the door. Afterward I'd shower and collapse on a cot for half an hour while Carolyn did laps in the pool. We'd dress, go back out into the rain, and hop a metro for home. At home, we'd do more yoga breathing. Then we'd throw some dinner together.

After that, we'd work on navigation, on French, on preparing a list for the next day, on making a phone list. We needed more supplies from New York. We needed Baggies. We couldn't find any in Paris. We needed a special lightweight racing battery from Germany. We needed to yell at Kaan in Austria. I needed to call six different people in Paris for information or help in getting sponsors. The lists were always longer than the time available to act on them. It was easier to call direct than to go to the office and telex. I'd call the office and have the incoming telexes read to me over the phone.

Many days we'd have to split up the chores, there was so much to do. We still needed visas for some of the countries we'd be traveling through. We'd gotten as many as we could in New York. Some countries wouldn't give us visas that far in advance of our trip and told us we'd have to get them later, in Paris.

I was working in the garage while Carolyn was out visa-hunting. She'd been gone all morning, then came back to the garage about two in the afternoon, in a state of high anxiety. She'd been at the Algerian Consulate. A nasty man there told her there was no way we'd get visas in Paris for Algeria, that we should have gotten them in New York. Carolyn told him we couldn't get them there, and why. She said he was abusive to her and told her there was no chance of us getting visas now. This was the most serious "You can't do that" yet.

Carolyn, being as determined as I am about never taking no for an answer, had immediately gone to the United States Embassy and enlisted the aid of someone who had called the Algerian Consulate, spoken to the boss of the *functionaire* who had made Carolyn miserable, and obtained the assurance that we would get our visas. But there was much rigmarole to go through. We needed a letter from the U.S. Embassy, which Carolyn had gotten, and a letter from the Rallye organizers, which we would have to get. Then we'd have to reapply for the visas, which we could only pick up the week before the start of the Rallye.

It meant getting photographs, filling out more forms, and making two more trips to the Algerian Consulate where people were treated like cattle. We would be left hanging by our fingernails right up to the end, wondering if there would be a last-minute snafu. Carolyn brought one piece of good news, though. She'd arranged for our visas for Mauritania. After I filled out my form and got some head shots taken, she could just go in and pick up both our visas.

This was everyday stuff. Behind the work in the garage and in the gym and at home at night was an ongoing bureaucratic hassle providing us with constant problems we didn't need. With customs, with shippers, with suppliers, with airlines. For example, my secretary had tried to ship the ammunition for the flare gun three times, three different ways. Each time she had been told that it was impossible and the merchandise had been returned. Finally I told her to put a few cartridges in a small box and air-mail it to me. She sent me a couple of small boxes a week for a few weeks. If we weren't home to receive a box when the mail came, I'd take the attempt-to-deliver slip to the post office and pick it up. It was that easy. And the French required visas to restrict the entry of terrorists. You could just mail them in!

I cringe whenever I hear someone say that something can't be done. With the effort it takes to find or manufacture a reason it can't, it can. There are people reading this who will say, sure, *he* can go off and do the Paris/Dakar Rallye. He's got the money, the time, the resources, the contacts, easy for him. But *me?* Never!

That's nonsense. There was nothing easy about any of this. But I also don't think there was anything particularly special about it either. There was only one reason we were able to do the Paris/Dakar Rallye. We had the determination to do it. Or maybe it's even simpler than that. We just didn't know that we couldn't. I'm convinced that most of the new or good or interesting or worthwhile things accomplished in this world are done by the truly ignorant. They're the only ones who don't realize that what they're doing can't be done.

Okay, so maybe the cost and nature of this particular escapade would be beyond the reach of most people. But how many of them will find equally powerful reasons for not going on a fishing trip or realizing some other goal that they *can* attain?

Of course we'd become disheartened and depressed when things failed to go the way we'd hoped. Or when some unanticipated obstacle presented itself. We became worn and frayed and ragged just from the daily grind, let alone the unpleasant surprises. Maybe we were lucky that it was such a complex and costly venture. It made it that much more unlikely that we would accept defeat and pack it in. In all honesty though, we often came close. I remember one day dragging ourselves toward the garage. We were shuffling down the Champs in the rain, burdened by bags of supplies. Carolyn said, "I can't take it anymore. Can't we have a day off?"

Without thinking, I said, "Look, honey, this isn't ballroom dancing."

Uncharacteristically, Carolyn had been complaining lately, about the work, about her cameras, about not having any time off. And it was getting on my nerves, which is why I had snapped at her. She looked at me, ready to explode, then shrugged it off. She was too unhappy, too spent to bother.

"No, it's not," she said. "It's marathon dancing."

At that moment, there on the Champs-Elysées, I sagged, for the first time truly sensing the accumulated pressure and fatigue that had been bearing down on both of us.

The next day we took off, slept late, made our one visit to a museum. The Marmottan, which had a magnificent collection of works by Monet until a bunch of thieves ripped some of them off a few days later.

Revitalized from the brief vacation, we poured ourselves back into the work.

In addition to the car work, we ran all over Paris. In the rain. Always the rain. Some days we'd go buy camping equipment, other days we'd shop for clothes we'd need in the desert. We needed an electronic Rallye computer. Kaan would install it when we got back to Graz. We needed a digital electronic compass. I was unhappy with the one we'd brought from the States. It would be relegated to backup. We needed maps. We needed a special Paris/Dakar survival kit. It contained a variety of medical and safety items, including a special radio transmitter to call for rescue if we became lost or stranded.

When we were not running errands, we would meet with people. Some days I'd have lunch with potential sponsors, but I was continuing to strike out. Other days we would have breakfast with people who knew something about the Rallye and whose brains we could pick. Once a journalist who had covered Paris/Dakar, another time someone who had run it, sometimes with someone who just knew somebody who had. Once it was a pilot who had flown along as part of the Rallye entourage. We always got something important or useful out of these meetings. One was T-shirts.

A journalist told us that the way to get help in the desert was to bring plenty of *cadeaux*. Gifts. The Rallye encampments would be thick with Africans looking for handouts. To earn them they would help by running errands, fetching water, what have you. The most desirable *cadeaux*, we learned, were T-shirts. That day I called my secretary in New York and asked her to send me fifty Fruit of the Loom T-shirts.

Many days we would go to Rallye headquarters to arrange for our passage to Africa, to pay a monumental number of expenses, to arrange to have the car shipped back from Dakar, assuming we got to Dakar. And always to get answers to our plentiful list of questions.

One day we walked in and before I could get a question out of my mouth, Patrick Verdoy, the head of the Rallye organization, greeted me by saying, "What do you want to know now? You already know more about the Rallye than we do."

This is when I first learned that for months they had been referring to me as "Mr. Telex." We decided to leave them alone for a few days.

I said earlier that I was never scared. It's true that nothing I knew about the horrors of the Rallye frightened me. What I knew, I could prepare for, face, and overcome. It's what I didn't know that bothered me. Not having done this before, there was much that I didn't know. The hidden terrors gave me sleepless nights. I was convinced that what I didn't know *could* hurt me. So I wanted to know everything, often making a pest of myself in the process.

This was nothing new to me. Having all the answers was something I was conditioned for by a life in advertising. This was like preparing for an advertising presentation. The major difference being instead of preparing myself for people who could kill my work, I was preparing myself to meet a challenge that could kill me.

I wasn't sure which was worse. I would walk into a conference room in which there were maybe fifteen people seated. Lately, more than ever, there would be a bunch of MBA middle-management types. These are the great inquisitors. They have all the questions and none of the answers. They'd fire questions at us relentlessly. And we had to be prepared to answer them all. Or months of work could be lost. A brilliant solution to a complex marketing problem could be sitting there staring them in the face. That didn't matter. What mattered was having the answers to the questions. Even if they were the wrong questions. After all the questions had been answered, they would leave, leaving the decision to someone else, someone who didn't have nearly so many questions. But they were covered, having asked them all.

I've always believed that the way to be happy, and to make money, is to stick to your beliefs no matter what. You don't change into something you're not just to adapt to external changes. You change, you adapt, you modify your working methods only to the extent that it enables you to adhere to your fundamental principles. You change, in order to stay the same. But when you find yourself working with people who don't share the same beliefs, you disassociate yourself from them and work only with people who do. No matter what the cost.

As a small, private company, that was the way we'd always worked. As part of a big, public conglomerate, the need to show a steady profit had taken precedence over my desire to flex my principles. Instead of grabbing a magic marker and scrawling STUPID QUESTION! on someone's forehead, I had gotten up from the conference table and just walked away.

It's much more rewarding dealing with the heads or owners of companies, rather than their probing sycophants. Frank Perdue is the chair-
man of Perdue Farms, one of the biggest poultry marketers in the world.
He could ask questions too. In fact, he looked at advertising the way he
looked at his chickens. Whenever I presented work to him, I knew I had
to be prepared for a good plucking. But at the end of the day, I could
look him in the eye and say, "Frank, do it." Nine times out of ten, he
would follow my advice. The result was one of the greatest ad campaigns of all time. One that has been used as a case study at the Harvard
Business School. Not that it seems to have done much good.

Anyway being prepared and having the answers to every conceivable
question had become a habit to me. In Paris, I was collecting answers.
Along with a lot of other stuff.

Philippe would arrive at the garage with his offbeat collection of
odds and ends. Scott Andrews flew in from Atlanta and began to rig
the cameras. We put him up in a cute little apartment a few blocks
away from us. Some days a runner would arrive from the office with
a fresh shipment from New York. The packing lists made as strange
reading as the lists I handed Philippe every morning: "4 boxes of
Baggies, 1 hunting knife, 1 pair of binoculars, 4 bottles of Loctite
cement, 4 dispensers of WetOnes, 20 pouches of rice and beans, 2
rolls of Velcro tape, one. . . ." The cannisters had arrived and we were
wrapping, labeling, and packing all the spare parts into them.

Thanksgiving Day went by almost unnoticed. That evening we
realized what day it was. I kept a daily diary, which some days I
actually had time to keep. A note at the end of the page for that day
read, "Yippee! Dinner out tonight."

A later entry, made with a different pen, read, "Dinner was ordinary."

We had yet to take the car out of the garage and drive anywhere
in Paris. One day we decided to take it to a car wash to clean off the
greasy handprints that covered it as a result of all the work we had
been doing. And just to run it around to put more miles on the engine.
After the wash, we both felt we had earned a brief period of goofing
off. So we drove to the Place de Vosges, a magnificent early seven-
teenth-century square near the Bastille. It's a beautiful place, and I
wanted Carolyn to see it. We parked the car in the square and walked
around admiring the architecture.

After this respite we got back into the car, started it up, and it
began to cough and splutter. It sounded like it was running on two
cylinders. We jerked and lurched our way toward the garage, thinking,

What now? Whenever we had to stop, the engine would die. So I kept it in neutral, racing the hiccupping engine. Back in the garage, we began to go through our check list. I thought maybe something had got wet in the car wash, possibly the spark plugs. But everything checked out okay on the engine.

Possibly some water had gotten into the gas tank, and that was causing the problem. I got under the car, disassembled the fuel filter, and found no traces of water. But at this point, water in the gasoline seemed the most likely culprit, so I pulled the car out of the box and located it over a drain. I unscrewed the plug under the fuel tank. Unable to get out from under the car quickly enough, I became soaked in gas. I let about seven gallons go down the drain before I realized that I had forgotten which was heavier, gas or water. If there was water in the tank, had it sunk to the bottom and by now run out? Or was it still floating on top of the gasoline that remained in the tank? Which was heavier, gasoline or water? It's times like these when I wish I had gone to high school. I screwed the plug back in and returned the car to its stall.

About that time Scott arrived from one of his many errands. He had been out having the cameras disassembled, strengthened, and put back together again. Much as we had been doing with nearly every part of the car. He had also gathered his own odd collection of nuts and bolts and sockets and wires to complete his job.

"What have you two been up to down here? I could smell the gas fumes out in the street!" he greeted us.

I told him about the problems we had been having and what we had done.

"Are you nuts?" he said. "Who knows where that drain leads? There are enough fumes down here to blow up half of Paris! They could hang around for days. Sometime next week someone could light a cigarette down here and the whole building might go up."

I felt like a ninny. I never said I was smart, just determined.

We took the car out and jerked around, demonstrating the problem to Scott, hoping for some valuable objective insight. The car was still stuttering and bucking. I hated driving it in that condition. A kid on a tricycle could have run rings around us.

Scott thought we might have gotten the ignition wet at the car wash. If so, it would eventually dry out. If not, he agreed water in the gas tank was as good a guess as any.

We took the car back to the garage, removed the plugs, and opened the distributor, letting them air out overnight. Then we headed for the gym.

The next morning we put the car back together and still had the problem. So we worked on other things, like reloosening all the critical nuts and bolts on the car, applying Loctite cement for added security, and retightening them. But our hearts weren't in the work what with the engine problem hanging over us. So we quit early and went to the gym. Later that evening we picked up Scott, filled a two-and-a-half gallon plastic jerry can with gas, and set off for the Bois de Boulogne, a big park at the north end of Paris.

I really felt bad about what we were going to do. But I didn't want to risk dumping the gas in the Paris sewer system. We could be too easily seen, and arrested. Or a pedestrian walking down a lonely street could flick a cigarette at a most inopportune time. Scott had me paranoid about this, and the Bois was the only unpopulated place I could think of. Anyway, our biggest problem that night wasn't the desecration of nature. It was with nature that had already been tampered with.

At night, the Bois is a haven for transvestites who go there to pick up passersby or to be picked up by them. Also, cars packed with tourists drive through, slowing down to gawk. As do those who have more of a visceral than visual interest in what is on display there. The transvestites parade up and down, strutting their unnatural stuff. That night it was hard to say who were the greater perverts, them or us, trying to illicitly dump our remaining eight gallons of possibly tainted gasoline.

We found a fairly deserted place, a small field of grass in a cluster of trees. I purposely chose a place far enough away from the roots of trees so as to minimize the possibility of damaging them. We got out of the car, grabbed the shovels, which were mounted behind the doors inside the cockpit in case we had to dig ourselves out of deep sand, and proceeded to dig a hole in the Bois de Boulogne instead. I backed the car over the hole, grabbed a wrench, and unscrewed the gas tank drain plug, once again becoming drenched before I could get out from under. The air was cold enough, but the gas cascading over my freezing skin was torture. Of course, it was also raining.

While I was doing this, Carolyn and Scott stood at the back of the car, blocking what I was doing from those leering out of passing cars. Cars kept slowing down, and people leaned out and ogled at us. They must have thought Scott and Carolyn were a couple of transvestites standing around looking for business. Who else would be standing out in the Bois in the cold and dark and rain? *That's all we need*, I thought, *for someone to pull up and proposition us. Or worse, for a cop to come along and arrest us on a morals charge, to say nothing of toxic waste.*

After the gush of gas slowed, I joined Scott and Carolyn, uncomfortably, trying to stand and help hide the slow trickle of gasoline still draining into the hole. We were standing there freezing, our teeth chattering, but between chatters, all laughing hysterically because Carolyn had started clowning. She wagged her hips and flashed big smiles. She even waved at some of the passing cars whose occupants were checking us out.

"Cut it out!" I told her, being as firm and serious as I could under the silly circumstances.

It turned out water in the gas wasn't the problem, for after we poured in the clean gasoline, the car still snorted and misfired.

I was standing in a phone booth, having finally reached Richard Kaan at home. We were in the lobby of the Hotel Lancaster across the street from the garage.

"Bad air," Kaan said. "Sounds to me like you've got bad air." This, after I had described the symptoms and all we had done to cure them. I put my hand over the mouthpiece and repeated to Carolyn, "Bad air. Sounds like we've got bad air," and gave her a shrug and perplexed look. I knew we had bad air. The car wasn't running. It was farting.

"What's bad air?" I asked Richard.

"A block in the fuel-injection system. I'll discuss it viss Helmut in za morning. Call me zen and vee'll tell you vot's to be done." His Austrian accent seemed to get thicker on the phone than it was in person.

Things were really bad. I could tell because I was starting to laugh a lot. Always a bad sign. Though the entry I made in my diary that night probably gives a more accurate view of my true state of mind.

November 30th
I don't have time to write this. I don't have time for anything. I don't have time for problems or breathing or exercise or romance. The relationship is in trouble. Carolyn is cracking under the strain, gets oversensitive and emotional and weepy at the drop of a hat. The greater the pressure becomes, the tougher I get, which just intensifies the problem. Maybe we should have attacked this whole thing like the amateurs we are and less like serious competitors. It's taking too big a toll. I

have become mentally, as well as physically absorbed by the Rallye. All my clothes reek of gasoline. So does my skin. I have no clean laundry. I am running out of $, the car doesn't work and we're not having any fun. Sex? What's that? Who's got time? Go to bed sore and exhausted. Wake up same. The Rallye couldn't be this tough.

I called Richard in the morning. Bad air was the consensus. They suggested I take the car to a Mercedes dealer to get the problem sorted out. Thanks.

I called Frank Perdue and told him I would like to have him as a partial sponsor. I explained again why I didn't want him to come in for the whole thing, but that as a partial sponsor, I felt the investment might be worth his while. Frank agreed to do it. As worried as I was about money, this took some of the load off my mind. Now I felt I could breathe a little easier.

Our expenses were astronomical. Forget the cost of the car, the cost of the trucks, the cost of our apartment, the cost of Scott Andrews, the cost of the racing lessons, the cost of our travel. Forget all that. In Paris, our laundry alone had been running a hundred bucks a week. Whenever you see a sign that says FRENCH HAND LAUNDRY, keep walking. That sign means two things. Expensive. And your clothes don't come back clean.

Even more than money, I had been worried about humiliation. I couldn't face the possibility of showing up at the starting line without something written on the car. To me it would have been like saying "Look everybody! Nobody believes in us!" Now I could get logotypes and there would be something for Richard Kaan to paint on the car. Maybe I could find a primary sponsor yet. There was still a little time.

Luckily, the company that bought my company had the Mercedes account in France, so I was able to get booked into a dealer who could make good my bad air. But I was thinking, I don't want bad air. Ever. Maybe we should switch from fuel injection to carburetors. My body would become exhausted, but my brain could not be stopped.

Around noon that day, we went to the garage and found water trickling out of the car and snaking its way toward the drain I had poured the gas into. "What now?" I said to Carolyn. Inside, one of the water tanks located behind our seats had split and the contents had run all over the inside of the car, soaking all kinds of stuff before it had run out and onto the floor. I had filled these tanks and strapped them behind our seats for just such a reason. To see if the weight and the pressure of the water in them would be a problem. Kaan strikes again!

He had given us tanks with seams in them, one of which had rup-tured under the rigors of sitting in the garage. What would have happened to them in the race itself? I charged upstairs to the phone booth in the Hotel Lancaster where I directed a voluble monologue at Richard Kaan in Graz. I reiterated all the problems and oversights for which I held him responsible, from leaky gas tanks to immovable sand tracks and now balky fuel injection and seamed water tanks.

At the end of this particular conversation, two things happened. Richard mollified me by promising that everything would be made right on our final trip to Graz, which was to be in just a few days. And the concierge of the Hotel Lancaster asked me to please make my phone calls elsewhere in the future, perhaps someplace where I would be assured of greater privacy.

In all fairness to Richard Kaan, some of these problems are quite normal in the preparation of a car for a race. That's why you try to do so much so far in advance. So the inevitable little unanticipated things that always crop up will have a chance to reveal themselves and become resolved. What made these problems so annoying, so intolerable, was Kaan himself. With his insufferably arrogant attitude, Richard set up a level of expectation he simply could not live up to.

We organized things for our trip back to Graz. Preparing lists of what still needed to be done and trying to figure out the logistics of carrying all the wheels and tires. The Mercedes dealer had unblocked the air in the fuel injection system and things settled back down to normal insanity. Scott completed the camera rigging, and we put him on a plane back to the States. We were just about ready to return to Graz, but first we had to attend a big Rallye press conference. At this event they would unveil the actual course we were to drive. We would at last meet the enemy face to face. And many more questions would be answered.

10

Behind the Eiffel Tower, running away from the River Seine, is a long, narrow, grass park. Wide walks run along each side. This is the Champs du Mar, where the presentation of the course was being held.

At the far end of the Champs seemed to float what appeared to be a large, brightly lit circus tent. Searchlights plied the rain-streaked sky. Lines of people converged from all directions. Traffic was tied up for blocks, so many taxis were stopping, as well as private cars. The area immediately in front of the tent was bedlam. Temporary wooden stairs had been erected and were now covered with people kayaking their way forward, using their shoulders as paddles, straining to pull up a place in the race to present their invitations.

From a distance, the scene could have been mistaken for a charity ball in progress or for an elegant government or society function. But close up you saw no black ties, no formal gowns. Windbreakers and blue jeans were this evening's dress.

"I've never seen such an attractive crowd," Carolyn said.

This was her immediate reaction. The first comment from a fashion photographer who works with beautiful models every day, and who had attended every glitzy premiere and glamorous party New York City had to offer. Of course it was also Carolyn being Carolyn. To a certain extent, it was a gathering of rebellious youth, her kind of crowd. Had they all been heads of state, she might have commented on their stuffiness.

There was a certain hypocrisy in this tendency of hers, and it bugged me. She seemed to delight in demeaning people, places, or events that would have been her natural milieu as a result of her upbringing. Conversely, she extolled anything that was unnatural or unlikely for one of her breeding. She seemed bent on hating anything her parents might approve of and loving everything that could make them uncomfortable. Possibly, she regarded me as one of the latter.

Though I admired and related to her quest for independence, I often thought she carried it too far. That it got in the way of her being her own person. That she was trying so hard to be the opposite of what she thought she was expected to be that she had lost touch with her true self.

There is nothing wrong with a little sophisticated self-delusion. What troubled me was the way it sometimes came out, in a form of naive cynicism. The conventional cynic is bored and disdainful of anything that is too familiar. The naive types belittle anything they are secretly afraid they may never be able to attain. I didn't mind that Carolyn approved of the unusual or disapproved of the accepted, but I thought it had become almost too predictable and really expressed a deep insecurity about herself.

In writing this, I realize that I possess in full measure that unfortunate human trait of being able to see flaws clearly in others though not so well in myself. I, too, tend to propound radical views simply for their anticonservatism—not necessarily their rightness.

Though at times disturbing, Carolyn's naiveté could be a joy when expressed in its purest form. One day we went into a drugstore. I'd never seen her wearing lipstick, yet she began toying with some of the tubes on display there, trying one on, blotting it off, trying another. We bought a color that suited her. That's when she told me she'd never worn lipstick before in her life, nor perfume, but would if it pleased me.

She wore the lipstick only once, then returned to her old self again.

She was right about the crowd though, even if she might have approved of it for the wrong reasons. This was a sea of young manhood oozing virility, each accompanied by at least two gorgeous young women, from the looks of it. Other than being accompanied by one of these, I felt totally out of place.

One doesn't usually think of people in motorsports as being the kind of perfect physical specimens as say baseball or football players. It's true there were few muscular giants here. In fact, many of the people were quite small, one thing that made me feel very much at home. But they were big in every other way. We could feel their fitness as we were pushed and shoved up against them by the crowd. They didn't give.

It was obvious that of the two thousand or so invitees, I was one of a mere handful of desk jockeys. What we had here were profes-sionals, many of them national champions from countries all over the world. There were even a few world champions. Those were the ones the press photographers clustered around and flashed at, as we all surged to get inside the big tent. There were Formula One drivers, motorcycle daredevils, professional sports car racers, off-road experts, professional rally drivers, athletes all. One thing was surprising. From the lips of athletes, one didn't expect to see so many cigarettes dangling. Maybe not so surprising after all, when you consider that many of these men earned their livings by flirting with death anyway.

Inside the tent, there was a stage. Parked on it were a car, a truck, and a motorcycle. Wooden bleachers faced the stage, stacked all the way up to the top of the tent. The place was already packed. We could only find a spot on a bench high up near the last row. Smoke hung in a foggy bank under the tent's ceiling. Where we sat, our heads were in it. There was no apparent ventilation.

"Jesus!" I coughed to Carolyn. "They're trying to kill us before they try to kill us."

People were lighting up all around us, and we made choking sounds and gave them dirty looks. It didn't do any good. The cloud of smoke grew and lowered as a man on stage began to drone out an excessive overture of welcome.

The French love to hear themselves talk. They go on and on and on, mostly about nothing. This man was performing for himself, rev-eling at the sound of his own voice coming back at him through the PA system. Even if he had been saying something meaningful, it wouldn't have meant much to us. We could read some French, we could speak some French, we could even understand quite a bit of French but only with some point of reference as to the possible meaning of what was being said and only when spoken *très lentement*.

This had become a major international sporting event. There were entrants from eighty different countries this year, but the French were still being French, making no concessions to the existence of other tongues. The route book for the Rallye would be printed only in French. All the meetings were conducted in French. That's why we'd been studying French. And why we'd brought along a tape recorder. That way we could get translations of the important French, if any, later.

After all the welcomes and thank yous had been made, after about an hour, during which I of course had to leave to pee, going outside and adding the Champs du Mar to the Bois de Boulogne as a target of my defilement, no facilities having been provided, they at last got to the important thing. The presentation of the course. René Metge, past winner of Paris/Dakar and the competition director for this year's Rallye, had laid it out. He presented it, using maps on slides, day by arduous day, all twenty-two of them. Paris to Barcelona, to Algiers, Ghardaïa, Ouargla, El Golea, In Salah, Tamanrasset, Achegour, Tombouctou . . . all the places we were destined for. Most of them were mysterious, meaningless names to us.

This year the course would prove to be a particularly challenging one for the navigators, we learned. As we received this information, Carolyn winced. And scorpions, I heard him say "scorpio."

We had been hoping that there would be more liaison stages. These are legs where you are allowed a certain amount of time to go from point to point. There were hardly any liaisons. Nearly every stage Metge announced was a speciale. And they were long speciales, too. Most of them over 500 kilometers, a few considerably longer than that. When he announced the 702-kilometer speciale stage from Dirkou to Anoumekerene, a groan went up from the audience, gradually becoming lost in the bank of smoke that now consumed the entire upper half of the tent. If that got a groan out of this crowd, what should Carolyn and I do, quake? I didn't know.

The names, the distances, they meant nothing. I had no inkling of their reality, never having done anything quite like this before, never even having noticed most of the places we were going on a map. Oh, yes, Tombouctou, I'd heard of that. To me, like most people, it was synonymous with the middle of nowhere. I'd once been in Morocco shooting a television commercial in the desert there. In Zagora, the town where I was staying, the main street ended at the beginning of the Sahara Desert. It just ended. There was a sign there. Painted on it was a primitive likeness of a long camel caravan. There was a faded red arrow pointing out into the dusty ochre nothingness. The words on the sign read TOMBOUCTOU, 52 JOURS. Now we were going there, to the middle of nowhere, where only camels dared to tread. It seemed funny.

Outside, we breathed a sigh of relief and gasped the wet, fresh air. We walked for a while, not really knowing what to think or feel. We didn't know if we were exhilarated or scared, impressed or let down. We knew what maps we needed to fill in our already comprehensive supply. We knew that the people competing were an impressive-looking lot. We knew there would be one rest day in Agadez and that we'd better try and make a hotel reservation there. The only other thing I knew was that I was very thirsty. Whether it was from the smoke, or anxiety, or both, I didn't know. We stopped at a bistro. I ordered a bottle of water. Carolyn had a vodka. I think she was wondering if she'd be up to the challenge of the navigation after all.

In the apartment, we had many books on navigation. I'd had them sent over from New York. Whenever possible, Carolyn pored over them, which hadn't been often enough. I was nervous about this. My nervousness was making Carolyn nervous. Navigation was a subject in which she now really had to cram. As far as I was concerned, it was her main job. Not car repair, driving, or even photography.

The next couple of days were spent filling in the missing maps, visiting Rallye headquarters for help in translating our incomprehensible tape, trying to get a hotel room in Agadez, unsuccessfully. All the rooms were already booked.

We didn't want to leave Paris to return to Graz. We felt a part of the action where we were. Graz was out of it. Besides, it was a long, tiring trip, which neither of us felt up to making. But we had to do it. There were still lots of loose ends that needed to be tied up.

We left early the morning of December 9th, my birthday. I was now forty-eight. *Too old to be doing this*, I thought.

Carolyn held a surprise birthday party for me in the car on the way. She had put together a delicious breakfast of fruit and French pastries. She had also made me a card and picked up some thoughtful little gifts. It took the edge off the unpleasantness we knew we would face in Graz.

This began even before we got there. When we arrived in Stuttgart in early afternoon, the gas tank wasn't ready. The people there weren't even expecting us. I called Kaan and unleashed another verbal barrage. Oh, he had forgotten to tell me. They decided to assemble the tank in Graz. We should just pick up the shell and bring it with us. Too casual, I thought. This wasn't the way I was used to doing business.

Between Stuttgart and Graz, we had an unwelcome misadventure. We had been trying to get an absolutely accurate measurement of the capacities of our various fuel tanks. I'd run the main tank down to the reserve and was now trying to determine exactly how far we could go on just the small kidney-shaped bladders imbedded in the waistline of the car. We'd run them down to the point where the red warning light came on and were on the lookout for a gas station. We had been passing them regularly, all along the way.

All of a sudden though, we found ourselves on a dark and desolate stretch of newly constructed autobahn where nothing was visible but a few twinkling lights off in the distance. That's where we ran out of gas, in about the worst imaginable place. We tried to flag down a passing car, but few were traveling this way. And it was cold, about fifteen degrees. Normally I'd be cursing myself for my own stupidity. But this was something we needed to do. I just wished we'd done it in a busier place on a nicer night. It was the first time I'd ever run out of fuel in my life.

Every racing car has gremlins, and as a rule a given car's problems will be of a consistent nature. One will be prone to electrical problems, another to brake problems, still another to suspension weaknesses. Fuel problems were starting to look like our weakness. First the fuel tank, then the injection problem, then out of gas in the middle of nowhere. I hoped, after Graz, we'd be seeing the end of these.

The third car we flagged down had a spare can of gas in the trunk, and the driver was willing to give it to us as a gift. I insisted on paying slightly more than fair market value. It was about ten o'clock at night and by the time we got moving again, we were in the shape we had grown accustomed to. Tired, cold, dirty, and reeking of gasoline.

We dropped the car at Kaan's shop in Graz at 1:30 A.M., switching to the beat-up VW, which held the keys to the flat. Again, we found there was no heat. And this time Graz was colder than before. We didn't even unpack. We decided to move to a hotel and treat ourselves to a little comfort for a change, saying good-bye to the SCHMUCK sign once and for all.

In the shop, the work proceeded apace. "The boys" attacked the car with renewed enthusiasm. Kaan, true to his word, set to making right all that was wrong. The car went into the factory for a thorough going-over for one day. While there, the hood and rear door went out to a paint shop and various logos and legends were sprayed on. The car came back to the shop, still minus hood and rear door, and the work continued. At night, it would go into the paint shop and the main body would be done.

As lax as things had begun to seem, this was a real turnaround. It was like watching a pit stop at the Indianapolis 500. With four men working, one to a wheel, the car would go up on jacks, the wheels would come off, the road shocks taken out, the racing versions installed, wheels back on, car dropped back down on its feet again. Two of "the boys" carried in the freshly painted hood. Another one hauled in the rear door. We drove in with a cumbersome four-wheel-drive vehicle and poof! it was changing into a racing car before our eyes. Water tanks were replaced. Still plastic, but unseamed. I asked Kaan if he thought these would be strong enough to hold up. He had anticipated my question and had a spare one ready, full of water.

"Here, Edvard, take it, try to destroy it."

I took it outside, held it up in the air, and dropped it on the concrete apron. I threw it on the concrete again and again. I placed it on the ground and jumped up and down on it. I tied a nylon strap around it and swung it round, crashing the container into a tree with all my might. No leaks.

"Satisfied?" Kaan asked, smiling, after watching my performance outside.

"Goot," I said, "Ver goot," mimicking Helmut.

The gas tank went back in. Even without it in the car, we had still been getting bad fuel smells. The entire fuel-breather system was ripped out, a new one engineered and installed. The cowcatcher was taken off and sprayed black. I had been getting kicks of light off of it, back into my eyes. The dash was torn apart yet again, the rally computer installed, lights, switches and knobs relocated and relabeled. The racing wheels and tires were sent out to be balanced. There was excitement, anticipation.

I felt a swelling of pride in myself as I watched the car come together. Carolyn had a dream, a dream that ignited a flame in me. Strange how a chance comment could generate this. We had come a long, long way in just eleven months. We had a car that would be well equipped and prepared. We both felt capable of driving it over long distances at high speeds. We were organized. We were fit.

From a sickly, recuperating specimen of dissipated middle age, I had become hard, in the best shape I had been since I was thirty. Thanks to the yoga, we were able to cope with fatigue, stress, and discomfort effectively. We spoke, or at least read and understood a modicum of French. Enough to get by. We knew how to maintain, diagnose, and repair the car. I had most, if not all the answers. My confidence soared with my pride. We were going to finish. We were going to do well. Just finishing would probably put us in the top twenty or thirty. Yes, we would do well. And in just over three weeks, we'd prove it.

As the freshly painted hood was slammed and locked into place, I could see that we even had a sponsor. Proof that we weren't the only ones who believed. On Second Avenue, I had told Carolyn we could do it. So far, I'd made good on that promise. I'd also told her it would be tough. I'd made good on that too. If anything, too good.

Yes, standing there in Kaan's shop I was proud. Proud of myself, proud of Carolyn, proud of all we had accomplished, proud of "the boys" and the great hard work they had been doing, proud even of Kaan who was now totally caught up in the spirit of the adventure. He was proud too, had painted his name on the car as well.

The last item to go into the car was a gift from Richard. One of the boys screwed it into the metal, in the center, just above the windshield where we could both reach it. It was a double-ended tool called a "lifehammer." Richard explained how to use it.

If we found ourselves turned over, trapped in the car and hanging upside down in our safety harnesses, we were to use one end of the tool to sever the harnesses and free ourselves. The other end was a hammer for smashing a hole in the windshield so we could crawl out.

"You think we'll need this?" I asked Richard.

"No. No," he said, laughing self-consciously. "Just in case."

Our last night in Graz, Richard and Herta invited us to their home for dinner. It was the best food we'd had in Graz, and it was a warm, friendly evening. Despite the problems, we had become friends.

At the end of the evening, Richard said, "Edvard, Carolyn, I think you're going to do it. In the beginning I vasn't so sure, but now I believe you vill do vell."

We left Graz for Paris at sunrise. There was a light dusting of snow on the trees and on the tops of hills. Everything was cast pink in the cold, weak winter light. Our white car was tinged with pink, the words lettered all over the car popping out in contrast to the soft background. The red PERDUE, the blue KAAN. Our names spelled out in bright red on each of our doors, followed by our blood types, mine O+, Carolyn's A+. On the back, in black, it said PARIS/DAKAR 1987, under that in blue, a big NIKON logo, right under the rear window with the lens pointing out. And across the front of the hood, the theme, the driving force that pulled us both along behind it, DO THE DREAM.

We drove toward Paris, fiddling with our respective toys. Carolyn was trying to sync up the rally computer with the tripmaster. The rally computer is really just a fancy name for an electronic time, speed, distance calculator. The tripmaster is a double odometer; one keeps track of overall distance, the other measures distances between points, either instructions in the route book, or landmarks. I was getting the feel of the new leather-covered steering wheel. White leather to reflect the heat of the sun. I sipped water through a tube. No more carrying of big water bottles. Now we had only the small plastic ones that were mounted to the roll cage. I would use these to pee into when the race was under way. For Carolyn, we had another arrangement altogether.

We were driving along happily, yet I was starting to be troubled. Something didn't feel right about the car. There was something wrong with the way it handled. They had installed the new racing shocks so the car should have felt different. But it felt the wrong kind of different. It should have been rigid and hard. It felt to me like we were bounding along on a trampoline. Too springy. "What next?" popped into my head again.

Again we hit a wall of rain entering Paris. But this time Carolyn and I were at peace with each other. Or were abiding by a temporary truce. I wasn't thinking about that. I was thinking about shocks, about navigation, about having the car preinspected in our own garage to uncover any possible infractions of the rules while we still had time to do something about it before the start.

I think it was on this trip that we decided to throw in the towel on the subject of getting a major sponsor. We were simply out of time. We decided to donate the car, other than the few spaces already occupied by PERDUE and the few spaces still reserved for the Rallye sponsors, to a talented young artist. We both thought it would be terrific to help someone whose work we liked to achieve recognition in this way. After our return to Paris, we spent days searching for such an artist. We found one, Robert Combas. But by the time all the logistics could be worked out, we were again out of time. He would have taken the car away from us for too many days. And there was still much to be done.

With two weeks remaining, what to put on the car in lieu of the name of a major sponsor and how to handle the wheels and tires were the two looming questions. I'd thought of sending Philippe to Barcelona with a truckload of racing wheels and tires. But what if he left them somewhere and we couldn't find them when we got there? It was too risky. Also, it would necessitate our running the Prologue on the racing tires, then changing to road tires, before handing the racing tires over to Philippe. What if we couldn't find the time to effect the change? And what if he broke down or became lost on his way to Barcelona? No, I had to find someone who was in the Rallye who had a truck going down there anyway. The rules required that we carry two spares that matched whatever tires we had on the road. So we were juggling six and six, the additional two racing tires would soon go on the trucks when they picked up our loaded cannisters.

Why not just leave the racing tires on the car the whole time? A good question. But I didn't want to do it. I didn't want to put that much wear on the desert tires. I wanted to save them for Africa. Also, the racing tires made the car handle very badly on pavement. On wet pavement they were slippery and dangerous. And by now I had come to suspect all 1,094 kilometers of pavement between Versailles and Barcelona would be soaked. Ideally, we would change to road tires after the Prologue and remount the racing tires when we got to Africa. But I needed the cooperation of someone with a truck. I'd talked to Knilli about this while in Graz. He'd waffled out on his earlier promises. I guessed he probably didn't even have a truck.

With these two questions continually haunting us, we bored our way through all the other final preparations. I even squeezed in lunch with the agency creative staff.

The first of our last two weeks was incredibly frustrating and tense. Kaan had struck again. I checked on the suspicious shocks by calling the manufacturer in Germany and reading them the serial numbers. I found that the shocks on the car were, indeed, not for racing. Kaan, of course, said that's what the factory had given him. I wondered if he *ever* checked on anything that he was responsible for.

Through a series of frantic phone calls and logistical legerdemain, we arranged for two sets of proper racing shocks to be sent to Kaan in Austria, then he would send them to me in Paris. I really didn't need all these calls and hassles. Even after it was resolved, I would still have to change the shocks, which I also didn't have time to do. When they finally arrived, I even had to pay $220 extra in shipping fees. Kaan sent them collect! That was the final straw. I sent the old, wrong shocks back to him the same way, hoping he'd be half as pissed off as I was.

At the same time all this was going on, Carolyn and I both came down with the flu. We both had fevers, chills, and sore throats. It didn't stop us. It just slowed us down and depressed us. We were still running around Paris in the rain. And I mean running around as in running around on foot. Both the Paris metro and the taxicabs were having intermittent work stoppages. Of course. It was Christmas sea-son. It was Paris.

We got a Rallye official to come to our garage for an early inspection. There were a couple of small things that needed correction. Nothing serious. He spent a lot of time checking our safety harnesses and the way they were mounted to the frame. Thank God I hadn't allowed Kaan to con us into those links. He also spent a long time staring into the engine compartment at our stock engine.

"You could have done much, much more, you know," he told us.

We knew. But our strategy remained the same. Finish. Total reliability was more important than flashy performance.

We decided what to do about painting the car. We wanted to thank everyone who helped us. Since we started, many had inspired us or had gone out of their way to help at a critical time. Many had provided valuable advice or assistance along the way. They would now be recognized. We compiled a list of a few dozen people, for the most part agreeing on who deserved the recognition and why. We designed the large, solid panels on each side of the car to carry the list of names in black, surrounding the big word THANKS, which would be in red. We thought this would not only show our gratitude, but it would also help our car stand out from the pack. Though why we ever wanted to do that I'm not quite sure. To flaunt our incompetence?

All the other cars would display commercialism, covered only with the names of companies or products. Ours would show some sensitivity by carrying the names of people. Also, it turned a disadvantage into an advantage, by making a virtue out of our lack of sponsorship. It turned out that someone else had our earlier idea anyway. His car had been all painted up by a serious artist. We had just read about it in the paper. It even showed a picture. It came out *really* ugly!

So we had a unique and nice idea. All we had to do was get it done. Easier said, as usual.

Through contacts I'd made at the French magazine *VSD*, we got the name of Jac the painter. He was all the way over on the other side of Paris, out in the far boondocks on the Left Bank. We wheedled him into coming to our garage for a look. It was a few days before Christmas. As we had hoped, he was captivated by the idea as well as the overtime pay. Jac would paint the car on the twenty-third and on Christmas Eve. We would pick it up the night of Christmas Eve.

We were still going to the gym every afternoon, going easy on the saunas, though, in deference to our fevers. Days we'd run and run and do last-minute car work. Shipments were coming in to the office at the rate of four a day. Our T-shirts arrived with duty due. Instead of paying for them and seeing me about it later, Lise took it upon herself to send them back. We scratched her name from the list of THANKS candidates. This was not a petty gesture. Much to do with racing has to do with jinxes and superstition. We didn't want to carry the name of anyone who in any way had slowed us down. I was often on the phone to New York, arranging for couriers to bring over last-minute stuff. We got our Algerian visas. One less last thing to worry about.

Nights we were still crashing on navigation and French. Also I was sealing dried beans, lentils, vegetables, and powdered soups into pouches. On this point my doctor had been emphatic. "Eat no meat during the Rallye itself," he'd said. So we had to avoid the tinned rations the Rallye supplied, even though we paid an arm and a leg for their availability.

Ever since I'd heard about the Indy driver's broken nose and kneecap in the Prologue, I'd been a little spooked by it. It had hung over me, a curse that needed to be exorcised. So the Sunday before Christmas, we drove out to look evil in the eye. It was a cold but sunny day. Our second day of sunshine in six weeks. Amazing how seeing light can lift bedeviled spirits.

The course was a six-kilometer serpentine that was still in the process of being built. Bulldozers were gouging out and shaping sections of it. Deep water stood in dips and valleys, while enormous boulders were scattered about at random, obstacles that had yet to be put into place. I walked around the course as best I could, in mud, sometimes up to my knees. This is the best way to scout a circuit that's new to you. Whenever I had raced on an unfamiliar one, I would try to walk it first. There was no hope of memorizing this one, though. There must have been close to a hundred turns in it. The best I could do was try to mentally catalog the most difficult and threatening parts.

We went out and drove around it at a snail's pace, the only car there. One lone journalist was on a hill, setting up angles with his videotape camera. The next day French television viewers were treated to a peek at Carolyn and me doing our homework.

We drove around five or six times before I began to pick up the pace. We'd brought our helmets just in case and were testing the intercom system and the equipment that would tape our conversations. Carolyn had loaded all the cameras and was testing them as well. We immediately destroyed one of them. We hadn't anticipated actually being able to drive the course, so we hadn't put the cameras into their protective plastic bags. But it had been an opportunity I couldn't afford to pass up. After one lap, it was too late. We plunged down off the crest of a hill, nose-diving into a deep pool of muddy water. We were set up for sand and dust. And these weren't underwater cameras. The low, front-mounted camera, the one with the 250-frame magazine, was out before the race even began, before the Prologue even began. Good thing Nikon had suggested I get all this equipment insured.

The damage done, we roared around the course. With the racing shocks still lying on the floor of the garage, the car pitched and sprang, sometimes completely out of control. It was absolutely wild. There were bumps, slides, chutes, dives, holes. We had mounted the road tires, which were smaller than the racing tires. The two road spares, which fit loosely into compartments designed to carry the bigger ones, flew out and would have joined us in the front seats if the nylon netting stretched behind us hadn't arrested their flight. The exaggerated gyrations of the car snapped the power box for the intercom system apart, and the nine-volt battery inside flew out. After one lap, I had no brakes, they became so wet. Still we kept going. The more I knew, the better we would be prepared. The better we were prepared, the better we would do. I was shooting for the moon, more than willing to settle for Dakar. Besides, it was fun. Great, tiring fun.

We washed a thick crust of mud off at a nearby car wash, considered making an appointment for the day of the Prologue, but didn't. Very unlike me not to get this organized. It proved to be a mistake.

We practically missed Thanksgiving. We'd both had birthdays while in Paris but hadn't done much celebrating of either one of those either. Now Christmas was almost upon us, and we'd hardly noticed. I was having the Christmas blues. Seeing the Christmas lights flickering all over Paris as we drove back into town inflamed us both with a sudden need to conjure up some semblance of holiday spirit.

We decided to take pictures of ourselves with the car and send them to our friends and relations. That night we drove all around Paris looking for a suitable location. Finally I had a brainstorm. The Avenue Montaigne was all lit up with Christmas lights. The Hotel Plaza-Athenée where I always used to stay when in Paris was on the Avenue Montaigne. It was about ten o'clock at night, very cold, a light snow was falling and blowing around. We parked just down the street from the hotel, under a cluster of bright Christmas lights.

I went into the hotel and got Jacques Vincent, the affable and always helpful concierge who had taken good care of me in Paris for years, to come outside and take our picture. Vincent—everybody calls him that—was surprised and excited that I would be running Paris/Dakar. Carolyn and I donned our racing suits and stood in front of the car, trying our best to smile through the cold. A smiling Vincent snapped away with Carolyn's Polaroid.

"Another one?"

"Just a couple more, Vincent."

We kept him outside for an hour, snapping and flashing until we had thirty-five nice photos. His face and hands were covered with snow and bright red. He wore only his little concierge jacket, no overcoat. Yet he never stopped smiling. He was trained to please.

Afterward, I was happy to give Vincent a generous Christmas tip. How many people do you know who would do such a thing, and happily, even for money?

The next day Carolyn and I split up, each doing separate errands. I went to the garage and changed to the racing shocks. Working alone, it took me six hours. Carolyn came and did final inventory. We had to provide an itemized list of everything we carried for customs clear- ance. This ended up running to eight typewritten pages. In the evening, we took the car to Jac. The last-minute Christmas rush was on, so the traffic was fierce. We got there at eight. Then to the gym. We got home at midnight.

Now, without the car, I had a little time to think. I thought I'd solved the wheel and tire puzzle. The race itinerary would take us to Rouen for the technical and safety inspection and final administrative controls. We were to be there at 10:00 A.M. on December 28th, a Sunday. We had received this info in the mail along with our assigned number, which was 248. Carolyn thought this was a very lucky number from a numerology point of view. I didn't know what she was talking about.

From Rouen we were to proceed to Versailles where the car would be impounded in a closed park. On Tuesday the 30th, we would liaison to Cergy-Pontoise to run the Prologue, returning to the closed park later that day where the car would rest until the start on New Year's morning. Between the Prologue and reentering the closed park, I thought we could change tires and while in Versailles find someone to haul the racing tires to Barcelona for us. There, we would just discard the road tires. In order to accomplish this, we had to first get the racing tires up to Versailles. Christmas Day was the only possibility.

On Christmas Eve night, we were to pick up the car from Jac the painter. This proved nearly impossible. Both the metro and the taxicabs had gone on strike. After two hours standing out in the cold rain trying to hail a cab, we finally called Jac and begged him to come pick us up with his car. At this point we wouldn't have been surprised if the phones had also been on strike. That's the way it felt, as though suddenly everything and everyone was turning against us. But Jac came and we went.

The car looked great. It projected a warm, happy feeling. Looking at it sitting there, saying "THANKS," you couldn't help but smile. We hoped the people we were thanking would be pleased. We knew a few whose names had been rather obviously omitted wouldn't be. C'est la vie.

We celebrated Christmas that night by having dinner at Jules Verne, the fancy restaurant in the Eiffel Tower that offers a splendid view. The view we enjoyed most was of our car parked below, surrounded by people grinning and talking about it.

Christmas morning we were awakened by the phone. Frank Perdue was calling from the States to wish us well. He asked me if I was scared. I told him there was no time for fear. Shortly after that, Richard Kaan called from Austria.

"I guess you're scared," he said.

I was starting to wonder if everybody else knew something I didn't. But it didn't really faze or scare me.

What got to me was Carolyn, who was filling out forms in another room, saying, "We need to give them the name of a Paris hospital we'd like to be airlifted to in case of an accident."

That made me think. What the hell was I doing here? We'd received the complete list of entrants. The first page read like a Who's Who of motorsports, except for "McCabe," who was listed right there along with the likes of Jacky Ickx, two time vice-champion of the world in Formula One, four-time winner of the world endurance racing championship, six-time winner of the twenty-four hours of Le Mans, and Henri Pescarolo, a mere piker, having only won the Le Mans twenty-four-hour race four times, along with his other seventeen world-championship racing victories. "Are you scared?" didn't scare me. But reading down the entry list for that year's Paris/Dakar made me quake in my racing boots. The thing I feared most wasn't death or injury. It was the fear of making a fool out of myself in this kind of company.

We hauled the racing tires to Versailles and therein lies a tale. We pulled into the courtyard of the Trianon Palace Hotel. A grand old hotel grown a little seedy, a bit of an old people's home, judging from the folks tottering around out front. We gave them quite a show. I'm surprised there weren't heart attacks.

Right out in front, we began jacking the car up and removing the wheels. I forget whether I jacked and Carolyn unscrewed or vice-versa. Anyway, off came the road tires, on went the racing tires, the road tires becoming a growing stack in front of the hotel's door. As I've said, these were all big heavy things, weighing nearly a hundred pounds apiece. And we were unloading, hefting, rolling and piling and unpiling a dozen of them. A skinny, little guy with this tall, good-looking girl. A crowd was forming, even in the cold drizzle. What was going on here? Some kind of whacko demonstration? They hadn't seen anything yet. All the jacking, lowering, and tightening done, we began rolling our dirty, muddy wheels up the stairs and into the hotel's lobby. On Christmas Day!

I fully expected to be stopped dead in my muddy tracks. Whenever I do something offbeat, I always assume the manner of someone who is behaving in a perfectly rational way and treat anyone who doesn't understand what I'm doing as though they're the ones who are crazy. Never allowing anyone time to come up with the inevitable "You can't do that!"

Rolling up to the concierge's desk and leaving racing tread marks the length of the hotel's lobby, I announced, "I'd like a room for my tires, and could you please help us bring them in? They're very heavy and as you can see, my partner is just a girl."

All the decrepit bodies scattered around the lobby were frozen in a variety of positions with horrified expressions on their faces. From the look of them, I thought they could do with a good dousing of WD-40. I had a can in the car. Once upon a time I would have gone out and come back brandishing it.

"Loosen up, folks!" I would have shouted at them.

But I was intent on more serious business.

"My name is McCabe," I said to the concierge. "We'll be spending a few days here with you. What's yours?" I asked extending my hand.

"Patrick," he replied and shook hands with a bit of a twinkle in his eye.

"Well then, Patrick, let's get to it."

The really amusing thing here is that Patrick, the concierge, didn't even blink. Acting as though people arrived and requested separate rooms for their tires every day, he came outside and pitched in without a word. Going me one better, he rolled *two* tires through the lobby. We followed his tracks right into the elevator. We rolled them down a long corridor, the muddy stripes becoming fainter as they scrubbed themselves clean on the Oriental rugs. We wheeled them directly into an empty room and stacked them up in front of a window. They had a lovely view, overlooking the formal gardens of the Palace of Versailles.

The tires all stacked, Patrick stood at attention and asked, "Will there be anything else sir?"

"No, Patrick, that will be all. And may I tell you what a pleasure it will be to be staying here with you," I said, slipping the French equivalent of seventy-five dollars into his hand.

He looked at the money, smiled, and said, "I'll be leaving for my vacation tomorrow, sir, but I will instruct my associates to be prepared for any other, ahem, unusual requests."

I thanked him again, and we headed downstairs for lunch.

En route, Patrick stopped and opened the door of the chamber next door. "This will be your room, sir."

"Oh, adjoining rooms," I observed.

He smiled as though knowing I would be pleased and led us downstairs.

The entry I made in my diary that night wasn't as cavalier as the entrance I'd made to the Trianon Palace Hotel.

Thursday 25, December
All along, strength has been my weakness. I'm in the best shape I can remember. Lean and mean, not brawn. But it's the basic lack of beefiness that bothers me. Two years living on fish and grain does that I suppose. I fear I need more bulk. Today, manhandling all the wheels and tires in and out of the car at Versailles, getting slammed in the shoulder by the fire extinguisher on the rear door, has left me feeling weak, vulnerable, scared. I only hope I'm tough enough. I'll work out till the last minute. Tomorrow we wrap up in the garage.

I only had two days to complete the miracle. Then we were going racing.

The water didn't taste a bit like Scotch or plastic either. I'd put half a quart of Cutty Sark into each tank, filled them all with water, and just let them sit there the last two days in Paris. After moving out of the apartment and just before locking up the garage for the final time, I poured the contents down the drain, leaving what had smelled first like a urinal, then a gas station, finally smelling like a bar. Then we topped up the tanks with twenty gallons of Evian. We'd been stocking up, each buying a couple of big bottles a day for weeks.

Except for the one night we'd spend in Rouen at the technical inspections, our headquarters for the next few days would be in Versailles, where the race would start.

Driving toward Versailles I savored the fresh-tasting water running into my mouth through a tube. That clown in Detroit had been right about one thing, I smiled to myself as I thought back to that, sipping into the first of my seven daily litres.

Most of the pressure was off us now. The Olympian training was over. Aside from coping with the vagaries of a route book, which was all in French and which would be presented to us the next day, all the work was done. I was at last beginning to relax and be happy. We had finished the race to the race. We had even beaten the flu. A few sniffles were all that remained.

We returned to the Trianon Palace. There was another Paris/Dakar car in the court out front. It belonged to a well-known English racing man named Ted Toleman. His name was painted on the door. I didn't notice his blood-type, but I did wonder if *his* tires had a room with a view.

Checking in, without fanfare this time, we stashed most of our gear in our room. Then we went down to have lunch in the dining room, which made us feel very young. Everyone there seemed to be over seventy. After lunch, we spent an hour or so walking the grounds around Versailles. We were enjoying our third day of sunshine, basking slowly along, yet a little edgy. It was the final moment of calm before the storm.

Until then we had felt we were only racing against ourselves. Now we began to feel that we were a part of something much bigger. First, the car at the hotel. Then, driving toward Rouen for the technical inspection, we began to see more cars. One all painted up and outfitted, just sitting there on the side of the road, the driver looking at a map. Then, the occasional entrant coming the other way, back to Versailles from Rouen. There was something in the air, an excitement, a crackle of anticipation as we rolled through the hills of Normandy. Going through a toll booth, the toll taker shoved a newspaper inside and asked me to put my car number and autograph on the paper for him. I wondered why the hell anyone would want *my* autograph but felt a mounting excitement as I scrawled it out for him.

We'd had a glimpse of the show-biz excitement that attends the Rallye when they'd presented the course in Paris. Now, nearing sunset, we'd arrived on the outskirts of Rouen anticipating a garage but instead came upon a carnival in full swing. The roads were choked up with traffic. Thousands of people walked around open, grassy fields as if at some kind of fair. Big tents and hangarlike buildings dotted the dense, human landscape. Mothers and fathers pushed carriages with kids flying balloons tied to their wrists. There were food stalls with people lined up in front of them. Some walked away with baguettes protruding from their mouths. But the main attraction was the cars, the trucks, the motorcycles, and the people who would pilot them. It was a jumble.

Motorcycles picked their way through the crowds. The driver of a white car that looked something like ours stood on the rail at the bottom of his door-frame, posing heroically in the purple light of a setting sun. The smell of charcoal and *saucisson* laced the air. Trucks trying to penetrate the crowded, hazy atmosphere blared their piercing air horns. A gendarme threw his arms in the air, surrendering any thought of trying to maintain order. We turned around and got out of there at the first opportunity. Tomorrow would be our turn. Our inspection was set for the next morning, and we had driven up a day early to avoid having to leave Versailles at dawn.

We went to a nearby motel, which was also the headquarters for

the Rallye organization's personnel during the technical controls. Suzanne Fournier appeared out of a crowd and asked if everything was
all right. She was about the only one on the staff who spoke English.
She told us that she would be going along on the Rallye and would
translate the key points of each day's driver's meeting for us. We were
glad to see her. Even though we could cope with French, we were
much more comfortable with English. She made us feel at home in this
strange place full of foreign speed demons.

The fairgrounds had yet to fill up when we pulled in the next
morning. We were about tenth in line, waiting to get into the big
tent. They served burnt coffee and greasy doughnuts. I passed, watching Carolyn grimace her way through the insipid brew. Huge heater-
fans whipped hot, stale air around the tent's small anteroom. It was
cold and raining again outside.

"Deux cent quarante-huit!"

Our number was being called. We entered the main tent. It was
enormous, with small booths lining all four walls, We were to pass
from booth to booth, carrying cards they had given us. As we completed
the interview at each booth, the cards would be stamped. When our
cards were all stamped, we were to proceed to our car and take it
through the technical controls.

Some booths were quite routine. One examined our passports and
travel documents.

"Thunk, thunk." We were stamped on our way.

Then a booth where our competition licenses, International Driving
Licenses, and racing permits were checked.

"Thunk, thunk."

Then our car papers. Then our medical histories. This is where we
had to designate an emergency hospital. We had chosen the St. Louis
on the advice of Parisian friends.

We thunked our way around the tent. Getting insurance on the car
in one. Insurance on ourselves in another. One booth was giving out
little plastic flare guns. I took one, thinking it would be useless for
self-defense. At another we received our Rallye wristbands and the
route book. The wristbands were little plastic ID bracelets, like those
worn by patients in hospitals. They entitled us to get food during the
Rallye, very little of which we planned to eat. The route book weighed
about seven pounds, came in two sections, each section being a good
four to five inches thick. Neither contained a word of English.

Then we came to the booth we'd been most anxious about. We had to answer a navigation quiz. We'd heard that this year they were giving the entrants navigation tests, and we were afraid we might get eliminated by some trick question. There were no trick questions, though. Just rudimentary stuff we both knew in our sleep. We heaved sighs of relief as the man there prepared to give us our thunking. Then he asked us an unexpected question in English.

"What *don't* you do if you become lost or involved in an accident?"

We looked at each other, not knowing what to say.

He smiled. "You don't leave your car. Our planes will find you within three days if you stay with the car. If you wander off, you may never be found. I hope you never have to follow this advice. Good luck."

He thunked us on our way. On the way out, we handed over our eight-page inventory list at the booth designated for that.

The technical controls were in an adjacent cinder block building. On one side, there was a row of cars and trucks up on steel ramps so the inspectors could get underneath. Down the center was a barricade, holding back the hundreds of spectators who leaned over, jabbering and waving for attention from the contestants. I wondered what it was about the French that will make them leave their cozy beds to look at people looking. That's all that was happening here. Officials were looking at cars.

Our turn came and I drove up on a ramp, swinging up and over the side rail of the roll cage nimbly and all the way down to the ground, landing on my feet in a crouch. The audience seemed unmoved by the deftness of my maneuver. Inspectors began going over the car with a fine-tooth comb. I hovered nervously, feeling a little foolish just watch-ing them look. Occasionally one of them would grunt approval. Then one called over two associates. They coagulated around the rear door, pointing at the rear window, the door, the wheels, jawing away in French too fast for me to follow. From the looks of it, we had a problem. I asked them in French if there was a problem. I was no good at French infractions, so I had trouble following what they were saying. Some-thing about the window and mud flaps. They called over a man who spoke some English. The same one who had come to our garage in Paris.

I had three problems, he told me. My mud flaps weren't the regu-lation length. The lock on my rear door was inadequate. Both he said

could be easily remedied before the start. But I had the word PERDUE
painted at the top of the rear window. And this was a bigger problem.
Advertising was not allowed on the rear window, he said.

I asked him why he hadn't told me these things when he'd seen the
car a couple of weeks before. He shrugged, telling me it hadn't been
painted when he'd seen it and that he was sorry but he had forgotten
to check the mud flaps and rear door.

I told him the Rallye regulations allowed for a four-inch strip of
advertising across the top of the rear window.

He knew, he said, but the regulations had been changed in a subsequent printing. Hadn't I seen them? No, I hadn't, I told him.

In fact, I had gone to Rallye headquarters, and using line drawings
of the car, had gotten clearance for everything I planned to paint. The
people I spoke to apparently weren't clued in to this rules change,
either. The problem, as he outlined it, was that if I finished in the first
four places in my class, I could be protested by a competitor and the
protest would be upheld, owing to the infraction.

"Oh, no problem," I said. "I'm willing to take my chances."

I didn't think I had a snowball's chance in hell of finishing in the
top four in my class, which was designated 4/1. Modified Production
Cars. That's for your Trivial Pursuit file.

There was much animated discussion among the group. Finally, they
passed me on, with the proviso that I have the rear door secured with
an additional safety strap and the rear mud flaps lengthened three
inches. The car would be checked every day by an official in Africa,
he told me, and if these problems weren't rectified, I wouldn't be
allowed to start. Again I was sore at Kaan, this time over the mud
flaps. He had the regulations and was supposed to have been following
them. Now I had something else to worry about before the start.

This may sound like making a mountain out of a molehill, but I
think it demonstrates the feeling of apprehension that always hung
over us. This one small incident was one of many that would constantly
rise up and plunge us into a state of nervous impotence, always a little
in the dark, always anxiously awaiting the next surprise that would
challenge us.

Physically, we were in pretty good shape. But mentally we were
sitting on a razor's edge, probably both as close as we'd ever come to
slipping off the ends of our tethers.

The third enclosure had a totally different ambiance and character
from either of the other two. The first had been hot and close. It was

brightly lit and reverberated with the sounds of shuffling feet, and hundreds of serious conversations being murmured under a continuous barrage of officious "thunks." The second was cooler, quieter, grayer. Not so brightly lit, sparsely populated, the most recognizable sound that of the occasional hoot of a spectator. At who, for what, I was never able to figure out.

The third, a long, narrow concrete structure, contained one long row of brightly lit stalls. A lineup of cars and trucks waiting to get in (the motorcycles must have gone through yesterday) ran down the middle, and a barricade held back a wall of blurred and waving fans. The stalls were each manned by a team of four or five persons, some of them women, yet I would still have to say they were "manned." These were some of the biggest, toughest-looking women I'd ever seen. The spectators were confined to the darker side of the building, yakking away more noisily than before. This was a kind of celebration, a graduation. The first two stops were for hopeful applicants. The third was for confirmed contestants.

Here one heard the pop of rivets as special Rallye plates were affixed to each vehicle, the rip of paper being peeled off of adhesive backing as numbers and sponsors' names were applied. While they were doing this to our car, we did some unofficial sticking and pasting of our own. I'd been carrying an envelope full of an assortment of stickers since we'd left New York, and we now put them in place.

Inside the top of the windshield, at the far left, we put a sign that read, GAUCHE! On the far right a matching reminder, DROITE! We had learned that through exhaustion it was not uncommon to forget which was which. Carolyn would be issuing instructions at me in French, which made such confusion even more likely. Also along the top of the windshield, directly over the steering wheel, I pasted another reminder: NO THUMBS! This had by now become almost a habit for me. But the sign was there to help me avoid lapses.

Finally, I applied two decals to the rear quarters of the car. Two small bulldogs standing with the letter "Y" given to me by my eldest son, Mark, who was attending Yale.

On the way out, we were given a card with the time stamped on it, a small packet of driving instructions, and were flagged on our way. The Rallye had begun. We were in it, actually participating in what was no longer a dream. From here on, everything would be real. There was nothing to imagine any more, no questions to ask, or not nearly so many.

On the way back to Versailles, we discovered how other competitors handled their tire problems. We were traveling along with two dune buggies, brightly painted things with skinny front wheels like dragsters who were obviously in the same team. It seemed they were trying to shake us, for they were going awfully fast for a liaison taking place on a crowded public highway. Shortly after leaving Rouen, they were joined by a small truck carrying a load of tires, which sped along with them. We had been staying close, just for the fun of it. But the three speeding vehicles made clear their desire to free themselves from our company. Not wanting to risk an accident or arrest so early in the game, I backed off and let them go their way. A few minutes later, we passed them off to the side of the road, changing from road tires to racing tires.

While doing research, I had heard that everyone cheats. This was a blatant infraction of the rule specifying that no assistance was allowed from any person or vehicle not actually in the Rallye. The way the factory teams got around this was by entering trucks and other cars whose main purpose was not really competing but assisting the serious contenders, and renting out haulage space to private entrants like us. These two cars were receiving help from an illegal source. Apparently, they would do the same thing on the leg from Versailles to Barcelona. I could have done this too. But I was an inexperienced goody-goody adhering strictly to the rules. So Philippe wasn't lurking in the woods with my tires. Carolyn and I decided not to fink on these guys. We figured they'd get their comeuppance some other way.

Had we been so inclined, we could have done a lot of squealing that day. All along the route, cars were meeting with trucks or were stopping off at gas stations where they had previously stashed tires. How had they known the route in advance? I then realized that no amount of homework can compensate for experience and local knowledge. We pressed on to Versailles a little bit disillusioned but otherwise undaunted. *Our* racing tires were already on the car.

We pulled in earlier than our schedule called for. Sometimes there is a penalty for early arrival on a liaison, but this one had specified "No penalty for early arrival." So we hadn't tarried, wanting to get to Versailles and back to the old folks' home for a rest. I needed it. I was coming down with the flu again; fever, sore throat, the works.

There were thousands of spectators already milling around the Place d'Armes, the big court in front of the Palace of Versailles. The palace sulked behind its big iron gates, looking uncomfortable and incongruous, a stranger in its own environment. A line of good-looking young girls, model types in white jump suits, beamed a welcome at us. Our card was stamped, and we were led to our assigned spot by an official riding a three-wheel motorcycle, which flew a red flag from a tall antenna. We followed it silently through a mass of black umbrellas. The drumming of the rain on the roof and on the surrounding umbrellas drowned out even the sound of the engine. We seemed to float into our berth. It was about three in the afternoon, but it looked like six, it was so gray and dreary. We hadn't eaten all day, so we locked up the car and headed for a restaurant just off to one side of the palace.

It was about six blocks from the palace to the hotel, a walk we learned well. We could have cut a block off the distance by going through the palace gardens, but the sandy walks were like bogs from all the rain, so we picked our way around the puddles on the streets.

It was about five or six in the afternoon, and the bed seemed to rise up and hit me as I fell into it. Sometime during the night, I got up covered in sweat, even though shaking with chills. I bundled myself with as many blankets as I could find, hoping to sweat it out for good. I felt barely strong enough to walk. And I had to drive the wringing Prologue day after tomorrow. I just had to shake this flu. It was about ten or eleven the next morning before I had a further thought.

I felt sick but better when I finally awoke. At least I had regained enough strength to walk. And walk was what we had to do today. We had to find a nylon strap to anchor the rear door. All my spares were already in cannisters on trucks. We also had to find a couple of pieces of heavy duty rubber with which to extend the rear mud flaps. I needed this like I needed another hole in my head. I looked out the window, getting a tire's-eye view of the gardens of Versailles. It looked gray and cold, but at least it wasn't raining. We had a slow and quiet breakfast along with a handful of late-rising geezers.

Mindful of the need to conserve our strength and avoid getting chilled, we bundled up and walked through town slowly. We found some straps quickly at an auto supply store. But the rubber wasn't so simple. We shuttled from a car repair shop, to a new car dealer to a shoe repair shop to a truck dealership before finding pieces of the requisite width. Then we went back to the hotel where I had a cup of broth sent to the room and lapsed into a further coma. I struggled awake at 6:00 P.M. We had to attend a drivers' meeting at 7:00 P.M.

While I had been doing all the sleeping, Carolyn had been going over the route book. She had done so late into the previous night, the next morning, and again that afternoon. I gathered it was a horror, filled with idiomatic French directions and warnings with which we were both unfamiliar. We were not shocked by its complexity. I had telexed for and received some of last year's book, and we had used it as the basis for our French tutoring. But many of the idioms had changed, and she was distraught with confusion.

Her confusion and my illness came with us to the driver's meeting. Through most of it, my face was buried in a handful of Kleenex. Carolyn fidgeted and looked around nervously. The whole thing was held in French, of course. A German stood up and in feeble French complained about the route book not being printed in German or at least in English, which most of the non-French-speaking contestants understood. *Good for him*, I thought, keeping my sentiments to myself, not wanting to be labeled as a whiner or complainer. What we were doing was hard enough without incurring the wrath of the officials upon whom we would have to lean for cooperation.

I did think it was ridiculous for an event of this magnitude and with such international pretensions to have not provided English transla- tions of all the printed matter. Lacking that, I thought it was even worse that all English verbal translation would fall upon the shoulders of one person who simply could not be everywhere at once. Suzanne Fournier was a lovely, friendly girl who had been around Paris/Dakar for some years. But Suzanne could translate only the highlights. By the time whoever was speaking finished speaking, there was never enough time left for anywhere near a full translation.

Also, she had other Rallye responsibilities, so she was not always available for help with translations of any kind. This put us at a distinct disadvantage. If not an actual one, certainly a psychological one. We often felt out of it, as though there were important gaps in our un- derstanding of what was going on. Even when there weren't.

For the most part, this meeting was a tedious rehash of the presen- tation of the course we'd attended in Paris. They seemed to have only one script and were adhering strictly to it. I even heard the word "scorpios" again. When the man said it, the audience laughed. I didn't get the humor. I don't find bugs funny. Nor have I met anyone who claims to be amused or entertained by them.

Insects bother me, physically and philosophically. Of course I un- derstand their significance in the ecological chain, but couldn't this function have been handled in some cleaner, neater way? Mankind has managed to find a way to take something beautiful—flowers— and profit from the manufacture and sale of fake, ugly versions of them. Why couldn't we do something like that with bugs?

Why not make beautiful versions of something ugly? Decorative, benign mosquitos, cockroaches, spiders, scorpions. For every one of these critters you'd buy, a percentage of the profits could be plowed back toward eradicating real ones in droves. I'd do the advertising for this free as a public service: BUY ONE. KILL A MILLION. People would buy 'em by the bunch. They'd have arrangements in their homes, bring bug bouquets to dinner parties. Guys would pin them on their dates. And we'd finally get rid of the little bastards.

After the driver's meeting, Suzanne was thronged with people wanting information and clarification. Carolyn had a list of abbreviations that had cropped up in the route book with alarming frequency. Words for which neither of us had a clue as to their possible meaning. But we were swept out of the hall by the crowds of people leaving, the list still untranslated.

Carolyn was confused and worried. I was sick and worried. We took our worries to the hotel bar. Carolyn drank strong coffee while I sipped weak tea. Many of the ancients had been replaced by Rallye competitors, which was obvious from the brightly colored uniforms and the lack of canes and walkers. We struck up a conversation with a tall, thin Dane who was with a group at the next table. We'd heard him speaking English. He turned out to be Ted Toleman's copilot and had run Paris/Dakar before. We told him of our predicament. He graciously volunteered to translate the list for us. He also offered to go over the route book with us and to clarify all our questions the next evening before dinner. We thanked him and said goodnight. Again, I crashed into bed. Again, Carolyn stayed up late, going over the route book.

The next day, the day before New Year's Eve, proved to be the most tense of the entire year-long experience. By now Carolyn and I had begun to grate on each other. We had been together with hardly a moment's break for months. We had been under heavy pressure, racing the clock to get where we were now. We hadn't seen or even spoken to our friends or relations since either of us could remember. We were also on edge about the upcoming Prologue. We'd both been sick with the flu. We were a couple of powderkegs whose fuses had flared up a few times, but now at the last minute, both kegs were about to blow.

Carolyn had stayed up until about two in the morning going over the route book, trying to make sense out of nonsense. Later, she had tossed and turned, having nightmares, talking in her sleep, in French. I slept fitfully, occasionally rising to mark degrees of magnetic variation on our maps and charts, listening to her fears coming out in a foreign tongue. Variation ranged from seven to thirteen degrees along the routes we would be racing. If we set a northerly course, that's how far we'd be off because our compasses would point to the magnetic pole rather than true north. If we didn't take this into account while fixing our position or plotting courses, we could easily become lost.

We were both cranky, irritable, and groggy when we awoke. It was another cold, gray, rainy day. Carolyn had had a really bad night, having nightmares about the route book. She was just lying there tense, probably scared too, while I got dressed. I said something like, "Well, I guess you better get up and start working on the route book."

She started screaming at me hysterically. Told me she couldn't do it. That she was having nightmares in French. That she couldn't cope with the language and was sure we'd get lost. I don't remember what I said. It didn't matter. To Carolyn, lately, everything I said was either patronizing and insensitive or critical and argumentative.

If I said, "There, there" and patted her on the head, she'd call me a condescending chauvinist. If I said, "I know it's hard, but we'll just have to get through it," she'd interpret that as giving her orders. I could see this was going to be one of those days, and I was simply out of patience with it. I probably said something like, "Let's cut the emotional crap and get on with it." Which was the kind of thing I'd been saying to her more and more lately.

Well, whatever it was I said, this time it made her freak. She began calling me all the names she'd used on me outside of Saarbrücken and a few more besides. This was the day before the Prologue, two days before the start of the Rallye itself. Standing there listening to her hysterical harangue, my mind pictured the same scene being played out somewhere else, somewhere in the desert in the midst of some desperate situation. As my attention dissolved back into the room, I didn't see my girlfriend, my fiancée, the woman I loved and wanted to marry. I saw my codriver disintegrating. I was so rattled by what I saw, I made a quick decision.

"We're not going on the Rallye. Forget the whole thing, we're not going anywhere. Look at yourself. You're in no condition to do it. I'm pulling the plug on the whole thing right now."

This, of course, made matters worse. When it did, my keg erupted. Then I stormed out of the room.

Outside, there was peace, there was calm. There would have been birds singing in the trees, if it hadn't been for the rain. I walked the puddled paths of the gardens of Versailles, simmering, venting my feelings into the little portable tape recorder I always carried. I include what I said not to attach blame or to present a one-sided picture of the episode but to give an inkling of the highly charged atmosphere that prevailed.

I'm going out for a little walk, just to get away from the hysteria and craziness in the room. I'm so flustered and I hate to think what state she's in. Must be worse. God, I'm so fed up with the Rallye Paris/Dakar at this point I could scream. Another dreary, cold gray day. Carolyn just freaked out and called me every name in the book because she didn't like the way I said something, and I've just had it. I've had it with the whole damn thing. It's too much pressure, too much hassle, too much expense. If I'm not happy about something, she just comes apart at the seams and I can't handle it anymore. I can't have someone around that's that vulnerable. I can't take the constant strain and expense and bickering and bullshit and her cracking and coming unglued every time I say something. As though I was criticizing her psyche or something! I can't take it anymore. I want out. I'm not going into this rally with this hanging over me. I don't think we could possibly do it. It's too dangerous.

If we're cracking here, we're going to explode there. So I pulled the plug on the whole thing. I just said "No! We're not going." I mean we're just fracturing and falling apart all over the place. But the bills keep coming in. A thousand francs for this, a thousand francs for that, ship this here, ship that there, this is collect. I mean the money is going and going and going and we're going nowhere. We're not going on any rally. And the money is still going out—thousands and thousands of bucks for nothing! For a relationship in a shambles and an event we're not even going on. It's a tragedy. I think we may be at the end of the line here, in every way.

After a while, I went back to the room and we got to work. Almost as though nothing had ever happened. "Hi, honey, I'm home." But if

I'd seen an unemployed male navigator loitering in the gardens of Versailles while out on that stroll, this might have turned out to be a whole different story.

Late that afternoon, bleary-eyed from hours of going over the route book and weak from what remained of my flu, I crashed for a nap. When I awoke, Carolyn was gone. I went downstairs to the bar. They were there, the beefy route book open on a flimsy little gilded table. Carolyn was intent on everything the Dane was saying. He was explaining some of the more arcane symbols that appeared throughout the tome.

The type and the graphic symbols indicating hazards were all oversize, as though prepared for people with poor eyesight. Traveling at high speed over bumps, it would be hard enough to focus on a page, let alone anything printed on it. The large, bold print would help. Hazards printed in gray were moderate, he was telling Carolyn. Those in heavy black were serious and could break the car or cause us to crash. He said we would be wise to mark the serious ones with a colored pen so that we would be less inclined to fly into a deep trench thinking it was only a shallow one.

From the looks of it, every page was filled with serious hazards. There were far more black symbols than gray ones. Some pages had as many as fifteen heavy, black warnings. In looking at one such page, I noticed it covered a total distance of only ten kilometers. Other pages had only spotty warnings and encompassed distances of more than a hundred kilometers. Directions for right or left turns were usually accompanied by compass headings we were to follow. These included small drawings of landmarks or peculiar topography to help us verify that we were on course.

The problem we were having with the route book wasn't with the French. It was with the abbreviated French. Bad enough that we had to translate the French into English. First we had to transpose the shorthand into French. And we had no idea what some of the abbreviations stood for. That's what we were trying to get cleared up. The Dane spent a good two hours helping us decipher the meaning of the Franco-cryptology.

I felt much better the next morning. All that remained of the flu was an occasional sniffle and a little weakness. I was still in less than optimum condition for driving the Prologue, but the show had to go on. That's what the Prologue really is. A show. An entertainment for the hundreds of thousands of spectators who turn out to watch the motorcycles, cars, and trucks splash, slip, and slide their ways around the muddy obstacle course.

Few competitors take the Prologue very seriously. It is regarded as a test that must be passed rather than a victory that needs to be won. Of course, there are always a few macho lunatics who go all out because they are unable to resist showing off for their friends and countrymen. And it's important for the factory team drivers to turn a good time because one's rank at the end of the Prologue determines starting position for the first "speciale" stage in Africa. The really serious contenders want to be as far up front as possible so they don't have to deal with the dangerous job of passing a bunch of slower cars while driving in a cloud of blinding dust. Behind the top twenty, we'd be driving blind from all the dust being churned up anyway. One hundredth or two hundreth didn't much matter. Dust is dust. So few drive the Prologue to the limit.

I just wanted to get through the thing. My strategy was to drive it quickly but smoothly, not risking damage to the car or to ourselves. I thought I was good enough to finish in the top half of the field without extending myself, which I was in no condition to do anyway.

So off we went from the Parc fermé at Versailles at about ten in the morning. We had been given a precise time to arrive at the course at Cergy-Pontoise. This time there would be a penalty for early or late arrival. We had to be there on the dot. This is where the navigation gets a little tricky. Carolyn had to keep figuring out the remaining distance and time as we went along, telling me whether I had to speed up or slow down. Better to go a little too fast in case you take a wrong turn or encounter some unexpected problem on the way. That's what I was doing.

All the other cars had the same idea, too. There we were in a race to a race again. We hit some traffic. Car 259, a bright yellow job, which looked to me like some kind of homemade special, more a sports/racing car than an off-road vehicle, had been riding my tail. Abruptly, he veered to the right, shot down the shoulder passing about twenty stalled cars before turning left from the right shoulder.

Jesus, I thought. *That guy's a maniac. Is he typical?*

This was a liaison on public roads. I couldn't imagine why anyone would be driving like that. I immediately nicknamed him "the Barger." The traffic moved and we began to catch up with him. As traffic choked up again, he did the same thing, barging down the shoulder and up higher into the slow-moving line of cars. We had been going about forty minutes and were getting close to Cergy-Pontoise. That's what the traffic was all about. Spectators were descending on the site from all over Europe. Cars were parked in the median strip down the center of the road, both sides were packed with parked cars, and pedestrians left them hauling hampers as though on their way to some picnic on the grass. Didn't they know it was all mud?

"How the hell do they expect us to get there at a precise time with all this traffic?" I asked Carolyn, as if she knew the answer.

I was getting nervous now, becoming a bit of a barger myself. So were all the other cars. It was madness. Cars sped through antlike trails of families and children, swerving, braking, dodging. Then we were stopped at the entrance to the course, in a solid mass of cars and people. We had four minutes to go before we had to have our card stamped. I asked Carolyn to run down the line and find a marshall, wait until the exact time, and have him stamp the card.

While she ran, I looked. There were thousands upon thousands of people here. And it was raining. Coming down even harder now than before. People were still streaming into the grounds, and no one appeared to be heading for cover. Probably they couldn't, planted as they were in mud up to their shins. Blue smoke rose from refreshment stands scattered all around. Grilled *saucisson*, again. The French amazed me.

Carolyn came back, the card stamped with the exact time we had been scheduled to arrive. Then real chaos ensued. We were meant to be running the Prologue according to number. The Barger, who was ten cars in front of me, was supposed to be eleven cars behind. So he had to be pulled out of the line.

What a moron! I thought.

Spectators were jammed up against both sides of the lined-up cars. Moving out of the lineup was practically impossible. What little room there was, was occupied by mud-drenched motorcyclists who were coming down the line in the opposite direction, having completed their runs. We sat there nervous with anticipation and amused at the mess.

Carolyn complained about the heat. I was overdressed and had the heater turned up full blast, determined to sweat out the last of the flu. I had the tube stuck in my mouth and was consuming water like a camel stocking up for a long caravan. Also, I had the windows closed and they were steaming up. We kept wiping at them, looking around and laughing at the stupidity around us.

In that limited space, they were trying to rearrange the lineup of cars. Some were turned partially around and had become stuck in deep mud. The only thing moving was the wall of onlookers along each side. Occasionally, one would rap on our steamed-up plastic, hoping for an autograph. As the only Americans in that year's Paris/Dakar, a fact that gave us a certain celebrity, there was awareness and appreciation of how far we had come and how hard we had worked to participate in this madness. Also, THANKS had attracted a lot of attention. Some people recognized names that were painted on the car. Other competitors as well as spectators rapped on our windows for brief chats.

We were thankful for the confusion, the disorder, and the interruptions. They distracted us from our private jitters. I had never stopped thinking about knocked-out teeth and shattered kneecaps, and I was trying to remember whether I was supposed to swing wide or hang inside entering the turn marked with the GET sign, a French aperitif. And I was concentrating on remembering to apply more gas through the tight left turn going up the hill before the precipitous drop.

In a two-wheel-drive car, when you lift off the accelerator in a turn, the rear end tends to break away. In a four-wheel-drive car, the opposite happens. When you lift, the car keeps going straight. To make the rear end break away, I had to do the opposite of everything that was natural to me. I had my eyes closed, and I was going around the course in my imagination as best as I could remember it, turn by turn, every so often asking Carolyn to review the map of the serpentine circuit and tell me whether it was in fact as I visualized it.

As we approached the starting ramp, I turned off the heater. I'd be generating enough of my own in a few seconds. We'd strapped ourselves down tightly, knowing that we were in for a thrashing even though I wouldn't be going all out. We tightened our helmets and switched on the intercom system, the battery now taped firmly inside, one lesson we'd learned here a week ago. That too felt like a distant memory, so much had occurred in the intervening week. The technical marshall came over.

"I see you got the safety strap for the rear door," he said approvingly. "Don't forget the mud flaps."

"I have the material," I told him.

We moved up to the top of the ramp, smiling back at Suzanne who was grinning and waving at us. Carolyn was handed another card as the starter held up a stopwatch so we could see the second hand jerk its way toward upright, our signal to go.

Months of thinking, planning, working, spending. It had all come down to a few trembling ticks of a frail and jittery second hand that was about to launch us on the scary first step of our long awaited adventure. Sweat was streaming into my eyes. I wiped at them with the backs of my gloves. This was the part I was most nervous about. If we could get through this—undamaged, unhurt—we could get through anything. I anticipated the last teetery jerk of the second hand, stood on the accelerator, and the Gelandewagen fishtailed off the starting line.

We shot down the ramp, building up speed quickly.

"What first?" I asked Carolyn through the intercom as we ran down a straightaway of well-churned mud.

Reddish-brown mud was banked up high on both sides of the course, and the banks all along were capped with a topping of spectators.

"Right," Carolyn responded.

"Right?" I queried her, that not jibing with my memory of the course.

"No, left." A pause. "No, right. A ninety-degree right."

"Make up your mind!" I snapped, moving left to set up for the right turn.

I was midway into it when we saw that the course went left. We were charging into a little escape road. I slammed on the brakes, half spun the car, and came to rest against an eight-foot-tall mound of mud. I put the car in reverse and began to inch cautiously back out into the course. The car that started behind me flew by, throwing an avalanche of mud toward us. We pulled all the way back out and made the left.

"Get it together, honey, get it together. I'll just have to pick up the pace a little now."

We'd lost almost a minute, a hell of a handicap to start out with. I don't recall if Carolyn had been holding her map upside down or had just become confused and disoriented, but from then on, she had it all together. We went through dozens of rights and lefts, getting them all correctly. We passed cars, some crashed, some stuck, some spun around in the mud facing in the wrong direction. I passed a couple of slower moving cars. But I was bugged about the one that got by me. It was Gooding, the Englishman, one of my neighbors in the Parc fermé.

I got through the hairy left leading up to the sharp drop where we had knocked out the camera. We were camera-free today, having learned our lesson. I also wanted to save the weight. Most of our heavy gear sat on the floor of our hotel room.

"Not so bad today," I said as we plunged down, the nose rearing smoothly up and out at the bottom, which was no longer a lake.

A couple of turns later, I caught up with another car and followed him nose to tail. We had been honking the air horn and flashing the lights so he would move out of the way. And we had been going much faster. But he wouldn't budge. With me tight on his tail, he broke into a skid, heading right for a mudbank. This was my chance to get around. But I was too close to him. My steering wheels were caught in the ruts he was making, and I was unable to break away from his tail. As he hit the mudbank, I plowed into his rear end with a crunch. I had anticipated the hit and slipped the car into reverse a split second before we hit, lessening the impact and keeping us from becoming entangled. Within a few seconds, I was out from behind and away.

"Fool!" I said to no one in particular through the intercom. "Why didn't he just move over?"

We were in the final third of the course now. Once in a while, I got a glimpse of Gooding up ahead, but there was no hope of catching him now. I was holding my own, though. On the final series of turns, two ninety-degree rights, which made up a big horseshoe, I passed two cars the hard way, sliding around on the outside, which put me in a perfect position to pass another car on the inside of the long sweeping left leading up to the finish line.

As we crossed it, sliding sideways and into position in front of the other car, I gave Carolyn a big smile and a "thumbs up," saying "All riiight" over the intercom.

We both knew we had done pretty well in spite of the foul-ups. From the looks of the course, which had been littered with cars, we figured we were in good shape. We stopped to get our card stamped and asked for our time. The official time wouldn't be available until later we were told. I was dying to know how we had done.

"What's the fastest time so far?" I asked.

"*Onze,*" a man replied.

About eleven minutes. I looked at our dashboard stopwatch. The minute hand was just then moving up to fourteen minutes. In the excitement, Carolyn had forgotten to stop it as we'd crossed the line. I felt pretty good, all things considered, as we were sent on our way.

The car was covered in mud. And the rain had stopped, so it was hardening fast. There must have been hundreds of pounds of it caked on. As we had driven, it had flown up at us in a near solid sheet. Carolyn had worked the washers and wipers as well as the horn. That was one of the good things Kaan had done. He'd installed controls for them on her side too. My hands had been too full and moving too fast to have taken them off the wheel even for a split second.

All along, I'd screamed through the intercom, "Wash! Wash!"

Even so, the washers and wipers had barely been able to keep up with the onslaught of the blinding, flying mud.

And I'd yelled, "Horn! Horn!" when trying to pass that turkey. That hadn't done much good either. I had my eye out for him now. I wanted to give that jerk a piece of my mind.

This may sound a little strange to you. I, after all, ran into him. Shouldn't he, in fact, be mad at me instead of the other way around? No. He was a slower car who had received fair warning from a faster, overtaking car, yet he had deliberately blocked me. I should have kept going, shoved him so deep into the mudbank that he'd never have gotten out. But that would have been cutting off my nose to spite my face. I was particularly peeved to be unable to find him in the snarl of cars afterward, missing my once-in-a-lifetime opportunity to be the indignant, fouled, faster car. I told you I was a bit of a fruitcake.

As we drove out of the paddock area, we saw Knilli there waiting his turn to go out.

"You did vell?" he asked as we crept by.

"Okay, I think," I told him, also telling him to watch out for all the cars stuck out there.

We saw Vatanen, the World Rallye champion, coming off the course. He was moving very slowly, and his co-pilot was riding outside on the roof of the car holding a wheel. Something had happened, but no one I asked knew what it was all about. Soon we were out of the grounds, heading back to Versailles. Cars were lined up at car washes and gas stations all along the way. Rather than stop close to Cergy-Pontoise where there were long lines, we decided to barrel our way to Versailles and find a car wash there. Hopefully one less crowded.

We had a lot of traffic heading in this direction too. Obviously, people were now leaving the Prologue and going to see all the cars in the Place d'Armes. We followed the example set earlier by the Barger, charging down shoulders, passing long lines of cars.

In the town of Versailles, we came to a car wash with Rallye cars lined up outside. We passed it in favor of finding one less busy. We had only forty-five minutes left to our allotted time. We found another with only three cars waiting. I got in line. While waiting, we surveyed the damage to our front end, which seemed minor, and filled up the gas tank, which was near empty. I'd purposely kept our load light for the Prologue. It took about half an hour just for the gas what with all the tanks and throwing valve handles and so forth. Every time I filled up, it cost about three hundred dollars. During the race I'd be filling up every day.

This is one of the reasons most all the competitors wore bulging money belts. We had money pouches on thongs around our necks, which we carried inside our clothing. I had thought it best not to advertise the presence of large quantities of cash, me being physically rather unintimidating and traveling with a girl.

Shortly after our tanks were full, we were next in line to have the car washed. We were standing there, feeling lucky about getting gas and a wash and making it back to the Parc in time, which we would just barely do if they started on us immediately. Just then who should drive up and barge right into the slot ahead of us? You guessed it. Good old #259. I began to go berserk. I had spent three hundred bucks on gas there in order to insure getting a wash. Now they were telling me the Barger had made an advance reservation for his wash, and they had to take him first. I didn't know who this Barger son-of-a-bitch was, had no idea of even his name. All I had was a color and a number to go by, but already I hated his guts.

We fumed out of there carrying who knows how much unwanted weight in rapidly hardening mud. Yes, I know. I should have made a reservation. I had even been forewarned. Should've, could've, would've. Knowing it was my own damn fault didn't make me feel any better about it, though.

We pulled into our slot in the Parc fermé and just sat in the car for a few minutes, catching our breath. Between recovering from the flu, the physical exertion of driving that obstacle course, the emotional relief at not having crashed and hurt either our noses or our kneecaps, I was drained. That and the frustration of sitting there in a still mud-caked car, all weighed heavily on me. Yet I was happy. I knew instinctively that we had done well despite our foul-ups. And tired as I was, I was wishing we could do it all over again, better.

Carolyn was upset with herself for messing up on that first turn. I was a little peeved, but I didn't make anything out of it. In fact, I spent some time in the car telling her how well she had done, that being her first time out, ever.

She was an odd girl. Nothing seemed to scare her, specifically. Smacking into that guy's tail, sliding around the course on the edge of control, this didn't seem to ruffle her in the least. She had kept an amazing cool.

Her fears were generic. She worried about not understanding the route book, about navigation, but never about crashing into walls or going off cliffs. In this respect, she was the perfect copilot. I hadn't got the feeling that she had doubts about my driving ability or that she was in any way nervous about placing her life in my hands. Her not worrying about me, at least not obviously so, was one less thing for me to worry about. I never thought I would, but then I knew that I wouldn't have to drive Paris/Dakar with a whining, white-knuckled girl in the seat next to me.

Though I sloughed off her mistake, I was still concerned about her ability to navigate us through the upcoming test, and her growing tendency to crack and become weepy had me worried, too. I prayed that it was a result of all the pressures leading up to the Rallye, a form of preflight jitters.

Rather than focus on what she had done wrong, or on what she hadn't done, which had been my tendency all along, and it was no longer working, I now praised her for all that she had done well. I needed to instill in her, and in myself, a fresh supply of self-confidence. This was a critical few minutes, just after the Prologue. Neither of us could afford to have doubts about ourselves now. We needed all the assurance we could muster. At that moment, neither of us gave any sign of being frightened. But how could we not have been?

It was the afternoon of New Year's Eve and pouring with rain. Cars and trucks, quite a few of them muddy like ours, streamed into the Place d'Armes, having run the Prologue. I took a perverse pleasure in noting this. It helped knowing I wasn't the only dope in the field.

I peered out through the windshield, out through the rain, looking for a car with a dent in its rear end. Then we scanned the list of entrants we had been given at Rouen. Number 259. The driver was a Frenchman whose name sounded Italian—Bravione.

Bargerone, I thought.

His car was called a Majorette.

We got out of the car and went to look for a truck that might carry our wheels and tires to Barcelona. There were thousands of spectators, but few contestants remained, most having locked up and gone off. It looked like we were destined to slip and slide to Barcelona.

We decided this was as good a time as any for me to attach the extensions to the mud flaps. While I worked on that, Carolyn puttered about the car, straightening out the cockpit, stashing our vitamin pills and supplements in the lockers under the seats, organizing all the car's papers and our driving documents. We tried to ignore most of the spectators who kept interrupting us with inane questions. We just pretended we didn't speak French. A very white half-lie, one that wouldn't keep us out of heaven.

We went back to the hotel and had a quick snack in the bar. As usual Toleman and his entourage, including his Danish navigator, were there. Somehow Toleman had found out that he finished in the top five, and they were all celebrating. We had no idea how we'd done for sure. The official, final results wouldn't be released until the next day, after the start. I went up to the room to take a nap. Carolyn went into town to have her hair done. We'd made an appointment for her the day before while out looking for rubber.

That night, we got dressed up and went out for a quiet dinner at a little seafood restaurant near the Place d'Armes. It was our last normal, pressure-free moment before the start in the morning. It was weird, trying to be low key and normal on New Year's Eve in a foreign country, the night before the biggest thing either of us had ever done.

We talked little, each full of our own private thoughts. We tried to smile and be happy, not that it should have been such a strain. We had much to be pleased about. But there was a certain sadness behind both our smiles. Like this was a commemoration of past events rather than a celebration in anticipation of those to come. More of a funeral than a baptism. Few people ever get as close to each other, and remain that way so constantly, and with such intensity, as Carolyn and I had over the past ten months. It was as though in rubbing ourselves together, we had created warmth, emitted sparks, and generated great heat, but at the end, we were each left with a little less of ourselves. I was wondering if, at the end of all this, either of us would have anything left to give to the other. I was also wondering if she was wondering the same thing.

Back at the hotel, before turning in for the night, we packed a suitcase with our civilian clothes. Jean-Pierre had arranged for it to be picked up and sent to us in New York. We also folded all our maps and charts and put them into the navigation case. We hugged and went to sleep, both too exhausted from the rigors of the waning year to be kept awake by the dawning one.

At four-thirty, the alarm went off and we cleared out of the room quickly.

On the way out of the hotel, we picked up the bags of food we had ordered the night before. The lobby looked like Times Square the morning after a New Year's Eve celebration. In a year when the sanitation men were on strike. It smelled like it too. The sour-sweet aroma of stale smoke and too much champagne still infused the air.

Our exit was quieter, but no less offbeat than our arrival.

"I have six wheels and tires in Room 209," I told the acting concierge in Patrick's absence. "Keep them, sell them, whatever you like. I have no further need of them."

"Yes, sir. Thank you, sir," was all the response I got.

As if *giving* them six wheels and tires was no more unusual than checking in with them in the first place.

We tried to hitch a ride to the start with Toleman's group, 13t their van was packed and they had no room for us. We asked about getting a taxi and told with a shrug that it was very early on a rainy New Year's Day morning.

We set off on foot down a shiny and puddled street through the blackness before dawn, asking ourselves, separately, what was to become of us.

12

Lugging our two big duffel bags and the navigation case, we turned right into the first street we came to and were swept toward the Place d'Armes by the force of thousands of celebratory spectators rushing in the same direction. We could only hope that this human wave would crash upon the Place and wash us up somewhere near our car.

We could see nothing. It was dark and pouring with rain, and we were surrounded tightly by people on all sides of us. We assumed we were headed in the right direction. Where else would they all be going?

Between the bobbing heads, we saw the sky brightening ahead and soon it became clear that we were not pushing toward dawn, but toward lights signaling the start of something unnaturally big. We could not move out of the mob. It was too big. It extended forever, in every direction, yet it moved in only one, forward.

It brought to mind one of my worst nightmares, one that I'd had two or three times before in my life but hadn't thought about for very many years. In it, I was a racing driver. My car was sitting on the starting grid surrounded by mechanics and swarms of onlookers. It was taking place in some kind of fairground and the grandstands were filling up with people. The announcer was calling the drivers to the grid. I could hear it from where I was, outside, in the crowd trying to get in. I would beg people to let me by, to allow me to go ahead of them.

"Please let me through," I'd say to the strangers around me. "I'm a driver in this race and have to get to my car."

"Yeah, yeah, and I'm A. J. Foyt!" one of them would retort. And they'd all laugh and kept pushing and shoving but refused to let me through.

The nightmare, in the illogical way of nightmares, would flash from scene to scene. In one, I'd be careering around corners in a car I'd commandeered, a half-dozen police cars on my tail, trying to keep me from getting away and into the fairgrounds. I'd screech up to a tall fence, jump out of the car, and climb it. Falling to the ground on the other side, I'd see that there was another, higher fence still to climb. Fairground ushers spotted me there and took up the chase.

Another scene would have me scrambling up a long flight of stairs and out onto a roof. I'd look down and see the roof of the grandstand below. Hearing footsteps thumping up behind me, I'd leap down onto the roof, bouncing, rolling, and scrabbling for a hand hold. But because of the way the roof was pitched, I'd fall back down into the crowd outside waiting to get in.

I'd somehow make it to the start. But I'd arrive just as they were pushing my car off the grid. I'd be exhausted and sweating and out of breath, and as soon as I climbed into the car, the race would begin. Then I'd wake up.

Trying to push through the crowd in Versailles, it was not surprising that old nightmare came back to me. It captured all the frustration involved in going racing. In going anywhere and doing anything for that matter. It's a killer, just getting to the starting line.

There are people who believe that winning is everything. I don't adhere to that cockeyed theory. To me, crossing the finish line first is simply an extension of the original challenge, which is showing up for the start.

That's what takes nerve, commitment, planning, training, the investment of time, money and energy. Arriving at the start, all suited up and ready for a go at the race. All the excuses and rationalizations for not trying in the first place having been put aside or overcome. Being willing to lay it all on the line. Wanting to win, but prepared to accept losing.

If winning was everything, we were setting off on a hopeless mission. Since winning was out of the question, why were we even bothering? What kind of personal victory could we hope to achieve here? In fact, the first personal victory had already been won. We had not been cowed by such supercilious bullshit as "winning is everything." We were going ahead and doing despite knowing that we couldn't win. Doing is everything. Not winning. Without doing there can be no winning, or losing. No experiencing.

We tried angling our way through the crowd. For every three or four steps forward, we'd sneak one to the right. After a couple of blocks, we saw glimpses of barricades. If we could get over to them, we might be able to sneak through somewhere. We had these big, heavy bags draped over us. And the rain was pouring down. We couldn't stop and rest. We'd have been trampled by the crowd, many of whom were greeting the New Year in mental absentia. They still wore party hats and waved bottles of champagne.

"God, I'm sick of all this," Carolyn groaned.

"Yeah, screw the fanfare. Let's go racing." I laughed it off. But it was getting to me too. We'd had enough overture. It was the performance that we'd come for.

A big gendarme who looked like Charles de Gaulle—they all looked like Charles de Gaulle, tall with long noses like caricatures in their round and peaked Legionnaires' caps—stopped us as we squeezed through a gap in the temporary fencing. We showed him our wrist-bands, and he let us pass across the open cobbles to another line of fences behind which the contestants' vehicles were impounded.

The crowd was thinner inside. Most of it was still outside the fences, rushing toward the main gate at the front of the Place. We had got in the back, close to the palace itself. We found our row, and then our car. I got in and started it up. Carolyn stuffed the bags into the back and battened them down.

We sat in the cockpit waiting for the heater to stop pumping cold, damp air. A Frenchman was babbling over the loudspeakers, prattling on about nothing as usual. A band was playing too. But we couldn't tell if it was live or recorded. Big arc searchlights were ranged all over the Place as though for a dozen movie openings. They shot beams of brightness hundreds of feet up into the murky black sky, spotlighting thousands of gallons of water falling down. We were soaked, inside and out. Inside, from our own sweat, generated while trundling the bags to the car. Outside, from all the rain that had fallen on us on the way. The two kinds of wet met and clasped their clammy hands, in celebration of the New Year.

The car warmed up a little, and I switched off to save gas. I could see a few motorcyclists standing around in colorful, heavy leather suits. They had their helmets on, not to protect their heads from being bashed in, but from being beaten on by the rain. Around the perimeter of the Place, out in the streets, there were rows of food and souvenir stalls, lit up and thronged with shadowy shapes.

Between where we sat and the stalls, we saw trucks moving forward in a line, toward the starting ramp, built up and mobbed near the head of the Place. The emcee's voice sped up and increased in volume, as he began to blare out the bios of the drivers. They were starting the trucks first, then the motorcycles, then the cars. The factory team cars would lead off. We'd go right behind as we were among the first of the private entries.

The Place had become practically filled with people. We'd heard that between a half million and a million were expected. It looked like they'd all come. They must have been parking their cars miles away and hiking here on foot. Or maybe they came by the busload. That had to be it. Some, no, many, were clearly too tipsy to drive. They shouted and staggered, bumping into our car, then cursed its hardness.

Many people tapped on our windows, looking for autographs. It interrupted our study of the route to Barcelona. We were trying to go through the route book, familiarizing ourselves with what was to come. But we felt obliged to be amiable. We were the only Americans there, ambassadors of a sort. So we tried our best to put on smiles and talk briefly with all who came along. As we were the only Yanks, and therefore an oddity here, people seemed to seek us out. It was as if we had big U.S. flags painted on the car, which we didn't. Maybe it was THANKS. Maybe that was setting us apart. That's what we had hoped it would do, and now we were suffering from our success.

"Maybe we should have made it '*merci*' instead of 'thanks,' " I said to Carolyn.

"Then they would expect us to speak French and we'd really have a problem," she quipped.

All our banter was jokey. It was as though neither of us wanted to consider the possibility that we might be doing something deadly serious.

The interior light went on in the car to our left. It was Gooding, the Englishman, and I could see that his copilot had scissors and was cutting up maps.

"I wonder what that's all about?" I asked Carolyn. "Why don't you go over and see what they're up to?"

After she left, a Belgian driver came over and introduced himself. He climbed into Carolyn's seat and began talking to me. He wondered why there weren't more American entries. I told him that not so many people in America know about Paris/Dakar and that those who did thought everybody in it got killed. He laughed and told me he had finished fourth last year, and in a two-wheel drive car, but that he'd never try *that* again. This year, he had a souped-up Toyota four-wheel drive. He pointed to it across the way.

It was a very shiny metallic silver, and I told him I had noticed it before and admired the paint job. He had bright, silver hair that matched his car. In America, I told him people often tend to have dogs that resemble them, here it was cars. He laughed again. He looked a lot like Kirk Douglas. He said good-bye and left, telling me that he hoped we could talk some more in Africa.

Carolyn came back and got some maps. Gooding's copilot was helping her get organized, she said. Any help she could get was a blessing to me. I didn't want to have anything to do with navigation.

There was a big fracas going on next door, on the other side of us. Guy Dupard, the driver of car 247, was sitting on his hood, drinking champagne and posing for a group of photographers. The area around his car was lit up like day from all the lights. They had a flair, this team, real promoters. The copilot passed out trinkets and souvenirs to the crowd.

They'd also held a press party on the Champs-Elysées the week before. Their sponsor, the Casa Nostra pizza chain, had an outlet on the Champs right next to our garage. One evening we had stumbled out and found their car on the sidewalk, all lit up. It was painted like a billboard, with a cartoon Italian chef holding a pizza in the foreground, and in the background were palm trees and sand. They'd even brought in sand and fake palm trees for the party, planting a make-believe patch of Senegal on the Champs-Elysées.

The motorcycles were starting to move up toward the ramp, and soon our turn would come.

Carolyn returned with the unnecessary parts of a lot of our maps trimmed off. Gooding's copilot had told her she'd be less likely to become confused if she used only the parts of the maps that covered the course itself. It was a good idea, I concurred.

I called over to thank Gooding for his help. He was out of his car and putting some padlocks through steel loops on his hood. I asked him why he was doing that. He pushed over to me through the crowd to explain.

The emcee was really going at it now. But all we could hear was distorted shouting and the sporadic roar of the immense crowd going up and drowning him out. We soon surmised that he had been calling the cars to prepare to start, for suddenly a lineup of marshalls in white jumpsuits materialized in front of our line of cars.

Gooding headed back to his car. How he would get there, I couldn't imagine. His car was only four feet away, but it might as well have been in China, so solid was the wall of people between us now. The line of marshalls had somehow managed to separate the front of our row of cars from the crowd. As they pushed backward against the hordes, space gradually opened up in front of us.

I had the engine going again and the heater was on full blast, so the windows were fogging up. Carolyn wiped at them as fast as she could.

Cars from the far right end of our line were moving past us now. We were going! Dupard was racing his engine, clearing the spark plugs, and beginning to inch his way forward in noisy, jittery bursts, the lightweight kevlar body twisting and untwisting from the torque. We would be next. Then Gooding and on down the line. Until we were no longer all there. Not that any of us could be rightly described as "all there." I've done a lot of wild and crazy things on the New Year in past years. But this, this had to be the least "there" yet.

Never have any two people been so ready and eager to get out of one place and on to the next. The fanfare, the carnival atmosphere had been exciting at first, then amusing, but it had begun to lose its charm. We'd been through too many carnivals already. We were champing to get the hell out of there. I pulled into line behind Dupard, feeling relieved. Here we were, beginning. But it felt like finishing. Almost like it was the end rather than the beginning. All the preparation, the planning, the last-minute surprises, they were all now, at last, history. There was nothing more to be done but the Rallye itself.

Again I felt an overwhelming sense of accomplishment. As though what remained was a mere formality. The eight thousand miles of bad and unfamiliar terrain that stretched out before us was the adventure, the fun. The hard part was over. As we crept toward the starting ramp in the relentless rain, through the solid chunk of spectators who parted like a sea as we moved, I was almost in awe of how far we had come. We were doing this dream. How well we would do *at* it almost didn't matter now. We were doing. We crested the ramp.

"Five, four, three, two, one . . ."

Going. We were going.

Flagged off the ramp, I'd thought we would at last leave the crowds and the hullabaloo behind. But we dropped down into a corridor of barricades whose walls were made of flesh. For as far as we could see, thousands upon thousands of people jumped, shouted, waved, and cheered in the gray dawn light. We had to go slowly. People were packed within inches of each side of us. They banged their fists on the sides of the car as we crawled along and they shrieked, *"Bonne chance!"* and *"Bon courage!"* Adorable little girls waved tiny fistsful of fresh flowers. One of the more demonstrative onlookers slid open my plastic side window and threw a handful of confetti inside the car. We picked it out a piece at a time for weeks.

All through France, the roads teemed with well-wishers. At the Trocadero checkpoint in Paris, someone rushed up out of the crowd to say we had done well in the Prologue. He'd seen it on TV. We still didn't have our official time, so we had no idea how we'd finished.

Just the other side of Paris, we pulled into a car wash and had all the caked-on mud steamed off. It took about forty-five minutes. The hollow chassis members had filled up with mud, which had hardened like rock, and we had a hell of a time loosening it up and getting it out, even with high-pressure hoses.

On the road again, we traveled in clutches of cars, which would change from time to time as one or another of them fell out and stopped to eat or grab a nap or pull off and make some hasty repairs or get washed. What an odd feeling it was flying down public roads in a group of cars that were clearly breaking the traffic laws yet were being applauded for it on all sides, even by the *gendarmerie* who held back spectators and traffic at every major crossroads in every minor little town we flew through.

We had a bag of healthy snack food in the car. That is, some fresh fruits and crisp vegetables we'd had the foresight to order from the hotel. Packaged "healthy" snack food is one of those compromises that doesn't work, for invariably that sort of thing is neither healthy nor tasty. Better to have greasy nuts or chips that taste good or fresh fruit and vegetables that *are* good than the insipid honey- and sesame-coated in-between stuff. It's people who can't make choices who are the product developer's and marketing man's dream.

"Hey, I've got it! Let's give them a candy bar with the pimple medicine built in."

After we finished our chunks of cauliflower and carrots, we each had a granola bar for dessert. You see, we were just as culpable as anybody else, only we weren't deluded about it.

We were holding out as long as we could for dinner. My strategy for the whole Rallye was to always get as close to the next destination as possible before relaxing and letting up. If we stopped now and had a mechanical problem later, there might not be enough time to deal with it. We were due in Barcelona at 4:00 A.M., with no penalty for early arrival. We'd already used forty-five minutes for the wash. Also, I couldn't drive much over seventy miles an hour on the slick roads. The car was practically uncontrollable, skidding and yawing all over the place. Stopping was sweat-inducing. The car would just keep going, aquaplaning, the tires refusing to grip the wet road. They were designed for biting dust. We decided to put off our dinner until sometime between 10:00 P.M. and midnight, after we had a lot more miles behind us.

It was still afternoon, somewhere in the lower half of France. There had been millions of people on the streets of Paris to wave us on our way. Since then the crowds had begun to thin. But the turnout was still amazing. Driving along the open highway, we'd pass a clot of spectators off to the side, the occupants all standing out in the rain, waving limp hankies as we went by.

In the towns, the streets were jammed as in Versailles and in Paris. They pressed right up against the barricades, drumming their good wishes on the sides of the car. The thumping was annoying and beginning to give us both headaches. Or maybe it wasn't the banging after all. Maybe it was the being up since four-thirty in the morning and eating little more than a few raw vegetables. Or maybe it was the fuel fumes inside. We still had some, not as bad as before, but just enough so that I was always aware of the fact that I was piloting a tanker.

One thing struck me as odd. Whenever we were going along the highway in a procession of cars, people on the sides would wave and cheer at each car going by. Then, as we approached, the jumping, waving, and shouting seemed to intensify. I had a revelation.

"I don't think everybody's getting this treatment," I said to Carolyn.

"What do you mean?" she asked.

I told her to watch the crowd's reactions as we went by, compared to the other cars.

"You're having delusions," she said.

But sure enough, they were showing an extra measure of enthusiasm at our passing. Then Carolyn noticed it too.

"Maybe there was something about us on TV," she speculated.

"I don't know," I said, "but *something's* going on."

We never found out what it was, but something was definitely going on. At one point we even passed under a viaduct crowded with shouting, waving fans. On the viaduct in big, blue graffiti-type lettering had been painted VIVE U.S.A.—M.B.

We assumed this display was for us, the Americans driving the Mercedes-Benz. Maybe it was delusions. Could be it was just some Frenchman named Michel Battiste showing his love for America. But that seemed less likely than the first delusion.

This turned out to be one of the most extraordinary days either of us had ever experienced. Even without any singular attention, the excitement and enthusiasm demonstrated by millions of people toward everyone in the Rallye was truly remarkable. It was something like the reception the Allied troops must have been accorded when liberating Paris near the end of World War II. And this was a lot easier and cheaper than fighting a war in order to earn such recognition. Though fighting a war was absolutely the only thing I could think of that would have been harder or costlier than what we were doing.

Difficult in itself, the Rallye was made much more so for us because our supply lines had been so long. So much of what we needed had come from the States, even the West Coast of the States. Communication had been costly and complicated. For a Frenchman living in France, doing Paris/Dakar would be much easier. Excepting the visa problems, the shipping and duty rigmarole, and the telephone and telex expense, and then the strain of working in an unfamiliar language, preparing and training for the Rallye could be done in one's spare time and for a lot less money.

But to do it from another country with no experience, one had to be well-heeled or heavily backed and have nearly unlimited time to devote to the enterprise. This doesn't even take into account the question of whether or not it's something worth doing in the first place. World opinion remains divided on this issue.

The Rallye polarizes people into two distinct factions: Those who approve, seeing it as one of the last great adventures in which man and sometimes woman can put themselves to the utmost test, requiring strength, courage, and sportsmanship in the extreme. These were obviously approvers who lined the roads of France, growing hoarse. Those who disapprove look upon it as an elitist outing for rich people who flaunt the worst of capitalism in the faces of some of the world's most poverty-stricken people, leaving little of value to the Africans, except a few handouts and a lot of garbage, which remains behind, tainting the beautiful landscape for years.

There is also now a third group emerging whose numbers grow every year and who are of the opinion that the Paris/Dakar Rallye is unnecessarily brutal and hazardous to contestants and spectators alike. The volume of their opinion grows whenever a driver is killed or an African is mowed down by a speeding car.

Carolyn and I had many discussions about this. Were we going to all this trouble to participate in something we should rightfully be demonstrating against? We didn't know the answer. At least we would be getting the facts firsthand. Whatever conclusion we arrived at would certainly be an informed one.

We were nearing the end of our first day in the Rallye. It looked as though we were escaping the accursed rain at last. Behind us the sky was steely gray and postboding. In front, the clouds were breaking up, revealing patches of blue. Streaks of red brightened the sky we were heading toward. The sun was up there somewhere, though it had yet to reveal its whereabouts.

We were hungry, tired, happy, and more than a little thrilled. In the descending dark, we could barely discern the cheering groups spaced along the road. But we felt their presence and agreed to each other that if something went wrong and we were knocked out of the Rallye right then, it would have all been worth it for that day alone.

By the time we made our scheduled dinner stop, there was no dinner to be had. All the restaurants that were still open had kitchens that had already closed. We settled for a cup of hot tea at a restaurant followed by a couple of granola bars from our own larder. I also popped some vitamins down the hatch and took the second of my weekly malaria pills along with those I would take every day until some time after the Rallye ended.

At the Spanish frontier, some Rallye officials were waiting, helping to hustle a lineup of cars through their paperwork. It was as easy as going through the Lincoln Tunnel in New York but with a lot less traffic. And we were driving much faster.

We hit the outskirts of Barcelona about 2:00 A.M. And then there was traffic. It looked like the entire town had come out to greet us. Later we learned that there were more than a million people on the streets there in the middle of the night. At times we inched along in the crush. When it opened up for a few blocks, we'd speed along flanked by Spaniards gunning their family cars who also smiled, cheered, and waved their national flags.

It was 3:00 A.M. when we finally crept onto the quai. The big ships bound for Algeria were there, waiting. But none of the cars, motor-cycles, or trucks that had been scheduled to commence boarding an hour ago had yet budged. We noticed that many contestants were taking advantage of the delay by doing maintenance on their cars. We decided to do the same.

I went over the car, giving everything a routine check while Carolyn unpacked and began mounting cameras. This is when we first learned we had a problem that affected the mounting of the lower front camera. The little incident in the Prologue had bent the cowcatcher and the bumper and the bolts that ran through it, which held the mount the camera would be placed in. The damage was minor, but the camera was unmountable. Carolyn was upset. This was her favorite angle, but we decided to leave this repair for later anyway. We were too tired, hungry, and cold to do anything that strenuous right now.

Not that it was cold. Compared to Paris it was almost tropical. We were cold because of hunger and fatigue. We went looking for food and bathrooms. Neither was to be found. We got back in the car to catch a few winks but were both too fidgety to sleep. We got out and wandered around the dock, to see if there was anyone we knew. At this point, Gooding and Dupard and a couple of others were the only ones we knew and they were nowhere to be seen.

I wondered why we had got here so early. Less than a third of the field had arrived. The rest had all probably stopped for large, sumptious, and leisurely dinners and nice long naps and would arrive in a few hours feeling fresh and happy. I began to second-guess my hurry up and wait strategy. I felt stupid. Still, if anything had gone wrong along the way . . .

We found out the cause of the delay. Some Algerian had been flexing his bureaucratic muscles and insisted on inspecting each entrant's pa-pers, one by one, and passing on them all before letting even one car go on board. I was working up a righteous hatred for Algerian bu-reaucrats. First the visas, now this. I spent most of that first night peeing on palm trees and trying to nap in the car. What little sleep we were able to get was constantly interrupted by marshalls who would move our cars around and into some master formation that was a mystery to us all.

At around five in the morning, I cracked an eye from my slumped slumber behind the wheel. The sky was reddish-gray. "Red in the morning, sailors take warning," flashed through my cloudy mind. *Christ, that's all we need*, I thought. *A gruesome crossing, holding paper bags to our green faces the whole way to Africa.*

We were lined up in twos now just sitting, waiting. I opened the door, swinging up, over and down onto the dock. In the dawn's chill light, I did some yoga stretches. We squeezed them in now whenever we could, which hadn't been very often lately.

The car next to me was a little Lada, number 185. This rang a bell. I reached inside my car for the list of entrants and looked it up. Sure enough, it was Jacky Ickx. I walked over. He was slumped as I had been before and was now yawning, contemplating the threatening sky. Seeing that I was coming to talk to him, he opened the door.

"Jo Hoppen asked me to say hello." I delivered the greeting, as promised.

"How is Jo?" he asked.

"Fine, I guess. Still with Audi."

I hardly knew what else to say, having only met the man for a minute in Ohio. But it served its purpose as a conversation starter with Ickx. He looked gray and bleary-eyed, as I guess we all did. I was a little awed to find this famous racing champion just sitting there on the dock next to me. To hear Kurt Knilli tell it, all the big-time factory team drivers stayed overnight in a hotel, then flew across to Africa, avoiding what can be a long, uncomfortable day and a half at sea. I asked him about this.

"I always take the boat," he replied. "It's part of the flavor of the Rallye."

This was no prima donna. I liked him immediately and resolved to stay close. I didn't have to work at it though, he was so friendly and outgoing. He seemed to know a lot about me, asked how I came to be doing the Rallye with a girl. I told him the story. He seemed charmed by it. He also asked how I came to be driving the car I was driving.

"If it was good enough for you to win with, I figured it would be good enough for me to finish with," I told him.

"Yes, it's a good car," he said. "Very safe. Very reliable. You made the perfect choice."

You can imagine how good this made me feel. The first evaluation of my judgment being a positive one and coming from a top, experienced pro. He came over to look at the car. As I was showing him around, Carolyn stirred. I introduced them. As we toured the car, I pointed out some of the modifications we'd made as well as those we hadn't.

He approved of everything, said I had done everything exactly right, including not tampering with the engine, including even the "owto-matic" gearbox. He quizzed me on my racing history. I filled him in, also letting him in on my strategy for Paris/Dakar. He concurred.

"It's a long race," he told me. "The surest way to Dakar is to drive it slowly."

Our line was moving up to the ramp to board the boat now.

As he headed back to his car, he turned and warned me over his shoulder, "Don't forget to lock your car."

The first of a hundred helpful tips and admonitions that were still to come.

I was grateful to have met this gifted and gracious man who was to be of so much help. I was also wary. I'd met someone who claimed to know him and who advised me to keep an eye on Jacky as far as Carolyn was concerned. He had a reputation for being quite the lady's man. Part of me was sensitive to this warning, and I hated myself for it.

Often I've observed that it is one of the baser components of human nature to see the worst of yourself in others. Social climbers suspect others of struggling for position. Moochers and freeloaders think every-one they meet is after something for nothing. Frauds always think the other guy is a fake. Guys with pussy on their brains believe all anyone thinks about is getting laid. Was this me? A skirt-hunter worried about getting poached upon? Disgusted with myself, I tried to shake the nasty, small suspicion out of my mind.

Mental shortcomings aside, I was feeling physically inadequate as well. This sensation was heightened by my shortness, obvious when standing among the rest of these guys while waiting to get into the dining room aboard ship for lunch. It was like finding myself attending the wrong convention. I was wearing the same wristband and carried the same credentials as all the others, but clearly, these were all life-guards. And I was drowning in their presence.

We'd spent the morning buying the required amount of Algerian money, getting our passports and visas checked. I'd yet to meet a pleasant Algerian. They all seemed to take a peculiar pleasure in making things as difficult and complicated as possible. I wondered why the Rallye didn't just go through Morocco instead.

The answer, of course, was obvious. That would have made it too easy. The Rallye *meant* to make things hard. It was part of the chal-lenge, part of the process of mental intimidation that the Rallye imposes on the *concurrents*. The program is designed to shake the weak links out as early as possible.

We'd heard that the organization did everything possible to eliminate as many contestants as possible, as soon as possible. That way they didn't need to transport as big a staff as the Rallye plunged deeper into Africa. Nor would there be as many mouths to feed. Every one of us was overhead the organization was out to reduce. Human degradation, deterioration, and elimination, that was their goal. Their financial success depended on our failure. And they went at us all with a vengeance. We were learning that there would be much more to the Dakar than driving fast. You are constantly confronted with unexpected pressures and obstacles. Forget the physical punishment. The challenge is to keep the extraneous stuff from turning your mind to jelly.

We were kept waiting for lunch for two hours, jammed into an airless, smoke-filled corridor as the ship rolled and heaved out into the Mediterranean. None of us had had much more than a few minutes' sleep in thirty-three hours. Carolyn and I hadn't eaten a real meal since our New Year's Eve dinner. That was forty-one hours ago. We were famished, we were tired, we were weak and queasy. And we were standing in line waiting to be admitted to a lifeguard's convention to which we were mistakenly invited. We were going to have life-saving drill at sea. I was the victim. As the floor under me tilted from side to side, I thought I was going to be sick. I was dreaming, asleep standing up, pressed so tightly up against the others that I had no fear of falling down. Only of drowning or choking on my own vomit.

The doors at last opened, and the inhabitants of the corridor moved inside en masse. We were near the end of the line. We looked around, blinking and rocking. All the tables were full! No. I couldn't cope with this. I had to eat. Desperate for food we plopped down at a big table occupied by a group of strangers. We didn't even ask if we could. If one of them had said something, I would have hauled off and punched him in the mouth. I was small but I was fast. I could run.

I then began to know why people resort to cannibalism when they're shipwrecked and hungry. The need to eat becomes a driving, blinding passion. I watched the caddy holding the salt, pepper, and catsup sliding back and forth the length of the table and was tempted to grab it and just start eating salt. That was how I felt. And we hadn't been through anything yet.

The food was horrendous. Some kind of mystery meat further disguised by a dark, disgusting sauce. There were greasy french fried potatoes, too. I was desperate for food, but I wouldn't bite. I ate bread. A lot of bread and a little lettuce. A few vegetables. Enough to allay the gnawing in my abdomen. I drank a lot of bottled water.

After "lunch," we went to our cabin. It was me and Carolyn in one over and under berth. In the two other over and under berths, four lifeguards were in repose. The air in the small, stuffy cabin was filled only with the sound of snoring, which was big. These were the luxury accommodations. There were only a few "private cabins," as these were called. I'd paid a premium to reserve this treat. I assumed many of the less fortunate *concurrents* were sprawled around the engine room or out on deck or . . . I awoke four hours later having failed to finish that thought.

Our German roommates were getting dressed in the dim light. I heard footsteps and voices in the hallway, commotion and activity outside. *Dinnertime*, I thought as I looked at my watch. We had to hurry. I couldn't face another long spell in the corridor. I woke Carolyn and ran down the hall to the head. There were no stalls, no seats, just holes in the floor one crouched over. And the stench was unbelievable. Never in my life had I smelled such an odor. The reek of hundreds of men in their first week of taking malaria pills. We'd heard that one of the most trying conditions on the Rallye was the primitive nature of the facilities, or rather the lack of them. I had just got my first snootful. I swiped a few sheets of the crackly brown toilet paper just in case, then went back to the cabin to fetch Carolyn. She was just heading to the toilet as well.

"Be prepared for a shock," I told her.

I went to get us a place in the dinner line back in the corridor.

The corridor was more jammed than it had been at lunch, and the line was even longer. The smell was higher too, everyone being a further six hours past their last contact with a bar of soap. With only our lunch experience to go by, we were in for at least a two-hour wait, it seemed to me. We were standing there, groggy and depressed, knowing that when the wait was done, the reward wouldn't prove worth it. But we were very hungry. As was everyone else standing in this linoleum-lined, fluorescent-lit container carrying us to Africa like so much freight. In fact, one of the sounds that one noticed standing there in that confined space—there were three distinct sound frequencies—was the background murmur and mumble of a chorus of a couple hundred empty stomachs. Above this bass discord, in frequency and volume, was the vocal chatter going on in French, a mass sing-song beyond our comprehension.

Above that was the hissing rasp of the shipboard PA system, which crackled out the names of the illustrious with annoying repetition. *"Monsieur Tambay. Monsieur Patrick Tambay."* As if to remind us that there were gods among us. *"Monsieur Tambay. Monsieur Tambay."* Rubbing our noses in who we weren't. *"Monsieur Ickx. Monsieur Jacky Ickx."* The B.O. was so bad I was getting a headache from it.

"Monsieur Vatanen. Monsieur Ari Vatanen." Was Vatanen here? I wondered. Surely the world champion took the plane. They say he knows no fear and is as cold as ice. I wonder if he's as crazy and dangerous a driver as everyone says. Last year he plowed through a crowd of spectators. *"Monsieur Pescarolo. Monsieur Henri Pescarolo."* That accident spurred an international rules change. The lightweight 600-horsepower cars of the type Vatanen had been driving were outlawed. But he was driving one here. This was one of the few places those cars were still allowed, this being a bit of an outlaw event—a "Raid." *"Monsieur Tambay. Patrick Tambay."*

These kinds of oddball events have always attracted me. Back in Chicago when I was very young, too young to be racing legally (I was nineteen, claiming twenty-one), somebody cooked up the idea of the world's first indoor grand prix. The race was to be run from building to building, through the old meat-packing and slaughtering plants of the Chicago stockyards. As soon as the plan was announced, the race was banned. *"Monsieur Ickx. Jacky Ickx."*

It was preposterously dangerous. As the cars thundered from one building into another, the course narrowed and you funneled from two lanes to one as you scraped through doorways. Steel girders stood all along the course, even on the outsides of turns. *"Henri Pescarolo. Monsieur Pescarolo."*

So a group of us entered, using silly assumed names so as not to lose our licenses. I crashed in practice, hitting a girder. It took them half an hour to cut me out of the wreckage with acetylene torches. I regained consciousness in the ambulance. As they put me on a stretcher to shift me to the medical facility, ghoulish spectators clamored for my autograph. I had the ambulance attendants put down the stretcher, and I lay there in my powder blue coveralls writing fiction on their programs. I had raced under the name of a man I particularly disliked, hoping *he'd* get into trouble.

"Monsieur McCabe. Monsieur Edward McCabe." Yessir, I was in the right place. Wait. I was jarred out of my stupor by the alien sound of the familiar name. I left Carolyn in line and went to the information desk on the main deck to see what this was all about.

The Rallye organization was inviting us to a small dinner in a private dining room for hot-shots and the press. Not feeling like much of a hot-shot, I assumed it was due to our status as members of the press. Or maybe it was our token-Americanism. No matter. No invitation before or since has ever been so welcome. I ran back to free Carolyn from the vile corridor.

We were so moved by the invitation, we arrived first. Other guests and our hosts started trickling in just seconds behind us. There was Suzanne Fournier and Patrick Verdoy of the Thierry Sabine Organisation, Jacky Ickx and his copilot, Christian Tarin, and many other shipboard luminaries. As it turned out, neither Vatanen nor Tambay were aboard, but there were more than enough interesting people and decent food to go around. There was a salad, which I wolfed down. And some kind of meat, which we didn't eat. But we dunked chunks of buttered French bread into the gravy and ate more than our fair share of vegetables. We were ravenous.

Responding to the page that was meant for me, a Scots motorcyclist named David McCabe had turned up by mistake. A burly, curly white-haired fellow with a rough and ruddy complexion and an infectious smile, his accidental presence and engaging personality brought some comic relief to the gathering. We sat with him, Jacky Ickx, and Patrick Fourticq, Pescarolo's copilot. McCabe and Fourticq fascinated me for reasons of a different nature than my fascination with the likes of Ickx and Pescarolo. I couldn't imagine what the allure could be to driving Paris/Dakar on a motorcycle. Nor could I quite fathom why someone would want to be the copilot in a racing car, a helpless passenger at the mercy of someone else's talent or lack of it.

In both cases, the reasons were simple and obvious. To D. McCabe, the attraction to doing Paris/Dakar on a motorcycle was as natural as it was for E. McCabe to want to do it in a car. He's a motorcycle person. It would never have occurred to him to drive it in a car any more than I would have considered doing it on a motorcycle. That's just the way it was. Still, I thought you had to be crazier to race through the desert on a motorcycle as opposed to the relative comfort and safety of a car.

Fourticq's motivations were even more obvious. It was almost the same as it was for me and Carolyn. He was more than Pescarolo's copilot. They were friends who shared the traits of daredevil adven- turers. Pescarolo is a great racing driver. So Fourticq would be the codriver in this adventure. Fourticq is a great pilot. He is the chief training pilot for Air France. After Paris/Dakar, they were going to circumnavigate the world in an old Lockheed Lodestar and try to break the speed record set by Howard Hughes. (They did, the following year.) Only in that adventure, Pescarolo would be copilot.

During the course of dinner, Ickx said to me, "You did well in the Prologue."

The official results had just been posted. We had placed 102nd out of 351, well up in the top third of the field, even with the mistakes. Nothing earth-shattering but respectable.

"Thanks. I didn't push and we made a couple of bad mistakes."

"It's silly to push. You did very well."

He pulled his chair in closer and began to offer some advice, like a father filling in the son on the facts of life. This was a role in which I had always felt comfortable. Throughout my career, I had been regarded as a bit of a "boy wonder," so I often found myself under the wing of older more experienced individuals who had helped guide me. Only in this case, I was the older man, listening intently to one who was seven years my junior. It felt funny, wrong. Somewhere along the line, I had slipped up into the less-exalted status of "man wonder."

Jacky Ickx is the opposite of an intimidating man. He doesn't put you off, he pulls you in. He is a magnetic man. Handsome, not tall, but with an athlete's build. You are drawn into what seems to be an almost naive openness, entering through the charming, boyish grin. I was riveted by this guy. I could see where women would be as well.

"Most people drive this race too fast, too soon," he confided to me. Usually, one-third of the field is knocked out in the first three days. Nearly half the contestants are out by the sixth day, never making it out of Algeria.

"Be cool, be steady," he advised. "Follow my advice and you'll be in Dakar in a good position."

He admitted that it would be hard on my ego, letting cars pass me and not passing cars I knew I could.

"Trust me," he said, "stop, relax, take a picture. Everyone who passes you, you will eventually pass."

"Do you study Zen?" I asked him.

"No." He smiled in his quiet, confident way. "I've done this before."

My mind was swimming with the advice as we went back to sleep amongst the lifeguards. At this point, we'd had a total of maybe five hours' sleep in forty hours.

The racket and bustle of people running down the hall knocking on doors woke us at six-thirty in the morning. It was January 2, but I didn't know what day it was. We'd started on New Year's morning. Since then, I'd lost track. Nights were already running into days, and it was to get worse. It took too much time to try to figure such things out, too much mental exertion. It was Day One in Africa, I knew that much.

We were rushed off the boat with a great sense of urgency and left standing on the dock waiting for the go-ahead to remove our cars from the sister ship. This came fairly quickly. I scrambled inside, picking my way over hold-down straps and chains, slithering through the narrow spaces between cars, finally squeezing into my own. Everybody was doing the same. As the chains were released, we moved forward in the big ship, all waiting to clear immigration and customs as we moved off.

All the running engines quickly filled the ship with noxious fumes, so I sat there coughing and choking on the poison, formulating a fantastic headache and a reasonable question. Why didn't someone tell these birds to keep their engines shut off until they actually had to move? I took it upon myself, walking up and down the lines of cars doing a choking and gagging pantomime. Some of the drivers actually took the hint and switched off.

I was a little worried about Algerian customs. So far the official-dom of this country had shown themselves to be a difficult lot. And my car had suspicious registration papers. At the last minute in Austria, Kaan had informed me that he couldn't get me an Austrian registration as was originally planned or I'd have to pay a 33 percent tax. Based on what this car had cost me, the tax would have been more than the price of *two* good cars. So Austrian registration was out of the question. Through a series of frantic last-minute calls, George Tradewell of Orion Motors got me a temporary Pennsylvania registration.

All I carried was a pink carbon from the application for temporary registration, chancy at best. I was worried that the Algerian bureaucrats would seize upon it as an excuse to detain, then possibly bend, fold, and mutilate me before my eventual slow execution, which would probably come as a result of being stapled to death. I have a vivid imagination.

When they looked at the pink paper suspiciously and started asking me questions in French, I pretended I didn't understand and spoke only English. Not wanting to be bothered with a hassle themselves, they stamped my passport and papers and sent me on with a bored shrug and an impassive look away.

Whenever we were stopped, which wasn't often, we went over the car. Tightening nuts and bolts, packing and repacking, that sort of thing. This latter mustn't be dismissed as a minor little nothing. Packing and repacking was Carolyn's job. In the back of the car, there were two large aluminum chests, two smaller aluminum cases, and a tool kit. Other than the case containing my killer flare gun and ammo and a first-aid kit, *everything* was in these five containers. No matter what we needed or when we needed it, these five cases had to be unstrapped, by loosening the big horizontal nylon strap holding them all together, the tool kit and the two smaller cases taken out of the car. Then the two straps holding down the big chests could be undone, the rearmost chest slid back so the lid on the other one could be opened.

We'd organized it so that items we needed to get to most often were in the smaller, upper cases. It was a good theory. But when we stopped and needed anything, we generally needed something from every case. So the whole affair had to be undone and put back together again. Many times each day. The tool kit and small aluminum cases weighed about fifty pounds apiece, the large cases about 150 pounds each. Just sliding them back and forth in their tracks required a major effort. Disassembling this stack of boxes was hard. Reassembling them was harder. They only fit back together one way. Lifting them, turning, adjusting, and refastening them drew grunts and curses from Carolyn every time.

Once properly back in place, she'd ratchet the straps tight; they had to be very tight. The slightest movement in these cases could set up a momentum over bumps or at high speed that could cause the heavy cases to shift around and snap the straps. This was one of our biggest fears. If one of those taut and powerful straps let go, it could rip right through the big gas tank. That safety risk and the knowledge that without the cases held securely down we could go nowhere kept Carolyn attuned to the tightness of the cases. Though her patience was often severely strained, like now, after she had redone the lot having organized our camping gear for tonight.

"I need the air compressor," I yelled back at her.

"Why didn't you tell me when I had the cases all apart!" she fumed.

"I just thought of it," I replied.

I needed to top up the spares with air. I would carry a lot of extra air in them, enough to add some air to all the tires on the car without always having to get to the compressor itself, which was stowed in one of the bottom cases. That's what we were doing that morning in Algiers. Getting ready. Going over the car. Getting on each other's nerves. We had no one else's nerves to get on.

As we waited for the last of the concurrents to be processed off the boat, that's pretty much what everyone else did. They diddled, fiddled, and fidgeted. In the beginning, there wasn't much walking around or talking or laughing or joking. There was a lot of seriousness in the air. Even here it was gray, though warmer. The air was dense and tense. The motorcyclists seemed to be the only ones moving. Really big, most of them were. Looking even bigger in their padded leather suits, color-coordinated leather boots, and gauntlet gloves, like some race of moon men set down on the wrong planet. They shuffled around, not talking to anyone, not even amongst themselves. There was a Finn, at least I think he was, maybe a Russian. He must have been six-ten easy. He had a big, round face with crazed black eyes, blond hair, and a dopey Jimmy Connors kind of haircut. Bangs all around. Gave me the creeps, this one did. The head moon man. He looked weird, even among the strange.

I was just sitting in the car watching all the others. Not just sitting. Squirming. My stomach was in an uproar. I had to go to the john, but there was no john to go to. I ripped my little plastic bottle from its Velcro mount and peed into it to relieve some internal pressure, hoping I'd be able to hang onto the rest.

They were going to parade us through Algiers to the starting point. From there, we had a 623-kilometer liaison to Ghardaïa. They lined us up according to number. I was between Dupard and Gooding again, and we were right up front with all the factory-team cars. The Barger, of course, didn't like this and moved up along the right and tried to squeeze in front of us and into a pack of Peugeot team cars. The marshalls had to put him back in his place again. This guy was in a hurry even when we weren't going anywhere. What a pain in the ass.

His need to speed just slowed things down for everybody else. *No way he'll ever make it to Dakar,* I thought.

We finally got out of there, moving through Algiers in parade for- mation.

It didn't look like Africa. At least not like anybody's common con- ception of it. The city seemed to consist of moderately wide avenues lined with a bunch of boring, concrete buildings. The tops of some of them were crenellated like castle turrets—the only hint that we might be in Africa, not Cincinnati.

There was less of the craziness that attended our arrival in Paris or Barcelona, but the Algerians were demonstrative nonetheless. Along the way, clusters of people stood on the roofs of houses, cheering and waving at us. We arrived at a bridge where we stopped, waiting for the motorcycles to be flagged off. We got out of the car and took a walk around. It wasn't that we needed the exercise, nor were we at a loss for other things to do. But we didn't know when we were going to be called upon to move, so we were reluctant to begin any serious work on the car. So, no harm in walking.

Carolyn had made friends with Mike Doughty, the copilot of Shekar Mehta in one of the Peugeot team cars. She went over to get some tips on navigation and some advice on marking the route book. An Algerian came up to me to talk. He made me nervous. Algerians made me nervous. This one was carrying a brown paper bag. Naturally I assumed there was a bomb in it, so I talked to him nervously, distract- edly. They all looked threatening to me. Many had severe facial scars, which looked to be the result of fighting with knives, and many had horrid pocked complexions, as though ravaged by disease. I don't re- member this Algerian's face. All I remember is his bag. And his dirty, black, pointy shoes.

"You American?" he asked.

"Yes," I replied, backing away a little, worrying that he was going to pass me his bag.

"I was in America once. In New Jersey."

"Oh, that's nice. Did you like New Jersey?" I asked him lamely.

"Yes, very nice. My brother is a doctor there. Long way away, America."

"Sure is. Yes, it sure is." I didn't know what to say. I didn't want to say anything, wanting only to be alone.

He wandered away, taking his bag with him.

At this point, everything, everyone, seemed threatening to me. Why was I being so paranoid? It must have been the strain, the unfamiliar environment, the fear of the unknown, the fear of the known, of what was coming. That was enough to get paranoid about. It's good to be on your guard. But bombs in bags? Come on, man! I had to pull myself together.

We just sat there, for an hour, maybe an hour and a half, all in a line, waiting. A few times we got out and walked around, or we'd sit in the car and try to snooze or talk about navigation. We looked over the damage to the front end and the camera mount again. Carolyn had the idea that a couple of strong guys could bend the whole thing back into position with their bare hands. Maybe. Bare hands with crowbars in them.

After a while they moved us out from under the bridge, around the median, and down the other side of the road, facing south toward the desert. We lined up Le Mans style, rear ends to the curb, noses out diagonally. Then everybody got out of their cars and walked up and down the line, chatting with friends, or doing last-minute car work. I stopped and talked with Dupard, which was hard because he spoke only French and very quickly in a highly animated style.

As we talked, he poured some liquid through a steel grate by the curb. After that he reached into the back of his car and drew out something which was wrapped in rags, long and thin, the shape of a couple of shock absorbers. With a flourish he unfurled the rags and as if by magic revealed a salami, which he then presented to me with great and obvious pleasure. I couldn't very well tell him that his treasure was wasted on us non-meat eaters, so I accepted it with appreciation. A Genoa salami, that's what it was. He reached inside again, this time withdrawing a bottle of chianti.

"*Nous ne bouvons pas*," I told him.

He gave me a sad little smile with a shrug and put the bottle back inside. I wondered what else he had in there. A pizza oven? I questioned the fate of whatever it was to myself. How much of this competition commissary would make it to Dakar? I was amused by Dupard, but he was not a joke. He finished thirty-seventh in the Prologue.

I walked up the line, salami in tow. I stopped and talked to Jacky Ickx. He joined me in my stroll. We stopped for a word with Pescarolo and Fourticq. Fourticq and Ickx then took me over and introduced me to Vatanen. Tall, blond, and good looking, he leaned against his car sunning himself, with his coveralls zipped open to his waist. The handsome Scandinavian face was slightly twisted in appearance due to a rather large scar creasing one cheek and his upper lip. He didn't act crazy. Seemed quite nice actually. I asked him about his problem in the Prologue. He threw a wheel in the middle of it. As a result, he would start the first speciale stage tomorrow in 282nd position, 180 places behind me.

I really had to go to the john. So I followed my salami back to the car and handed it over to Carolyn for safekeeping.

"What are we going to do with *that*?" she asked in too loud a voice.

I whispered, "It's from Dupard and I couldn't refuse. Act like you're happy with it." I whispered some more, "He's watching."

Dupard was standing right next to us, smiling with anticipation, as though he expected Carolyn to run over and give him a big kiss in gratitude for his chivalrous act.

As if she could read my mind, Carolyn went over and gave him a kiss in thanks, all the time smiling and babbling very quickly in English, something like, "What's wrong with you, you silly French goofball, don't you know we're vegetarians and will throw your stupid salami away as soon as we get a chance?"

Of course Carolyn knew that Dupard didn't speak a word of English. He thought she was praising him to the skies. She was always doing things like that to shake me up, pulling jokes that made me uncomfortable and nervous.

We were parked in front of the Algerian version of a shopping center. Which means it was pretty much like any small shopping center anywhere, only here they ran out of cement about halfway through. There were a few stores, shops, and restaurants standing brightly between unfinished, unglazed black spaces. It looked like the inside of an old man's mouth. I managed to find a toilet, becoming aware that I'd contracted some kind of bug. Maybe it was my system adjusting to the malaria pills or all the vitamins and supplements and salt tablets I was taking.

Feeling a little better, I found a coffee shop on the way out, got myself a tea, a coffee for Carolyn, and a couple of croissants. All either of us had eaten so far that day were a couple of granola bars and some dried rice cakes. It was about two o'clock in the afternoon. All the waiting made me lazy and lackadaisical. It seemed like they'd never get us going. I shuffled out, taking my good, sweet time.

As I emerged back into the street, I saw that the car in front of Dupard was being flagged off. I ran, sloshing hot tea and coffee all over myself. Carolyn was beside herself. Where had I been? We would have incurred a major penalty if I'd been one minute longer. This is why you're never supposed to leave the car. Vacations, even brief ones, aren't allowed. If you are unable to start when you're called upon to start, they start you last. But they start the clock on you from the time you were originally meant to go.

We got off, unable to finish our coffee and tea, unable to even get ourselves strapped in. We were due in Ghardaïa at 1:14 A.M., knowing little of what lay in between.

A liaison is not supposed to be a race. You are allowed adequate time to reach your destination without risking life and limb. Didn't all the other cars know that? As soon as we reached the outskirts of Algiers, Gooding passed me, going like a bat out of hell. He was no slouch as a driver, had finished forty-second in the Prologue. About where we would have been if it wasn't for the mistakes.

Damn! Watch out. I had to keep a leash on my ego or it would get me into trouble.

For a while I trailed Gooding down the narrow tarmac road, reminded of my old rallying days when we blasted down back roads outside of Chicago. We didn't have to race. It was our egos made us do it. Slipstreaming Steve Wendt at night on narrow little country lanes at over a hundred miles an hour. In the rain yet. Crazy days. This guy Gooding even looked like Wendt. Soon the Barger blasted by both of us. No surprise there. He was always trying to get to tomorrow today. There must be something about the present that he found unacceptable. And he struck me as the kind of driver who would soon be relieved of that burden.

The sun was blinding off the tarmac. The road looked like it had been paved with a mixture of tar and old broken mirrors.

About three-thirty in the afternoon, I saw a gas station up ahead on the right, so I peeled off of Gooding's tail and turned in. I didn't need gas, but Suzanne said to get it whenever we could. It only took a few minutes to top up. On our way again, cars kept rushing by. This was an open two-lane road, the road that led to the desert, though we could see the desert was already beginning off on each side. Crusty reddish rock was becoming interspersed with wind-rippled puddles of sand.

Every so often a car would come up from the opposite direction. Some local heading toward Algiers, I supposed. That didn't stop the loonies who, not satisfied to just pass us on the straight parts, would slide by us on the outsides of turns, which must have given heart failure to some of the drivers of oncoming cars. What was wrong with these guys, I kept wondering. Couldn't they wait to die?

By 4:30 P.M., the sand puddles had grown into lakes with a six-inch chop disfiguring the surface. The rock was still red. But there were now only lonely slabs of it floating in the sand and a few boulders strewn around looking rusty and ravaged, like abandoned cars. We drove through occasional rocky passes, climbing up into and down out of them rather quickly. We were going about seventy or eighty miles an hour and each successive ridge became lower, as though setting the stage for the fact that we were gradually descending into some hellish pit and the devil himself had filed down these ridges, tilting us too easily, unsuspectingly, into his loathsome realm.

Snaking through one such pass, car 213, a Range Rover driven by René Boubet, roared by at well over a hundred. Coming out of the pass minutes later, there was a non-competing car stopped by the side of the road, and a police car coming from the opposite direction with its lights flashing. A large cloud of dust hung in the air. Off to the side and down in a ravine was Boubet's car, with a wrinkled roof and no windshield. The scenario was obvious from the squiggle of black tire marks in the road. Boubet had obviously swerved to miss the oncoming car and plunged down into the gulch. I was reminded of that line from the film, *The Godfather*, "Pain in the ass innocent bystander!" I didn't stop. The police were there. They must have been coming the other way and seen the whole thing happen.

Shaken by danger's near proximity, I pulled off the road a few minutes later, in need of a deep breath and some hot food. We were past hungry. The sun was setting and cast a cold reddish-purple light over the dry sea of sand. And the temperature sank with the sun. In the chill, we unstrapped the cases and broke out our camp stoves. Hot soup and some brown rice was what we needed. I siphoned some water into a pan from my tank and put it on the stove to heat. We made vegetable soup, drinking it out of large, clear, plastic mugs, warming our hands gratefully on them. I drained some more water into another pan, this one for the pouches of rice. While putting it on the stove, I was shaking so much from the cold that some water sloshed out of the pan and onto the stove, squelching the flame with a quick, cold hiss.

We'd been there over half an hour already, the sun was almost gone, the wind howling and whipping up eddies of sand. We were at the approach to the Sahara Desert, the reddish rock piles having become more scattered, revealing large open expanses of sand marked only by occasional clumps of dead weeds. We crouched behind the car to protect ourselves from the wind, and the cold dug at us like we were getting acupuncture with icicles.

I've been to Minnesota in the winter where it was so cold my pee tinkled onto the snow in solid, golden pieces. I've spent time in northern Sweden, where even long saunas and massive doses of alcohol couldn't warm me. But I've never felt cold like this. We were warned, well warned. The cold at night in Algeria, everyone had told us, was unbearable, indescribable. It was. It was so cold, most of the brain cells I need to describe it were destroyed in the act of experiencing it. It is a hollow, silent cold that makes you feel turned inside out, your most vulnerable parts hanging outside of you. It is a sneaky cold that penetrates your organs before you ever notice it on your skin. And once its chill slips its blades into you, there is no getting them out. Not even in the hot sun of day when your skin is burning. Your insides still shiver. You feel the painful memory of it slicing through your chest, as though you've eaten too much ice cream too fast.

In this sort of atmosphere, we weren't about to fumble around trying to get the stove relit. Why people call this time of day "nightfall," I've never quite understood. It's the day that falls. Here, it plummeted, leaving us standing in the icy instant night, trembling and afraid.

We packed up and left, hitting the road with the heater on high to keep the unseen ghosts that had crept into us from getting the upper hand. As we drove, we ate more granola bars. But they just kept us alive, not really relieving our deep, inner emptiness. About nine that night, we came upon a gas station with a long line of Rallye cars, waiting. We joined the line.

I was beginning to realize what the racing was all about. It was to earn seniority in the gas lines. There were twenty-five or thirty cars waiting there for one man with one pump. There were bright fluorescent lights bathing the area around the pump. In the darkness, ringing the edges where the light lacked the strength or the will to penetrate, eyes stared out at us.

While waiting, Carolyn was doing her unpacking/packing routine. She'd taken the safety strap off the rear door and put it down on the ground. As she turned back inside the car, a pair of eyes flew out of the dark, whisked up the strap and back into the darkness, settling into their spooky vigil once again. The driver of the car behind us came up and warned us not to take our eyes off of anything for even a second, gesturing to the thieving eyes lurking in the shadows. From then on, we were unable to give anything our full attention, a part of us always on guard, on the defensive. As if we weren't already edgy and defensive enough.

We decided to take advantage of the delay. Carolyn had a good idea.

"Let's take our tow rope," she said, "attach one end to the bent front bumper, the other to a telephone pole, and try to pull the bent bumper back into place."

We pulled out of the gas line. I tied one end to the front of the car, walking the other end toward the pole. There was a cop standing nearby directing traffic in the line. He came over and put a damper on the plan, not being very nice about it in typical Algerian fashion.

"Okay," I said to Carolyn, inspired by this negativism, "let's attach it to the car in front. When he pulls forward, *he'll* straighten it out."

The driver in front agreed to try. But the cop didn't like that idea either. The maneuver required taking up an extra car length, and the cars were now lined up out into the main road. Carolyn and I gave up, conspiring to find an unguarded phone pole somewhere down the road. Another driver came up to talk. Most of these chats were held in French, mind you. From him we learned that this station only had regular gas. We needed super. He told us there was a station with super a few miles down the road. We left having lost one hour and one rear door safety strap. Our only gain was a few additional degrees of dislike for Algerian officialdom.

Now I began driving a little crazily like Gooding, Boubet, the Barger, and all the rest. We were running out of time. Every car that passed us I now saw as a threat, every one we passed a gain. I wanted to beat as many as I could into the next gas line.

We came upon another station about 11:00 P.M. This one had super as well as an even longer line. I didn't see any eyes staring out of the dark, but I knew that they were there. We began the unpacking procedure, looking for a spare strap to replace the one that had been swiped. The unseen eyes materialized into a gang of ragged children who surrounded our gear stacked up on the ground. Carolyn tried to shoo them away. They stood their ground, looking at our cases and duffels greedily. I guarded the stuff while Carolyn unearthed a spare strap from the bowels of a chest, the second of the pair we'd bought in Versailles. A couple of them ran up to the front of the car.

"Go guard the front!" I told Carolyn.

She rushed up, trying to chase them away from there. I spoiled their tactic by standing firm in back, watching over the piled-up cases. They moved off in search of easier pickings.

Though this line was longer, it moved a little faster. We were out of there about twelve-fifteen. We had an hour to go, and we figured we could make it to our destination in half an hour. So we drove along fairly slowly, on the lookout for a pole. We didn't have to work too hard at that. There was a full moon, a cold, blue-white disk hanging opaquely, a million miles in front of a transparent purple-black sky. This moon was so bright any stars that might have been out faded into the depths of the background.

Any poles trying to escape our notice were dreaming. Their long shadows bent sharp and black across the silvery road. We passed a whole row of short, stubby posts, markers lining the edge of a curve. I pulled over. In the eerie light and under the almost superfluous glow of our headlights, I wrapped the tow line around the bent bumper and around one of the poles, motioning Carolyn to back away slowly. The line went taut, and quivered.

I urged Carolyn back, afraid that the line would begin to twang, sending out a cry for help to the dread Algerian police. Back she inched and a small creaking sound began to form, expanding, extending itself into a plaintive wail. And then the post popped right out of the ground. Surrendered without resistance. *Strong car*, I thought. Either that or all the poles in Algeria are wimps. That must have been why they needed police protection.

We made it to the end of the stage with only minutes to spare. I started out thinking I had all the time in the world, wound up barely having enough. Our card was stamped, and we lumbered over rocks and boulders into the immense dish-shaped bivouac. There were lights everywhere. Bright driving lights mounted on trucks, car's headlights, and driving lights, free-standing floodlights on skinny metal stands, and hundreds of people walked around with bright little miner's lights shooting shaky rays from their heads. We had these too. It looked like some kind of night mining operation going on in the crater of an extinct volcano.

For a place we were supposed to be going to sleep, there was an awful lot of activity. Cars were up on jacks while crews worked on them under the glare. Some people were putting up tents. I was sorry we didn't have one, but Suzanne had told us in Paris that a tent wouldn't be necessary. That it was just another thing to worry about.

We drove through this bizarre display of energy being expended in the middle of nowhere, getting the feel of its strangeness, looking for a spot to park and bed down for the night. I picked a place away from the center, where there was a little less noise and flashing of light. But the rumble of generators, the crack and hammer of tools powered by compressed air was inescapable.

We found a vacant patch of dirt and began clearing it of rocks. It seemed like all this light, all this noise, and all these people should have had a warming effect. Not even a little. It was cold. Bitter cold. It was nearly two in the morning, and we had neither the strength nor inclination to set up the camp stoves. While Carolyn put out the sleeping bags, I went to find the chow line, bringing back mugs of hot soup and chunks of crusty bread. We disposed of this quickly, and I went back for more. We finished these and Carolyn continued to put our camp in order. I surveyed the area immediately around us, propelled only by an undying trickle of nervous energy and a serious fear of getting undressed in that cold.

I stumbled across Boubet, working under some lights. He was unhurt and in the process of stretching chicken wire across the gaping hole where his windshield used to be. I talked to him. The accident had occurred as I'd imagined. He told me he'd asked the Range Rover factory team to lend him a spare windshield and that they had refused because he wasn't a member of the team. *The bastards*, I thought.

I looked down at the stony ground, and the realization of what was going on here hit me. Here was a guy going to race across the rocky Algerian wastes without a windshield! He'd be pulverized by flying stones and gravel. The chicken wire could only prevent the entry of boulders bigger than eggs. I was so moved by this display of courage and determination that I went and got Dupard's salami and brought it to him, handing it over with great reverence in an even sillier ceremony than the one in which Dupard had presented it to me.

13

About four-thirty in the morning, an icy gust of grit sailed into my sleeping bag. *Jesus, it's colder than it was when I went to "bed,"* I thought. The sleeping bag was inside a vinyl outer bag. Inside those I wore a pair of long underwear pants, two long-sleeve undershirts, a cotton jumpsuit over that, a pair of heavy cotton socks under a pair of heavy wool socks. A woolen hat covered my head. Yet I was freezing.

As tired as I was, the thought of returning to sleep was unthinkable. It was simply too cold. I guessed it was about fifteen degrees, which is not really all that cold. Statistical information can be very misleading. It felt colder than many below zero temperatures I've experienced. The sleeping bag was rated for temperatures down to zero. But it wasn't coping very well with this. Perhaps it was designed for the zero of a less hostile continent. I pulled on my camp boots, put the miner's light over my hat, grabbed a handful of the wooden paper I took from the Algerian ship and a shovel, and beamed my way up and over the rim of the crater. My stomach was in turmoil.

When I returned, the camp was coming to life. I woke Carolyn. We had to be at a drivers' meeting at 5:00 A.M. While she dressed and packed up the sleeping bags, I headed for the chow line. Zombies dragged themselves around the rocky bivouac. Dirty, unshaven, grim, and hollow-eyed men, they looked like refugees, shuffling around in tired circles. And the tiring part hadn't even begun. I got us coffee and tea, some more chunks of bread, and treated myself to a bowl of dry cereal. Carolyn had a stove going when I got back. At last we could have a hot pouchful of brown rice. We ate the rice in silence until a voice over a microphone summoned everyone to the meeting.

The concurrents stood in a solid block, tramping in place, hitting themselves with their hands, exhaling megaphone-shaped clouds of breath. Floodlights lit up the area. Still, it was dark. We saw Patrick Fourticq, David McCabe, and a few others we knew. We didn't talk. This wasn't a social gathering. Everyone was intent on the day's hardships, which were being outlined for us by the Rallye director who droned on endlessly, mindless of the fact that about a thousand people were standing before him freezing to death. Afterward, Suzanne translated the high, or low, points. It was unnecessary. We had understood most all the French. Today we had a short liaison, then a speciale, then another short liaison, about 450 kilometers in all. We were going to El Golea, wherever that was.

After the motorcycles were flagged off, beginning at 6:00 A.M. one every thirty seconds, the cars and trucks would begin. We would start in the order of our finish in the Prologue. Today we would start in ninety-eighth position. We had moved up four places since the Prologue. Four cars that had been ahead of us had already dropped out. One of the victims was the amiable, silver-haired Belgian who'd slipped into my car for a talk in Versailles. His souped-up engine had exploded on the way to Barcelona.

We had time to prepare for our start. Carolyn loaded film into her cameras. All except the lower front one, which she was very upset about. I sympathized with her. But getting the car ready was more important than the camera. A fact she accepted, but reluctantly. I taped the battery into the intercom system again. We couldn't risk this going out in the middle of a speciale. I would never be able to hear her warnings and instructions over the screaming engine and the noise of rocks hitting the suspension and the floor of the car.

I marked the steering wheel with tape at the point where the wheels were straight. That way I wouldn't accidentally come down from a jump with them turned and flip. I went through the daily maintenance routine. Checked the oil, emptied the dust separating valve on the air intake to the fuel injection system, beat the dust out of the filter pads covering the fuel cooler, tightened the lug nuts on all the wheels to 180 pounds of torque, checked the fluid level in the steering reservoir. While I was checking the air in the tires, Jacky came by in his little Lada, a lightweight Russian-made car that looked like a grasshopper skittering over the ground.

"Fairly straightforward today. Hard-packed sand. You shouldn't have any trouble."

I asked him about tire pressures. "Two point five," he advised. "And remember, take it easy. Don't race!"

He needn't have worried about that. The only racing I did that day was for the bushes, what few I could find. I had the runs. Lack of food was upsetting my system. Or maybe it was the salt pills. Or the lack of sleep.

After the short liaison, the Rallye wasted no time in getting down to the business at hand, that of beating the shit out of *all* the contestants. The first fifty kilometers or so of the speciale took us down a narrow, sandy trail with humps in it. We were often airborne, coming down with a prayer that there was no deep hole or other hazard where we crashed down on the other side. Occasionally we'd fly up at a leftward tilt, landing on the other side of a big hump, down on a trail that unexpectedly had a rightward tilt. At seventy or eighty miles an hour, our left wheels would touch down and we'd travel maybe fifty yards before the right wheels found the earth. Then for a hundred yards or so, we'd rock from side to side, wrestling with the gravity that wanted to throw us over.

Georges Groine, the man who ran the team of trucks that carried our spares, had defied gravity and lost. He was driving a huge Mercedes truck, one of two that had finished ahead of us in the Prologue. We came off a hump and there it was, framed in our windshield, over on its side. It was the size of a big-city garbage truck. Luckily for us, this particular truck carried none of our spares. Groine was a short, silver-haired, and chubby man. We'd met him at dinner on the boat. We saw him standing next to his overturned truck, looking small and puzzled, his hands on his hips. The crew was ranged around it with ropes, obviously hoping to pull it back upright. This looked to me like trying to bring a dead elephant to its feet. *Might as well try moving the Empire State Building*, I thought.

We dodged around the mammoth obstruction. Seconds later, we passed a motorcycle, also down on its side, off on the right. Jacky was right. No need to hurry. We'd do well by default.

We were in the Sahara now. The Sahara is not *a* place any more than America is *a* place. The Sahara is a collection of deserts. And they're all different, each with its own beauty and horror.

On this day, the scenery we raced through was reminiscent of the East Coast of the United States. Low dunes rolled up from each side of the track we squiggled down. There were no trees, only low-lying

clumps of yellowed grass. It was the seashore bemoaning the loss of
its sea.

Our wheels churned up billows of dust, which had a spicy pungency
to it. Where the aroma came from, I couldn't imagine. Perhaps it was
the grass decaying in the sun, releasing its last gasps of fading chlo-
rophyll. My impressions were fleeting, for we went very fast over
unfamiliar ground. My eyes—my entire repertoire of sensory
detectors—were too occupied for much mundane enjoyment. I con-
centrated on watching the ground fly toward the car, and on the
mirrors to make sure no one was overtaking, and on the compass,
always checking that we were on course. I listened for irregularities
in the beat and scream of the engine and drivetrain, sniffed at the air
focused only on detecting more fuel fumes than usual or the telltale
stink of burning wire that presages an electrical problem.

Carolyn looked out for long-distance dangers, that is anything over
fifty yards in front of us, the outside range of my attention span. Though
I do remember a long, long stretch of hard-packed sand, a flat maybe
fifty miles wide and seventy-five long. We were going along at top
speed, over a hundred miles an hour, with Carolyn calling out kilometers.

"Three."

A pause.

"Two."

A pause.

"Slow down, it should be coming up fast now."

She was alerting me to the location of a wadi that cut through the
flat. Suddenly we'd see it. Just a faint line in the sand, rapidly growing
into a trench three or four feet wide up close. Some of these were four
or five feet deep as well. They were dried-up streams, some of them
riverbeds. Some we had yet to meet were deeper and wider than the
Ohio or Mississippi rivers. Whether they were hundreds or thousands
or millions of years old, we had no way of telling. Some of the smaller
ones might have been formed as recently as a year ago, sometime when
a raging torrent of water moving too fast to penetrate the parched
ground had rushed along the surface of the desert, gouging out a
convenient course for itself, much as we were doing cutting across the
desert now.

Whenever we came to one of these wadis, we had to practically
stop, creep in, and then out the other side. If we hit one at high speed,
we'd flip end-for-end a half dozen times and the car would simply

disintegrate around us. I'd resume the high-speed run, slowing down only when approaching another wadi or when answering the call of nature, which must have rung at least ten times that day. I had a violent case of the runs.

Farther on, we came to a steep sandy pass and made it only halfway up before getting stuck. A few cars were dug in deep. It looked like they'd stay parked in the hill forever. There were press cars at the bottom. Photographers ran all around. A Chinese journalist I'd met at lunch on the boat came over and told me the best way to take the hill was at an angle from lower right to upper left. He suggested we back down the hill and take a long running start. We backed off nearly half a mile and charged at the wall of sand. The front wheels bit into the bottom of it at about eighty miles an hour. We churned, crablike, up and across, barely making it over the top just as we ran out of momentum. In my mirror I saw people waving and cheering as we popped over the top.

There was a fork in the trail then. Carolyn thought we were supposed to go left. We did. Soon we saw a car that had made the same decision coming back the other way. It was Ted Toleman in his green Land Rover, apparently lost or confused. We kept going. Not seeing another car, I asked Carolyn if she was sure this was the right way. She thought we were going correctly. I wasn't so sure and turned around. Soon we met a car coming the way we had been going. We stopped. So did he. We asked if he was sure this was right. He thought so.

So we turned around, heading back in the original direction. Ted Toleman tore past, having obviously concluded that this was the correct way, after all. This sort of thing was going on all the time. Cars coming and going in opposite directions. If you weren't sure of your navigation, it could become very confusing. It undermined your faith in yourself. Being inexperienced, we were particularly vulnerable to this.

It seemed like every car in the Rallye passed us that day. We'd be going along, doing very well, then I'd have to stop and answer the call and a half-dozen cars and trucks would pass. Just before approaching the finish line, in the late afternoon sun, Vatanen shot by in his factory Peugeot, sideways at about 135 miles an hour, his rear end eager to overtake everything in its path including its own front end. These Peugeots were amazing machines. In effect, they were detuned Formula One cars wearing little yellow plastic body shells that could fool you into thinking they were economy sedans—economy sedans that cost about a million bucks apiece. Vatanen had moved up 180 places in one of them, in one day. I wondered how many places I'd moved down.

We felt a wonderful sense of exhilaration as we crossed the finish line, but it was built on false hopes. It was about 5:30 P.M., the finish of the first speciale, our second day in Africa, but that was nowhere near the end of the day. There was still a liaison leg to go. Short though it was in distance, only thirty kilometers, it was absolute murder. We had to traverse maybe a dozen wadis. Some of them were half a mile wide and as much as forty feet deep, the bottoms full of boulders, unexpected patches of deep, soft sand and punishing cracks and ruts.

We came to the smallest, narrowest wadi at dusk. A car was stuck in it, blocking the trail. We went around to the right, looking for another place to cross. I found a ford (there was no water there though water had once formed this gulch, so I guess I can call it a ford) and made it through to the other side. Shortly after that, we rejoined the trail. Carolyn wanted me to back down the trail and pull the stuck car out. It was good karma, she said.

"You'll see, something good will come to us," she said, after we pulled out the car.

Farther on, in the dark, we came to a large, flat oasis of palm trees standing in deep, soft sand. We could see it clearly because of all the headlights. There were twenty or thirty cars and trucks spaced around facing in all directions at various degrees of crazy tilt, mired in the stuff. Ted Toleman was one of them.

Pass me, will you? I thought as we churned by, my big desert tires somehow pulling and paddling us through. Maybe it wasn't the tires, but our recently earned good karma.

Soon we came to the top of a hill, saw lights twinkling below, and followed a long, sandy trough that ran under high-tension wires down to the bivouac in El Golea. It was very dark, the moon being strangled by clouds, and I had on all the lights so we could pick our way around and between the poles.

I'm gluing these pictures together out of broken fragments of my memory. They do not go together with ease. I have kept these details piled in one large mound and covered with a sheet for some time now, preferring to retain and view the experience as a whole, an immense sculptural monument standing out from other occurrences and dimensions in my life. I have taken comfort in its abstraction, in its lack of specificity.

Now, as I yank off the sheet and try to examine each piece of minutiae, hoping to find clues pointing toward an overall meaning, the specific shape and substance of the event are still lost on me. Its overall significance or lack thereof remains shrouded in mystery, a puzzle I'm not sure ever needs to be solved.

"What was I doing there?" is one of those questions that may not need answering. If I was wise, I believe I would understand that it does not even need to be asked. I was there. What I was experiencing made little impression on me at the time, and little more even now. But I was experiencing. That meant I was alive. How many are alive without really knowing it? Still, I feel unwilling to settle for that.

In El Golea, broken shock absorbers littered the dusty main street, and I remember being revolted by it. The Rallye had been here before. Neither the defilers nor those defiled cared enough to do anything about it. I wished I wasn't there. I was in a line of cars waiting for gas. The line stretched the entire length of the town, which was small. Still, there must have been a hundred cars in it. So many days and nights I spent in these lines, yet I rarely saw a truck or a motorcycle in them. Where did they get their gas? Another question that didn't need answering. Or asking.

While we waited, we worked on the car. Carolyn emptied and reloaded the cameras. I torqued the wheels and so forth. There were always some small repairs to be made. We tried to sleep, but it was impossible. Just as we'd doze off, the car in front would move up a place and the inevitable Algerian cop would tap on the car, motioning us to move up or we'd lose our place in the line. Never had I suffered such hardship in order to pay anyone three hundred dollars. And always, the little scavengers, darting up to us and back, waiting for the best time to pounce.

These lines weren't all bad. While we waited we would squeeze in some yoga meditation, and that would bring us back to semiconscious-ness. This was the only time during the Rallye in which some degree of social interaction was possible. In this particular line, the car behind us was also crewed by a man and a woman. They were Swiss. He was also considerably older than she was. She was quite small and girllike, dark haired and pretty. I wondered how they were managing. We talked a little. The outcome made no lasting impression on me. All I remember is that they had a Range Rover with a five-litre Porsche engine. A very fast car. They told us there were three or four other man/woman teams in the Rallye and one all-girl team. I wondered what kind of steroids they all took.

Also in this line we met Klaus Seppi. A tall, handsome Italian who was driving a car almost identical to ours, one difference being that it had a lightweight kevlar body. Another difference was that he was in forty-eighth place. We had fallen to two hundredth. Although we weren't to learn this until the next morning.

Every morning the results of the day before were passed out at the driver's meeting, so we all knew how everyone else was doing. Every morning you were either exhilarated or embarrassed. For me, the fourth day of the Rallye, the third day in Africa, it was the latter.

I was moping around the car after the meeting when Jacky drove up, beaming.

"Congratulations! You lost a hundred places yesterday. I'm very proud of you."

He wasn't being facetious. He was completely in earnest, steadfast in his insistence that the quickest, surest way to Dakar was slowly. After congratulating me on my lousy performance, he briefed me on what the new day would hold.

"Put two bar in your tires. After the early rocky part, there's some soft sand. You're doing great. Don't race. After today you'll start moving up."

I was having trouble believing this. Already I was feeling a little punch-drunk, like a battered boxer whose trainer is in his corner telling him to hang in there for one more round and victory would surely be his.

We were hanging in. Four and a half hours, we had waited in that gas line. By the time we cleared a campsite of rocks, made ourselves some hot soup, and crawled into our frosty sleeping bags, it was well past midnight. Then we were up again at 4:00 A.M., fiddling with the car and the cameras, just to keep warm if nothing else. I got some tea, bread, and dry cereal from the chow line. All through the Rallye, the bread was good, baked locally and delivered every night. After break-fast, we listened to the outline of the day's course, then sped out into the desert to compensate the compass. We did this every morning.

Finding a large flat area free of metallic interference, we'd drive around in a big circle until the electronic compass corrected itself and locked in on a heading. It was a great piece of equipment. It could either display the heading or be programmed for a specific heading, and it would display the degrees plus or minus that we were off course. We'd use that format only when running flat out on long straight stretches. Other times we preferred the security of seeing our actual heading.

The compass corrected for the day, we'd drive back to the bivouac and get into the starting lineup. Luckily, the worse we did, the later we had to start. Unluckily, the later we started, the later we finished, arriving near the tail end of the gas lines, which Jacky had told me would get worse every day. That was because they became more primitive and therefore slower the deeper we moved into Africa. He continued to advise us to go slow though, even if it pushed us farther and farther back in the lines.

By this time I had no idea whether this was the third or fourth day of the Rallye. I was too hungry and tired to care. I think it must have been the fourth. I hoped so. That was better than the third. It meant there were only eighteen days to go.

I hadn't had a complete meal since the dinner on the boat, and that wasn't much of one, either. A shower? I couldn't remember back that far. It must have been five days. In the car, we ate dust and granola bars. I was beginning to suffer severe hunger pains, but at least the runs were going away. There was nothing more in me to come out.

Today we had a short liaison from El Golea to Chebaba. Then, a long speciale, five hundred kilometers, from Fogaret to In Salah. These names, they meant nothing to me. They were then and remain now as meaningless to me as they must be to you. They were not places we were meant to notice or stop in and enjoy. They were obstacles we had to get past. The terrain we crossed in between is memorable only in pieces.

Mostly I remember the dust, the driving blind. The choking and coughing, even though we wore paper filter masks. I remember the tiredness, the nodding off at the wheel, even when we were going very fast, the feeling of hopelessness and futility at keeping going. I can still taste the chalky dryness in my mouth. My lips became caked with mud from the dust that coagulated as a result of water dribbling out of the tube, which was as much a part of my mouth as my tongue, only much more useful. On the bumps I would bite the tube and the tongue. The tube didn't bleed. I remember blowing my nose and being astounded at how any human system could continue to function on what I had been inhaling. By now, the skin on my fingertips was shredded from the stitching on the wheel. My racing gloves had already worn through.

There were incidents, little meaningless incidents that have stayed in my mind. At the end of the first liaison of the fourth day, I headed for the hills to go to the john again. I remember taking down my pants and being scared of scorpions. This was the place they had been talking about, the place where the organization had seen them when they had come through a few weeks before, checking the route. As we lined up for the beginning of the speciale, I backed up to get into position, and backed into another car. I was tired, not paying attention to where I was going.

You'd think I had killed this guy's child. I scratched his car, and he carried on like I couldn't believe. By now, most of these cars had already begun to look like they'd been parked for the summer on a driving range. And this guy was yelping over a little dent and a rather nasty scratch. Didn't he realize it was highly likely that before this race was over his car would be ripped to pieces? This was more of a demolition derby than a *concours d'elegance*. I was sorry, but quickly stopped feeling bad about it because of the way he went on. He must have been delirious too. We were all delirious. Why else would any of us be doing this? What else could we be, doing what we were doing on little or no sleep?

The day had dawned clear and cloudless. At about 10:00 A.M., as we lined up for the speciale, the sky held an iridescent blue. It seemed low and glaring, even when the sun was not directly in my field of view. The entire sky lowered itself down, and I felt its full weight pressing in on my eyes. It made me feel weak. The flu was trying to come back, but I was fighting it off with extra vitamins and stubborn refusal.

We took off into rocky wastes, covered with a thin film of sand. Just enough to kick up a blinding cloud of dust, obliterating everything our lives depended on us seeing. The stony track was much harder on us and on the car than the sand had been. It was rougher, with sharp, jagged rocks jutting out and up at us from every angle. We passed many cars that had stopped for tire changes. The rocks were less red and more granite-colored now. The sun glinting off the glassy little flecks in them hit me in the eyes with cutting kicks of light. We drove into an overall blinding whiteness from the dust. Like climbing out of the uppermost cloud in a plane.

What I could see was disturbing. What I couldn't see, that was worse. A couple of times, driving fast in these conditions, some inner voice bade me to just jam on the brakes. We'd sit for a few seconds and wait for the cloud of dust to clear. Once I was about to go off a cliff, another time I was a foot short of crashing into a big boulder. Both times we just sat there, shaken, catching our breath before moving on. Hoping some car or dreadnaught of a truck that was also flying blind didn't crash into us from behind.

Out in the barren, open, sandy stretches, I fought the wheel. The car kept wanting to drift to the left, and I had to force the wheel to the right to hold the car in a straight line. I was worried that I'd already knocked the front end out of alignment on the bumps.

We would go along feeling the day but would actually see it only in shreds and patches. Against the azure crispness of the sky, everything else looked vague, somber hues whose contrast to the sky were useful primarily for signaling the difference between up and down. Even these directions became confused, balled up within each other, because we were so often disoriented from the gyrations we experienced in the cockpit while rollicking over ruts and mounds. And from giddiness induced by being deprived of food and sleep.

We felt the day more than we saw it, mostly by sensing the heat of the sun and because of the tiring blue brightness that hovered at the outer edges of the bleached cloud we continually traveled in. As night crashed down on us, we drove in the same cloud, a little more blinding, perhaps, because it threw our own lights back into our faces and the periphery of it was black rather than blue. That was the subtle difference between night and day. The only other delineation being the cold that crept into the car and jabbed at us even with the heater on. Then I'd wonder what it must be like for the motorcyclists, the cold they must be feeling, the abuse they must be taking. And poor Boubet with his porous windshield. Poor, crazy people.

Occasionally I still had to stop and relieve my jittery stomach, though not as often as the day before. Carolyn was finally forced to abandon the last vestiges of feminine vanity and would no longer try to run off and hide. She'd just squat beside the car like me. Like everybody else. This *wasn't* ballroom dancing.

Fewer cars seemed to pass us, though. I didn't know if it was because I was going faster or if I was so far back in the pack that anybody who could pass already had. It was a long day, I remember that. But whether it was the third the fourth or fifth day, I had no idea. Now, I know it was the fourth. But then, it was all just one long day that sometimes grew cold and strangely dark at the edge of my perception.

We didn't sleep at all that night. We got in late, waited in line for gas until four-thirty in the morning, only to rush breathless and still unwashed to the drivers' meeting at five. After the meeting, we were working on the car when Jacky tooled up in his.

"You only lost twelve places yesterday. The worst is almost over. Soon it starts getting much easier."

He knew I was in need of propping up.

I told him I thought I'd knocked the front end out of line.

"Which direction is it pulling?" he asked me.

"To the left. I have to hold it to the right," I told him.

"Don't worry about the car," he said, "it's the wind."

Of course! I was driving in a crosswind. Again I felt like a ninny, but there was no way to know. At sea, you have the surface waves to help you read wind direction. On land, you look at the trees. In the desert, lost in a continuous cloud of dust, there is nothing to go by but your experience. And of this, I had none.

He briefed me on the fifth day's race, a long one, about six hundred kilometers of speciale with a couple hundred kilometers of liaison thrown in. The early part would be rocky, mountainous, and slow, then it would become flat and fast. Finally, there would be a very long, badly undulating stretch.

"You have to drive this part very fast," he warned me, "or you'll shake your car apart."

"How fast?" I asked. "A hundred?"

"A hundred-twenty is better. Go back to two point five in your tires."

"You ever do anything easy?" I asked him, jokingly.

He didn't joke back, saying only, "It's hard." And after a long pause, "Very hard."

14

his day—the fifth—has stayed as clear to me as the previous one remains hazy. There is no explaining this phenomenon other than perhaps to say that some days my mind was blurred with fatigue and others it was sharp, though no less fatigued.

Because we were starting a little later every day, as we fell behind, we had some more time in the mornings to organize things. As always, I went over the engine and wheels, checking and tightening. Carolyn would unload and reload the cameras. These had her more than a little distressed. She wasn't getting many pictures, she said. As sophisticated as the camera rigging was, they kept shaking loose from their mounts from all the bumping and pounding. The lower front camera remained unmountable due to the damage sustained in the Prologue. The inside cameras hung limply from their ball joints, pointing down instead of out, like dead flowers. Only the rear camera and the one on the right front fender had been working. These cameras and the problems she was having with them had begun to bore me.

"I've got to go find our trucks," I told her. "Please will you forget the cameras and go over the car?"

Aside from all the checking and tightening of the car, the seemingly simple task of straightening up and getting the cockpit organized for the day was a prodigious one. Morning would always find it strewn with maps, torn-off pages from the route book, odd bits of scribbled-over paper, food wrappers, scuzzy plastic bottles that contained the residue of the previous day's mineral supplements, as well as bottles full of more personal waste.

"But I've got to get pictures. It's the reason I'm here," she complained, near to tears yet again.

"Forget the damn cameras," I snapped at her. "We'll fix them when we can. The car comes first. We can survive without the pictures but not without the car."

I understood her desperation to get pictures. She had virtually dropped her photography business to go on the Rallye. She had been counting on coming back with great photos. I was just as sorry she wasn't getting any as she was. I had got her cameras, film, a car to put them on, and a rigger to install them. But my patience was wearing a little thin from her carping.

I went off to make contact with the two trucks carrying our spares. We hadn't yet had a moment to seek them out. I found both trucks, introduced myself to their crews, and made a mental note of the location of our chests and tires on each one. I had a hunch we'd soon need to get at some of the parts they carried.

When I returned to the car, I brushed my teeth, I think I shaved and made a feeble attempt at washing. Then we headed off into the desert to compensate the compass. Carolyn was still emotional about the state of her cameras. I was becoming hardened to these displays. I didn't have the energy, just didn't have enough left over to devote to commiseration. I had a long, long race to drive today and was falling asleep at the wheel before it even started.

Fifty-four cars and trucks were already out of the running. I wasn't counting motorcycles. You could see in the bivouac how the ranks were being thinned. The chow line was less crowded. Those still there were looking more and more like displaced refugees. The starting lineup was less crowded too. I think the guy whose car I scratched went out yesterday. Anyway, I didn't see him anywhere near the start.

Toleman was out, and his nice Danish navigator with him. Boubet was still going strong, even with no windshield. He was in 17th place only minutes behind the leader, who was Mehta in a factory Peugeot. Vatanen had moved up to ninth place, having caught and passed most of the field. He wasn't world champion for nothing. Jacky Ickx was in 10th place, right behind Vatanen. In 13th place, fueled by salamis, was Dupard. Behind Boubet, in 18th place were Pescarolo and Fourticq. Seppi, in the Mercedes like mine, was in 36th position. Gooding was 40th. I had plunged to 212th. Now there were only seventy-six behind me. At least I was still in. And as Jacky said, if I hang in, I'll move up.

My last meal and my last good night's sleep were becoming faint, distant memories. Yet my head was remarkably clear. Almost as clear as this day, which had risen as quickly as the one before fell. It was clear, bright, and sunny. The ground was a dusty, white hard-packed sand. It gave off a pulsing dazzle that reached up to the sky, bleaching out the blue. We were flagged off with strained smiles. The TSO personnel were starting to look as beat as the contestants they were trying to destroy.

We started off with a long run on what looked like a salt flat. Intermittent ripples disrupted its seemingly placid surface. As we sped along, we were often airborne. I was depressed about our poor standing and kept my foot to the floor. In the beginning, the course was marked out with stakes. I went outside of them, seeing that there were fewer undulations there. Cars and trucks bucketing along the lumpy track were unable to match our pace. I passed about six. Every so often I paid for it. The surface was hard and flat, but now and again we'd hit a ridge, larger than the lumps on the marked out track. Hitting one at ninety to a hundred miles an hour launched us into the air where we'd remain for a nerve-racking interval before landing heavily, rocking precariously and noisily.

We were heading toward a mountainous pass. The highest and longest we had yet encountered. I couldn't see it yet, but Carolyn could, on our maps and a couple of pages ahead in the route book, which was full of dark, black warnings. I wanted to get some passing over with before it became too dangerous to do so. We knew where we were headed passing would be next to impossible. We raced on for another hour or so, at top speed, catching and passing many cars and all but a handful of the trucks. Then the going got pretty rocky.

After the world was created, after the sixth day, there were some leftovers. They were all dumped here. All the stuff nobody wanted. All piled up and solidified through millennia. We were entering a no-man's-land, a moonscape on earth, so grotesque it was beautiful.

Most of the rock was black and porous. An unearthly volcanic slag heap. It was piled high in places, in vast heaps, perhaps a couple thousand feet high. We were bouncing up into it. The rock was all pocked and gouged, layer upon layer of it. Much of the stone was loose. The big Michelins clawed into it, but the surface would shift and slide underneath. At times we would be going nearly straight up. Up steep vertical inclines with shaky, moving surfaces, praying that the tires had a grip on something solid somewhere or we'd begin sliding backward with no hope of regaining our footing.

Other times we'd be heading nearly straight down, the surface rock scuttling out from in front of us as I applied the brakes. It raced ahead of us down the hill. I snapped the wheel back and forth, sliding through turn after turn, worried that the sidewalls of the tires might be stabbed by the black, needlelike daggers that thrust their points at us on the outsides of every turn. Or worse, that they would prove too small and insignificant to arrest our sideward momentum and that we'd roll over and plunge down out of sight over the edge.

From the higher vantage points, we could see that we were strung out in a line of cars and trucks, all trying to pick our way through the petrified garbage. Cresting one of these ridges and heading down the other side, the trail widened slightly, enough for me to squeak by one or two other competitors before heading up the other side. Then I pulled away, gaining considerable distance on whoever was behind. Unlike cars that were built for flat-out speed, ours was made for this. I swear the car could go up a greased pole.

We were halfway through the pass, having gained maybe a dozen more places and about to cross over the highest jagged peak of rubble when Carolyn started yelling "STOP! STOP!" through the intercom. That brought back memories. I looked at her quizzically, lacking the energy or will to speak.

"I want to stop and take a picture," she said.

"Can't you get it with the fender camera?" I asked her.

"No, I want to get out and get a wide angle of the whole thing. Please."

I remembered Jacky's words, "Stop, take a picture." I pulled over onto the side. There were no shoulders on these tracks, so the car was heeled, two wheels up on the chunky, black rubble. I walked up to the peak with her, and she shot a whole roll. I've never seen Death Valley. I don't need to. There were three more, and slightly lower ridges still to cross, then the valley stretched out beyond for a distance of forty or fifty miles. The day was hot, the sun was high, yet a chill coursed through my body. I looked at endless acres of baked white powder sitting in a vast black dish, emanating quivering shafts of torrid complaint back up toward the heavens that left it burning there in eternal misery. Black stone boulders were strewn helter-skelter across the surface, relics of a forgotten era lying there, throbbing in the heat. I turned away and shuddered.

The stop cost us three or four of our newly gained positions. Oh well, if I could stop to relieve myself of the intestinal jitters, I guess she could stop to snap pictures of the environment that was generating them. We moved on, me sucking water furiously in preparation for what was to come.

The deserts all looked menacing, but it was the entrances and exits to them that were really threatening. We passed through the valley fast, without incident, shooting up a tall plume of white dust and passing a few more cars and trucks along the way. Like so many things in life that seem frightening or impassable, the perils of the valley turned out to be more symbolic than real.

Coming out the other side, we found even the ridges less intimidating than those going in.

We entered the fast part that Jacky had told us would come. The powdery white sand changed into a coarser variety, deep yellow and hard-packed. For about an hour, we drove flat out on it, between 105 and 110 miles an hour. Way off in the distance, on both sides of us, roseate lines of cliffs walled us in but not very tightly. It looked as if we were on the floor of what had once been a large lake or a sea, now being sailed over by an armada of strange landships.

The oddest looking, of course, were the trucks. Out here in the desert, far from civilization, we looked off into the distance toward one of the rock walls and saw a smear of black smoke across the top of it. Somehow one didn't expect to see an enormous truck emerge at the end, belching diesel smoke and shattering the boundless stillness with its air horns. It was like encountering a mammoth in its original, prehistoric habitat. And being stunned to find that it was made of metal and trumpeted along at over eighty miles an hour. I'd begun to grow accustomed to these strange visions, yet remained awed by their surreality.

Racing along this former lake, the contestants were stretched out in a line maybe thirty miles long across a front a few miles wide. A gauzy curtain of dust hung in the air a hundred feet high, and I raced along one side of it. Inside the car everything was coated with dust. We had given up on the dust masks. Coarse unfiltered dust was no harder to digest than the fine filtered variety. Besides, the masks made us feel claustrophobic. Now our faces were free to breathe directly the stale and dusty air that hovered thickly inside the theoretically sealed car.

Sometimes I spit fresh water into my daily diaper, which by this time every day was brown and mud-caked, and wiped my face with it. It didn't get me clean, just wet the dust, which redried in streaks. But for the moment, it felt refreshing. For food, we'd taken to cutting open the pouches of brown rice and eating the contents unwarmed as we went. We rarely had time to get our camp stoves going. Whenever we tried they hadn't worked very well anyway. The venturis in them kept clogging up from the gasoline we were using for fuel.

For some time, I had been aware of hunger pains. What started out as a subtle clawing in the midsection had grown into a hot poker imbedded in my left side. On these easy fast stretches, I drove one-handed, pressing the other into my side, which gave some relief from the pain. My arms were weak from wrestling the wheel, my shoulders ached from the harness cutting into them, and my legs were cramped from the long hours of sitting in the same position. I'd hate to think what it would have felt like without the yoga training.

As the sun slid down behind the curtain, I wanted to go to sleep. No, I didn't want to sleep. I wanted to stay awake. I had to stay awake. But the fading light and accumulated fatigue lapped over me in narcotic waves. I caught myself nodding off and told Carolyn to keep talking to me no matter what.

One-handed, half-asleep, I'd be driving over a hundred miles an hour, trying to remain a little alert for the rogue bump or gash that sometimes interrupted our hasty progress over the desert. As we neared the end of this eerie dried-up lake, these disruptions became more frequent, and I had to slow down.

Now with the flat, wide open area closing into a narrow funnel, cars and trucks joined up and came together. And as the day died, so did many of them. First we passed a car stopped to change a flat. Then one with the hood up, smoke pouring out. Squirting out the small end of the funnel, we found ourselves on a rutted track with deep ravines on each side. An organization truck was pulling a battered car out of one of them.

The track degenerated into a corrugated ribbon. It looked flat because the depressions were filled with dust. But it didn't feel flat. Jacky, as usual, was right on. Between 110 and 120 kilometers an hour, the bumps smoothed out. We'd fly from the top of one hard little ridge to the next, not feeling the worst of the jolts. There was one problem, though. I was closing in on big trucks going 90 to 100. We got caught up in their dust trails and couldn't see or breathe. I had to back off. Passing blind here was out of the question. Both sides of the track were lined with nasty, jagged rocks.

Washboard is a word that can describe the surface, but it can't begin to describe the experience of driving over it. Washing machine is more like it. We were being tossed around like a couple of T-shirts inside of one. So intense were the bumps that the speedometer snapped loose from its mooring in the dashboard, adding to the surrounding racket. We could *see* screws unscrewing themselves from the car around us. The spare windshield broke away from its mounting overhead and began to bang against the roof, resounding like gunfire. The spare wheels worked themselves loose and bashed up and down on the wheel wells with such force that the metal began to fracture.

I had to speed up. Like a plane passing out of turbulence, everything quieted down. But in seconds we were back in the cloud of dust, nose to tail with a truck. It wasn't just that I couldn't see; the dust reflected the rays of the powerful driving lights back into my eyes, actually blinding me. I tried a new tactic. I moved as far to the right as I dared, until I was half in and half out of the dust cloud. Carolyn could see a little. I couldn't. She acted as human radar, trying to talk me around trucks and cars and on down the track.

"Right a little. No, too much. Left! Okay. Hold it now. Hold it."

Once in a while, we made it past someone this way. In spite of the bumps and the precarious driving conditions, I had to fight to keep myself from nodding off. So far that day I had been driving thirteen hours. I asked Carolyn how much farther.

"A hundred and eighty kilometers," she said.

I knew she was lying on the low side. I acted like I'd bought the lie; I needed to buy the lie to keep me going. But it didn't keep me from moaning at the pains ripping into my side or from groaning in disbelief at the possibility of making it to the end.

"I'm not going to make it, honey. I don't think I can do it."

Even with the excruciating pains I was having, I kept nodding off to sleep.

"Pinch me, hit me, hurt me!" I screamed at her through the intercom. "Please don't let me sleep!"

Shaking and chattering along the track, I began to hallucinate. I saw strangely striped and colored animals standing in the road and played chicken with them. Which of us would weaken first? I'd always win. They ran off into the dark. Though once I swerved to avoid hitting a particularly stubborn and oversized imaginary cat.

Carolyn screamed, "What are you doing?" over the intercom, snapping me out of it.

Now she was carrying me. I was failing fast. She remained focused on the tortuous track, bolstering me, talking me around every hazard and refusing to acknowledge my wimpering self-doubts.

"You can do it! You can! You're almost there."

Ideally, we should have switched places. But I was afraid she didn't have the strength to drive this abusive stretch. And she knew I didn't have the wits left to navigate. We accepted the groggy status quo.

Nearing the end of the speciale, we saw headlights coming toward us. A few cars and trucks were coming the other way. We stopped and asked what was going on. The control wasn't where it was supposed to be, we learned, and they were all trying to find another track that might lead to it. We turned and followed them for a while, but they all split up and went off in different directions. Now we were alone and lost, picking our way over a large, rock-topped plateau, trying to find another track.

We got out of the car and looked for signs of life from our lonely lookout. We saw only blackness and were both now as frightened as we were hungry and exhausted. We spent nearly an hour trying to find our way off of the barren shelves of rock and back to the original track. After a time we found it, and for many miles we followed a fast-moving truck that had come along. We clung to the red glow of his taillights, traveling in a common cloud, which we could only hope was headed home to food and sleep. When we crossed the finish line, my arms fell into my lap like lead and my chin fell into my chest. For fifteen minutes I was unable to lift either one.

The reason for the confusion was that the organization had arbitrarily moved the control fifty kilometers farther down the track than the route book indicated. We complained, as did many others who had managed to find their way. An official responded by reminding us that the Rallye was eight thousand miles long and that there were bound to be some mistakes.

"Besides," the man said, "everyone faces the same difficulty."

Now they were using psychological warfare on us.

Another enraged driver told us the route book was always wrong, that you couldn't go by it. We had been clinging to the route book like torpedoed sailors clutch life preservers. If we couldn't trust the route book, who or what could we trust? Surely not ourselves.

We still had a liaison to contend with before we arrived at the bivouac. Just past the control, as we pulled off the dirt track and onto a busted-up tarmac road, we thought we saw a mirage. A gas station was hidden in a copse of dust-covered trees. There was only one car and one truck waiting. This was too good to be true. We pulled in and filled up.

The bivouac was practically empty when we dragged in about midnight. Most of the cars and trucks seemed to be arriving just then. The catering truck was still setting up for dinner. We must have had a good run. Maybe many in the field had been stymied by the moved control.

It was very cold, and we were sent to stand in line outside a tent. It was Algerian customs. Sometime tomorrow we would pass out of Algeria and into Niger. But we had to complete the customs formalities here. I didn't know where here was. The bivouac was just a large and stony dirt field, pretty much like all of them, somewhere near the end of Algeria.

The Algerian soldiers inside the tent had heaters going and were passing a bottle around among themselves, making a regular party of it. They delighted in chattering amongst themselves while leaving us exhausted racers standing outside shivering. That seemed to be their retribution for drawing such unpleasant night duty. When my turn came, the Algerian threw our passports back at me with a growl. He wouldn't even look at them without my car papers. I had to run back to the car and rummage through the locker under my seat for the worthless pink piece of paper. Carolyn held a place in line.

When I returned, the Algerian looked at the paper, snarled, and threw the passports back at me again. He took another swig from the bottle and leered at his friends, who laughed. I was getting angry now and went into my "no speaka da French" routine. If that didn't work, I would just rip the Adam's apple out of this cocksucker's throat. The fact that they were all carrying automatic rifles didn't make much of an impression on me. After what I'd already been through, I felt bulletproof. Lead couldn't hurt lead.

As I stood there not moving away, he either sensed the defiance rising in me or looked upon me as just another foreign retard, for he impatiently motioned for me to hand the papers back. Without looking at me, he stamped and shuffled, tossed them back, and lifted his nasty gaze to the next victim. Someday I'd like to torture these guys back, send them a case of wingless flies. We were about to see the best part of Algeria. The last of it. And it wouldn't be soon enough for me.

Carolyn coaxed one stove to crank out enough heat for cups of soup. Life would have been a lot easier if I could have just gone to the chow line and dug into some of the tinned military-type rations they handed out there. But they were mostly heavy meat dishes swimming in suspicious sauces. Better to starve than to poison myself. Also, my stomach had shrunk from eating nothing for so long. I didn't need much. Still, I grabbed some bread and a piece of cake.

The dirt, the cold, the hunger, these petty things didn't bother us anymore. We were beyond noticing such trivia. We crawled into our sleeping bags and enjoyed a solid four hours of oblivion.

It was now the sixth day, and Jacky came by after the morning driver's meeting somewhat less than his usual jovial self.

"You gained more than twenty-five places yesterday."

"Not bad, huh?" I smiled, full of myself.

"Too good." He let me know of his disapproval. "More than twenty-five is too many in one day. You're going too fast. You'll break your car, and you won't have time to fix it. Then where will you be?" He shot off.

Student of his own teaching, he was laying back in eighth place, an hour or so behind the leader, who was still Mehta. Vatanen had moved up to fifth.

I was surprised Jacky had a second to waste on me. I was grateful for his advice and support. Everything he had told me so far proved true. Cars were starting to drop like flies. About thirty went out yesterday, along with a few trucks. It seemed every car that went by us in the morning, we'd pass in the afternoon. In their hurry, they got flats. Or broke their suspensions. Or burned up their gearboxes. So far we'd had no problems with the car, although a lot more was in need of tightening that morning than usual. Our biggest problem was us. We hadn't had a real meal in at least five days. Dust-coated granola bars were still our major staple. For the week, we'd gotten maybe eight hours' sleep. But on the morning of the sixth day, we were still there and so many weren't. We were in 184th place. And we still had fifteen days to Dakar in which to move up. Or out.

15

Upon my stupified-not-quite-aware-
ness, a pattern was being tattooed. The Rallye was beginning to become understandable to me. Each day's race seemed to be coming
at us in thirds. In the mornings there would usually be some fast,
interesting racing. A lot of curves and turns and bumps and hills, like
the road racing we had done in Atlanta, but without the road. After
they got us good and worn out with a few hours of that, we'd get a
rest. There would be a few hours of going flat out through boring
emptiness, which would lull us into a state of dopey lassitude. The
worst kind of preparation for our descent into hell at night. They
always saved the worst for last, when we were least prepared to cope
with it.

The sixth day was running true to this form. The whole first third
ran twisting through a long, wide wadi. It was like racing through the
Mississippi River a million years before it filled up. Running down the
bed, we'd go up on the banks, which were exactly that. Banked. No
man could create a better race course. We'd shoot from the bed up
onto the banking for the turns. We were in heavy traffic, racing bumper
to bumper and wheel to wheel with many other cars and a few
large—they were all very large—trucks. We were sideways much of
the time, a huge rooster tail of dust spewed up behind.

I diced playfully with other cars, pushing more than Jacky would
have liked but not pushing really hard. Old techniques were coming
back to me. I'd dog a guy close, right up on his tail. Going into left
bends, I'd slide up the banking, above him on his right. Invariably,
he'd move up to block. On the next left bend, I'd anticipate his upward
blocking move, drop down into the bed, and pass him inside. I'd do
the same on the rights, tricking other cars. One I caught up with, a

bright yellow car from Argentina, would have none of it. He matched me move for move. We had a grand race before he pulled over with a flat tire about an hour later. I didn't know it then, but he was in thirtieth place. I didn't know then either that we were destined to meet again later under less uplifting circumstances.

We were now passing cars the way they had been passing us earlier in the race. Carolyn kept urging me to slow down. She was worried that I was going too fast. Her concern was for the car, not for her own safety. I never saw her afraid, even in the most hair-raising conditions. She was a far better passenger than I could ever be. The first day I would have said, "Are you crazy? Let me out of here!"

By now I knew the car's capabilities as well as I knew my own. My skill as a driver was growing. But the car wasn't getting any better. It was what it was. I was becoming able to push it to its limit and hold it there, exactly what Jacky and now Carolyn didn't want me to do. And what I also knew I shouldn't do. But I didn't like being in 184th place. Get it while you can, I figured. You never knew what might happen next.

Then all of a sudden, it happened. We had come flying out of the wadi and tore out into the open desert. Instantly we were alone. This was a strange sensation. At one minute we were embroiled in heavy competition with other cars all around, the next it was as though we were the only car, the only people on the continent. We would begin to feel small, vulnerable, and lost, an insignificant speck, a nothing in the capital of nothingness. Navigation was easy when a bunch of us were going down the same track. In open expanses with no one else in sight, we always doubted the correctness of our headings. We knew they were there, the other cars, mere minutes ahead of and behind us. But the lack of definitive visual corroboration troubled us. We saw tracks too. But sometimes these criss-crossed and headed off in all directions, adding to our confusion and concern.

Sometimes along the confusing tracks, we'd catch a glint. These were empty cans of Nergisport tossed out of cars as they sped on their way, lying there reflecting the sun. It had taken me five days to figure out that the breakfast line was also the lunch line, and box lunches could be picked up there. Every box contained a little cheese and a lot of heavily sugared date and fruit and nut bars, along with a can of Nergisport, a mineral-laced soft drink. They called these boxes "high-energy lunches." They looked to us like sugar in a variety of forms. I guess the Rallye people hadn't yet caught on to the fact that complex carbohydrates were a better source of energy than sugar. In any event, we ate the cheese and an occasional fruit bar. The only other thing of value to us were the cans of Nergisport, which we didn't drink, but followed after they'd been cast off by others.

It was another day of bright, white light, bleaching out both sand and sky. We couldn't discern detail. Looking out the windshield was like sitting in a dark room and staring at a lightbulb. It hurt to blink.

Cutting through the bleached whiteness came flashes of silver. At first we thought it was just a bunch of abandoned cans, but they grew bigger and brighter. Soon we saw hazy shapes of rippling colorless cars and trucks stopped ahead, the sun bouncing down on their windshields and fracturing off in silvery shafts. There were about twenty of them, the drivers all outside, holding a heated conference.

We stopped and asked what was going on. The route book was wrong again, someone said. They had all been down this track, and the markers were nowhere to be found. It was a repeat of last night, which seemed so long ago. As quickly and as unexpectedly as we had come upon them, they dispersed in all directions and were swallowed by the emptiness. We were alone again, not sure of what to do. We went on, following the tracks over which they'd gone and come. We went farther on, following past where their tracks had turned to return. After eight or ten kilometers, we still saw no markers, only an expanse of paleness. We turned back too, not really knowing where to go or what to do. We followed the tracks back to where we began and set off in the direction a few of the others had taken. The sun had passed its peak and was rolling down the other side. Now we could see the nothing we were in the midst of. Low rolling dunes of crusty sand becoming yellow as the sun gradually lowered itself down toward the horizon. This is where it hid out nights, out where no one could possibly find it.

We probably should have just stayed put and waited. Surely some-one would have happened along who knew more than we did. If we were lost before, we were worse now, miles off our original course, scanning the horizon for a black-faced cliff that was indicated as a background landmark in the general direction we wanted to go. All the cliffs off in the distance looked pink now. Maybe it only appeared black in the morning light when we were meant to view it? Maybe we were staring at it now and couldn't recognize it. We began to look for black beneath the pink, deceiving ourselves that, yes, one was a darker shade of pink than the others.

Maybe that was it! We were disoriented and becoming desperate. We could have talked ourselves into believing anything. We could wishful-think ourselves to death. Far off the Rallye track now, maybe out of the sweep of the Rallye search planes, I decided to double back once again. Back to the commencement of our confusion. We arrived back at the spot. It was four in the afternoon. It looked an entirely different place, bathed as it was now in late afternoon purplish light. We got out of the car and scanned the horizon with binoculars. Off in the distance, a car was speeding along! We set an intercept course and caught up with it in a few minutes, honking our airhorn and flashing our lights. It was the Jeep of Leclercq and Piccin.

No one in the Rallye had first names. Everyone was listed by sur- name, McCabe/Jones, Ickx/Tarin, Pescarolo/Fourticq. Even when fate brought you close together, you never knew if someone was Sam or Pierre, never had time to find out. Somehow it didn't seem important then.

Leclercq/Piccin were as lost as McCabe/Jones. Piccin, the copilot, was as pudgy as he was friendly. He wore a tight red sweatshirt and looked like a meaty saucisson. To me, he became the Little Red Fat Man.

Considering he was in the same boat we were, he seemed awfully sure of his navigation, telling us he was positive that the way to go was straight on from there, the way we had first gone, the direction from which the other lost souls had come. While we were discussing this, six or eight more cars caught up and then a couple of trucks. We all conferred and agreed that the Little Red Fat Man seemed right. We traveled in a group, a ragtag gypsy caravan, jet-propelled. Sure enough, we found the markers, twenty kilometers farther on than the route book indicated. We had been looking for these very markers only a mile or so to the west of where we were now. That's why we hadn't seen more tracks. They were all over here. Our heading had been only a degree or two off, and it had cost us four hours. At the driver's meeting that morning, they'd told us today would be a chal- lenge for the navigators. So it now seemed.

Our group sped along, meeting all the markers the route book in- dicated, a metal barrel here, two tires there. Now we were looking for three tires at which we were to make a right turn. I thought I saw them off on our right in the gathering dusk, but the rest of the group roared on. We caught up with two or three more cars. Now there were about fifteen of us in all. A miserable company. Soon, the pack came to a stop as though controlled by a single set of brakes. We were lost again. No one of the fifteen knew what to do.

I said I thought I saw the three tires back a way and would direct the group back toward them. Everyone followed us. It was pitch black, with a few lights flickering here and there off in the distance. We couldn't imagine what they were. The part of the desert over which we now raced was quite lumpy. We'd soar into the air, come down with a crash then take off again. Again we stopped and conferred. The others wanted to go back to the smooth area we were on before. Our cars were taking too much abuse this way, some of them felt. But I thought I'd seen the three tires.

Just then we saw a flashing blue light heading for us out of the blackness. It was an Algerian Army truck. Yes, we were still in Algeria, but only a couple of miles from the border with Niger. These army men turned out to be the first decent Algerians we'd met. There was a Rallye checkpoint a few miles from there, and they offered to guide us all to it. We got there just before ten o'clock when it was getting ready to close up for the night. It was the halfway point for the stage. The sixth day was coming to an end. But not for us.

We all received four-hour penalties for our late arrival. That, added to the slow time we'd had anyway, dropped us even farther back than we already were. But we were back on track. And that turned out to be by far the worst penalty.

I've seen hell and I can tell you exactly what it looks like. It looks like the next seven hours.

First we had to cross an enormous sand dune. The word "dune," while literally correct, is not applicable here because in most people's minds it has come to mean something else. A mound of sand along a beach to run over, play in, or roll down. This was not that sort of dune at all. Imagine the great pyramids, try to picture the biggest, tallest one. Good, now double, no, triple, quadruple it. This dune was the size of Denver.

We still traveled in a caravan, even more tightly now. Before leaving the checkpoint, we agreed that if one stopped, we would all stop to help the one in trouble. We each knew that we might be in need of help, so we cleaved to the safety of our numbers. We were all weak, hungry, exhausted. I vaguely recall someone saying we were about to cross the largest sand dune in the world.

We couldn't see what was coming, for the sky was even blacker than the circles under our eyes. Nothing stood out. All we saw was sand made yellower than sand is supposed to be by our headlamps and the dark, unclear forms of palm trees off to the sides where the yellow abruptly fell into blackness. Slowly, we headed up the steep incline, the palm shapes rolling away from us on each side. At one point, the Range Rover of Belgians Van Damme/Cnudde became stuck. We all stopped, got out of our cars, and shouldered them out of the sand. It was warmer now than it had been and a ground fog had formed, giving all our bodies a ghostlike aura. The air was uncomfortably still.

Now other cars became stuck, having lost their upward momentum. Next we all tramped up the slope to push the Little Red Fat Man free of the sucking sand. Then another, I don't remember who. All I remember is that our cars were splayed all over the base of this dune at a variety of crazy angles as we gnawed our way up. It took us an hour just to reach the top of the base.

There we found a small plateau, a toehold from which to mount the next phase of the climbing expedition. From where we sat, we could see a trail rising between two sandy peaks. It was very steep, a nearly sheer cliff of sand with deep ruts riven into it. Cars had climbed here before. We chose the most powerful and lightest car to make the first attempt. Then we all got down on our hands and knees in the sand. Not to pray, though we probably should have. But to let air out of our tires. This improved our traction in the sand. I fell asleep with my face up against the tire. The sound of the first car racing his engine and making a running charge at the cliff woke me. I crouched there by the wheel and watched. He fishtailed halfway up before turning sideways and sliding helplessly back down to the bottom.

We decided to send the truck piloted by Spaniards. It was a big Pegaso. They *had* to make it on their own. There was no hope of our pushing or pulling this huge thing to the top. If they made it, they could toss down lines and help pull up the cars that became stuck. The next thing I remember is waking with a start, alone on the little plateau. Everyone was gone! I shook Carolyn awake. We both looked around. Someone was walking toward us, I think it was the Belgian driver Van Damme.

They had all made it to the top, and now it was my turn. I'd been out cold for two hours. I remember thinking, I hope Carolyn took pictures.

We missed a lot of action. After the truck made it up, many of the cars became stuck halfway and had to be pulled the rest of the way with ropes, while the stronger members of the group bullied them up with brute strength from behind. They had left us to our sleep.

Now we made our running charge and the incredible Gelandewagen twisted its way up the eminence as easily as an iguana slithers over an anthill.

At the top, everyone was waiting for the last of us to scale the peak and anxious to go. Van Damme asked if we were okay. I said, "Sure. Sure, go ahead." They all took off in a pack, the truck lumbering behind in a tremendous cloud of dust.

As soon as we took off after them, I realized that everything was not okay. They had all refilled their tires, using the truck's compressor. Ours were still nearly flat. Great for climbing walls of soft sand, but now we found ourselves on a hardpacked downhill washboard and our car slewed along the track with an ungainly side-to-side rolling motion, its performance badly impaired.

I carried a small compressor of my own but had burned it out somewhere along the way, sometime when my mind was in a cloud and I'd left it running inside its case unable to breathe. By now a lot of things no longer worked. The oil temperature gauge went out on day two, as I'd predicted it would to Helmut back in Graz. Ah, Graz! How I'd have liked to be there then, bathed in all its many comforts.

Nothing has positive or negative significance in and of itself. We view all things in relation to something else. What I once thought of as hell seemed as heaven now, with the new comparison. The Rallye brutalized, then enlightened you.

The tape recorder connections burned out after the first day of riding over the burning hot, uninsulated "owtomatic" gearbox. They couldn't take the heat. None of the doors fit as snugly as they once did. All the twisting and bashing contorted them out of their original airtight seal. Now puffs of dust blew into the car at will. Instead of the reassuring tick of the Halda counting off the kilometers, it now gave off an ominous "clack." The speedometer was no longer mounted in the dashboard. It just swiveled and shook around in its hole. The windshield washers and wipers were slowing down and looked ready to pack it in any time now. Why didn't we?

This is a question that only comes up now, after the fact. Quitting never occurred to us. The Rallye was trying to knock us out, and we were intent on thwarting "them." The Rallye was a bucking bronco that had a burr under its saddle. That burr was me. Every day, every kilometer, every painful inch of the way, the Rallye was trying to throw me, telling me "You can't do that."

"Oh, no? Watch me," I was saying back.

Somehow surrender and the justification for it didn't fit in. All that mattered was catching the truck, that compressor, which was flying away into the night, leaving us lumping along like cripples in its wake. A couple of times, we managed to catch up with it and pulled alongside, honking, flashing, and gesticulating wildly at our tires, hoping that they would notice their sorry state and stop. The driver didn't understand. He just looked over at us with a vacuous and toothy grin, then waved back. We couldn't keep up. At anything over a hundred kilometers an hour, the car wobbled violently, threatening to snap out of control. I backed off, resigned to slow and mushy progress.

Even though we were now on one of those long, straight downhill runs and could see miles ahead, the taillights of the cars had gone a misty pink in the fog and faded out of sight. The giant truck was being whittled down to our size as it, too, pulled away.

The road deteriorated rapidly. By "road" I mean a trail down which two cars might pass, assuming they were piloted by very daring drivers. By "track" I mean a one-lane cut across the topography, upon which we traveled at great risk. Everything else was simply impassable cross-country terrain, which we were obliged to pass over anyway. I couldn't remember the last real road we'd seen. We were riding across the body of Africa. Since no road cut across smoothing out its lumps and deformities, we felt everything, every tremble and quake. I found myself hating this writhing giant and wishing it dead.

As we descended the back of the dune, chunky rubble was piling up on both sides. It was as though all of Algeria was a fulsome dung heap from which the meatier, heavier pieces broke off and rolled down the sides, collecting. No one ever came along and picked them up. Partially obscured by the mounds of natural debris were rifts torn into the land. Jagged chasms unexpectedly shot across the road, and we had to bear off until we came to their shallow, narrow points in order to cross. Clearly even Algeria was unhappy being in Algeria. It wanted to be something else, somewhere else. It just sat there flexing its plates, trying to get away from itself, and tore itself to pieces in the process.

We felt our way along, from abyss to abyss, following the dim and hazy glow of our own headlamps and an ever-changing compass heading, becoming dizzy and confused as we tacked back and forth across our intended track. It was getting foggier, too. Once we saw another car picking its way through the maze. We were only five feet away from each other, but he was on the other side of a deep chasm, heading the other way and we soon lost sight of him, never to make contact again. It took us two hours to go twenty kilometers.

We came to a wadi, and our course undulated between dried up little islets dotting the desert stream. We didn't know if it was miles long or wide because we couldn't see far enough to make any sense of it.

By now we were convinced that we were lost and out of the Rallye. We'd changed course maybe fifty times and were traversing land with no trace of a track. For some time now, we had been without confirmation of our position. We saw none of the landmarks mentioned in the route book. We had no idea where we were. We were tired but were more frightened. The fear propelled us on, way past the point of exhaustion.

Coming up one bank of the wadi, we found the ghost of a track. We so wanted to find a track heading somewhere that we would have followed anything believing, wanting to believe, that it was something.

The landscape, what little we could see of it, in the dust and fog, was gnarled and grotesque. Dead, contorted trees reached out at us menacingly. They looked spectral, coated in gray dust. We were both having hallucinations now and as we went along, they grew more vivid and frightening. Hideous animals sprang out at us from moving shadows. I thought I saw a fire, and we went off the track searching for it, hoping to find life. We never even found the fire. Worming our way back to the track, what we assumed to be a track, we saw a sign on a stand marking the track as it plunged into another wadi. It was a triangle indicating "men working." I suspected it was a trap. Bandits had put it there to slow us down so they could beat, rob, or kill us. I turned around, going back to look for the fire, which was probably the robber's camp. At this point, Carolyn suggested that she should probably drive. It was about three in the morning when we stopped and switched places. I immediately began to nod off.

I was passing in and out of a conscious state, but even when semi-awake I was deranged. At one point I noticed Carolyn was passing the MEN WORKING sign. I began screaming, "STOP! STOP! GO BACK! IT'S A TRAP!" Carolyn ignored me and I nodded out again.

Every so often I would crawl back into consciousness, mutter some incoherent nonsense, and drift off again.

I didn't know how long I'd been out. Probably no more than a few minutes. I jerked into wakefulness and was horrified by what I now saw. Everything, *everything* was covered with a fine grayish-white dust that smelled rank and ancient, like decayed and cremated bones. The track was made of it, and we were sunk deeply into it. I could hear it clawing at the underside of the car as we scraped our way over it. The twisted and spindly trees were coated with the stuff. As our headlamps hit them, they seemed to float and glow. The car was covered with the ashen powder. A spooky cloud of it hovered inside the car. Carolyn looked like a luminous wraith.

We were passing through a deathscape. No one could live here. No one could survive here. Or so I would have believed if it hadn't been for the hundreds of white rats scurrying everywhere through the gruesome setting. Our exhausted minds hadn't invented these. They were real. We could tell because their little yellow eyes became transfixed by the headlights and we heard them crunch as our wheels ground them into the dust.

We went on like this for hours, shrouded in the dank and disturbing mist, annihilating rats. We couldn't avoid them. There were two deep furrows in the track, and these furrows owned us for a time. About five in the morning, we came across another car and then another one, running in deep ruts of their own on each side of us. From behind us came a truck, the big Spanish Pegaso carrying the air we no longer needed. In this soft mush, low tires pressures were better.

My God, I thought, *we're all back together, all still lost.* Then we saw the orbiting yellow beacon of the Rallye checkpoint. I couldn't believe it. Carolyn couldn't believe it. We were convinced we were approaching it from the wrong direction and would be given an even bigger penalty than the one we'd already received. We couldn't possibly be on course, it was inconceivable that we were *meant* to travel the route we had gone through.

We were back in the running. Late, very late, but not yet out.

We asked the man in the control booth for directions to the bivouac. He didn't know where it was. And so began the most frustrating and nerve-racking hour we'd yet had. We were in a town called Arlit in Niger. And there were few signs of life at this time of the morning. The other cars and truck had all disappeared. To where we hadn't a clue.

We drove to the airport on the edge of town and found a Rallye official there. He couldn't help us either, he said. They'd moved the

bivouac the night before, and he wasn't sure where to. More psychological warfare. We were becoming hysterical. We had survived the
horrid day and night, and now we couldn't find our way back into
the Rallye. Why wasn't there a sign somewhere? Why were they
doing this to us? Wasn't it hard enough? Hadn't we earned our way
back in? One more day, just give us one more day, please. We scoured
the town, stopping to ask the occasional living person, usually an
African native who would point in this direction or that. We would
charge off blindly, looking, but couldn't find the bivouac. How could
they hide a couple hundred cars and trucks from us in a little town
like this? Were they in an underground cavern? Under camouflage
netting?

Both of us were near to tears. I was ranting and raving and screaming
and cursing the vile and insensitive creatures who could do this to us
when a car popped out of a gap in the sand piled high along each side
of the town's one tarmac road. It was a Rallye car! I swung a U-turn
and entered the gap. There, in a depression, behind a wall of sand,
was the elusive campsite.

16

Far from the stupendous spectacle that left Versailles, the Rallye had become a fraction of its once gran- diose self. The body of contestants had been whittled down to less than half its original stature. In the beginning, these bivouacs had been scenes of sprawling bustle and noise. Now here was only a tight little bundle of survivors who were just now, quietly, coming to life.

I found Jacky immediately. One look at us was all he needed to know our whole story. Carolyn ran off to cover the drivers' meeting.

Jacky began slapping me back to consciousness verbally.

"You're out of Algeria. You've made it through the worst part. Now, it will become fun. Look how small the camp has become. Believe me, it gets easier now."

I was as close to defeated as I've ever been and began to whine. "I haven't had a meal in six days, I haven't slept, I need gas and there's no time to get any."

The motorcycles were already lining up to start.

Jacky arranged for me to get gas from the Lada camp. He helped roll a big drum of it over to the car. I began to pump it from the drum into my tank with the little portable hand pump we carried.

We'd gotten in too late for the computers to record our arrival and rank us in time for the morning meeting. So we'd been listed as missing. Friends who saw that we were, indeed, not missing, ran over to offer their help. Kurt Knilli was one of them. He looked at me as though he'd seen a ghost. I'll never forget his startled expression. He didn't look so hot either. The Rallye was turning us all into the driving dead.

Jacky gave me two boxes of granola bars that he said packed more energy than the kind I was carrying. He also gave me some vials of special liquid-energy supplements along with some huge vitamin pills.

He told me how much to take and when. And he told me that after I finished pumping the two hundred liters from the drum, I should take whatever additional gas I needed to fill up completely. Today, we were racing out into the Tenere Desert.

I looked around for water. I had been buying water and topping up the tanks whenever I had the opportunity. A native offered to sell me six liters for thirty dollars. It was off-road robbery. I passed. We had enough to get through today with plenty left over.

We were in Black Africa now. The natives were no longer Arab. Some wore colorful robelike costumes. Most wore Western garb, khaki pants and filthy, torn T-shirts. They went barefoot or wore rubber flip-flops on their feet. There were hundreds of them in the camp, swarming over the contestants, and as the sun got higher, they flew out of it, lighting on us like flies on excrement. They buzzed around, begging, grabbing, and badgering. As long as you kept moving, it wasn't so bad. Stop, and it was as though you were a dead carcass, fair game for the hungry flies.

"*Cadeau, cadeau*" (gift), they'd cry. When I turned my back, they'd grab for whatever they thought I couldn't see. They'd open the sliding plastic windows and reach, grasping, into the car. It was a scene so disturbing and confusing, I couldn't think straight. I'd seen poverty and want before, but never anything like this, without a scintilla of pride. The Sahara is a hard place to live, an even harder place to continue doing so. Here, a man takes something simply because he has nothing. There is little concept of value. It didn't matter what a thing was or what it was worth. Why should it? In a world where even life has little value, the value of a thing is measured not by what it is, only by who possesses it.

The Paris/Dakar Rallye is not the finest forum for expressing one's liberal leanings. In my sleepless, thoughtless daze, I recoiled from the spectacle, not caring or even thinking about the plight of these unfortunate Africans. I thought only of self-preservation, following the natural instinct to protect myself and Carolyn, to keep going, to survive. So I hardened myself to their pleas. Later I realized how easy it is to maintain a concerned and caring attitude toward the unfortunate. It's simple, as long as the concept remains abstract, removed. Like the man who gives generously to support the homeless, but backs away from the stoplight whenever one steps up to clean his windshield.

The Lada man wanted to get paid for the gas. Another guy wanted to borrow my gas pump. I paid a native to pump the rest of the gas

for me while I began to do some maintenance on the car. After a couple
of minutes, he just wandered away. I went after him and dragged him
back with the promise of still more money.

I had about seventy-five liters left in the small tank. That, plus the
two hundred liters from the drum, would bring the car almost to its
capacity. I was running out of time. So when the drum was empty, I
loaned the guy my pump. Carolyn returned from getting a private
translation of the driver's meeting. We tightened the wheels and added
some oil. Then went looking for the truck that carried our spares. We
needed air for our tires and a fresh supply of dusty diapers to wash
ourselves off with.

All this time I had been charged with adrenaline and was in a
clammy, dirty sweat. Again, we also had to compensate the compass.
We made it to the starting line with only a couple of minutes to spare.
I downed the first vial of gooey brown liquid Jacky had given me and
feasted on two granola bars, relishing the slightly unfamiliar taste.
They were German, I think, and I remember their name. Korny Bars.
Carolyn and I laughed about the name. We still had our sense of
humor if not our wits.

At this point I had no idea who was winning the Paris/Dakar Rallye.
Oh yes, I did. The Rallye was.

Day seven began on a sandy track that wound its way through scrub
trees. Except for the occasional clump of palms or an interesting little
village still looking oddly arabesque, we might have been on Long
Island. I slung the car sideways over and over again as we followed
the winding little trail around and through the trees. It was a single-
lane track, yet I passed many cars, slewing and fishtailing past while
brushing the trees. We came upon a small one-lane bridge over a deep
defile and I passed a car on the verge of it, barely making it up onto
the concrete slab in front of him. How strange it was to be crossing
a bridge over sand. Why?

Before I could form an answer, we were off on the other side, sliding
through a left turn and passing still another car. We were moving to
the left and I had the wheel full lock to the right, and for a moment
I was amazed at my own aptitude. Turning my head in slow motion
to give Carolyn a smiling glance, defying gravity without even looking,
like a matador who turns away at the last second knowing that the
horns will just brush past, indulging in a langorous second of grace
and power.

A bright, hot sun beat down on us. Our heads throbbed inside our helmets, inside the hot, dusty cockpit, which was much hotter now that we were out of Algeria and into Niger.

All along Algeria had been an artificial finish line. Something like the start of the Rallye had been to us. Rallye statistics were often quoted along the lines of how many went out in Algeria. How many went out by the third day in Algeria. How many never made it out, had become lost and never heard from again. Tales were told of break-downs in Algeria, the unfortunate crews having to abandon their cars, there to become part of the wretched landscape because the Algerian bureaucracy made it impossible to get them out. Jacky's words: "You've made it out of Algeria. The worst is over."

As beaten down as we were, we were euphoric. We had crossed an important line, getting out of Algeria. It seemed to us as though we had escaped from hell, only instead of going from there to heaven, we had been sent somewhere else bad. But, compared to Algeria, that was fine with us.

Jacky's potions were taking effect, so I pulled out all the stops. This was a long, long speciale—692 kilometers—and I wanted to drive as much of it as I could before dark.

For a long time, we ran on sand, sometimes soft, sometimes hard, and often deeply rutted. There were switchback turns so tight the car almost turned back in on itself. It was similar to the Martha's Vineyard and Chappaquiddick Island tracks we'd practiced on in the summer. I felt more comfortable racing here than I had at any time, and my driving skills had sharpened themselves immeasurably. I drove very fast, much faster than I'd gone in the race thus far. I asked Carolyn if she was scared. No, it was beautiful to watch, she said. God knows I'd had enough practice. I'd driven more hours at speed in the last week than most racing drivers do in a year.

The ruts were traps. If my wheels went into them, the friction of the sand slowed us down, so I flew the car rather than drove it, keeping the wheels up on the upper edges of the ruts. For hours, I was in a continuous skid, spinning the wheel a full turn one way, then a full turn the other way, just to get a degree or two of correction in the front end. I think Jim Fitzgerald would have approved of my handi-work, which was far from lazy that day.

In the next three hours, I must have passed between twenty and thirty cars. At one point I remember passing three cars in a hundred-yard stretch. There were two cars off to the side of the track, the drivers talking. I knew one of them; it was Mano Dayak, who was a citizen of Niger. As we shot past the three cars, I could see Mano and the other guy clapping, cheering us on. We made up so much time that I decided to take a rest. I couldn't have kept up that pace much longer anyway. Neither could the car. I'd been giving it such a flogging that the right rear shock absorber had broken and the other was close behind.

I turned the wheel over to Carolyn, advising her to watch out for the springiness in the right rear due to the broken shock. I wouldn't say that Carolyn is good for a girl. She's good for a guy. Just inexperienced. After a while, some of the cars I'd passed began to catch up. Carolyn had never driven in wheel-to-wheel competition before, and I think the reality took her quite by surprise. A car began to pass us on our left. She moved right. Another car was trying to pass us there. The shock of it jolted Carolyn. As they passed, closely on each side, she braked and swerved just behind the car on our right, went up an embankment and down the other side where our front end plunged into a sandy depression about five feet deep. We came to a sudden, jarring stop.

The car wouldn't move forward or back, and the gearbox was making funny, grinding noises. This time we were out for sure, I thought. Carolyn was crushed and teary-eyed. I was mad, not so much at her but at the sudden rudeness with which the dream had been dashed.

I crawled under the car but could see no evidence of damage. We had to get the car out of the hole before we could really assess the problem. I attached our tow line, gave the other end to Carolyn, and asked her to flag down help. A passing truck stopped and hauled us out. It took less than a minute. Good karma was coming around and back to us it seemed.

Now the Mercedes was standing on flat ground. Still I could see no damage anywhere underneath. No broken half-shafts or universal joints. Yet the gearbox still made the noises and the car wouldn't move. I got inside to shift into "four-wheel low" and found the problem. The shock of our sudden stop in the hole had popped this shift lever out of "four-wheel high" and into neutral.

"We're not out yet, you bastards!" I screamed at no one in particular as we took off. I was driving again, and like a madman. Within five minutes I caught the truck that had helped us out, passed them shouting "Thanks" and flashing my lights. Soon I had the cars that had retaken us and a couple more besides.

Then we came to Adrar Chiriet.

I had heard that there was some religious significance to this place. Or maybe I hadn't heard it, only felt it. Anyhow, there was *something* special about it. I felt an overwhelming sense of *déjà vu*. I knew I'd been here before and that I was meant to be here now.

We were coming upon a sandy oasis, clawing our way through foot-deep sand, yellowing in the afternoon light. There were palm trees and water holes but no signs of life. The oasis was large, maybe a couple of miles square. There were clusters of palms on different levels of elevation. It was like finding a dozen oases in one convenient location. A dying man would become frustrated and confused deciding which one to head to. We were winding our way through this installment-plan oasis, looking for the pass that would take us out into the Tenere Desert at the other end. Around and around we churned through the deepening sand and under the lowering sun, not finding the pass, over and over again passing pockets of paradise but never in exactly the same direction. The beauty and peace and promise was taunting, and it was all bathed in a golden light.

We saw a pass off to one side, not on the compass heading we were meant to follow, but I headed for it anyway, over Carolyn's objections. Down we went into a hidden valley, coming upon a tiny village of stucco huts with pointy thatch roofs, occupied by sheepherders from the looks of it. It was a cul de sac, a dead end offering no apparent exit to the Tenere, because a semicircle of high, unbroken red cliffs rose beyond. It was magnificent. For a time we just sat and stared at the view, riveted to our seats by its powerful presence. Realizing that there was no way out, we headed back to the oasis to pick through there yet again, looking for the elusive pass.

Again and again we churned around, becoming mesmerized by the majestic silence and amber glow being generated by this place. The sun was near setting, and we would soon lose visibility. We had to find the pass.

We found it, finally, the easy way. We came upon a competitor who had broken down and asked. He told us we were right in the middle of the pass we'd been searching for. We'd been going around and around looking *for* it without realizing that we were *in* it. This was one of the navigation problems we'd been having right along, the problem of scale. And it's where our lack of experience continually got us in trouble. We could follow the headings and fix our position,

but when the route book said we were to go through a pass, we thought
we could see it. We thought the pass was a half mile wide opening
to the desert, and we'd be looking for the cliffs that delineated it.

In reality, the pass was maybe ten miles wide and the cliffs bordering
it were twenty, thirty miles off in the distance. That's why we could
never find anything for sure. We were trying to reduce the desert
down to an understandable, human, scale. How were we to know that
the desert wasn't understandable? The scale of it is staggering. And
it was the least human place either of us had ever been.

Having wasted hours on a meandering tour, we now faced the most
difficult part of the stage in the dark.

Jacky had told me that when in doubt, "Just follow the tracks."
Simple advice, but first you had to find them, which wasn't always
easy. There were still a couple hundred vehicles in the race, maybe a
hundred ahead of us even with all we had passed. But the desert is
an enormous place and finding the tracks of a hundred cars in it is like
trying to isolate a few seconds out of eternity. When we did find tracks
to follow, they didn't all lead in the same direction but went back and
forth across each other in a confused tangle. Sometimes we'd come
upon tracks and were unsure whether they were those of the Rallye.
In our exhausted mental state, it never occurred to either of us to ask
ourselves who the hell else would be out here in the middle of nowhere.

Racing along nonstop, day after day, noise and blurs all around us,
we thought we were always moving through a heavily trafficked area.
It never quite got through to either of us that the odds were a few
hundred thousand to one that any track would be anything but a
Rallye track. Somewhere along here, a man jumped out of the dark,
frantically trying to wave us to a stop. As we pulled up to him, we
saw a Rallye car off to the side. It had broken down, and the driver
asked us to report his location when we got to the checkpoint so he
could be rescued.

"Of course," we told him. Carolyn wrote down his number and
approximate location so we wouldn't forget. We never remembered
to look at what we had written down. And it would be days before
we would recall the incident and begin to feel guilty about it.

We were going down a steep sandy slope, now, in the darkest of
black. There was no mistaking the tracks our lights illuminated. They
were those of the Rallye. One minute we'd be following what appeared
to be hundreds of them. The next, there'd be no tracks at all. None.
They seemed to evaporate. We'd get lulled into a sense of security

and all of a sudden our security blanket would disappear. Each time this happened, we became more confused and disoriented. And more despairing, frustrated, and angry at each other.

We were in a mountain range of dunes, lost among white powder piles. We couldn't see our way out. There were no landmarks, nor vegetation, just the sand that glowed like phosphorous as our driving lights washed over it.

"Can't you please just give me a heading you're sure of?" I asked Carolyn. No, she couldn't, she said. She didn't know and couldn't figure one out. She wasn't a professional navigator. I didn't appreciate the timing of this unexpected confession.

I probably told her that if I'd known that, I wouldn't have taken her along. I don't remember what I said. I was beyond thinking, beyond knowing much of what I was saying or doing. All I know is we began to argue on an emotional as well as navigational level. All our frustrations and anxieties bubbled to the surface at a most inopportune time.

"I told you to do more navigation homework."

"If only you hadn't wasted all that time going into the valley."

This, of course, got us nowhere but angrier on top of being dirty, hungry, exhausted, and nearly lost yet again.

Earlier, I had fallen asleep in the middle of braking for a turn. I didn't wake up until after I'd sleep-driven my way through it. I was in no condition to drive, let alone drive a race. My lights were going out.

I was completely delirious now. I made repeated attempts to drive over a dune that wasn't even on our course. I saw it there, looming big, and decided it needed to be overcome. I hurled the Gelande at it time after time, like The Little Engine That Could. Only it couldn't. We'd get halfway up only to come sliding back down. Once, we became badly stuck and it took us a long time, jerking backward and forward and spinning the wheels until the tires smoked, before I was able to work our way out. I remember some of these charges, but there are parts and sequences missing that I will never know. I was lapsing in and out of consciousness.

Later, Carolyn told me she had been very frightened, too frightened to try to coax me to stop my maniacal attacks on the dune. She thought I had gone insane. I probably had, for I awoke with only the sketchiest recollection of mere bits of it.

I had passed out completely, slumped at the wheel. Carolyn must have conked too, for when I snapped awake, it was two hours later and she was out. The car's engine was still running.

"I can't go on. First we sleep, then we go," I told her. "If we make it, we make it, if we don't, we don't."

I was sad and depressed, part of me knowing that I was throwing away everything we had worked so hard to do. But there was just no going on. The Rallye had all but KO'd us. There was still a sliver of hope for a comeback, but not without a little sleep.

Carolyn agreed. Whether it was from fear of my insanity recurring or realization that it was the only thing that made any sense, I don't know. I never asked.

We pulled off, behind a lower dune, threw our sleeping bags on the sand, and collapsed onto them.

At dawn on the eighth day, we awoke, looked at each other guiltily, knowing our self-indulgent nap had jeopardized all. We hadn't yet finished the seventh day's course. We now had to make a desperate last-ditch run for it. By the time we threw together a makeshift break-fast and packed up the car, we had less than four hours to make it to the control before it closed. We might just make it in time. So we'd incur another big penalty. At least we'd still be in the race. Way behind, but in.

It took us a while to find our way back onto the track. There were no signs reading "to the race" out there. But when we found hundreds of parallel lines scribed across the sand, we knew what they were. Even through our deep and drugged sleep, we'd both occasionally heard the zooms of cars and trucks shooting by.

We had a hair over three hours to go three hundred kilometers. I had to average a hundred. But our speed was controlled by the sand. When it was hard-packed, I could go about 110. In the softer places, our speed would fall to 90. Talk about touch and go. For two hours we kept up this madly fluctuating pace, the engine shrieking without relief at 6,600 revolutions per minute, the tires spinning, trying to gain a grip on the sand.

This entire section was one long, straight stretch of sand with no vegetation, no rock formations. It was interrupted only occasionally by lines of dunes. We'd run at them as fast as we could go, our momentum slowing as we neared the tops, then picking up speed as we shot down the other side. All along we passed cars. None moved. Some were abandoned, imbedded in sand that went halfway up their sides, looking like cankers growing on the face of a dune. Others were off to the sides, jacked up and being worked on by their crews. On the far right side of the wide track, a helicopter was hovering over a car that was turned over on its side. It was like a battle scene, after a massacre.

We flashed along, not perceiving the frustration or anguish that must have been felt by all these others who had faltered along the way.

The gasoline warning light started flickering. I hadn't even looked at the gauge, hadn't even thought about it for the longest time. Out of habit, I'd been regularly opening the valve to allow gas to pass from the big tank into the smaller one, which was now close to empty. Once again, I opened the valve. But ten minutes later, the needle on the fuel gauge still pointed to E. All the time, the engine was shrieking, winding past the red line on the tachometer. I was concentrating only on getting to the checkpoint before it closed, worried only about the engine exploding before we got there. But gas, now I had to worry about gas.

I kept the valve open, hoping a few litres, ounces, drops, or even a few fumes would find their way into the other tank. We had an hour left and a hundred kilometers to go. We were right on target. We could still make the checkpoint before it closed! But I couldn't go so fast anymore. I knew it was eating too much fuel. The warning light that told me I was burning emergency rations stopped flashing and held a steady red glare. Reluctantly, I slowed a little, trying to make up the difference with body English. I let up on the accelerator and pushed harder with my being. But it didn't work.

Ten kilometers later, the ninth Paris/Dakar Rallye dribbled to a pathetic halt for car 248 as the Mercedes whispered to a stop a mere ninety kilometers short of its goal. That's all it did. The engine just stopped, and the car coasted for about a hundred yards. Even then we both pushed with our bodies, trying to keep it moving, willing it on, hoping the engine would find some hidden supply of fuel and splutter back to life. But the reservoir of miracles had run dry on us.

End of the line . . . Thatcherville. Everybody out!" That was my first thought as the Mercedes crept to a stop. It was a tasteless joke to myself, referring to the fate of Mark Thatcher, the prime minister of England's son. He had been lost and stranded for days in the desert a couple of years before, causing consternation in high diplomatic circles.

Carolyn and I sat in the car in silence for a long time, not getting out, not knowing what to say. We both knew we were finished. Still we sat there, as though making any move or sound at all would force us to face our failure. Even if a car came along now and we were able to get gas, it would be impossible to make it to the control before it closed. It had been that close. Acting the optimist, clinging to a shred of hope, that would have been pointless now. Better to hoard these resources for our future survival. For now, we were down and OUT.

Recriminations, blame, rationalizations? Why? What would have been the point? They couldn't get us back into the Rallye. Of course I felt deep disappointment, defeat, anger at all the time and money that had been invested in . . . in what? In failure.

But I felt it only for a moment. What possible value would there have been in hanging on to such feelings? I think the yoga had taught me that. It had trained me to let go of pain, physical pain. But mental pain was equally hurtful, and I found I was able to let go of that with similar facility. Besides, there was really no point in being miserable after the fact.

Even the suddenness with which the dream collapsed didn't take us by surprise. We'd had our disappointment practice, before, when we'd crashed into the hole. Then again, when we'd stopped last night to sleep. Only this time no one could come along and pull us out, no more last-ditch, all-or-nothing efforts were possible.

It was like skiing. Somewhere up the slope, I'd made a bad turn, lost my balance, and never quite recovered from it. I'd been teetering for days. Now there we were, our own momentum having dragged us so much farther along, before we finally fell.

We sat for a while, still strapped into the car. Finally, I removed my helmet and broke the heavy silence.

"Next year we need a mechanic, a larger gas tank, and two shocks on each wheel," I said, turning to look at Carolyn for the first time since we'd stopped.

She looked over to me with a tired smile and picked up the thread, ". . . and move the Twinmaster so I don't have to reach so far."

"Get some paper. Write it down so we don't forget," I suggested.

We sat there in the car, reviewing our needs for next year, making a lengthy list. After all we had been through, the first thing we thought about was going through it all again!

I didn't know whether either of us really intended to do Paris/Dakar again or if the notion rose out of a subconscious need to mitigate our feelings of defeat. "We'll show them next year." That sort of thing.

Much as a long, hot shower allows one to remove and distance oneself from the real world, a neutral zone in which to make a transition from the work day to the social night, or from gentle slumber to hectic morning, our daydreams in the car helped us adjust to our abrupt arrival in a new reality.

If our plunge into the hole and sudden stop had been earth-shattering, what was this? It was the same idea but on a far grander scale. It was a cosmic dislocation. We had gone, instantly, from everything to nothing. And neither of us was quite prepared for the shock of that. It wasn't the suddenness so much as the contrast. And the quiet.

Swinging myself down out of the car to the ground, I was squashed by the silence. The strained scream of the engine, the whine of the gearbox, the nearly constant chatter over the intercom, the clamorous rattle of objects within the car, the frenetic beat of the race, the other cars zooming alongside, in front and in back of us, the desperate rush of our own pulses and desires pushing us toward the next turn, the next landmark, the next day, these were all gone. The needle had been lifted from the record in mid-dance.

I had the urge to cover my ears with my hands to protect my

eardrums from exploding in reaction to the sudden weightlessness. I felt the heat of the sun cascading down on me in layers. Yet it was not so menacing as the silence. The penetrating stillness denounced the very existence of life.

Carolyn scrambled up onto the top of the car and scanned the desert with binoculars. For 360 degrees there was only sand and desolation. And the tire tracks. Vacant traces of the life that had so recently, and quickly, passed by.

We had pulled off to the side of what we had come to believe was a road. We still clung to this absurd belief. At least I did. I asked Carolyn to walk back down the road and set up the red warning triangle in case a straggler came speeding up behind us. I was not only convinced that we were off to the side of a road but that we were in a depression, invisible to oncoming traffic. The triangle was a futile gesture. There was no road. There would be no traffic. The feeling of being in a depression was an optical illusion, a trick of the eye that tilted us into a hole in the midst of the great emptiness creating a near horizon, an imaginary barricade that kept the infinite nothingness from moving in and swallowing us.

While Carolyn trudged off with the triangle, I took a crowbar from the tool kit and etched the word FUEL in huge block letters in the crusty sand. Just in case we were spotted from the air. This was more than a mute cry for help. This was also a summary, a metaphor for the entire race as far as we were concerned. All along fuel had been a problem. Our nemesis. I looked at the word staring impotently up at the empty sky. FUEL. It said so little. It said so much. It both begged and explained.

The word, just gaping there, forced me into a period of self-flagel-lation.

If only I'd filled the tank all the way to the top as Jacky had told me to.

If only I hadn't fallen asleep at the wheel with the engine running.

If only the tank had been bigger in the first place, we could have carried more fuel.

Instead of FUEL, maybe I should have scrawled in the sand FOOL. But such acknowledgment couldn't help us now. It was too late. Now it was time to revel in the sheer joy and relief of being out of it. But before we could openly admit to such heretical feelings, we had to keep up the pretense of disappointment a few minutes longer. We had a final sad ceremony to attend, and we both needed to act as though we didn't enjoy it.

I took the emergency radio transmitter from the survival case, placed it on the hood of the car, and we both stared at it dejectedly for a minute before I reached for the switch and flicked it on. This made our failure final. Then we fell into each other's arms unsure of what was the right thing to do next, to laugh or to cry. So we did both.

Your best attempt at imagining the desolation in which we then found ourselves will most likely fall considerably short of reality. To do it, you can't fantasize. You can't use your imagination at all. You must do the opposite. Close your mind down, isolate it from the intrusion of any sensory memory. You must see only a blank tan sheet of sand without even a wrinkle in it, over that a blue sky so high and far away that its being there didn't even matter. There was no other thing. Nothing.

No petrified, contorted tree standing gaunt and withered off in the middle distance. No small cactus whose outstretched arms ending in flat hands with sharp nails reached up from the ground in defensive welcome. No artistically twisted piece of windworn wood tweaked our imaginations. No bleached and bony steer's skull paid homage to the passage of life. No tumbleweed blew anywhere, giving clue to the existence of any other destination. No line of smoke on the horizon offered the faintest wisp of hope. Not a breath of breeze stirred our senses. No vaguely familiar aroma haunted our memory. No sound startled us. Nothing was visible, audible, smellable. It defined the word *desert*. It was a totally senseless place.

But—it was big.

In the face of it, I had been anticipating, had even been willing, to be deflated by the sheer hopelessness of contending with so much nothing. Instead I actually began to see and feel myself—growing. I was buoyed by a growing sense of my own enormity.

My profile, that vague awareness of one's own configuration, normally only perceived out of the corner of an eye, gained stature and dimension, etching itself heroically against the no-dimensional backdrop. My arms seemed to stretch out in front of me for yards and my hands looked huge as paddles, like one of those humanized animal characters out of a Walt Disney cartoon. Propped atop the bleak expanse of tan, under the frightening and faraway sky, the car, sitting there alone, seemed gigantic, distended in length and height as though photographed through a radical wide-angle lens. Carolyn looked taller than I'd ever seen her. The crowbar lying on the sand stretched itself into a baseball bat. The dinky little red plastic triangle we'd put out, though a hundred yards away, now seemed to tower into the lofty sky. Even our voices seemed to have grown in timbre and volume. We had to whisper to keep from becoming overwhelmed by ourselves.

I didn't know if this was a mental aberration or a psychological necessity, but in our pathetic smallness and vulnerability, we had expanded to meet the challenge. Like a pair of game little kids puffing themselves up, flexing their mini-muscles, standing on tippy toes to face up to a gang of older, threatening bullies.

Looking back, I don't know why I should have found this surprising. Carolyn, me, the car, the crowbar, the few packing cases, we were the only objects anywhere. Of course we looked imposing. A line of soggy wash snapping with false bravado against an ominous and unending sky.

Plunked down into this soundless, wall-less, and endless prison, I began to plan our escape. Spreading a shiny, metallic survival blanket out upon the ground to reflect a call for HELP into the air, something caught my eye. Something so small it would be beneath notice in any other environment. A couple of tiny black specks. At first glance, they seemed that they might be no more than floaters, imperfections within my own eyeball. I thought they might be small stones a couple of hundred yards away. These inconsequential objects would never have caught my attention except for the fact that I was on my hands and knees and just happened to be looking for something to anchor down the corners of the survival blanket in case of wind. So I walked out to explore. The sand was hard, like pavement, with a thin layer spread across the top. It issued a dead "thlock . . . thlock . . . thlock . . . thlock" as I walked across it toward what was looking more and more like just a couple of black stones.

I came upon these objects, now also grown larger just as we had. Just as I began to lean over to pick them up, I noticed that they were not rocks at all, but rock-hard remnants. They were the vestiges of a black bird whose talons were locked in a death grip around the skeletal remains of a snake.

I am not an archaeologist. But even I could read some disturbing history into these particular artifacts.

1. It was not ancient enough history for me. What was left of the bird still had feathers on it.

2. Part of the snake still had snakeskin on it.

3. From the shape of the snake's skull, I surmised it was venomous.

In addition to these suppositions, I also had some questions. Did the bird carry the snake here from some other place? Or did the bird swoop down on the snake on the snake's home ground? Who ate the top two-thirds of the bird? Did the snake have relatives living in the neighborhood?

I took my unanswered questions away, left the reception committee to their eternal disagreement, anchored the blanket with tools, and made a command decision. We would sleep inside the car that night.

Most of the time, we just sat in the car and fidgeted, waiting for help to arrive. Initially, I had a pipedream that the helicopter we'd passed, hovering a half-hour behind, would fly over, see us stranded there and set down to give us fuel and we'd be on our way. That wisp-of-the-will evaporated after a couple of hours. The helicopter didn't come. I also thought one of the cars we'd passed might come limping into view and give us enough gas to get to the next checkpoint where we could fill up. It was only ninety kilometers away and was called "Texaco." This led us to conclude that it was a gas station where we could obtain fuel even after the Rallye had moved away. The name Texaco and its proximity taunted us, adding fire to our frustration over the painful subject of fuel. No car came.

As the sun swung into its late afternoon position, we began to resign ourselves to spending the night there, began to wonder how many nights we would have to spend there before help came.

"They *will* find us, won't they?" Carolyn asked.

"Of course," I answered. "I only hope it doesn't take them too long."

"Well, we've got plenty of food," Carolyn said, brightening and getting out to fix us some dinner.

"Yes, but not so much water," I said, eyeing the measly five liters left in one tank.

At our previous rate of intake, that was less than half a day's supply. Now we would have to ration. We might have to stretch that for three days. They *did* say they'd get to us within three days. But what if they didn't? If they didn't, we were doomed.

If only I'd paid the native the thirty dollars. I reproached myself for that too.

Even though we were loaded with food, we couldn't spare the water needed to cook it. I allotted a small amount for heating up pouches of brown rice. There could be no soup, we would prepare no dried vegetables. What water was left after heating the pouches we would use for a single cup of tea.

It took Carolyn an hour to clean and assemble the stove. Every time it was used, it would clog up on the gas and required elaborate cleaning before it would work again. Stupid stove! Didn't it realize what a luxury it was to have gas to run on? I thought of pouring the gas from the little stove tank into the car, which would be grateful for it. But there wasn't enough in there to bother about.

The stove worked for five minutes before flickering out, leaving us with a useless pan of water not warm enough to cook with. I thought of shaving with it. I hadn't shaved or washed in days. But realizing that water was now precious, I poured it back into the tank.

We sat outside on our aluminum cases and had two pouches of cold brown rice and beans each. It was the biggest meal we'd had in over a week. Eight days we'd been running on little more than adrenaline and hope. Now we were out of hope too. Eight days! More than a third, less than a half. Had we accomplished much or little? Is the glass half empty or half full? It depended on how you looked at it. And I wasn't ready to look. We never talked about this.

As we ate, we watched an amazing sunset. The sun itself was no big deal. Just a big red ball falling off one end of the earth. What made this so unusual and spectacular was, there, we could look behind and to each side of us and see all the other ends of the earth at the same time. We could see a multicolored sky forever. It was the first sunset we'd had time to notice or appreciate since we'd been in Africa.

It got cold very quickly. Not as bad as Algeria but cold enough for long underwear, sweatsuits, two pairs of socks, and an unzipped sleeping bag as a blanket in the cockpit. Still we were chilly.

The seats weren't designed for sleeping, either. They were meant to hold us ramrod straight for racing. But we were so tired it didn't matter.

During the night I awoke, thought I saw a light on the horizon, grabbed my flare cannon, jumped out of the car, and fired a few flares into the air. Apparently we were the only ones who saw that show.

I don't know if it was the exhaustion or the cessation of demand on our nervous energy that made us sleep through the night and doze on and off throughout most of the ninth day. Probably both. It was a good thing too, for it helped us conserve our energy and therefore our water. In the occasional wakeful moments, we'd hallucinate and day-dream. We didn't speak much about anything. What was there to say? Talking aloud parched us, creating the need for more water. I had rationed us to one cup every two hours. Carolyn, as usual, thought I was going overboard. I was too tired to argue with her about it. The tank with the water in it was behind my seat and in my control. So every two hours I just silently passed her the tube and let her take her few sips. In between, I drifted. From absurdity to lucidity and back again in a blink.

Does anyone know? Does anyone care?

Surely, Jacky will miss us and tell them to send a plane out looking for us.

Tomorrow morning they'll parachute fuel and water down to us and we'll get going again.

I'd better start setting up a solar still.

The thing I most worried about was water. We could have survived out there for days, even weeks, but not without water. I had boned up on desert survival back in the States, reading many books on the subject, committing to memory the essentials of contriving a solar still. This, basically, involves digging a hole in the sand, placing a container in the bottom of it, covering the hole with a sheet of clear plastic with a weight in the middle of it forcing the plastic to a point over the container. Condensation forms on the underside of the plastic, drips down into the container and collects. That's the theory.

It was middle afternoon, and we had been there more than twenty-four hours without a sign of help. We had stayed in the car most of the day not just because we were tired but also to save our strength and avoid exposing ourselves to the strength of the sun, something else I'd learned in the books I'd read.

In the waning heat, I grabbed a shovel and the sheet of lightweight clear plastic, which I'd gone to great lengths to find, even in New York, and walked off to dig a hole. I made a jab at the sand. The blade went into it an inch or two and clanged to a stop, sending painful vibrations back up my arms. Under the sand there was a crust hard as pavement. I cleared a small area and began to hack away at the black crust. It was impervious to my thrusts. *Great*, I thought. *So much for theory.* I decided it was better not to work up a sweat over it.

There was another job I had to do. One I could do slowly and deliberately without becoming overheated. Streaking toward this place at high speed, I had noticed the car tending to run hot. The engine had a four-bladed fan mounted on it. We knew that at some point we'd have to switch to a more efficient five-bladed fan. This was as good a time as any. I wanted to be ready to roll when help finally came. If help came. About that, I was now beginning to worry.

I spent the next two hours slowly and methodically removing the old fan and installing the new one.

Again we watched the sun fall off one edge of our world, awestruck by the beauty of the desert before being smitten by the cold and fearsome emptiness of it. That night we decided to take full advantage of our predicament and get a good, comfortable night's sleep. We put out the sleeping bags. Surely the bird carried the snake there from someplace else? We hadn't seen a sign of a bird or any other kind of life. Out there, we would see and hear the approach of a snake when it was still a day away no matter how fast or quietly it could slither. Besides, we were too tired to really care.

We both heard it at the same time the next morning. A distant hum moving toward us. It was a plane! We leaped out of our sleeping bags and rushed to get the signaling mirrors from our survival case. We knew what to do, having practiced using them the first day. A bit of foresight that paid off. Before the plane became visible to us, our flashes must have been visible to him because, soon, we saw a small plane flying right into the light shafts we were beaming up. They glinted back down at us off of the fuselage. The pilot circled. I grabbed the metallic blanket, upending all the tools weighing it down onto the sand. We held it, one of us on each side, moving it up and down, catching the sunlight. The plane flew over and waggled its wings at us. We dropped the blanket, did all the cliché stuff. Jumped up and down, screamed, laughed, hugged. Then it was gone. Back in the sudden silence, we wondered what would happen now, if anything.

An hour later, we got an answer. We thought we heard another plane but couldn't see one anywhere. Then, on the horizon, a speck. A speck growing into a spot becoming a car. No, a truck. It was a truck coming out of nowhere, going to nowhere, and pulling up to us there in the middle of nowhere. We couldn't believe it. It was a truck filled with drums of gasoline. The Rallye, the plane must have radioed for it.

A crew of about eight Arabs and Blacks manned the truck. I spoke in strained and broken French with the one who seemed to be the leader, a pock-marked Black man with a stringy little beard and an olive drab turban. Yes, they had gas. Yes, they could sell me 250 liters.

As you know, I held more than 300 liters, yet I only asked for 250. An instinct, I suppose. A silly subterfuge to keep them from understanding the true depth of our plight. As if 250 represented shallower shit than 300.

"*Combien?*" I asked.

He quoted me a price in francs. Fifteen thousand of them. That was about twenty-five hundred dollars.

"*Combien?!*" I asked again in disbelief. Then, shaking my head to signify my negative reaction, said, "*Très, très, très cher! Trop cher!*"

Thus began a tense desert bargaining session that went on for hours.

Soon, it dawned on me that these people had not been sent by the Rallye. I also knew that we had been spotted by a plane, probably the Rallye's. So our situation seemed a little less dire than it had before. I could afford to bargain and stall for time.

The real head man emerged. He looked more Indian or Pakistani than Arab or Black, and he was big. He was wearing a khaki fatigue jacket, what looked like a pair of Pro-Keds, and a massive gold Rolex. With only the looks of him and the rest of his gang to go by, I was somewhat surprised to see the watch mounted on this particular wrist, and not dangling from his belt still attached to a severed one belonging to the original owner.

"I speak English," he said.

"I understand you've got gas, and I'd like to buy some," I told him, "but the price your friend here mentioned is far too high."

Much chattering in a strange foreign tongue ensued among the bunch of them. The head man crouched, drawing a number with his finger, slowly, in the sand.

"10,000."

Ten thousand francs was about seventeen hundred dollars.

I responded verbally to his handwritten offer, "That's ridiculous!"

He glanced up at me. "That is Sahara," he said in a cold and menacing tone, pronouncing it Suh-hah-ra.

With my foot I reached over and erased his asking price. Then I crouched, took a large screwdriver that had been holding the blanket, and made a written counteroffer.

"1,800."

He wiped the number out of the sand, replacing it with a new number of his own.

"6000."

These guys must figure I'm desperate, I thought and stood up.

"Forget it," I said. "We were spotted by a Rallye plane just before you came. They'll be bringing us gas any time now."

Carolyn shot me a plaintive, questioning look. Later she told me she was beside herself wondering why I didn't just buy the gas at any price. I don't know what kind of movies I'd been watching but just instinctively knew you don't let sharks smell blood.

Carolyn had often accused me of being untrusting and overly sus-picious. I think she tends toward the naive and unrealistic. If the truth is somewhere in the middle, at a time like this, you play it my way. I answered her look with an urgent whisper.

"Take pictures!"

I was a little miffed at her. After all the trouble and expense I'd gone to getting her camera equipment, and after all her complaining about not getting any pictures, here we had the photo opportunity of a lifetime and I couldn't understand why she wasn't jumping on it.

"We sell gas to Rallye. That's our business, me and my partners here," the head man was telling me.

Maybe. But I suspected they were desert brigands who had stolen the gas from the nearby Rallye control and were trying to unload it quickly for a huge profit. In fact, I thought it might have been their lights I'd seen on the horizon night before last, roaming around the deserted bivouac. After poring over our charts, I had no doubt that the lights I'd seen had come from the camp.

"Look, the Rallye people will be here soon with free gas for me. I don't need to pay that kind of price." I shrugged and turned away.

He dropped his price. We struck a deal: The French equivalent of $750 for 250 liters.

"But first," I said, "I want to try twenty liters to see if it's any good."

I seemed to have a fathomless reserve of bullshit, bravado, and self-delusion at my disposal. I was still glued to this crazy notion that the Rallye would bring me gas. After all, whenever I'd written an ad in the past, I'd always got results. As for the bravado, it was all a bluff. I just prayed these guys wouldn't call it.

One of them gave me a can, and I poured the contents into the tank, started the car, and drove around in circles leisurely, hoping to project a false nonchalance.

I drove the car alongside the truck so they could pour the gas directly from the truck into the big tank whose filler was located high up on one side. It took four of them to do this job. Three to upend the big drums and pour, one to handle the funnel and hose.

The ones who weren't busy with the gas started circling the car. The head man came over to where we were standing and asked Carolyn's name. She told him.

"You are very beautiful, Carolyn," he said to her.

One of them was hanging around the driver's side door, looking inside. I got back into the car and made a show of taking the flare gun from the dash and placing it on the empty seat next to me. I don't know which was more daunting, the thought of having this thing fired at you or the thought of having to fire it. Since I'd shot it off before, my whole hand had turned black and blue.

I wanted this guy to see the gun. He knew as well as I did that the odds were eight-two his favor. But I wanted him to think it through. If I managed to get two, there would still be six. But would he, personally, be one of the unfortunate two or one of the lucky six? It was like I could see into his head, the gears, him weighing.

He moved away.

Then the first guy I'd talked to, old pockmarked stringy beard, came over.

"Give us T-shirts," he demanded.

All of a sudden, he knew English.

"Why should I?" I asked.

Now in a rage, he demanded again, "Give us T-shirts!"

I just stared at him until he walked away.

An older man wearing a burnoose and a filthy djellaba came over. He had a classic pointy Arab nose and rotten brown teeth.

"Do you have any aspirin?" he asked in French.

"Where does it hurt?"

He pointed to his stomach.

"Aspirin is bad for the stomach."

He began to walk away, then turned back, having learned English in the interval.

"Why won't you give him some T-shirts?"

All this time, Carolyn was packing up our belongings, which had been out of the car all over the sand. When they were not hectoring me, these guys crouched or sprawled on the ground near Carolyn, picking at our stuff as though it was all for sale or free for the taking. I stayed in the car acting big, hoping that I was fooling someone but sweating bullets as big as the flares for my gun.

"Why should I give any of you anything?" I asked the Arab.

"We give you good price on gas," he whined.

"Okay, I'll give you three T-shirts."

"There are more than three of us," he smiled, baring awful teeth.

"That's too many T-shirts. I'll give you three. Then I don't want to hear any more from you."

The deal was finally done. I got the three T-shirts out of the back and gave them to him. I still had about thirty T-shirts left, but I wasn't about to give them out frivolously. We still had to buy our way across three thousand miles of Africa before we got to Dakar.

Some of the others, smelling T-shirts, came over. They began arguing with each other over how they would reconcile the problem of eight into three. I gave the head man forty-five hundred francs. I was tempted to ask him for water but was afraid it would be too telling. Besides, who knew what kind of water they had and what we might catch from drinking it?

"Why don't you come with us to Arlit?" the head man asked me.

"No, we're going to Agadez, to catch up with the Rallye."

"It's faster to Agadez through Arlit. Come with us. We take shortcut through hills. You don't want to go through desert. Very dangerous. Better you come with us."

"No, the Rallye people will be here to meet us any minute. We're going to wait."

As quickly as it had appeared, the truck became a spot, diminished to a speck, then evaporated. I'll never know if this was a truly threatening situation or if it just seemed so. Whether the suggestion to follow them to Arlit was a friendly gesture or the overture for an attempt at robbery or kidnapping. That sort of thing happens all the time in the desert.

Carolyn told me she thought there was no problem, no danger. It was all just my paranoia. I was finding myself at odds with Carolyn more and more now. It was as though the rules we had been playing under had dissolved when we ran out of gas. I felt like the captain of a ship lost in a strange sea, the crew on the verge of mutiny.

Carolyn wanted to take off immediately. I insisted we stay put. We had a heated argument over this, as if our situation wasn't hot enough already.

We'd been spotted, I was certain, by a Rallye plane. If we took off and ran into trouble alone in the desert, there would be no help for us. The Rallye had moved on from the Texaco checkpoint two days ago. What if we got there and couldn't find water? Where to from there? No, the only sensible thing was to wait for the help I knew would come.

About an hour after the truck left, another plane flew over. I got out and fired some flares at it, switching from green ones, which meant we were stranded but okay, to red ones which meant we needed help fast. While I shot off the flares, I asked Carolyn to smear out the "FUEL" in the sand and write a big "H20" in its place. It didn't erase the existence of the fuel problem that dogged us from the start. It just added dimension to it. We were now out of human fuel, and our need for this was more urgent.

The plane circled overhead three times, finally dipping its wings at us as if to say "I read you" before droning out of sight. I was positive they had us covered now and began to relax. We had about a pint of water left in the tank.

We'd been stuck in this spot for fifty-three hours and twenty-seven minutes. Two days of nothing, then a plane, then the gas truck, then another plane. Now we heard something else. A car. Then we saw it. A car, followed by another car. Two stragglers were pulling up to us. Needless to say, we gave them a warm welcome. Other than the Arabs on the truck, these were the first humans we'd seen in days.

We all sat in a circle in the sand for a few minutes, talking. One of the cars was crewed by Frenchmen. The other was a Land Rover piloted by a Venezuelan, Bernard Cave. This was the same bright yellow car I had spent so much time dicing with on what, the fifth day? We told each other our stories. The Venezuelan had been in thirtieth place but had blown his gearbox. After two days of working on it, they could now only limp along slowly. I forget what problem had befallen the French people. But they were badly in need of fuel. They had a diesel engine, and diesel fuel was even rarer than gasoline in the desert. And we, of course, needed water.

We decided to caravan to Texaco, hopefully finding fuel for the Frenchmen and then spend the night. From Texaco we would proceed to Achegour, which had an ancient waterhole marked "poison" on our charts, but which we could treat chemically if we were desperate enough. From there we would caravan to Agadez. The Rallye had gone east, made a big loop in the desert, and would arrive back in Agadez tonight. Tomorrow would be the mid-point rest break. We could make it there before they left the next day.

Bernard had been in the desert even longer than we had. He said he loved it, the peace and beauty of it. He said he wished he could stay out there longer, but once his car was running again, he knew it was safer to move on. I was surprised neither Carolyn nor I had noticed him stranded as we sped by. He'd seen us though, he said, going by so fast, so far behind the pack.

We sat there in the late afternoon sun, quietly talking about such things. No one complained about his problems or railed at the fate that had shattered his aspirations. All the disappointments were buried, and the urgency to move forward was as evident with us as I imagined it was with those who were still in the Rallye. An attitude of wanting to get on with it, to seize life and whatever it brought with it, never looking back. A far cry from so many of the people I knew in New York who spend so much of their lives examining and trying to understand the past, distancing themselves from the present. As if by doing so they can avoid confronting the future and whatever frights it holds.

Stranded in the desert, I had time to think. What did I think about? The past, my life, my children, my successes, my failures? No. None of these. Being possibly close to death, I thought only of life as I then knew it. My world had contracted into a sphere that for the moment contained only Carolyn, Jacky Ickx, Guy Dupard, Kurt Knilli, René Boubet, David McCabe, Ari Vatanen, Gooding, Pescarolo, Fourticq, the Little Red Fat Man, Van Damme, and the others. Maybe my life had expanded, not contracted. One by one, I had thought of them all, wondering where they were and how they were doing. Were they all still going strong or out of it like me? I hadn't once thought of my old life or anything in it. Another life had interposed itself between me and my former one. And that is what I wanted and why I had embraced this crazy idea in the first place.

But now I began to view my recent travail, stranded without fuel in the middle of nowhere, as analogous to my life. End of the line, everybody out. Was that it? Was my career at an end, stalled as I had been in the desert? Were my career and my life inextricably intertwined? Or was my life separate, a moving thing that could not be stalled or sidetracked no matter how confused I was about my career? Would my life go on, leading me to wherever it needed to go? That's what I was banking on. That was the positive side of the analogy. I was free of all former encumbrance and restraint. Free to go wherever I wanted, now that I had fuel. As soon as I made up my mind.

As we headed off into the desert with the other two cars, it struck me as funny that it wasn't until then that I began to wonder where I was going, where my life was taking me. We have an innate priority system that tells us what's important. Obviously, my career worries were only of consequence when there wasn't anything truly important to worry about. That told me something. That reassured me. If I could only wait until it became important, then it would take care of itself.

18

Texaco was a disappointment. But so is everything in life that you have too high hopes for. Whatever I had in mind, this wasn't it. No female attendants wearing the scantiest of short shorts and provocative bustiers roller-skated up to clean my windshield and check the oil. There was no gift shop, no luncheonette, no arcade. No showers for us gritty long-haul desert truckers to refresh ourselves under. There were no refreshments of any kind. Not even a crummy old Coke machine at which to pause, or a water cooler that couldn't quite get it up.

Texaco was a derelict way station on an abandoned petroleum pipe-line. A ramshackle collection of walls and pipes and doors whose bright colors had long since faded, it processed nothing. It just sat there, commercial residue that flapped and groaned in the desert wind, look-ing very much like a miniature version of the Pompidou Museum in Paris, fallen down.

We pulled up just after sunset, having been joined by an organization truck full of bedraggled dropouts that had been picked up along the way. For some reason this "sweep-up" truck was running two days behind schedule. The driver apologized for our long sit in the desert and actually seemed a little embarrassed about it. We all sat around a big campfire, about twenty of us, not trading war stories. Everybody knew that everybody else had an interesting one to tell, so no one bothered to. Sort of like Bush and Gorbachev being washed up on a desert island after a nuclear disagreement. What would there be to say—"Sorry?"

We were a sorry-looking bunch of survivors, sitting at the feet of this industrial phantom. Most of us hadn't washed or shaved in more than ten days and looked as though we'd been through exactly what we'd been through. We stuck our pans in the fire and made ourselves a good, hot meal.

An Italian mechanic whose specialty was the Mercedes Gelande-wagen helped me change a wheel. I'd ruptured the sidewall of the right rear tire when I'd run over a large rock at high speed and broke the shock. We found a store of oil drums, most of them empty, but some still contained traces of fuel. The other two cars in our party stayed up most of the night, rummaging through them and pumping fuel into their tanks with a tiny, underpowered electric pump. I got two litres of bad-tasting chemically-treated water from the Organiza-tion truck, which is all they could spare, before turning in for the night.

At dawn we got up; Carolyn took one look at me and ran for a camera. She took a photograph, which is far from the most flattering ever taken of me but one of the best to come out of this adventure, for it perfectly illustrates the exhaustion, the strain, the discomfort, the Rallye subjects one to. And it captured the maniacal determination written on the faces of all who go through it. Or try to.

Having tried to go through it, and failed, I now found myself in a peculiar position. I didn't know how to feel. I was in a mental quan-dary, not knowing whether to feel like a failure for having failed to finish or like a hero for having tried. We had tried to do the world's hardest race, the hardest possible way. With no one to take over the car when we came in at night like the pros had, we had driven ourselves senseless. In any event, eight days was the farthest any American had ever made it in a car. But was that anything worth bragging about? Maybe. It was a joke among French journalists that no American could make it more than three or four days in Paris/Dakar because they couldn't go any longer than that without a shower. Well we'd shown them. And we both exuded the not-so-sweet smell of our success.

Now we were going on, not as competitors but as journalists. We were obliged to deliver a story to *Esquire* magazine and to *The Au-tomobile*, a secondary motivation, at best, for continuing to suffer the tortures of the Rallye. We had to go through with it for another reason as well. We needed to get to Dakar in order to have the car shipped back to the United States. I wasn't about to park my enormous in-vestment in the sand and walk away from it.

If anything, the next ten days were more hellish for us than the first ten had been. For we now lacked the driving, single-minded sense of purpose that had brought us this far. Discomforts we hadn't even noticed before now began to annoy and eat away at us. Freed from the all-consuming pressure of competition, we were now able to observe and reflect. We had to hurry to catch up with the Rallye. Once we'd caught it, we'd have to hurry to keep up with it. We were now being manipulated by outside pressures we were able to understand and analyze and therefore wanted to reject.

I noticed more, felt more, and remember more of every hour of the next few days than from the entire ten days that preceded it.

The three cars, mine, Bernard's, and the Frenchman's, caravanned slowly toward the water hole at Achegour. We could go no faster than Bernard's badly mangled transmission would allow. We set out at eight in the morning and estimated that we would arrive in Agadez at eight that night, in time to catch up with the Rallye. Twelve hours of slow grinding through deep sand that was soft and tried to pull us down into it every inch of the way. The days were getting hotter and hotter now. We were deep in the Tenere Desert—one of the many deserts that make up the Sahara. And this was one of the most desertlike of all.

We plowed through what seemed to be an endless open expanse of sand, arriving at a broken-down straw shack next to a raised concrete platform just before noon. This would have been the center of the town square, if there had been a town or even a square. It was the well at Achegour. That's all there was to Achegour, a well. A holeful of tainted water. We were all desperate for water. There wasn't another drop for three hundred miles in any direction.

A big bucket dangled from a frayed rope down into the cool darkness of the well. We stood around in a circle looking down into it. The sun pounded on our backs and pushed us down toward the coolness we could feel reaching up to our faces out of the black. Bernard's copilot, a muscular and surly young Venezuelan, whose competence Bernard had bemoaned, wielded the bucket. He hauled it up, straining, and passed it around, each of us scooping out some water and drenching ourselves with it to cool off. It was surprisingly cold. After we were all refreshed, he hauled up more buckets and we each filled one of our water tanks with it. I handed around the treatment tablets, and we all put in half again as many as the instructions called for.

Soon after leaving Achegour, Bernard's transmission finally gave out. He piled into the cockpit with us, his co-pilot rode with the Frenchmen.

Carolyn gave up her seat to Bernard and straddled the fire extinguisher in between. For hours we went along like this, the transmission
in four-wheel low, the wheels spinning through mile after mile of sand.
The sun beating down on us was hot, the sand underneath was hot,
and the transmission tunnel over which Carolyn sat grew intensely
hot from its labors. I could see that she was in extreme discomfort
both from the heat and from the hardness and smallness of her perch.
A part of me commiserated with her. But she had made the grand
unnecessary gesture. I was annoyed that she had made it. For I was
suffering along with her in stupid sympathy with her self-inflicted
punishment. Bernard would have been happy to ride in-between. Many
times Bernard had offered to change places with her, but she stubbornly
refused, seeming to enjoy playing the martyr.

An interesting character, this Venezuelan. A Caracas real-estate
developer who apparently did pretty well. The fact that he had twenty
homes around the world as well as a private plane were clues that
came out as we went along.

We were on the Trans-Saharan Highway now. Don't be misled by
its name. It is nothing more than a sand-track marked with sticks, six
lanes wide though.

We plowed along, hour after drowsy and sweaty hour. At eight
that night, we weren't in Agadez as we hoped we'd be, but lost in
terrain as bad as any we'd encountered in Algeria. Boulders, chasms,
mangled scrub trees, white rats, the full panoply of horrors. We'd
taken an offshoot of the Trans-Saharan, thinking it was a shortcut to
Agadez. We'd lost the Frenchmen who had been tailing us, had no
idea where they'd gone or where they were. The offshoot turned out
to be a dud, so we spent hours grinding around in circles, looking for
a way out.

Seeing that this was getting us nowhere, I picked a heading and
stuck to it no matter what obstacles we came across. It was The Little
Engine That Could all over again. We crawled over huge rock heaps,
went into and came out of a succession of abysses, once in a while
stopping to shoot off some bright, white flares to light our way
through them. Eventually we came to a road under construction,
thirty miles the wrong side of Agadez. Carolyn had long ago moved
to the back of the car where she rattled and shook up and down
on our luggage like a sack of potatoes. The heat and the cramps
generated by her seat in the cockpit finally got the better of her. By

the time we pulled into the Agadez bivouac, it was three in the morning, and we were as badly beaten and disheveled as we'd been on any night of the Rallye.

The Rallye had shrunk still more. The few people we saw there in the morning were mostly strangers to us. Anyone we knew who might still be in the running must have already left. We had caught up with the Rallye, but it was, literally, running away from us. We found Suzanne. She gave us a quizzical expression as if to ask "What are *you* doing here?" Then she explained. We were no longer part of the Rallye and would not be allowed in the Rallye bivouacs or to eat the Rallye's food. That was no problem. We hadn't anyway.

I explained that we had not only been competitors but were planning to go on as press, covering the event. We had registered ourselves as press from the outset. We would have to talk to the Rallye director, she told us. But she thought it highly unlikely. The rule was, once you're out, you're out.

The Rallye would be moving from Agadez to Tahoua, the following day from Tahoua to Niamey, the capital of Niger. We could leave Agadez the next day, take a shortcut, and catch the Rallye in Niamey in time to get our press status sorted out. In the meantime, we'd spend an easy day, get needed food and rest, and do some overdue mainte-nance on the car.

Walking back to the car, we ran into René Boubet and asked him how it was going. Not well, he told us, smiling. He'd gotten a wind-shield and managed to replace it, all the while holding a very good position. Then yesterday he had rolled the car and lost his windshield again. He'd fallen way behind and thought he might drop out tomor-row. He was happy, friendly, smiling. These Frenchmen amazed me. They were all like this. No gnashing of teeth or complaining. They were the best sportsmen I'd ever seen. Boubet, for me, epitomized the French and their sporting flair. He was even washed, clean-shaven, and was wearing a fresh ascot. He sauntered off to his car, ready to face another grueling day in the open air.

"Did you *look* at him?" Carolyn asked. "And look at yourself. Aren't you ashamed of how you look?"

Actually, I was looking good compared to how I was to look a few hours later. I found my trucks just before they started and got oil, shock absorbers, and a few other odds and ends out of the chests. Even with the careful packing, the contents had taken a beating. The spare battery had cracked in two, a can of brake fluid had split open and leaked all over everything, the spare Halda had come apart, gears and little springs were scattered all through the sand and dust lining both chests. Opening them was like opening ancient Egyptian crypts.

With Carolyn's help I changed the rear shock absorbers. After that, I got under the front of the car to drain the engine oil. I had a plastic can under the car with me to catch the oil. I completely misjudged the direction and velocity of the filthy stream. Instead of pouring straight down under the drain plug as I'd anticipated, it shot out to one side, splashing right into my face, soaking my hair. I tried to push the plug back in to staunch the flow. Then it just ran down my arm inside my coveralls. By the time I rolled out from under there, the hot, sticky, dirty stuff covered every inch of my body. Now Carolyn had an airtight case against the way I looked.

After the third shampoo, most of the sand comes out. But it's not until after the fifth that you begin to get the oil and dust. Even so, my hair didn't feel completely clean, and I knew it would remain slimy and gritty for some time to come. I stood in the concrete stall shower at the Hotel Telwa in Agadez, watching my last twelve days merge with the cold water and swirl down the drain. It made me feel lighter, as though I would emerge twelve days younger. I also felt a little sad, watching what had been so much a part of me gurgle away under the gray suds. I saw a dead frog lying there on the floor of the shower with his outstretched bloody feet and left it there.

I flopped on the bed. Carolyn went into the shower and I lay there, relaxing, waiting for her scream.

The Hotel Telwa was about as far from a luxury hotel as you could get. It was a bare-bones cinderblock oasis. But, oh, what a paradise it seemed. When we drove up, a native at the front door offered to stay up all night and guard the car, for a fee of course. I know of no hotel in New York that offers this much-needed service.

Abahi was the name of the boy. Abahi did everything. He was the hotel laundryman, ran the hotel car wash, ran errands, supplied water. Whatever you needed, you just had to find Abahi and it was done with a smile. Abahi was about twelve or thirteen, so black he appeared to have fluorescent teeth, which were always switched on, bathing his entire face in a happy light. He was in awe of me and Carolyn, as he was of everyone else who drove the Rallye. He collected decals and stickers from the cars and sponsors. Unfortunately we had no decals, but we gave him a T-shirt and a few little trinkets we picked up in Paris. Eiffel Tower key chains and such.

Abahi was standing outside the open door to our room, waiting to pick up our laundry when the scream came.

"Eeeeeek! There's a frog in the shower!" Carolyn predictably cried.

"Oh, good, you found it," I said enthusiastically. "There's a little boy here looking for it. It's his pet."

"It's dead!"

"Oh, no! Have you killed it? It was alive and kicking when I saw it."

Carolyn was not amused. I went into the shower, removed the body, and tossed it outside, into the dirt corridor, beaming a big one back at Abahi.

"She hates the French," I told him.

He didn't get it but kept smiling anyway.

That'll teach her to tell me I don't look good, I thought, enjoying playful retribution. Lunch was couscous. Now that the worst of the pressure was off, I figured I could get away with eating some meat. It was the first legitimate meal Carolyn or I had had since the dinner on the boat. We both ate way too much, but it was wonderful nonetheless.

The Hotel Telwa on this day, the twelfth day of the Rallye, served as a way station for displaced persons. Going out of the hotel, we bumped into Bernard coming in. He was arranging to have his car brought in out of the desert. Going back into the hotel, we ran into Gooding and his copilot coming out. They had broken their front suspension the day before yesterday and were trying to get their car back, too. We saw the Frenchmen we'd become separated from the day before. They were very mad at us for deserting them. We told them of our terrible night, and that seemed to mollify them.

It was like we were all meeting in the revolving door of a building to which we had all gone to apply for the same job. It made me feel better, knowing I wasn't the only one interested in this lousy position.

That afternoon we wandered around Agadez sight-seeing. There wasn't a lot to see. It was a bustling village of a few thousand inhabitants. Wide, dusty streets lined with white stucco walls hid the sights and the squalor from view. The town had a huge souk for one of its size and population. It was a trading post for people who came to Agadez from all over the Sahara. Camels and mules piled high with sacks were tethered in the streets, their handlers goading them into position and unloading them. The market sold everything from fruits and vegetables to wood carvings and custom-made shirts, which were fabricated on the spot by batteries of natives at sewing machines.

As we moved, browsing from stall to stall, a group of raggedy black children began to form and grow around us. They all begged for *ca-deaux*. We had anticipated this and carried a supply of the trinkets we'd bought in Paris to pass out. We distributed a few token gifts and gave a little boy of about six a tiny toy camera. His eyes bulged with wonder as he looked it over, trying to figure out what to do with it. He clutched it hungrily.

Suddenly, a bunch of the bigger, older boys leaped on him, pum-meling him, trying to wrench the toy from his grasp. Before we could do anything, they twisted the camera out of his little hands and ran off, leaving him crying on the ground in the dust.

Carolyn ran after the others, caught them, and took the camera back and brought it to the blubbering little boy. Such happiness. But it was sad. For we knew it couldn't last. As he held the camera, we could see him looking around with fear in his eyes. He would be beaten and lose it yet again when they were all out of our sight. Here was a case where it would have been better not to give. A situation where giving caused pain. I wished we had brought only hundreds of ballpoint pens, something we could give democratically that they could all use pro-ductively. But even that wouldn't have been enough to meet the need. And there would always be one who wanted two. The memory of this experience rode with us for the rest of the trip, and the fear of reliving it tended to make misers of us.

We used the hotel phone to call the States. Carolyn talked to her parents in Pennsylvania. I called my secretary in New York, and asked her to contact all our friends and relations, and tell them that we were out but okay and would be pushing on to Dakar with the Rallye to the end. We might as well have been talking on an interoffice phone, the connection was so clear. Somehow, I hadn't expected that. I didn't like it. It pushed me mentally back toward my life in New York, made it seem too close, too real, like this was, in fact, the dream and that was reality, waiting for me to return to it.

I had begun to see it the other way around. This was the reality I wanted, not that one there. This was where life was. The discomfort, the danger, the consuming need to overcome a succession of obstacles, these challenges made both today and tomorrow seem more worth living than they had ever seemed before. No scenario I could conjure up seemed to hold half as much allure. New York and all that it stood for seemed threateningly near. It threw me into a state of apprehension verging on depression. In the best of all possible worlds, in my own private production of this dream, the telephone connection was supposed to be awful.

The next morning we were out of there, our laundry still damp, but clean, our water tanks full to the tune of a hundred dollars. Steep, but that is "Suhahra" the natives kept saying. Abahi stood in the street and waved us on our way, beaming as always.

It was Tuesday the thirteenth of January. Just outside of Agadez, on the road to Niamey via Tahoua we come upon an amazing spectacle. A camel caravan was crossing the road and heading out into the desert. It looked to be about two miles long. There must have been three hundred camels in it. Neither of us had ever seen anything like it before. A living, breathing, stinking, fly-infested freight train. While we sat and watched it move off into the desert, I wished I could hop aboard and let it take me wherever it wanted to go. I could feel an end coming. I was still in search of a beginning.

A pale magenta cloud floated on the horizon. Driving toward it and then into it, we came to realize that it was a sandstorm. The visibility was as bad as it was when we were racing, and even though we now traveled on a paved, public road, the journey was not without risk. A high wind deposited drifts of sand across the road, which we could hardly see. We traveled in a generic, undetailed brightness that made me groggy, and over and over again I caught myself nodding off at the wheel. I snapped awake when we came upon a mangled car being raised out of a gully by a tow truck. *Nobody could have lived through that,* I thought, as I stared at the twisted wreckage and drove on with newfound wakefulness.

We got to Niamey and tracked down the Rallye director having dinner in a large modern hotel that was acting as Rallye headquarters. Patrick Verdoy turned out to be one of those pretentious French bureaucrats whose minds are too small to wrap around anything bigger than a rule. He smiled a lot, making us feel small, treating us as though our major reason for now wanting to go along with the Rallye as press was to sponge off their food.

We wanted to continue as though we were still competing so Carolyn could get some good action pictures. She'd gotten very few when we were actually racing. She wasn't going to get any more either. TSO Officialdom wouldn't budge on this. The best they would do was let us run along at the tail of each stage, as press, keeping in touch with the Rallye and in that way getting our car to Dakar. Patrick warned us, however, that under no circumstances were we allowed to help a competing car in any way, no matter how much they begged, cajoled, or offered to pay.

In retrospect, I think Patrick made the right decision not letting us continue to act as though we were competing. It would have been unfair to the other competitors. Also I think he was right to have cautioned us against helping others, for many appealed for our help as it turned out. But his manner was so annoying, I wanted to smack him on the ear. With his condescending smile, he intimated that of course we could be swayed to help someone if the price was right, as if he thought we needed the money.

We went looking around for our friends in a shitty frame of mind. Many people we knew were out, and we found quite a few of them hanging around this hotel. David McCabe had become so tired and senseless that on the tenth day he put diesel fuel in his bike by mistake and melted his pistons. Kurt Knilli lasted a day longer than I did. He said his car just mysteriously burst into flames and burned to the ground. He was still filthy, covered with smoky stains and streaks. Pescarolo and Fourticq went out the day before us. I couldn't find out the cause. Guy Dupard wasn't there, but someone told us his engine exploded on the sixth day and he would be coming to Dakar. I wondered if he'd show up with some salvaged salamis.

I learned that the car I'd seen being pulled out of the ditch belonged to a journalist who had been trying to keep up with the Rallye. He was killed, the first fatality so far. A lean year. I assume he just fell asleep at the wheel. Traveling alone, he didn't have anyone to keep him awake.

We found Jacky in the lobby and summarized our adventures for him. It didn't feel good finding him. I felt we had taken his help and counsel under false pretenses and let him down. He seemed much less interested in us now than before. He seemed to have other concerns now. We were just history. He was in tenth place. Vatanen had taken over the lead and was extending it day by day. One of the big trucks was in seventh place, a piece of news that astonished everyone. Seppi, in the Mercedes like mine, was in eighteenth place. Way to go, Seppi! I was rooting for him for sentimental reasons. Out of the 311 cars that started, only 117 were left. The Rallye continued to grind people and cars into the dust.

Some people were barely hanging on. The Little Red Fat Man was fourth from last. Of the three cars behind him, one was that of the Belgians Van Damme and Cnudde. The big competitive story, of course, was being written among the leaders, the top ten or fifteen pros slugging it out for money and glory. But I was attracted by the drama I could see building around the little people, the burrs that wouldn't be shaken from under the saddle. To me, the Little Red Fat Men were bigger heros than the Vatanens. Theirs was the greater glory. For they had no tents, no mechanics, no sleep, no help, no hope, no great driving talent, and little business being there. They had only dreams. Dreams whose fading relevance made them all the more essential to pursue with even greater tenacity. Not surprisingly, I related to this.

We felt like outcasts among both groups. And being there was not a pleasure. First the organization, then the contestants who were still in it, seemed to be giving us the cold shoulder. We felt like members of a leprous band of gate-crashers and began to wish we could just go away and disappear. We resolved to go along with the Rallye only when we had to, taking shortcuts on our own whenever we could. We slept that night in our sleeping bags on the hotel's mosquito-infested lawn. There was no room for us at the inn.

We took the direct route to Gao, the next stop on the Rallye's rampage across Africa. But in the Sahara, even the straightest route takes strange and unexpected twists and turns. Every few miles we came to a "border crossing." After the first six or seven, we wised up to the chains stretched across the road in every little village through which we passed. Natives, some dressed in official-looking military garb, would come up to the car, ask to see our passports, then beg us for T-shirts, pens, lighters, anything they could get. Which in our case was nothing.

I now regarded our *cadeaux* as precious currency to be paid out only for services rendered, or for those clearly deserving, not extorting, unless it was absolutely necessary. So I began driving right around the chains at high speed, watching the natives scatter like khaki-clad chickens. After nineteen of these, we came to the last, the official one on the Niger/Mali border. Here, the uniformed officer took our passports into a little stone shed with a dirt floor. We followed him and after a few minutes of just standing and watching him sit, I asked for our passports back.

"Do you have some T-shirts for me?" he asked.

I went out to the car and brought him two. He looked them over, not liking what he saw.

"No writing on them," he complained.

"That's all I have."

He snorted contemptuously and tossed them on a table behind his desk, stamped our passports, and handed them over. I asked myself what would have happened if I hadn't had any T-shirts at all. The firing squad, I guessed.

After successfully negotiating our way around and through all these extortion points, we were relieved as hell to be getting out of Niger and into Mali.

It's a beautiful, colorful country, Mali. Out of the parched, drab, and dusty earth upon which we'd been traveling, a lush oasis seemed to sprout. We were now in a country whose surface had been painted by a primitive artist, one who was not afraid to experiment with color. The flatness gave way to plains with slight undulations in them. Rather than sand, the desert seemed to be made up of pieces of polished terra cotta, like pebbles worn smooth by the sea. The buildings, even little native shacks, were more stylish, more tastefully designed. In the villages, there were long, low apartment dwellings made of red clay with crenellated ramparts. These abutted the edges of the road. Brightly dressed inhabitants lined the roofs, waving welcomes, wearing smiles as bright as their clothes.

Between the villages, which were few and far between, there were occasional huts with bleached white stucco walls and neatly trimmed thatch roofs. Some of them appeared to be made entirely of straw, with interesting patterns woven right into the walls. Some were surrounded by liberal plots of land, the boundaries fenced off with artfully arranged pieces of sunbleached driftwood. Off in the distance, we could see lush bursts of emerald green. The river Niger was an ocean blue and looked cool and inviting in contrast to the sunburned copper-colored plains.

If I go on a bit about color, it is only because it washed over our dulled senses and cleared our vision, revealing something truly new. It was as though we had driven through a decade and before our mental film of it was completed, technology progressed from black and white to color. The sky was a brilliant deep blue, and we couldn't see a mote of dust in it anywhere. Nor any of the flies that had so recently clouded over us. It was as though we were in the American Southwest, the way someone who's never been there would imagine it. The American Southwest the way a gifted artist who had never actually seen it would paint it from inspired imagination. For a time, being there felt clean and good.

Caught up in the beauty of the place and the magic of the moment, we took pictures. We stopped in front of one of the more picturesque of the native huts. Carolyn rounded up a family of about ten kids, their parents and their grandparents, yakking away at them in English, calling them all out of their hut, gathering them in a group and positioning them for the camera. She took a picture of me standing with them in front of the car, in front of their primitive dwelling. We moved on. Every mile seemed to become more beautiful than the last. The Niger looked wider, bluer, cooler. The levees grew larger and even more verdant.

We passed through fairytale villages whose buildings looked like chocolate sandcastles with bright blue doors. The buildings were placed haphazardly yet somehow perfectly correctly from a design point of view, even the most nonsensical arrangements seemed to make some kind of visual sense.

But all this was chimera. We were being sucked in by the beauty of one of the world's ugliest places. Beneath the tranquil surface layer, there was pentimento as yet unseen. An underlying image of corruption and brazen thievery that, once viewed, can deface the beauty of the place in your memory, forever.

We were the first to pull into the Rallye bivouac in Gao at about five in the afternoon, having gotten gas at a station with no line. As beautiful as the day had been, that's how ugly this country looked to us now as the day began to shrink into the nearing night. The camp was disgusting. A fenced-in field covered with shards of broken glass, pieces of tin and aluminum, and much evidence of more personal human waste. We set up camp under a long-dead tree. We hadn't been there three minutes before a swarm of ragged children, ranging in age from seven to twelve or thirteen, surrounded us. One would dart in at us from the perimeter, try to grab something and dart back into the circle that undulated around us. We were standing back to back, verbally fending them off.

"Cadeau, cadeau," they whimpered and whined, taking turns making strafing runs at us, becoming more forward and insistent with each attempt. We couldn't unpack and set anything up. We'd lose it all. So we stood there yelling at them to get away. I began assembling a pile of rocks, for a campfire and, possibly, for self-defense.

Motorcycles and cars were streaming into the bivouac now. Having made it clear to the kids that they would get nothing from us without a hell of a fight, some began to lose interest and moved away in search of newly arrived and possibly easier pickings. Still, they left six sentries to keep their eyes on us. It seemed as though they had this down to a system. If some worthwhile booty appeared, they could always send for reinforcements.

We found this more disturbing and wearing than the Rallye itself. We had to keep so alert and on guard that we couldn't relax for a second. No one in the Rallye seemed immune. Even the big teams with all of their burly personnel had trouble defending themselves.

At least we ate. I paid off a few of the young sentries to go gather brush for a fire, and we made a great feast of lentils and vegetables, distributing the leftovers among them. They watched us eat from the shadows around the smoldering fire, their wide, white unblinking eyes ever alert for some sign of weakness upon which they could pounce.

We didn't dare sleep. So neither of us was in condition to drive the speciale to Tombouctou the next day. But we had to. And the long, 590-kilometer one the day after from Tombouctou to Nema in Mauritania. It was the only way we could get to Dakar. We had to cross some more desert wastes, and even the unwelcoming Rallye officials told us it was best to stay with the Rallye for our own safety. Safer to drive along in the world's most dangerous race than to cross this country at our leisure alone. We were now revising our early Pollyanna feelings about Mali.

This speciale was short, only 418 kilometers, but it was brutal. Hot and dusty with heat and dust the likes of which we hadn't felt or seen before. It was about 110 degrees outside, and twenty or thirty degrees hotter than that inside the car. The heat was stifling, but the dust was downright suffocating. Dust we'd experienced before was lightweight stuff compared to this. Now it billowed into the car in hot waves, having been previously baked in the sun. It was an inch thick on the floor of the car. As I cranked the wheel from one side to the other, my elbows hit my sides, raising further clouds of dust, so much was imbedded in our clothing. Occasionally we had to stop just to allow the dust cloud inside the car to subside so we could gasp for a clean, hot breath.

Despite the stopping we were going hell-bent for Tombouctou and Dakar beyond. And this was our biggest problem. Not the heat and dust and violent bumps, which would catch us completely by surprise because they were hidden under the fine sand that covered the track. These would jolt and snap our helmet-heavy heads with great force and frequency. The problem was our speed. We were catching and passing too many cars and trucks that were still in the Rallye.

To be perfectly polite and play by the rules, I should have lingered behind. But I was both physically and emotionally incapable of this. To go slower meant becoming bogged down in the sand. To start last and stay last meant having fewer opportunities for help in case we encountered a problem along the way. So I didn't push, but I didn't dawdle either. Most contestants still in the Rallye but at the back of the pack were simply no match for us. Some of them were victims of prior accidents. Every day there had been three or four crashes reported and many injuries treated. Burns, broken arms and legs, and such. Some suffered mechanical difficulties, yet pressed on regardless.

We gobbled them up, leaving them in our dust, adding insult to whatever injury had already been inflicted. They knew we were out because we'd X'd out our numbers. I know how it must have rankled. Had I been in their place, I would have gone berserk. But I did the only thing I felt I could do. I sympathized with them, then passed. Whenever I caught up with a car or truck that was still going strong, I held back, chasing after them. Sometimes I'd get bored even with this and seeing a cross-country opening veering off the track, I'd take it, rejoining the main track somewhere ahead.

Whenever I took these little detours, the car would pay for it. There were petrified dead trees sticking up out of the powdery sand all along this route, and they had hard, sharp barbs on them. Every time we shot through one of the narrow trails off to the side, it was to the unnerving, dissonant screech of steel fingernails clawing across a blackboard.

Occasionally, we'd speed through a small village. One I remember consisted of about six huts and a couple of small clay buildings. A lone black man stood by the side of the trail that cut through his village. He was wearing a flowing lavender robe that billowed out in the gusty breeze left by passing cars. A fine veil of crimson dust lingered over the trail. He stood just clear of it, standing out sharply in the sunlight. He looked about sixty, was tall and muscular, with knotty features and graying hair. He was frozen in midstep, as though caught by a camera, and his face was fixed with a stoic expression, one of dignified puzzle-ment. He just stared at our car as we flashed past and Carolyn shot a picture.

We speculated for a while, probing each other for the possible mean-ing of this seemingly ordinary occurrence.

All year long the man walks or stands there in his little village and absolutely nothing unusual happens. Then one day all these motor-cycles and cars and trucks show up. They zoom through making loud noises, spurting flames from their turbocharged engines and kicking up dust. Where does he think they all came from? Does he know that they traveled all the way from Europe? Does he have any idea where Europe is, or even that there is such a place? Maybe he thinks this is some kind of natural phenomenon that occurs in his village once every year about this time. Does he know that it happens in other villages up and down the line too? Does he think we all fell from the sky?

Does he believe the gods have cast these objects into his midst? Maybe he just accepts what he sees as a fact that he can't hope to understand. Is he amused, angered, or confused by our presence here? Or has he simply denied us our relevance, just waiting for us to pass so he can cross the road?

We arrived at the Tombouctou control well up in the middle of the pack. It was late afternoon, and the sun was getting ready to set. As we slowed to signal our arrival to the Rallye officials, we sagged, limp and relieved inside our shoulder harnesses. The soft, muted purple of the desert dusk washed over us in a relaxing ebb. Then blurred, moving colors appeared and flowed alongside of us. Magenta, bright yellow, steely gray, fluid running colors like a watercolor hastily daubed. It was a pack of children ranging in age from maybe eight to fifteen running alongside us. We headed toward the main village, unable to go more than about ten miles an hour, so thick were the children around us. We saw the bright clothes were ragged, but the children did not look dirty. It seemed they all had their hands outstretched toward us even as they trotted alongside.

While we were moving at this reduced speed, one of the kids opened the rear door, clambered up inside, and made off with Carolyn's duffel bag. Carolyn started yelling and pointing. It happened so quickly I didn't even see it, but she had. I jumped out of the car and ran as fast as I could after the small vanishing figure scrabbling up the face of a dune at incredible speed, considering he was carrying a duffel bag bigger than he was. From the brief glimpse I got of him dragging the bag over the top of the dune, I'd say he couldn't have been more than nine years old. Seeing that catching him was hopeless—he was that fast—I dashed back to the car, got in, and roared off after him. Twenty or thirty kids had broken out of the main pack and were running ahead, behind, and on each side of us.

Carolyn was in tears and acted as though she had suffered the final blow. She had reached her limit. The incident put me into such a blind rage I could have ended up doing life in a prison there. We chased the boy into a tiny village of about ten squalid huts. It was like stepping not only into another country, another culture, but into another time in history. The huts were round, like Navaho hogans in Arizona, but of white stucco with thatched roofs. There were no doors on them, nor cloth hanging at their entrances. We could have just stepped inside any one of them. A powerful instinct told that would be a potentially disastrous mistake, a mantle of sense quieting my trembling rage. There was no sign of the boy anywhere.

Carolyn got out of the car and made a teary plea for information on his whereabouts. He was obviously being hidden by someone in one of the huts where they were divvying up the loot, which was of little value to anyone but Carolyn. The bag contained her underwear, clothing, and toilet articles, not much more than that. But it was all she had in the world then and it meant more to her than jewels would mean to someone in more familiar and less threatening surroundings.

I said the huts were squalid, but not as miserable as you might imagine, given the degree of apparent desperation. It could have been that many were forced to live in each one of these little dwellings. But at least they had shelter. There was no evidence of starvation. To be sure, there were no fatties in sight. Yet none of the natives appeared emaciated.

There were few adults to be seen. Were they away, working? Where were the parents of all these marauding children? Had they abandoned them at birth? Were there simply too many kids to care for? Were there no schools for them to attend? Was there no law to keep them in check? Could it be that we in the Rallye were their only hope for help? Would a lone tourist passing through be picked clean to the bone? There was much I didn't understand. Maybe I was missing something obvious. Maybe I was too angry to reason. Something didn't track. I had difficulty sympathizing with what I could not understand.

We were standing outside the car in the middle of this tiny hamlet, fully exposed to the circle that was slowly beginning to tighten around us. I seemed to sense that we were standing on the site of a central campfire, but it may have been my imagination making me and Carolyn into unfortunate missionaries whose inopportune arrival at the cannibals' village made life very hot for them. Even so, I could see that they were more scared than we were, what with this crazy man who had driven boldly right into their village and the distraught girl standing there screaming at them. In poker, a full house beats three of a kind. But in life, an empty house beats everything. Something I learned on the streets of Chicago is, the one thing that can frighten and intimidate even hardened and violent killers is an unpredictable lunatic. Clearly, just by being there, Carolyn and I were not playing with a full deck. And I could see in those astonished faces that for the moment anyway, we held the upper hand.

Looking around and seeing that none of the Rallye contestants nor any of the officials who, incidentally, had witnessed the whole thing, had come to our aid, I thought it best to give up and get out of there. Before all the villagers came out, came to their senses, and realized they had us outnumbered and surrounded.

We had dinner in a big—that is, big by Tombouctou standards—hotel that night. It was not really so big, nor was it entirely civilized. This was the first place we'd been where there was no evidence or apparent knowledge of something called Coca-Cola.

Everyone we saw commiserated with Carolyn and tried to cheer her up. Zanussi, an affable Italian who was one of the Peugeot factory team drivers, gave her a T-shirt. The Peugeot team not only had thermometers on their shock absorbers and special water pumps that could be operated by the copilots to cool them, not only did they have dozens of mechanics who rebuilt the cars practically from scratch every night, but they seemed to have an endless supply of T-shirts, jackets, duffel bags, and other color-coordinated paraphernalia to hand out.

Seppi came over and was very solicitous. I asked him how he was doing. He was in fourteenth place and going strong. But an acquaintance, also driving a Gelandewagen, wasn't doing so well, he informed me. He needed a driveshaft and wanted to talk to me about cannibalizing my car so he could go on. I didn't want to get into such a discussion there, so I told him to have the guy look me up in the bivouac after dinner.

The campsite was located next to the airfield and was aswarm with ragamuffins. The whole campground was alive with the shouts of concurrents trying to chase them away. But there were so many of them they practically looted at will.

The man with car problems came to see me. Reading the desperation in his eyes, it seemed he would kill to get the parts he needed. The Rallye not only brought out bravery, heroism, and good in people, it pushed some to cheat and do possibly much worse in order to keep their hopes alive. Out of both sensitivity and fear, I didn't give him a flat refusal. I explained to him that the Rallye Organization was watching us like hawks because they knew we would be approached for help. I told him I'd love to be able to help him, but that he would surely be caught and disqualified. That got me off the hook.

The Rallye now contained less than a quarter of its original population. Aside from the elaborate little tent villages of the factory teams whose mechanics labored under lights all night, there was only exhaustion to be seen. The motorcyclists and truckers no longer encamped in separate areas. It was now one small cluster of holdouts trying to get to Dakar. Where their methods of transport were once a segregating force, the common goal now bound them together as one.

Everybody seemed to conk out at night now. Few stayed up working on their cars. One stood out. It was the Barger, bent into his engine, working under dim lights in the ghostly campground. I began to feel a grudging respect for this Bravione who now seemed so aptly named.

We got into our sleeping bags. I couldn't sleep. I lay there all night watching small shadows carrying large bags. They slinked through the fence and slithered out across the airfield dragging their booty behind. It wouldn't have done any good to chase after them or even to shout and raise an alarm. They were too fast. And their victims were too spent to do anything about it. Or even to care.

I, and I supposed Carolyn as well, was swamped with a sense of ennui. Our lives seemed to have lost pace and bogged down. It wasn't that the events we were now living through and experiencing lacked vitality. They lacked purpose. Out of the Rallye, there was no thrust or direction to our journey other than to get to the end. We were existing and that wasn't enough.

With no worthwhile goal, no dream to pursue, I was beginning to feel lost, disinterested, just as I had felt in my business. Even isolated events and adventures, interesting in and of themselves, seemed less so than they could be, or had recently been, because they popped irrelevantly into our now aimless journey. There was an irony to this. I had looked upon this endeavor as a distraction, as a cushion against the letdown I was sure I would feel from having left advertising after so many years. Now even the cushion had been pulled out from under me, and I came crashing down to the floor stunned and bewildered. How was I to know that those few days of incredible intensity that had so quickly passed would prove harder to live without than a lifelong career? Excitement, danger, these are powerful drugs. I needed more. I was suffering the early symptoms of withdrawal.

19

The next day's speciale from Tom-
bouctou to Nema was as hard as anything we'd experienced when
we had gone at it for real. Needless to say the primary elements were
heat, dust, and bumps. It was a jarring and exhausting sixteen-hour
day.

The Gelandewagen, staunch as it was, finally showed signs of buck-
ling under the torrent of abuse that kept coming at it. The horns no
longer blared, nor even squeaked. The windshield washers wouldn't
wash, and the wipers wouldn't wipe at all. There was no estimating
how many hundreds of pounds of dust they'd cleared away over the
last sixteen days. The electronic compass was giving us hysterical
headings. We had to double-check all our courses with a hand compass.
Little things were coming apart all over the car. And every mile we
sweated that something big might finally let go.

We were caught in a kind of a bind. If we went fast and passed
too many other cars, it got noses out of joint. And it increased the risk
of something going wrong. If we hung back, took our time, and had
a mechanical breakdown, we could have been left behind. By now,
even the sweep-up crews were rushing toward Dakar. They were
departing only a few minutes after the last competitors. So, we raced,
primarily to insure that there would always be plenty of potential help
in back of us. But, in all honesty, it was more fun than just poking
along.

Since our first day in Mali, the topography had become bleak. No
shining blue river with emerald deltas lured us toward it. Gone were
the artistically designed huts, villages, and the sun-tanned plains. We
were in a dusty, gray landscape, driving in gullies between low hills
of sand. There were scrub trees, some of them quite large, black, dead-

looking. We had to dodge and slide around them. We couldn't see where we were going. Not only because of the blinding sun and dust. Always there was a hill ahead, a hill behind, and hills on each side. We were walled in by the landscape. It was like driving in a maze. And there was no air. If there had been a breeze, it couldn't have reached us. It was about 130 degrees in the car.

For hours, we didn't see a village or any sign of life. Just other cars and trucks and most of these we passed. It was difficult not to. Quickly we caught up with the part of the fleet that had been badly mauled in battle and was now staggering home. Every day this forced march of the wounded had grown longer, slower moving. We no longer felt sorry as we passed them, only sorry knowing that despite their valiant attempts, some of them would never make it out.

Cars with caved-in roofs from having flipped or dragging fenders that had come adrift in crashes were commonplace. Large trucks that once appeared invincible now had taped-over, shattered windows. Some were minus glazing altogether. One car we passed appeared to be held together with yards of messily applied tape. Some cars had doors tied shut with rope and wire. And many of the crews inside were patched up as well. Many had engines about to give up the ghost. They puffed out clouds of blue smoke as a result of broken piston rings, or vaporous white mists from ruptured head gaskets. Or from cooling system leaks, the precious liquid boiling away on red hot exhaust manifolds.

So it didn't much surprise us when we came sliding around a bend and chanced upon a car slowing down in front of us, a thick column of black smoke rising from it. The entire rear end of the car had just burst into flames. Before I slid to a complete stop, I had the fire extinguisher out of its holder, jumped out, and handed it to one of the crew. They emptied their own fire extinguishers, yet the fire still raged. Bright orange flames leaped all around the gas tank in back. The whole thing could have blown any second. I noticed it was a Gelandewagen like ours, but with the rear body panels cut off, so there wasn't even a shell of protection between us and the blast that seemed sure to come.

While the driver shot at the flames with my extinguisher, I ran to get another one. I could see that his arms were being burned by flames shooting out from the car. And I saw Carolyn standing there taking a lot of pictures, pleased that she'd finally, reluctantly, adopted the role of reporter rather than artist, but at the same time frightened that she might be hurt. My big fire extinguisher seemed to have done the trick, for when I returned with another, the flames were out. Only the oily, black smoke continued to roll up into the sky.

We seemed to be on the outskirts of a village, because suddenly we were surrounded by men in military uniforms. They seemed to materialize out of nowhere. Or maybe we were so focused on the emergency that we had subconsciously censored their existence. One already had his hands around Carolyn's camera and was trying to tear it out of her grasp. She was screaming at the man, not without reason, but this looked like a situation that called for a little caution. I stepped between the army and Carolyn, demanding to know the meaning of this. The man with his hands on Carolyn's camera spoke some English.

"No pictures allowed," he said. "We take camera."

"No, you will not," I told him. "Who do you think you are?"

"This is restricted area. No photographs allowed."

"We took no photographs of your restricted area. We are with the Rallye and she was only taking pictures of this accident."

"You keep camera, but we take film," he said, grabbing the camera again and trying to pull it from around Carolyn's neck. Her response was more emotional than considered. She started kicking at him and screaming, "You're animals, bastards, heathens!" Something like that. Her exact words I don't recall, but they were familiar, similar to those that had been directed at me on a few occasions during the last year.

About a dozen uniformed black men glowered at us, each carrying an automatic rifle. I tried to reason with her.

"Why don't we just give them the film and we'll be on our way."

This, of course, made her even angrier. As though I was a traitor to her cause. She kept screaming expletives at them and then they started to get mad and shouted back at us in some African dialect. A few moved in closer to help their leader wrest the camera from Carolyn's life-and-death grip. This was clearly a no-win situation. I gave up reasoning with her.

"Give them the fucking film and let's get out of here."

She opened the back of the camera and yanked it out, pulling the film out of its cannister, and exposing it to the sunlight. She threw the celluloid tangle at the main man, the one with the biggest, gaudiest epaulets in any event. I started to back away, pulling Carolyn with me. They backed off too, then tramped away. The men whose car had been burning thanked us for our help. They spoke very little English, one of them saying only, "Terrible. It's terrible," and shaking his head.

Then, seeing that we were driving the same make of car, he asked me if I had a spare set of shock absorbers I could let them have. I shook my head too, saying, "Sorry. I'm sorry."

What I had already done was strictly against the rules. A car out of the Rallye is not supposed to help another car in trouble, and we had even been warned not to. But what was I supposed to do? Let it explode and melt, perhaps injuring, maybe even killing the crew in the process? After seeing that fire, it was painfully obvious that they were out of the Rallye anyway. But they were as crazy as all the rest, not yet accepting that they were out, recognizing only that they needed new shock absorbers to keep going.

I apologized to Carolyn for not fighting harder to save her film, explaining that I thought she'd got the action anyway, with the bumper camera, as we pulled up. We'd had the bumper straightened by one of our truck crews, and for the past few days she'd been able to mount a camera up there and get some action shots. That was another reason I'd been going fast, to help her get some photos. But she didn't think she'd got it with that camera. We'd been too far away for that particular lens.

I felt for her. First the difficulty of getting any pictures at all, then the disappointment of dropping out, then losing her clothes, and now this latest insult. And as if all that weren't bad enough, when we later told someone about our military confrontation, he said, "Oh, you didn't give them the film, did you? You shouldn't have. That's not what they were after at all. They use that film ploy around here all the time. You should have just given them some T-shirts!"

The Paris/Dakar Rallye, if nothing else, is a lesson in learning to live with disappointment.

Later that night we had our closest brush with death or injury yet. As we approached the border crossing into Mauritania, we found ourselves on a hard, dirt track filled with both holes and bumps. It was pitch black and my driving lights were not quite adequate for the job, as I was driving very fast, trying to bound from bump to bump and avoid the holes, which caused the most damage. We were leaping downhill at about seventy miles an hour when I charged into a left turn that was a little too tight for the speed we were traveling.

Coming out of it, sideways, I hit a bump with my inside wheels. They came up off the ground, and the car tilted precariously over onto its two right wheels. It just kept going that way, on two wheels, unsteerable for what seemed an interminable time. We were headed for a large tree. I couldn't use the brakes or we'd roll over for sure. I sawed the steering wheel back and forth with no effect. I turned it all the way to the right, heading, if anything, even more directly for the tree, hoping the loose dirt building up under the inside of the right front tire would create a drag so the left wheels would come back down to earth.

It didn't happen soon enough. It was the pressure of the trunk of the tree grazing our roof that set us right again. The car rocked violently for a time before settling down on all four feet. The adrenaline generated in those few seconds was all I needed to keep me awake until the end that night. I never told Carolyn how close a call it had actually been.

We arrived at the Nema bivouac, in Mauritania, at one o'clock in the morning. Dazed men stumbled in weary circles around the bivouac site, another of those lumpy, dirt fields the Organization was never at a loss to find. It is hard to describe or even to imagine the degradation, both physical and mental, that had taken place since the Rallye began. Aside from the occasional fastidious Frenchman like Boubet, who was now out, this was a pack of filthy, dead-eyed animals. The only thing keeping most of them going was their own temporary insanity. That must have been it. Anyone whose brain still functioned would simply drop out.

This mindless dedication to a forgotten goal was clearly illustrated to me when I ran into Raphaël de Montremy, the French motorcyclist whom I'd met in Paris and had occasionally spoken to in bivouacs throughout the Rallye. He was carrying a blanket, looking very much like a live version of Linus in the Snoopy comic strip. He shuffled past where I was standing, next to my car. He looked like a sleepwalker, for his glazed eyes stared straight ahead, transfixed on some ambiguous destination. Even here, he moved with vacuous determination, not looking at me as we spoke. I moved along with him. I don't remember what we talked about, nor I'm sure does he. He moved with me, changing direction slightly to match mine from time to time. Still, his eyes stared straight ahead, blankly. After a hundred feet or so, he just fell over, face down in the dirt, asleep.

We had been happy to get out of Algeria and into Niger. Happier still to get out of Niger and into Mali. And happier yet to get out of Mali and into Mauritania. The first thing we noticed was the absence of thieving. No bands of scavengers marauded the camp. The next thing we noticed were the flies. Here, they were more persistent and malevolent than any that had buzzed us yet. We gave Mauritania the Golden Fly Award.

We broke off from the Rallye the next morning, having slept way past the start. Safely out of Mali, no small accomplishment in itself, we could now go on our own until the end, the finish in Dakar, which would be in four more days.

We headed for Noukschott, Mauritania, a sizable town on the coast through which the Rallye would pass. We got onto a two-lane paved road and stayed on it for thirteen hours, trading places behind the wheel whenever I started dozing off. On each side of the narrow, concrete strip were sand dunes. They looked to be between twenty and maybe a hundred feet high. But there was no way to tell for sure. There was nothing in the foreground, middleground, nor in the distance to measure them against. Just pile after pile of sand, lined up in rows, their surfaces waving with ripples as a result of the sand being dropped on them in layers by the wind. It was a steady wind that lifted the tops off of the dunes and sent a spray of sand along before it, making the hills of sand appear like big waves curling and cresting toward a beach.

Visibility was poor. A cloud of sand floats over this entire country and blows out into the Atlantic for hundreds of miles. The sand itself was near white with just a hint of yellow. Yet the cloud in the air had a crimson cast. It must have been the color of the sun trapped inside the billions of particles floating in the air. The saliva in my mouth felt like gritty paste.

Every so often we had to stop and wait while a sand plow scraped a large, freshly made sand dune off the road. I wondered where these earth movers came from, where they were kept. I thought of an old Volkswagen commercial and paraphrased it for the Mauritanian market. "Have you ever wondered how the man who drives the sand plow gets *to* the sand plow?"

Other times we had to stop and worm our way around a portion of the road that had caved in, presumably from the sheer weight of a dune that had recently sat on it, resting its weary tons, before being scraped or blown on its way.

We drove nearly the entire length of Mauritania on this one road, passing through only a few small villages along the way. They were all pretty much the same. Small, white stucco or concrete buildings huddled close, cleaving tightly to the edges of the road, as though afraid to venture out into the desert where they would be swept up and lost in the enormous sea of dunes. That's where the Rallye was that day, out there. I felt happy to be on this boring road instead.

Near the villages, we saw people walking along the road. They were always men or teenage boys, in pairs, walking hand in hand or with their arms around each other. They seemed closer than just friends. They wore loose-fitting pale blue or lavender gowns with little caps in matching colors. In shape, something like the kind butchers wear. Compared to the places we'd been, the people looked clean and happy. I don't remember seeing either women or children in Mauritania, but they must have been there. Perhaps it was just that I was struck by seeing so many males blatantly coupled that I didn't notice. I remember wondering what the AIDS situation was like in Mauritania.

Accompanying us the length of this arid country was a buzz, a throbbing hum as though there were underground generating stations all along the way. It was the sound of the flies. There were hundreds of them in the car. I couldn't figure out how they got in. More pervasive than the air, and oblivious to our swatting, they seemed to grow in numbers and perversity as we traveled along. It was as though they'd been in control here for centuries and wanted us outsiders to learn, first hand, of their ascendancy.

About two-thirds of the way to Noukschott, in the late afternoon, Carolyn started complaining of a headache. She said she felt really awful. I touched her forehead, and it was burning hot. There was nothing to do but keep going, though. We were still far out in the desert with dunes stringing out endlessly on each side. Darkness came and Carolyn drowsed in her fever. I began to think I had one too. I thought I was seeing things. Taxicabs, all over the place. Every few minutes one would be coming toward us or we'd pass some heading in the same direction, their little "TAXI" lights glowing in amber absurdity. I felt my forehead to see if I was all right. These apparitions had me baffled until the next day when I found out that most of the private cars in Noukschott are also taxis. They pick up anyone on foot heading in their direction. It's the major form of public transport in the area.

By the time we found and checked into a nice, modern hotel, it was past midnight and Carolyn was in bad shape. I had to half-carry her to the room and put her to bed. All the next day I nursed her, going out only to try and find a doctor or to get some ice. Her temperature was over 104.

The hotel was another of those Rallye way stations, filling up with dropouts as well as officials setting up for the Rallye's arrival in the area the next day. I finally found a doctor attached to the Rallye and brought him to the room. He examined Carolyn and said she had all the symptoms of spinal meningitis, but he couldn't be sure without blood tests. He gave her pills to ease the headache pain, some antibiotics to try to reduce the fever, and referred us to a doctor friend in Dakar. He told us we should head there as soon as she felt well enough to travel.

In the meanwhile, the Rallye plowed on, generating accidents, injuries, incidents, and stories. Vatanen looked invincible in the lead now. They were still giving the navigators hell. On the seventeenth day, the course through the Mauritania dunes was so tricky only six cars found the way. A total of 105 cars and trucks couldn't and received big penalties. Seppi was one of the lucky six and moved up into fifth place. Jacky Ickx was long out of it. His engine blew on the fourteenth day.

On the nineteenth day, Patrick Tambay turned in a feat of driving virtuosity unparalleled in the Rallye's history, finishing the stage a full forty minutes ahead of the next place car. The all-woman team went out. De Montremy went out. The Little Red Fat Man went out. The Belgians, who had been hanging on to next to the last place for days, went out and dragged into the hotel in Noukschott. We had dinner together while Carolyn rested in the room. It was from them and others that I got updated on events in the Rallye.

The hotel dining room was a study in wild contrast. The rested and refreshed mingled with the filthy and exhausted. It was easy to tell who had gone out when. The more you looked and smelled like a regular, living, breathing human being, the longer ago you went out. Most of these were very recent dropouts, and the room reeked of their disappointment. They all wore the vacant expressions of madmen. A heavily bearded motorcyclist came over and berated me for going along with the Rallye as long as I had. Apparently one of the slower cars that I'd passed had complained about it to the officials, and this guy had taken it upon himself to take up their case.

"If Thierry Sabine was still alive, you wouldn't be allowed here," he said to me.

"Why not? I'm press."

"This Rallye isn't what it used to be. It's all wrong," he muttered as he wandered away, shooting me crazed, angry glances over his shoulder.

De Montremy sat in a corner by himself, staring out into the room and shaking his head slowly from side to side, as if he just couldn't come to grips with where he was.

The Belgians told me about their last few days' travails, about how the gas lines were so long and slow moving that by the time their turn came they were too late to start. They had to fight with the Rallye officials to be allowed to keep going. Then, a couple of days ago, their car broke down and they had to walk for miles until they came to a native hut where they got food and sleep and regained enough strength and determination to go back and fix the car. But by then they were too late to continue. Their eyes were like little round ball bearings, shiny and hot and steely.

As they told the story, it was obvious to me that only their bodies were present in the hotel telling it. Their minds were still out in the desert living it. And there was no telling if that part of them would ever come back. But there was a small piece of them, a little chink of sanity they'd never own up to, still clearly there. It was a secret sliver of a smile behind the outwardly deranged expression. It said, "I'm happy, happy to be finished with this insanity at last."

Late the next morning, we organized a kind of garage sale. Everything was free. Gathering all the needy-looking locals who had begun to loiter around the parking lot of the hotel, and also the guards who were incapable of keeping them out, we began unloading the car and gave away all the stuff we no longer needed. We passed out all our leftover provisions: dried rice cakes, dried fruit, dried vegetables and soup, pouches of lentils, brown rice, and beans—there was enough to feed a small village—including our little trinkets and all but three of our leftover T-shirts. It felt so great, giving this stuff away to people who we knew were needy. But what made it feel best was giving it to those who hadn't asked.

Carolyn was still in pain, but her fever had abated so we decided to move on to Dakar, get her to the doctor, and arrange to have the car shipped back to the States before all the other cars arrived.

We thought it would be fun to try driving down the beach, along the Atlantic all the way to Dakar. That's the route the Rallye would take in its final push to Dakar in two days.

Wide, sandy flats stretched between Noukschott and the sea, pocked occasionally with large, shallow puddles. I checked the sky. It had the same dusty haze as before. No sign of rain coming or going. We could have turned south anywhere along this vast apron of sand. But I wanted to drive along the sea. It was weird being on a beach, yet unable to see the water.

The flats must have been five miles wide, with a single line of dunes separating them from the ocean. It took us a while to find a break in the dunes, and then we dropped down onto a strip of beach only about twenty-five feet wide, angling steeply to the sea. Almost as soon as we drove onto it, the car sank down in wet sand. It was like mush and our spinning wheels just bogged us down more deeply into it.

Naturally, the tide was coming in. Luckily there were some native fishermen down the beach who saw the predicament we were in and came running over and helped push us out. It was the only time in the Rallye that we needed to use the sand tracks. The few minutes we were stuck there, with each wave lapping successively a little closer to us, was for me, personally, the most frightening time during the entire journey. It was the only time I felt completely helpless. Much later I learned that Noukschott has the highest tides in the world, with a swing of about thirty-five feet. And those puddles up there on the flats, they hadn't been made by rain.

We proceeded back to the main road, opting for less danger on the way to Dakar. After a couple of hours, we came to a river with a small ferry hauling a few cars and a lot of basket-carrying natives to the other side. The natives wore more brightly colored costumes than any we had yet seen, and they were festooned with jewelry. Our spirits lifted to the glitter only to sink again as they swarmed upon us along with the flies. I was exhausted from the constant struggle and Carolyn was beyond that. So we just got into the car and locked the doors, trying our best to look impassive, trying to ignore their begging.

The river was the dividing line between Mauritania and Senegal. Floating across it on that little barge in our locked car felt like sailing safely out of a bad dream. It continued in other minds in other lives somewhere behind us. But even they would float out of it soon.

You'd think I'd have been mighty happy to be getting the hell out of there and back to civilization. I wasn't. A large part of me was sad to be leaving it all behind, the hardship, the frustration, the Sahara. Before Carolyn became ill, we had considered turning around and going back out into the desert, alone. Both of us had felt drawn back, to appreciate the beauty of the place we'd hardly seen, in peace.

Like former soldiers who revisit scenes of great battles in peacetime, it's not the place they go back to. They are trying to return to themselves. To touch and reacquaint themselves with themselves, the way they were in a place where they saw, found or felt something that made them, somehow, more intensely human. They might have been sad, desperate, uncomfortable, sickened, yet they were profoundly enriched by the experience. And they long to feel it again. To relive the hardships that once made them feel so alive. We were of such a mind.

On the other side of the river, we drove for a few miles and the wide, sandy banks began to erupt in foliage of junglelike density. Palm trees and greenery flourished all around us. We were out of the Sahara and into the northern reaches of central Africa. There was still sand, but out of it now sprung life.

Soon we came to a ramshackle village. A few dilapidated wooden houses on the left and a small concrete building squatted on the right of an akimbo dirt street. Some cars were lined up, blocking the tiny street—not Rallye cars but the real cars of real local people. This brought us to the comforting and disturbing realization that we were out of the middle of nowhere at last. Comforting, for the nightmare part of the dream we'd done was at an end. Disturbing because the novelty and wonder of it was evaporating too.

The inevitable group of natives hung around the line of cars. But these weren't begging, they were selling. They were money-changers trying to sell Senegalese money. Not up to the negotiating, I got out of the car and went into the concrete building, which turned out to be both a police station and Senegalese customs. The ranking cop sat at a big, wooden desk. I walked over and handed him fifty French francs. He looked at the bill, then at me, then back at the bill, and then up at me again, with a somewhat perplexed smile.

I explained to him that I wanted to change French francs into Senegalese currency, but I didn't know the fair rate of exchange. I told him the bill I had placed in his hand was his fee for acting as my agent in this transaction.

He called over one of the native money-changers hovering by the doorway. I snapped ten two-hundred-franc notes out onto the cop's desk one by one. The native picked them up and started laying down the Senegalese bills in exchange. Whenever he stopped counting and laying, the cop cuffed the air with his hand, signifying, "Come on, come on, keep counting."

When the man finally finished counting out the bills and had turned to leave, the cop called him back and said something gruff in an African tongue. The guy threw up his hands and mumbled an angry response. Then he dug into his pocket and came up with a couple of additional small bills and a few coins and, reluctantly, laid them on the desk. I scooped these up and said "Merci" to the cop.

I'll bet I got the best exchange rate in Senegal that day. Maybe any day. Of course, in all likelihood, I still got screwed. But at least it was official.

We had a small problem getting out of there after that. Our visas weren't valid in Senegal until the next day. I'd purposely had them dated to coincide closely with our planned arrival date with the Rallye, leaving the extra days at the end in case we ran into snags getting the car out or if we just wanted to hang around and rest. I solved this problem with the application of an additional fifty francs. You win some, you lose some.

On our final stretch into Dakar, a military cop in crisp, khaki uniform and oversized Ray-bans flagged us over to the side of the road. He detained us for a long time asking questions about our visas, our car papers, about the Rallye. That done, he came to the point, sheepishly asking, "Don't you have a little gift for me?"

"Oh, fuck off," I said, spinning my wheels as I pulled away, leaving him standing in the road, his neat uniform and highly polished holster covered with a layer of dust.

At the same time, only a few miles away, Hubert Auriol, who'd been leading the motorcycle category throughout most of the Rallye, grazed a tree stump and was thrown from his bike, breaking both legs. Another cyclist came by, carried Auriol back to his downed bike, and set him up on it. Auriol drove the twenty-five kilometers to the end of the stage, where he collapsed after crossing the line, out for good on the next to last day.

Heroism, absurdity, the Rallye had it all. Only sometimes it was hard to tell which was which.

One thing is for sure. If they ran the thing the other way around, made it the Dakar/Paris Rallye, a lot more people would find the will to make it to the end. The garden spot of the world, Dakar is not. It's a big, boisterous city, half-resort, half-metropolis, and there is an uneasy tension between the two. To us, it was a surrogate New York, a town full of hype whose streets were, if anything, even more unsafe. Our arrival stamped the end of our adventure with just as much finality as if we'd arrived home.

As we drove up to the hotel, a modern, glass tower that could have been in Miami Beach if it weren't for the mangled race cars parked out front, a native in T-shirt and jeans, wearing cool sunglasses and an L.A. Raider's cap, took charge of our car. He ran the car-guarding concession in the parking lot. A lucrative job, judging from what he extracted from me. Every time we came in or out of the hotel, he waved as though we were long lost friends and swim-walked over to give me the high five.

We'd been confined to the Gelandewagen for eight-thousand miles, most of them sheer hell. So in getting around Dakar, we chose the luxury of riding in taxis. Also, the car attracted the attention of the needy, many of whom wandered the crowded streets of Dakar. And we'd been warned that here, many of their outstretched palms would be holding switchblade knives. As I said, it felt like home.

Cab-going proved to be another kind of sport altogether. We'd get into one, typically a very old and beat-up Japanese car, give the driver the address of the doctor's office, the blood lab or whatever, and ask him for a quote on the fare. It was always an astronomical figure, the equivalent of a few hundred dollars. So we'd sit and bargain. This took about fifteen minutes, just sitting in the back of a hot taxi in front of the hotel, arguing, all the while still being waved at by the cool parking attendant.

After allowing himself to be beaten down to three or four dollars, the driver would ask for the money in advance. Then, as though a green flag had dropped, he'd pop the clutch, and peel away from the hotel, throwing us wildly around in the back seat. Squealing around corners and rattling to beat the band, we'd race to the nearest gas station. There the driver would buy fifty cents worth of gas. Then he'd proceed, very slowly, to our intended destination. I was always afraid that we'd run out of gas just shy of it. That seemed to be a bad habit I'd picked up somewhere along the way.

Carolyn had typhoid. There was no telling where she got it. Maybe from the Achegour water, even though we'd treated it. Typhoid vaccinations weren't mandatory, so we'd passed on them in New York, having become sick enough with nasty side effects from those we'd already received. I'd informed my doctor of this in London, and without my knowledge he'd slipped me a typhoid vaccination along with some others he thought I needed. That's why Carolyn had got sick and I hadn't. But once properly diagnosed and treated, she began to recover quickly.

We hung around Dakar waiting for the end to come. Ours already had, so we hated being there.

At one time, we'd talked about sailing from Dakar to the Caribbean, hitching a ride back across the Atlantic. We'd even talked of possibly getting married at sea. But that seemed a long time ago. Our hearts were no longer in that idea. Even so, we went down to the docks to see if there was a sailboat going to the Caribbean. Dakar, as well as being a commercial center of Western Africa, and a beach resort, is a bustling port. Many big ships were moored in the harbor, derricks dropping large burlapped bales into their holds. We had to walk all around the commercial docks before finding where the private yachts were moored. But all the skippers we talked to were bound for South America.

If our arrival in Dakar is beginning to sound like one of the great anticlimaxes of all time, you should have been present at the "finish" on the last day. The big wind-up was a silly little parody of our Paris send-off.

The main event was a staged finish, a recreation. The actual end of the Rallye occurred on the beach outside of Dakar the night before, with few spectators. This reenactment had all the drama of a block party in a small town.

About eleven in the morning, the few finishers were marshalled, paraded into town, and parked a half block from a fake "Finish Line" where a set of bleachers had been erected. These were filled with maybe two hundred people. In front of them, there were dancers in the street—about a dozen girls in bright red and green native outfits banging tambourines on their hips. Cavorting with them were a few musicians, about a dozen press photographers, and a man in top hat and tails up on high stilts. It was a sort of mini Mardi Gras. A detachment of military police moved into the street and cordoned it off from the few hundred spectators who weren't pushing and shoving to get past them. All the time, the cars, trucks, and motorcycles sat in full view of everyone, just up the street. Most of the occupants were asleep or groggily waiting for the signal to move down the block so they could get their picture taken. Then they could head for the showers and about seventy hours of sleep.

When the signal came, the first vehicle to inch toward glory wasn't Vatanen's Peugeot, which had won. Nor was it Cyril Neveu on the winning motorcycle. Neither was it the Dutchmen in their winning DAF truck. It was Patrick Verdoy, all dressed up in fresh, white coveralls, standing on a platform built onto an organization car. He smiled and waved at the crowd, held both arms high in the air, and carried on as though he'd won the Rallye or at least done something more difficult than talk his way through it. I was so outraged by this pompous and insensitive performance that I was tempted to break through the police line and go yank him off the car. It was an affront to everyone who followed.

Behind the popinjay, their triumphs thus belittled, the winners followed with all the other finishers behind. They paraded past the grandstand with agonizing slowness. About sixty cars, twenty-seven trucks, and twenty-four motorcycles. It looked like a procession en route to a junkyard, trailed by an assortment of mangy stray dogs whose noses poked at wheels, appearing to roll the whole heap along.

Carolyn and I stood there unable to believe that our year of aspiration and struggle had come down to this. She looked pale, gaunt, hopeless—like a homeless person—wearing one of our oversized *cadeau* T-shirts and a pair of my baggy cotton desert pants, too short over sockless sneakers. Beneath my pants she wore a pair of my jockey shorts. She had nothing left she could call her own. I had my own clothes, but I still wore less than I started with. I'd dropped fifteen pounds of myself somewhere out in the Sahara. I now looked like a cadaver. But I felt stronger and healthier than I had in years. And despite the absurdly dinky end the Rallye had come to, I felt that we had accomplished something. We both came away with something immeasurable, perhaps incomprehensible, to anyone who hasn't done anything quite like this.

No, we didn't even finish. No, we hadn't contributed anything major to mankind. And compared to a true epic adventure, this wasn't all that much of one. We had no pretensions. Carolyn had wanted to come away from the experience with a lot of great pictures. She got very few. I was looking for something, I didn't know exactly what. So it's hard to say whether or not I even found it. The lessons learned and the experience gained will be years in coming.

Was it worth doing? That's hard to say, even harder to really know. I do know that it matters not. Some things are worth doing whether or not they're worth doing. The Paris/Dakar Rallye is one of those. You never appreciate life until you risk losing it.

Certainly the Rallye has little enduring or redeeming value. Though to those who condemn it for flaunting wealth in the face of poverty, I would point out that the Rallye provides many poor Africans with food, money, and gifts they wouldn't ordinarily receive. Where is the nobility in the notion that poverty is best left in place, in peace?

For the contestant, particularly the amateur like me, the Rallye offers a rather unique and adventuresome experience, which perhaps causes a temporarily inflated sense of self-importance. This as a result of having done, or in my case having tried to do, something that is damned difficult.

As Ari Vatanen, the winner, said to me at breakfast the morning after his victory, "It is impossible to overestimate the difficulty of this event." That made me feel good. All my insane preparation suddenly seemed vindicated. Then he proceeded to tell me I had made the one unforgivable mistake anyone driving Paris/Dakar can make and that is to run out of gas. Then he laughed. That didn't make me feel too good. So much for self-importance.

The finale was not without emotion. As the parade of finishers shuffled past, there were a couple of shocks. The winning truck finished sixth overall. And, against my expectations, the Barger made it, finishing twenty-fifth. We had a moment of cheer. Seppi ended up in fifth place. And later, a pang of sadness. The Little Red Fat Man floated across the line, having hitched a ride on the back of a truck. He saw us standing there and flashed us a brave smile along with a "V" sign. He was wearing a tight, green sweatshirt. The Little Fat Man was Red no more.

There was no more. The stands emptied. The photographers left. The dancing girls and musicians wandered off. And the man on stilts jumped down to the littered street, tucked his sticks under his arm, and walked away.

The palatial backdrop remained oblivious to the hubbub immediately in front of it. Overhead, a blue-black sky kept its cold lid tightly screwed down on New Year's Day. It was much colder than last year, but at least it wasn't raining.

As I pushed through the crowd, I saw Vatanen's blond head sticking up. He was mobbed with photographers and spectators. No chance of getting close to him, I moved down the line in search of more accessible friends. A few cars down, I came to Pescarolo and Fourticq. I introduced them to the girl I'd been seeing for a few months. Fourticq knew that Carolyn and I were kaput, so he wasn't surprised. We'd spent some time together in New York, just before he set his around-the-world flying record. Then, he'd been surprised.

A few months after our return to New York, Carolyn and I decided to go our separate ways. We'd seen the best of each other, and we'd also got to see and know the worst. And this had exhausted us both. Nothing either of us could imagine doing together seemed to hold as much promise as what we had already done. We'd pursued Carolyn's one big dream, at least the only one she ever told me about. She had no particular interest in any of mine. She wasn't into fighting bulls or sailing around the world. For a time we tried concocting new schemes that we could both get excited about. Windsurfing through the Strait of Magellan, stuff like that.

It didn't take either of us too long to figure out that we were reaching, straining to find something that could hold us together. Glue applied dry doesn't stick.

Some said the Rallye broke us up. I prefer to think the Rallye exposed weaknesses that were already there. Some joked that I'd taken Carolyn out on the world's most expensive date, implying that I had been taken *for a hell of a ride. If we used each other, I don't think either of us did it consciously. For a complexity of reasons, we both needed to do the Paris/Dakar Rallye, and we each made it possible for the other.*

"You're not driving?" Fourticq asked the rhetorical question with a note of surprised disappointment.

"No, I've just come to see my friends, to wish you all a happy New Year."

"Oh, that's terrible. Why you don't drive?"

"I didn't have time to get my car ready. And no team offered me a ride."

"You should have asked me. We could have found you a car to drive."

"Maybe next year," I told him. "Have fun."

Maybe coming here wasn't such a good idea after all. It was making me sad. I felt like a war widow, staying behind while all the men went off to fight. But I couldn't have made it. Between the customs rigmarole, the DOT conversions, and changing the engine to meet U.S. emissions standards, it had taken ten months for me to get the Gelandewagen back in my hands. I had spent an additional fortune. And I wasn't up to going through all that again. Yet something had drawn me here anyway, like going home for the holidays.

"Call me. Whenever you're in France, come and stay." Fourticq shouted the invitation as we moved off down the line.

We came to Mano Dayak, a Paris/Dakar stalwart. Mano lives in Agadez, in Niger. A tall, dark, muscular guy with piercing blue eyes, Mano is a little scary-looking, but a kinder, more gentle soul I've never met.

"I saw you're not driving. Is very sad."

"Maybe next year. You have fun." I was having to force a smile now.

Next I introduced myself to Malcolm Smith and wished him well. He was an American professional, driving for the English Land Rover team. I told him all he had to do to set a record was stay awake for nine days.

Up and down the line we strolled. The reactions to my being there and not driving were all the same.

"I didn't see you, but you're driving?" Bernard Cave asked enthusiastically.

"No. I just came to see you off."

"But why not? You have a good car."

I told him the same thing I told Fourticq, the same thing I'd been telling them all.

"Here's my number in New York and Caracas. You call me. If you're ever near Venezuela, you call and I'll send my plane."

"Have fun, Bernard. I'll call you for sure."

Knilli was Knilli. No surprises there.

"Vy didn't you tell me? I could haf got you a factory team car, no problem."

"Thanks, Kurt, maybe next year. You have a good time."

I spent a few minutes talking to Van Damme and Cnudde, the Belgians who struggled so hard the year before. I wished them well and explained why I wasn't going along. Van Damme winked at me and whispered, "That girl, is she your daughter?"

Jacky seemed so genuinely sad and depressed that I wasn't going, it made me want to cry.

"Get him to take you next year," he said to my girlfriend. "He's done it. He knows how."

She told him it wasn't her kind of thing.

"That's why we're together," I told him, "because it's not her kind of thing."

He grinned and stuck out his hand. "We'll all miss you."

"I'll miss you too, Jacky. Have fun."

You never tell a racing driver good luck. It's considered a jinx, the kiss of death.

The French spectators didn't seem to know that because all around us they were blabbing, "Bonne chance!" and "Bonne année!"

The trucks were starting to grumble, and some of the motorcycles were firing up. The emcee's volume was cranked up into the stratospheric distortion range. One by one the searchlights blinked out as dawn began to break. And I wasn't going. A part of me felt bad, yet an even bigger part felt glad. Sure, it would be nice to try again, maybe finish, get to Dakar. But it no longer felt like something I needed to do. I no longer had the burning desire I once had. I'd done it. Not as well as I would have liked, but I'd done it. And it wasn't even my dream in the first place.

Leaving the noise and excitement behind, we walked against the human tide still seething into the Place d'Armes. We needed warmth, a cup of tea. The only place I knew that might be open so early was the Trianon Palace Hotel, so we gravitated toward it. Inside, the lobby was deserted and looked a mess. We walked through it and into the equally deserted and messy dining room. I found a woman in the kitchen to make us a cup of tea.

Just sitting there, warming up, my mind wandered back to the year before and all those memories came racing back. The race, the cars, the trucks, the places, the people, the discomfort, the exhaustion, the thrill. Too good to let lay, unshared. I knew then what I would do next. Found it in one of those rare, unguarded moments when I wasn't even looking.

On the way out of the hotel, I was startled by the sound of a voice calling my name.

"Monsieur McCabe, Monsieur McCabe." A familiar figure came running over. It was the hotel concierge.

"My name is Patrick, do you remember?"

"Yes, of course, Patrick. It's good to see you again."

"You're not racing, Monsieur?"

"No, Patrick. Not this year. Maybe next year." More and more as I said this, it was clanging untrue in my head. Inside I knew I'd probably never do Paris/Dakar again. Unless I could sell it to someone with desert racing aspirations, the Gelandewagen would become a beach buggy carrying a load of memories.

"We still have your tires."

I gave Patrick a puzzled look. The tires? I'd forgotten all about the tires. Surely they'd have sold or given them away or chucked them out by now.

Patrick insisted on taking us up to the room to prove that he was serious.

He'd moved them to a smaller room, one with no view. They just sat in a stack filling the air with the pungent smell of unexercised rubber. Seeing and smelling them brought back more memories. I started laughing. I couldn't control myself. It seemed so ludicrous, the three of us making this pilgrimage upstairs and barging in on a bunch of tires having a peaceful sleep there in their room.

Patrick realized it and started chuckling too. Then my girlfriend cracked up. All three of us were laughing so hard we had to wipe our eyes. And we kept it up, savoring it way beyond its funniness, none of us wanting to quit, all of us somehow knowing this would be the very last laugh in a dream that had come to an end.